BLOODBOUND
DRUADAN LEGACY
BOOK THREE

AMELIA COLE

Copyright © 2025 by Amelia Cole

All rights reserved.

Interior illustrations and formatting by Amelia Cole

Book cover by Seventhstar Art

This book is licensed for your personal enjoyment only.

This is a work of fiction. Names, characters, places, brands, media, and incidents are either the product of the author's imagination or are used fictitiously. The author acknowledges the trademark status and trademark owners of various products referred to in this work of fiction, which have been used without permission.

No part of this book may be reproduced in any form or by any electronic or mechanical means, including information storage and retrieval systems, without written permission from the author, except for the use of brief quotations in a book review.

*To Isaac, Morgan, Kyle, Chris, and Brandon.
My OG fans, my loudest cheerleaders. Thank you for tolerating me
flirting with all the NPCs in our campaigns.*

To the players of Fallout who wished you could ride horses and bang hot guys

CONTENT WARNINGS

Bloodbound is book three in a series where the main character will end up with multiple love interests.

It is a dystopian sci-fi romance and includes elements of violence, death, drug use, mental illness, torture, harm to animals, sexual situations, war, emotional abuse, cults, threat of SA, and infertility.

It is intended for mature 18+ readers

SHADOWBOUND AND SOULBOUND RECAP

A thousand years ago, the oceans rose, leaving the continents as small islands.

Venovia is what remains of the northwestern part of the United States.

Humanity had barely recovered from the flooding when mystyl emerged from the seas. Nearly transparent, these squid-like creatures have tentacles with deadly venom.

Some horses showed a resistance to their venom, and soon after, druadans were created from nine original stallions.

The lines were: Galaxy, Shade, Raven, Ghost, Inferno, Solara, Gemini, and Obsidian.

The war with the mystyl lasted for decades until the fledgling government called Circuit dropped poisonous bombs that killed everything within hundreds of miles. The war might have ended; however, the cost was thousands of square miles that had become inhospitable, the air and ground too poisoned to sustain life. These areas were dubbed "Toxic Zones" or TZ for short.

Centuries after the war ended, the druadans are now used

for exhibitions only. They're no longer bred, but cloned from the original prime samples. However, years of the frost-thaw cycle have led to fewer and fewer viable samples, and fears are rising among druadan stations that the druadans will soon become extinct.

Only stallions are cloned, and therefore, only bond with a single male rider with whom they form a telepathic bond. Some highly attuned riders are able to sense their fellow riders' moods and attitudes via the bond as well.

The bond, however, comes with a cost. The men are rendered sterile and have a shortened life expectancy of around ten years due to their increased metabolism and chronic fever, inducing an illness called brimming, which can lead to flaring out and death.

Various ways of staving off brimming include exercise, consumption of alcohol, riding or proximity to their druadan stallion, and sex.

In search of her sister, Sharice, Brigid Corsair interviewed for a public relations position at Meridian Station, one of the few druadan stables.

There is she meets the manager, Heath Lockwood. A very handsome man with black hair and dark eyes. He is the son and heir of Lockwood Industries, an extremely wealthy business family.

Upon hiring, she meets Carter James, a sandy-haired, green-eyed master rider with a reputation for being one of Venovia's most notorious playboys. She grows close to him, seeking answers for the clues to her older sister's disappearance.

Soon after, she meets another master rider and head of security, Logan McCelroy. He's intimidating as hell with his six-half-foot height, shoulders wider than most door frames, and hard steel gray eyes.

SHADOWBOUND AND SOULBOUND RECAP

When she discovers Heath hiding her sister's comm, she confronts him and learns he knew of her identity all along despite her different last name.

Heath also reveals the station's deepest secret. One of the three remaining druadan eggs in the world, which is kept on display at Meridian, is a fake.

The night Sharice went missing, so did the egg.

The three of them work together to piece together what happened to make Sharice leave, with all clues leading to her being coerced into stealing one of the druadan eggs.

Every day she is there, Brigid feels called to the druadans, and senses a connection. One night, she goes to the barn and is attacked by mystyl.

Galaxian, Logan's stallion, protects her, and Logan finds her injured.

Concerned about what or who has brought back the deadly creature thought to be extinct, the four enlist Circuit scientists to investigate.

Carter and Logan ride out with the scientists and discover a cave with broken crates and evidence of mystyl activity. One scientist is spooked and accidentally shoots Carter's stallion, Ember, injuring him. Galaxian retaliates and kills the scientists.

As it is forbidden for a druadan to harm a human, Galaxian bolts into the desert and is now called a rogue druanan.

Logan is placed on probation until a suitable punishment can be determined.

Circuit is limiting funding for stations, and therefore, Brigid's priority is ensuring the fundraising gala is a success to raise money for the station.

The night of the gala, however, a mysterious attack and they soon discover a secret terrorist organization called ITM, the Inherited Terra Movement, is responsible.

SHADOWBOUND AND SOULBOUND RECAP

During the chaos, Carter, Heath, and Logan defend the station, and Brigid sees her sister, Sharice, there attempting to steal the other two eggs.

She stows away on their truck, which then crashes, and one of the eggs breaks. Her sister and the rebels then surround her, and fearing her doom, she fiercely protects the egg.

Galaxian appears, having phased near her, and she rides with him and the egg into the desert, escaping.

The three guys find her and bring her back to the station.

Circuit then tells them to relocate all of Meridian to Blackhawk Station, a much larger and better-protected station to the north.

Upon arriving, the three riders have difficulty settling in and find they must earn their master rider status among the fifty or so other skillful riders.

Brigid and Carter grow closer, even enjoying a sexy liaison in the orchards and tasting the rare fresh apples. Carter's mother, General James, convinces him to become the leader of a covert druadan group as riders are capable of seeing the nearly invisible mystyl and assisting soldiers with the attacks.

The lead Master Rider of Blackhawk is Marshal Clemmons, and Brigid soon learns is her half-brother. The two try to connect, and she learns her father is named Arlin Clemmons and is in rare contact with Marshal.

Heath's fiancée Jessica Drakeford moves to Blackhawk as the wedding preparations commence, which tests Heath and Brigid's relationship.

Lockwood and Drakeford family businesses are attempting to merge, and if they don't, many people will lose their jobs as the filtration plants— large factories that help keep the toxic air from spreading— will close.

The egg hatches, revealing a female druadan, known as a druanara. She names herself Oriana and is the first female born in centuries. Brigid feels drawn to her and Heath, and they begin researching druaneras in Blackhawk's archives. They discover a series of journals by one of the last druanera riders named Rosaline.

Determined to become Oriana's rider, Brigid works to convince Marshal and the leaders of Blackhawk.

Meanwhile, Brigid discovers that druanera riders can manipulate other riders' bonds, and she realizes she has been seeing theirs all along.

She learns that Jess and Heath's parents' merger is tenuous, and that the Bloodland pact would unite them, saving thousands of jobs.

They must have a child, however. Brigid formulates an idea that she can pull Heath's bond back just enough to allow him to be fertile for a night, potentially impregnating Jess.

She, Carter, Heath, and Jess then share in groups sex, in the hopes that this occurs.

Logan is charged with assault for defending Brigid against Garrett Peterson, the Circuit's president's son, and fellow rider's advances.

He is stripped of his rank as a rider. During the trial, Brigid learns Oriana is sick and soon might die.

Desperate, she calls Agent Zane and, upon speaking with her sister's old friend and former ITM member, goes to Uncy'lia to talk with her estranged mother.

Her mother drugs her, and Sharice kidnaps her.

And now the story continues with Bloodbound....

One

BRIGID

T his must be death.
 This cold vacancy. This nothingness.
 White light sears my eyelids, and I strain to regain any sense of reality.
 I wiggle my fingers, then my toes. Everything is working, and I couldn't do that if I were dead.
 Right?
 I force my eyes open, letting them adjust to the harsh light as I prop up on my elbows. Memories slam into me, fragmented images of faces and voices, that are whisked away like a fog.
 This isn't the same room I fell asleep in last night.
 The walls are painted white with that specialized coating

used to seal shuttles. The square space is nearly featureless, with no windows and no decorations, consisting only of ivory walls and a formidable-looking steel door.

Dammit.

I never should have left Blackhawk.

In my frantic impulse to save Oriana, I made the one mistake I warned Heath and the others against: I underestimated Sharice.

My comm is gone, so whatever messages I might get from my friends or the guys are being left unread.

I stare at the whitewashed walls of the room, my thoughts circling back to them. I don't regret leaving. I knew it was important. I wrote that stupid note thinking I'd be back soon with answers to save Oriana.

She's the first druanera, female druadan, born in centuries. An impossibility, born from an egg thought long dead. And with the return of the once-extinct mystyl, the deadly squid-like creatures they were bred to fight, ensuring the future of the druadans is critical to protecting the people of Venovia.

I close my eyes, willing their faces to the surface of my mind.

Heath wears his steadfast gaze, and jet-black hair that's literally made for me to run my fingers through. And Carter, with those incredible emerald eyes and his irresistible smirk that promises me we'll get into all sorts of trouble. And then there's Logan with his towering frame, broad shoulders, and intense gray eyes. He's all hard edges and steel, but I glimpsed a tender side underneath that he reserved only for me.

Or so I thought.

"We were better off before you." His last words to me before I left still cut deep.

I *hate* this. All of this.

The need to rage takes hold, but there's nothing to break or throw.

I take a deep breath, trying to calm the swirling tempest that is my mind. I can figure this out. I need to think rationally, starting first with where the hell I am.

I twist into a sitting position. My mouth tastes like cotton, and a pounding headache squeezes my skull like a vice. The sensation crawls through my body like the worst hangover ever. I try to swallow, but my parched throat refuses to cooperate.

Someone has changed me out of my clothes and into a beige jumpsuit and slip-on canvas shoes, and my comm is missing.

I swallow down the rising surge of nausea that some stranger touched me while I was asleep, and start to piece together the bits of my hazy memory.

Without any windows, I can't tell if it's day or night, so assuming yesterday was the day I met my mom in Unc'lyia, and I only slept one night, then I've only been here a day. Maybe two.

I breathe a deep sigh of relief. Okay. That's not so bad.

Plenty of time to return to Blackhawk and apologize to the guys so they don't lose their shit and do something extreme like report me missing. Once I can explain everything, and they hear why I left, they'll understand. They have to.

I pivot, swinging my legs off the side of the twin-sized bed. It takes a second for the dizziness to stop, but when it does, I ease onto my wobbly legs and stagger the three steps to the edge of the room.

My yelling sends a surge of white-hot pain ricocheting through my skull. I wince, digging the heels of my hands into the side of my head as the throbbing intensifies.

"Good morning, Brigid." I flinch at the sound of my sister Sharice's voice. "Happy to see you're up and about."

I drop my hands and whirl to locate the source of the sound. Goosebumps prickled my arms at the thought of a hidden camera, and she was watching me the whole time. "Sharice!" I say, a little quieter this time. "Oh, thank God. Please, let me out of here!"

"I promise I'll explain everything soon, but you need to stay in there for a while. It's not safe to let you out yet."

Not safe? "What do you mean? Tell me where I am!"

"I promise I'll explain everything soon."

"That's not an answer," I snarl.

There's a pause, and I imagine her debating how to answer. "You're at one of ITM's primary research facilities."

ITM. The Inherited Terra Movement, the terrorist group my sister is a part of.

No. Not a part of. *Leads.*

My earlier rage dissipates, leaving only the hollow ache of cold despair settling in my chest. "Please just let me go," I plead. "I swear I won't tell anyone where you are. Blindfold me, cover my ears, whatever you want. I made a mistake and need to get back." The sob building in my throat spills over and cracks my voice.

There's a long pause this time, and I wonder if she walked away, leaving me to stew in my misery.

Finally, the speaker crackles. "If I let you out now, you'll die."

"Why?"

"The air inside here isn't clean, but we make it livable with procedures like these. Still, there are leaks, even with our best precautions. You're in an acclimatization chamber where your lungs can adapt. I must warn you, it might be uncomfortable for a while." There's a mechanical hiss and a slight change in the atmosphere. I gaze at the vents shadowed in the recesses of the zigzagging pipes, listening as the slow, controlled filtration begins.

Holy shit. We're in a tox zone. Or at least dangerously close to one.

My breath hitches, and the rasp feels like sandpaper scraping my throat. The air tastes sour, like rotten milk, and I gag, falling to my knees.

I am so *very* fucked.

"How long?" I wheeze. I dread the answer, but I'm desperate to know.

"Seventy-two hours." Her tone seems unfazed by my suffering. "Possibly more. Unfortunately, the first twelve hours are the worse. Most people experience lung spasms and shortness of breath, so make sure to rest and drink the water provided."

A cough builds in my chest, and I try to stifle it, but the itch intensifies until I succumb to a fit. I crawl on my hands and knees to the bed but am too weak to get on it, so I collapse on my side, curling into a ball on the cold, hard floor.

"Try and rest. It'll be over soon. We're not trying to harm you. We're trying to prepare you."

My diaphragm cramps, feeling like razor blades are scraping the inside of my ribcage. "Prepare me for what?" I say, grimacing.

There's a moment of hesitation, then, "For everything you're going to become."

Two

HEATH

"In the past forty-eight hours," Fiaro says, standing at the head of the long table in the meeting room. "Everything has changed."

The Blackhawk station manager taps his comm, and a statement with the Circuit National Security letterhead appears on the digital screen affixed to the wall. "All the stations received this message this morning," he says, "and I wanted to share it with you first before informing the whole station."

I scan the three paragraphs of typeprint, stating how ITM's violence has escalated, and curfews are being implemented nationwide for businesses. The holiday parade is being postponed, and the last major soccer tournament of the year will be held in an empty stadium and live-streamed on the Network. Once finished, there's a solid ten-second delay before I hear murmurs and groans from everyone else.

"To be clear," Fiaro continues, "This isn't a lockdown yet, but as an abundance of caution, all shuttle activity will be limited to emergency station-related tasks and restricted to certain departures and arrival time slots. I trust all of you to enforce the new rules. Should there be any pushback, please notify me, Master Rider Clemmons, or Deputy Lugsen. Blackhawk Village is also implementing similar measures. However, as a government facility, we are considered a higher valued target and therefore at greater risk of an attack."

"You can't honestly believe ITM will come here?" Mack, our head of IT, says. "We have the ocean at our back and a hundred-foot ravine at our front. They'd have to be crazy to try anything." His words sound strong, but there's a mild undertone of panic laced throughout them. It's clear he's trying to convince himself that we're safe, as he's worried about his wife, Carla, and their unborn baby.

"You might be right," Fiaro replies, "But given the fact ITM has targeted a druadan station recently, we're not willing to take any chances. As such, we're implementing a curfew for all riders to be back at Blackhawk from any visits to the Village."

"Which means no late-night lolly-gagging at the pubs," Lugsen adds.

There is a series of grumbles, as expected. The station has a kitchen and commissary, but the alcohol selection is limited, as is the company of the female persuasion.

Fiaro taps off the screen and returns to his seat, the expensive fabric of his suit straining slightly across his round belly. The leather chair groans beneath him, its arms polished to a shine where his hands have rested over countless years. He's a businessman, not a rider like most station managers. But while

I couldn't keep Meridian safe for even two years, Fiaro has shepherded Blackhawk through budget cuts and privatized corporate takeover attempts for decades. I might not agree with everything he does, but I respect him.

"The station deputy and I," he continues, "have discussed increasing security teams from two to four and employing double shifts. The financial department has approved overtime pay to any staff who wish to earn a little extra while also supporting station safety."

I don't miss he used the word staff specifically, not riders.

Our schedules are packed as it is, and our salaries rival those of professional athletes. Financial compensation for the shortened lifespan, the toll on our bodies, and the risk of working around one-ton animals with not just powerful hooves but also teeth sharp enough to tear through flesh if they're startled or angered.

While Fiaro moves on to the next item on the agenda, Carter drums his fingers on the table beside me. His restlessness is subtle. He's become good at masking it, but it's a case of striker shivers.

He's overdue for a dose, and his body is detoxing. Orange Striker is addictive as hell and expensive, not to mention illegal, although with everything going on, the police aren't monitoring it as closely as in the past.

Carter's used O-strike off and on since Vanguard Academy, but back then, it was reserved for weekends and parties. Now, it's every day.

Our metabolisms run hot, so we're able to handle the comedown better than regular people. For them, the next day is like the worst hangover times ten.

Fiaro gestures to Lugsen, who stands. "As I'm sure you've all heard," he says, "our public relations coordinator, Brigid Corsair, left abruptly last week. We've reached out to her friends and family for information but have yet to receive any word on why she left. We have agreed to hold her position for the time being should she return. Until then, Carla Danby has agreed to take on her duties, and we have two interns from DU coming for the off-season to assist her."

At the mention of Brigid's name, Carter shifts in his seat but doesn't look up, keeping his eyes locked on the network news streaming across his comm's screen.

My eyes drift to Marshal seated to the right of Lugsen, and he senses my gaze and lifts his head from the digital tablet with the meeting's agenda. Our eyes meet for a second, and he offers me a small, reassuring smile and a nod.

He knows I'm thinking of Brigid.

Lugsen returns to his seat and nods to Fiaro. "Now," he says, eyes passing over all of us, "for the next point of order. As you all well know, former rider Logan McCelroy was recently stripped of his rider rank and position. Due to this, he has remained on administrative leave until another suitable position could be found."

Hearing Logan's name, I sit up a little straighter in my chair. He's notably absent from the meeting, whether by his choice, which is pretty typical for him, or Lugsen's, I'm not sure.

"However," Fiaro continues, "several staff members have encouraged me to reposition McCelroy as a security officer. I, for one, believe McCelroy is an asset to this station, and his expertise is invaluable in times such as these, where recruiting knowledgeable and trustworthy staff is difficult."

It's only half the truth. If they don't keep him here, they can't keep an eye on him.

He's a wild card, and if there's one thing our government fears, it's someone they can't control, doubly so when that person is a skilled fighter, built like a tank, and knows all the station's security secrets.

If he leaves, ITM rebels will scoop him up the second his shuttle lands.

Lugsen leans forward, resting his hands on the table. "I know some of you might disagree that it's unconventional to keep a rider on like this. Therefore, I suggest we put it to a vote. All those in favor of McCelroy assuming this new position, raise your hand."

I raise my hand along with five others, including Marshal. Carter's remains in his lap.

My jaw clenches, but I keep my face neutral.

Fiaro nods. "And those opposed?"

Carter raises his hand, as does another master rider, Darren. It's not surprising since he's friends with Garret Peterson, the novice who charged Logan with assault.

Lugsen raps his knuckle twice on the table like a gavel. "Then it is agreed. McCelroy will move to staff apartments and assume his new role as a member of security."

Fiaro rises to his feet. "Are there any other matters to address?"

Silence.

Fiaro nods. "Very well, this meeting is adjourned."

Carter is up and out the door before anyone else.

Once out of the meeting room, I grab a wrapped sandwich from the mess hall for dinner, then retreat to my room.

A small paper-wrapped package is waiting for me at my door.

I carry it inside and tear it open when inside the apartment, I still share with Jess. She's in Delford closing a deal on a condo building and won't be back until tomorrow.

The living arrangement is odd, but since she's gone most of the time, I rarely see her.

Inside the box, I find a wax-sealed bottle of Northern Gold whiskey and a red velvet box containing a new wrist communicator. The latest model with a stainless steel band and gold-plated edging. It's lighter than my current one, and the screen is slightly wider. The engraving on the back is a modified Lockwood Industries logo.

L&DI. They added a D for Drakeford.

A printed card inside that reads, "Congratulations! Lockwood and Drakeford United are leading Venovia into a new future." Stamped on the bottom is my father's signature.

I toss the comm back in the box and pull out the bottle.

The old ass did it. The merger went through even without the news of a baby.

I twist off the cap, breaking the seal, and pour it into a glass I used earlier that day.

Seated alone in the apartment I share with Jess, I sip the whiskey as the sun disappears behind the rooftops of the village to the west.

I should return to the barracks, but I'm not ready. My comm buzzes with the new curfew rules, and I scroll down to find Carla's sign-off at the bottom.

I tip back the rest of my glass, then refill it.

This morning, a pack of mystyl was spotted at a military base, and a storage facility with mostly weapons and gear was raided.

I put the glass to my lips and sip. The single malt gold burns less than I like, but goes down smoothly. The others don't know. I went through three bottles since she left a week ago.

One week without her, and it already feels like an eternity. I'm losing grasp of her voice, her smell, her taste.

After discovering her note, Carter, Logan, and I went to Marshal immediately. He's concerned but insists we need to wait and trust she'll come back when she finishes with whatever she's doing. All of us tried calling her, half-expecting her to answer, laughing that she found it all too much: the attack at Meridian, Oriana hatching, and her newfound ability to sense our bonds. She fled.

However, I know her better than that. We all did. Brigid had an impulsive streak, something I find both exhilarating and terrible for my peace of mind.

Chasing colts through dust storms, kissing Logan just as he was about to leap from a window, galloping full speed on a druadan with an egg in tow, each reckless act sent my heart pounding.

But a coward? No. That she is certainly not.

She wouldn't leave without good cause and not on a whim.

So, with Marshal's help, I talked Carter and Logan down from burning the country to find her, and we gave her three days to contact us or return.

On the fourth, we all agreed something was terribly wrong.

We debated for hours on what to do. Logan reviewed the security camera footage with Marshal, and I dug into my personal account to hire an investigator my dad swore was one of the best.

We contacted a police detective, but they said unless there is evidence of foul play—blood, a ransom note, or mysterious circumstances—there's little they can do and pretty much shrugged us off. Of course, Logan's threat to break the guy's fingers if he didn't at least look at her picture didn't help our case.

In the end, we did what we could, but people are reported missing every day.

Especially lately, with the terrorist attacks and riots.

I pry myself from the chair and drift to the bed. My finger

traces the rumpled sheets where Carter, Jess, Brigid, and I had lain together.

Yesterday, I scared the poor housekeeper off, demanding she leave the bed as is, even though it's been a week.

A foolish sentiment, but it is all I have.

Proof that Brigid is real and was here.

I sit on the bed and pull a pillow to my face.

Vanilla and lilac and the light musky scent of...arousal.

My dick hardens to iron instantly, and I rub the crease in my pants. The ache deepens, and I stroke it harder over the fabric. I shift and lie face down on the bed. I imagine Brigid's blue eyes heated with arousal when she sat on the chair and watched us pleasure ourselves. The image morphs until she's on her knees in front of me, peering up expectantly, and it is *her* hands that are unbuttoning my pants.

I inhale the faint, lingering scent of her on the sheets, my hand sliding down to grip myself. The swollen tip of my cock presses into the bed, and my mind conjures the tantalizing softness between her thighs, a softness I only ever explored with my eager fingers and tongue.

My hips rock instinctively, thrusting into the tight circle of my fist.

But it's not enough.

The ache deepens, a desperate need gnawing at me. I spit into my palm, then resume my grip. The wet warmth slicks my grip as I stroke myself harder, faster. My other hand slips lower, cupping and caressing my balls with a gentle, teasing touch that sends shivers up my spine.

A low groan escapes through clenched teeth, raw and primal. The fantasy of her face sharpens, vivid and all-consuming. I can almost feel her warm breath brushing my cheek, hear the soft, breathy gasps spilling from her lips as I imagine thrusting into her, claiming her.

Mate female. Shadowmane's presence washes over me, fueling the feeling of desire and want.

Shadowmane's presence surges over me like a powerful wave, an untamed energy that sparks every nerve in my body with burning desire and an unyielding need. His stallion consciousness blends with mine, a deep fusion of instinct and intent, and I feel the intensity of his ancient, wild urges becoming my own. Shadowmane yearns to breed, to claim, and create life, and as his thoughts intertwine with mine, I find myself mirroring that same deep-seated hunger. The need to possess, to mark, to fill courses through me with a force I can't ignore.

My mind drifts to Jess, to the moment I released into her, consumed by a desperate fantasy of Brigid. That act of impregnating Jess while lost in thoughts of another awakened something buried within me.

A repressed part of my subconscious awakened by the merging of my stallion's primal drives and my own desires. I want to claim, to breed, to see life bloom from my seed, a need that feels as much a part of me as it is of the stallion whose spirit pulses in me.

My breath quickens as the memory of us in this very bed materializes with stark clarity at the front of my mind: Carter matching me thrust for thrust. The soft sounds she made, and how she was blindfolded, so didn't know I watched her the entire time I fucked Jess.

I groan between clenched teeth. Then, hear the door open and close.

Jess appears in the bedroom doorway, wearing white jeans and a black-and-white striped turtle-neck.

Hand still clamped around my dick, I freeze, too stunned to move.

The room is lit only by my bedside lamp, and she doesn't

see me. She goes to the closet and sifts through the clothes on the hangers.

I pull my hand from my boxers and sit up, clearing my throat.

She jumps and spins around. Her eyes narrow as it takes her a second to recognize me.

"Holy Shit, Heath," she says, breathlessly. She presses a hand to her heart. "I didn't think you were here. What the hell are you doing?"

Her eyes drop to my shorts, and she curls her lip in disgust. "God, no. Never mind."

She turns, yanking a blazer from the closet before striding to the open door. "I'm staying in the Village tonight. That stupid curfew might be for everyone else, but I don't see why it should apply to me."

Yet, surprisingly, she's respecting it, at least for now.

"Wait."

She turns to face me. Her left, perfectly shaped brow inches upward. "What?"

Confident I no longer have an erection, I sit up further. "You know what. Have you taken the—?"

She lets out an exasperated sigh. "They were out of tests, so I have to wait until more are delivered tomorrow."

I bite my tongue, wanting to lecture her about why she hadn't gone to the Village to pick up more, but stop myself. I'm not in the mood to argue. While I'm eager to know if I'm going to be a father, there's a selfish side of me that wants her gone. Brigid's scent hovers around me, leaving my balls aching from the interruption.

The bond ratchets tighter, but I shove it back, allowing my sensible side to win. If we're going to be tied together with a child, I should keep a modicum of peace between us.

It's the least I can do, considering the implications for her are far greater than mine.

"I know it may seem like I don't care, Jess, but I do. Whatever happens next, whatever the outcome. I'll be here for you."

Her mouth twitches, and the ice in her frosty look melts just a little. "Well, good to know. I'm capable of managing this on my own, but I won't lie. It'll be easier if you're involved."

She adjusts the blazer draped over her arm. "I'll take the test first thing tomorrow and let you know."

Then, without another word, she leaves. A second later, the front door opens and locks shut.

I collapse back onto the bed, placing an arm behind my head as frustration tightens around my chest. I reach down to touch myself, but there's nothing there. The overwhelming stress and the appearance of my ex-fiancé erased everything. It's vanished.

Fuck.

The image of Brigid fades.

Before I change my mind, I get up and start to strip the bed. Silky fabric bunches in my fists, soft and weightless. I press my knuckles against it, the lingering ghosts of her, of something that isn't even real anymore. But I can't hold on to ghosts.

I force my fingers to move, to gather the sheets, to peel them away from the mattress. The air shifts as I pull them free. It's as if the room itself exhales. The scent, once so sharp, so unmistakably hers, is barely there.

A week ago, it clung to every thread. Now, I have to close my eyes and inhale deeply to catch the last traces. And even then, I'm not sure if it's real or just a memory.

I grip the sheets tighter, my jaw locking as I push through the ache coiled in my ribs.

I chose this. Still, my hands hesitate.

Just one more breath. One more second.

But it's gone.

Her scent. The last piece of her…

I swallow hard, shoving the sheets into the hamper with more force than necessary. My fingers linger on the fabric before I rip them away. Done.

The mattress is bare now, and I exhale as I enter the bathroom.

I turn the shower to cold and step inside.

I don't chill easily since my bond keeps me with a low-grade fever, so it takes the edge off.

Stepping out, I look at the gilded vanity. I wipe the steam from the mirror and study myself. A towel hangs around my hips, and I stare at the tattoo on my chest. The dark edges around the inked horseshoe seem to blur as I trace them with my finger. Everything's blurring these days. The endless meetings about security, my focus, my purpose.

The thought of Brigid hits harder than usual tonight. I should have pushed more for her to join the riders who fought the system that kept her waiting. Instead, I let her slip through my hands.

How damn naïve to think my presence alone was enough to make her stay.

It's an hour until curfew, and my bond is muddied from the tension of the day. A ride will help me clear it. I dress in my insulated pants, tall boots, and schooling jacket. I slip the new comm around my wrist and toss the old one in the trash. All data is saved on Network, so any messages or images are automatically transferred as soon as I turn off the old one. It's lighter and, regrettably, more comfortable.

Perhaps I can have the engraving removed.

I walk the length of the hallway past the other staff apartments and descend the four flights of stairs to the stables in the bowels of Blackhawk.

On the way down, I send my parents a short message, thanking them for the gift, and they respond with false promises of getting together soon. They're not leaving their penthouse for anything. If the country was on edge before, it's dangling from the precipice by its fingertips.

Businesses are shuttering, filtration plants are on lockdown, and several hospitals have closed entire wings due to a lack of medical staff. Every medical professional, analyst, and active or non-active duty military personnel are summoned by Circuit to aid in the fight against the resistance. ITM's claws dug into every part of Venovia.

Small towns, suburban neighborhoods, or prestigious city blocks in Delford, the terrorist group is wreaking havoc indiscriminately.

Vanguard's dean sent word that they're contemplating closing the school for the winter semester for the first time ever to let the students return to their families until the situation eases.

Down in the stables under Blackhawk, I fetch Shadowmane for a ride. I pull on my heat-protective gear, gloves, pants, and boots. The stallion's hide is nearly hot enough to fry an egg.

As soon as I sink into the saddle, all is right in the world. The clamor of voices evaporates as if a switch has been flipped. It's just me and him.

"You are worried," he says, his tone flat.

"I am."

No use in lying to him. He knows, just like I know, when he's tired, when he's hungry, or when his thoughts stray to mares, which is frequently, but in reverse order.

"Time to fight?" he asks.

"Not yet, just practice."

"You practice. I am ready," he says, with the confidence I

admire. He's the eldest druadan here and never lets me forget he's nearly twice my age.

Upon joining Specter Team, the covert druadan riders unit used to detect mystyl and aid the military, Carter began drilling us, running formations with the other eight riders he handpicked. His mother, General James, would arrive next week to oversee the progress of our training.

Mostly, it's been weapons and holograms, but they've also sent instructors to work with us on hand-to-hand combat, code phrases, and tactical approaches based on various scenarios.

I guide Shadowmane into another precise turn, feeling the familiar surge of satisfaction as he responds to my slightest cue.

We haven't been deployed yet, but General James insists we maintain constant readiness. She won't elaborate on the specifics, but the haunted look in Carter's eyes after he hangs up on a call speaks to her, confirming my suspicions about what's coming.

War.

And us detecting the mystyl will be the only key to keeping thousands from dying.

Voices draw my attention. Marshal walks along the rail to the stables with Dr. Gideon trailing behind him. Marshal's outfit, jeans, worn sweatshirt, and hair rumpled like he's been up all night. If I didn't know better, I'd never peg him as one of the best riders on the station.

I nudge Shadowmane to the edge of the arena and dismount.

Marshal glances over at me with a look of surprise. "Hey Lockwood. Sorry, didn't see you out there."

I rub a gloved hand over Shadowmane's forehead, straightening the stitched browband on his bridle. "Couldn't sleep, so decided to get a late ride in."

"Ah yeah, I get it," he says. "Well, we'll let you get back to it."

It's unorthodox to ride at such a late hour, even by a Master Rider such as myself. He should be reprimanding me for setting a poor example for the novices and listing the safety risks riding alone imposes, but he's not.

My gaze darts between Blackhawk's head rider and a very guilty-looking Dr. Gideon.

"What's going on?"

Marshal's eyes shift to the doctor before going back to mine. "We don't want word getting out, but we're moving Oriana."

"Why is that?" Shadowmane tosses his head, agitation bleeding into me.

"No take female," he says in my head.

I tug on the reins gripped under his chin and press calming thoughts into our bond, trying to regain control.

Dr. Gideon adjusts his glasses. He looks like he hasn't slept in days. Caring for the druanera filly round the clock has obviously taken its toll. "I heard back about the blood samples I sent to Lannet," he says, "They confirmed, as I suspected, that the humid air is aggravating her immune system. She needs a specialized maintenance dose of medication to stabilize."

Asthma and allergies are uncommon in druadans as most genetic disorders were culled from the prime DNA, but it's not unheard of. Shadowmane does better with a dose of antihistamine before a performance.

"Then have them send it up here," I argue.

Dr. Gideon shakes his head and rests a hand on his hip. "If she were an adult, I would, but she's too young and considered fragile. We're not equipped to handle this." My stallion pins his ears, my own annoyance reflecting through as a self-fulfilling loop. "This isn't permanent," Gideon adds quickly, "Just until she's a yearling. After that, I'll request to bring her back."

Seeing his escape, Dr. Gideon goes toward Oriana's stall.

I want to argue, but Marshal moves closer, arms resting on the wall. "Listen," he says in a low voice, "I know this isn't what you want, but I'll stay on top of it. Lugsen even said he'd make monthly visits, no matter what, and if he can't, I will. We won't lose her, I promise."

His eyes grip mine, and I know there's a double meaning in his words.

Marshal cares about Brigid. That much is obvious. But his connection to her is new and still raw. They only recently found out they're siblings. He's worried, sure, but it's not the same for him.

"Thank you." My words sound hollow, and Marshal nods.

"Spread the ground poles a few more inches," he says, stepping back and gesturing to my pawing stallion. "I noticed him dragging his hind a bit."

I still my tongue at the comment. It's been some time since I was schooled on riding. "I'll make sure to do so." Feeling like a novice again with a damn colt instead of a seasoned stallion.

Marshal and Dr. Gideon leave, heading down the alleyway to the right where Oriana is kept. I remount to finish our session, but Shadowmane and I are both distracted, so call it quits after five minutes.

I lead my stallion to the crossties at the left of his stall to remove his tack. I wipe him down. The repetition of the mundane task settles my nerves, and I bask in the stillness in my chest where the tether to our bond is strongest.

From down the hall, Marshal and Gideon speak in hushed tones. As I step out into the alleyway, they bring a canvas stretcher past me. Oriana's golden form is small and frail, but long legs dangle off the side of the sling. The young filly's eyes are closed, and a tube runs from her nose into an oxygen tank.

Marshal's eyes meet mine for a moment. He's grim-faced and determined, although the tightness around the corners eases as if trying to reassure me.

They move past, easily carrying her to the double doors and ramp that leads up to the station's shuttle pad outside.

And then they're gone.

The door Brigid had so adamantly shoved ajar to allow her to bond with her closes. All the effort and time we put into researching druaneras and their riders was for nothing.

Marshal and Gideon don't return.

Not ready to call it quits, I prep Shadowmane for the night and convince him that the female will come back and there's no need for him to try and paw his way through his stall walls.

Afterward, I grab a rag and polish my saddle and bridle until they gleam. When I'm done, I pick up Carter and Logan's gear, giving them the same treatment. Logan doesn't ride anymore, but I can't stand the sight of dust gathering on his equipment.

I straighten the helmet rack, stacking it neatly, and make a note to order more bit guards. Every motion keeps my hands busy, but my mind is buzzing. Oriana. Brigid. This knot of things I can't control.

My comm alerts me to an update from the investigator.

Better go find Carter and Logan. They'll be pissed if I make them wait until morning.

Three

BRIGID

A week has passed.
   Seven days in this stale, windowless room, with only my spiraling thoughts and guilt for company.

I know this because of the three meals of canned meat, vegetables, and cup of water brought along with my once-a-day visits from my sister telling me good morning and asking how I feel.

I dig my fingers into my hair and claw at my skull, hunching over on the cot shoving away the despair. After Sharice left that first day, I struggled to stay awake but despite my efforts, exhaustion eventually won the wrestling match.

Which in truth, relief only comes when I am asleep.

My dreams are the one place I am free.

And when I awake, there are trays of food, fresh clothes, and hygiene. There is a small bathroom, though no shower, but there are towels, and I wipe the grime and sweat off myself as best I can.

The first night, I screamed until my throat was raw, and between that and the poisoned air, my voice is a hoarse whisper.

Throughout each day, I pound at the door until my fists ache and my arms feel like jelly.

I demanded to be free.

I demanded to speak to my sister, and when those demands were unanswered, I resorted to pleading.

I make promises I'm not proud of.

Offers of my entire life savings and bargaining with propositions to not turn her in and keep her secrets forever.

But isolation does that to you. Twists your sense of self, and your moral compass begins to spin until you no longer know what is right and wrong.

I will do anything to get out of here.

However, it's not like I'm being tortured.

They bring me dogeared books to read, and puzzles and cards to play when I'm bored. Then, when I'm tired of that, I throw myself into exercise. Squats, sit-ups, and my shaky-armed push-ups, not giving a shit to whoever watches on the camera.

I'm desperate to burn off this restless energy, so I'll stop driving myself crazy trying to figure out where I am.

So far, I've concluded these walls are different from the quarried stone as Blackhawk, nor are they new concrete like in Delford. They're not the corrugated metal like in Uncy'lia either, which tells me I'm someplace I've never been.

The door is reinforced steel, and the lock is a giant deadbolt. I've made a thousand guesses as to what it is. An old jail.

A mental asylum. Or maybe some sort of military base where they keep fugitives before questioning. There's no writing on the walls. No markings. And the only sound is the contestant vibration which I assume is generators and the muffled voices of people as they walk past.

A slit of a window in the door had revealed itself when a hatch was slid open on the outside.

I noticed it immediately on day three. It's barely big enough to peer through, but I can press my face against the door just right to peek outside at a narrow hallway lit by temporary cables of lights like they used in construction. It goes to my right and left and is flanked by doors that match mine. With nothing else to pass the time, I spend hours standing there, watching, and once in a while, I see other people being led in and out of those doors. Some are my age, others older, and they wear clothes similar to mine. However, they all have one thing in common.

The burns.

Ghastly red welts on their hands, neck, arms, and even faces. Anywhere the clothes don't cover, I see the wounds, lines of bright red, raised skin. Sometimes, they're fresh and oozing. Other times, they're crusted over and beginning to scar.

I've seen enough mystyl burns to recognize them for what they are.

She released them at Meridian, so it's no leap to assume they have some here. Perhaps growing them, housing them, preparing them for future use.

Still, you think they'd be more cautious working around such dangerous creatures.

Unless they aren't workers at all but test subjects for studying mystyl burns. What if my sister isn't breeding them at all? What if she's catching wild ones, bringing untamed mystyl into the facility? The random patterns of burns, the increasing frequency of injuries...it fits. And if she's hunting wild mystyl, how many more are out there?

I know better than to assume anything when it comes to my sister.

Like mine, their clothes are worn, mismatched, and often dirty. Some have stained white button-up shirts and drawstring pants, while others have dresses cut to be long shirts and faded sweatpants.

There are more people than I realized. I start to recognize the faces and routines of regulars walking past.

There's Sad Broom girl. And Tall Glasses Guy, who carries crates of cans with Mr. Overalls throughout the day, and a woman around my age with dark brown skin and a tan long coat, has her nose buried in a digital tablet. She's always so preoccupied with whatever she's working on and narrowly avoids bumping into others, so I nicknamed her Dr. Busy.

When I grow bored of people watching, I move to the small table and thumb through the three books they brought me. One is a mystery about a Parnian fisherman who went out to sea and returned alive years later with no memories of what happened.

I already read it twice, so I know the twist ending.

He never left but sent his boat out without him when he'd grown tired of the dull routine of his life and, with a disguise, had assumed the role of the mysterious new owner of the inn.

Only to reveal himself when his wife, who was in mourning, decided to marry again.

The other two are nonfiction. One is about Venovian soil compositions, and the other is a high school-level biology textbook.

The pages are yellowed, and many are missing, which is not surprising given students haven't used physical books in hundreds of years.

I take a book and open it to the first chapter of *What the Ocean Forgot*. As I read, my focus wanders, my thoughts inevitably drifting to Blackhawk and my deal with Agent Zane.

My attention wavers from the book as the questions I don't have answers to seep into my mind like a receding wave in the sand.

Is Oriana still alive? What did Zane tell the others? When I didn't return to the shuttle, did he look for me? Did he lie to them? Or assumed that when I didn't reappear with my sister, I had betrayed him and run off to join her? What about my mom? Didn't he speak to her? Asked her where I was?

There had to be cameras showing me talking to Marcus. I wrack my brain for anyone who saw me at the police station. But days of isolation and the lingering effects of the sedation make any focus difficult.

I start chapter two when the lock on the door clangs and Sharice steps inside.

It's the first time I've seen my sister since being locked in this room. She wears a crisp white shirt out beneath a man's gray jacket. A purple scarf drapes elegantly around her neck and her chestnut-colored locks are pulled into a low bun.

"Times up!" she says, grinning. "The readouts on the monitors looked good. How are you feeling?"

A thousand reactions surge through me. I want to lunge at her, to scream, and demand answers for every second I've been trapped in this room, but days of isolation have left me drained and exhausted.

All of it— Oriana's impending death. The heartbreak of never seeing the three men I thought I'd share forever with, and the acceptance that I might never return to my old life — makes me want to cry, let loose all the tears I've held back since they brought me here. But I don't dare. Not in front of her.

"Fine," I say flatly.

She smiles but it doesn't reach her eyes. "Good to hear it. If you do experience any headaches, lightheadedness, or nausea, let me or one of your attendants know."

I glare at her, my body tensing.

"Now, then, I'm going to venture a guess; you're wanting to get out of here?"

Before she finishes, I'm on my feet. "You're letting me go?"

Sharice sighs and tilts her head like I just said the most idiotic thing.

God, I forgot how much I hate it when she looks at me like that.

"Don't be ridiculous. You can't leave." Her mouth twitches. "Not yet, anyway. Besides, you're acclimated now, and I really want to show you everything I've been working on."

I want to snap at her, tell her I don't give a crap about whatever she's doing with ITM, but hold my tongue.

I still need answers from her, and if I have any hope of getting them, I need to stay on her good side.

The ventilation system kicks on, and a warm breeze wafts over my face. "All right," I finally say with a heavy sigh.

Sharice offers me a reassuring smile. "Excellent. Follow me."

We step out of the room and into the hallway. Two attendants rush in, carrying cleaning supplies. They start stripping down the bed and stuffing the sheets into a white bag.

"We have others coming in who need the acclimation room." Sharice turns left and begins walking. "Since I haven't had a chance to tell you, I want to say I'm glad you're here. Believe it or not, Brigid, I missed you. I felt awful missing your graduation. I streamed the ceremony live on Network. On your twenty-second birthday, I wanted to message you. We had a contact working at Tritan, and I tried to think of ways to leave you a card or flowers. But in the end, it was too risky. It tore me apart that I couldn't tell you where I was. You understand that, right?"

Before I respond, she hugs me, and I hate that I like it.

Hate that I like my big sister telling me everything will be okay and being lulled by the belief she's right. I hate that I lean into her embrace and breathe in her lily-scented perfume. I hate that it reminds me of our childhood, of hiding under the covers, staying up past bedtime, and giggling about some biology site we'd found in the school's Network library with its naked anatomical photos.

She breaks the hug, stepping back. Reaching into her pocket, she takes out the bracelet. The silver chain is repaired, and it looks like it's been cleaned. I stare at it as sadness envelopes me in frigid arms.

"Please, just take it?" Her voice is softer, pleading, and my resolve etches away.

It's just a bracelet. It doesn't mean I believe her or her cause. I take it and slip it over my wrist.

"But," she continues, "I also need you to know this is more important than you or me or any single person. I sacrificed everything for this. We're not the bad guys you think we are. We're the ones trying to save everyone."

"By releasing those monsters? How does violence and death help anything?"

Her left eye twitches. "An unfortunate but necessary action. It was the only way to gain Circuit's attention and prove to them we're serious about our threats to expose their lies."

"Where's mom?"

She blinks, clearly caught off guard. "She's here as well. I finally convinced her to take a sabbatical. As you can imagine, her expertise is invaluable and well-received. She's quite busy, but I'm sure we'll see her soon. She's been asking about you."

The casual way she says it makes my blood run cold, but I keep my expression neutral. Mom is here? With Sharice?

The speculation that she's been working with her solidifies. She wasn't coerced into drugging me; she actually *wanted* me here, too.

"Asking about what?" I say. "How it feels to be drugged and betrayed by the one person you think you can trust?"

Sharice tilts her head sideways, peering at me. "She feels awful about that; I assure you if we had any other option, we would have—"

"You *had* other options." The words burst out before I can stop them. "You could've talked to me, told me what was happening."

My sister stops and pivots to face me. "Tides, Brigid. For one second in your life, would you stop and just think?"

I blink back the sting of the insult.

She folds her arms and pops out a hip. "Be honest. If I told you that attacking Meridian station and stealing the egg was for the good of the world, would you have believed me?"

I don't reply.

"There you go." She gestures with one hand; a sharp movement that makes me flinch. "If I told you what you wanted, you would have left, and it'd put everything we've worked for and everyone here in danger." She leans forward, close enough that I can see the swirls of caramel in her seal brown eyes. "I needed you here. I waited long enough. I need to show you."

"Show me what?" I ask. "You haven't even told me where we are."

She laughs and resumes walking. "Nice try, but you know I can't tell you. On the very small chance you did find a way out of here, I can't have you revealing where our base is."

I narrow my eyes at her, and she scoffs. "I hate it when you look at me like that. I'm not your enemy, you know."

"Oh, yeah?" I gesture to the barred door behind her. "From where I'm sitting, it sure looks that way."

"Very well. I can't tell you the exact location, but I can tell you this much." She motions to our surroundings. "This was a shopping mall, back before the chem bombs hit and wiped out every living thing within a hundred-mile radius. Thirty-thousand people"—she snaps her fingers— "Gone. Just like that."

Holy shit. I understand why she'd had me in an acclimation room for so long.

We're in a Tox Zone. But which one? And more importantly, how?

"The acclimation rooms were converted from food storage freezers behind the food court, and there are holding rooms for shoplifters that have been converted nicely into secure storage."

This place must've sat empty for centuries. Water damage has left its mark on the walls, rust creeping up old pipes and across the decorative railing on the second floor. Some sections were cleaned and reinforced, and transforming them into something like this must have taken time. *Years.*

As Sharice leads me on the tour, I try to absorb it all in. I'm far from a strategist, but this is the time to pay attention. There's no telling if I'll ever get a chance like this again to see the entire base. So far, I haven't seen an exit, whether that's intentional on Sharice's part or not, I'm not sure. My best option is to find a comm someone left unattended and send a message to the others letting them know where I am.

We pass a group of four men in fatigues with bulletproof vests. My eyes immediately dip to the pistols at their hips. The math is simple: four armed guards, one unarmed me, and Sharice, who might or might not stop them if I ran.

Shit. Like it or not, I'm stuck here for a while, but if Sharice is in a showing mood, I might as well learn what I can. My sister has always had an ego.

Maybe I can use it against her.

Once they armed men are a good distance away, I stop to face her. "Before we go any farther, I need to know something."

Her steps falter, just slightly, before she glances back.

"Why did you steal the egg from Meridian?"

A faint flicker of relief crosses her eyes. "When I first took the job there, it was to satisfy my curiosity about how cloning an animal that bonds with humans continues to be successful or decline over time. But when I saw those three eggs, it all changed. Suddenly, I couldn't stop thinking about them, spending all my free time in the hall to gaze at them. They were a puzzle I needed to solve. The questions kept me up at night. Why didn't they hatch? Lannet checked for viability every few years, and the readings and ultrasounds showed viable embryos in them, but they stopped developing. So, I spent every free moment looking into why and then the team was encouraged to collect field data."

"Collect field data? Is *that* what you're calling the attack on Meridian?"

She frowns, and a crease between her brows. "There's still so much you don't understand, but yes, although not so crudely. We learned there are very crucial factors surrounding druaneras. One, a hatching can only occur when they're in proximity to druadans in danger. While we're not entirely sure how this triggers it, we believe it has something related to the vibrations of their voices. And then once that has occurred, it must be saved from that said danger. I'm unable to find anything specific in the records I've gone through, but as far as I can tell, in the past, there were rites to earn your druanera. Trials that riders had to be put through, all while caretaking for an egg, to prove their worth, and it still didn't guarantee it would hatch but it would increase the probability."

I stiffen as the pieces snap together.

My upper lip curls into a snarl. "You placed the egg in harm's way, with the *hope* that someone would try to save it, and it would hatch?"

Sharice presses her lips together, and a flicker of irritation passes over her face. "No, not someone. *Me.*"

There it is. The reason she sounded so bitter when she told me I was lucky Oriana hatched for me was because she had wanted to connect with her. But she was jealous of nothing. I can't deny there is a connection between me and Oriana, but we are far from bonded.

"It's true. Mistakes happen in uncontrolled environments," she continues, clipped. "I was warned by the research team it could fail. But the ITM leaders pushed for it. They knew we needed that egg to strike Circuit where it hurt, to gain their attention." A pause. "And ITM has encountered and overcome obstacles before. It's our ability to adapt and learn from our mistakes so we don't make them again."

The hard edge to her tone says she means me. I'm the mistake.

In uncomfortable silence, we continue walking, only to stop again near a window. It's coated in dirt, and cracks were sealed with silver tape, but it's my first look outside.

The remnants of an old parking lot stretch out beyond, its asphalt fractured into jagged lines as if some immense hand had clawed through it. Tufts of grass and wiry saplings sprout from the cracks, their roots breaking apart what time and neglect hadn't yet claimed. Mounds of windblown dust and debris gather in uneven heaps, creating small hills where smooth pavement once lay.

Rust-eaten shells of cars dot the lot, barely recognizable

under layers of corrosion and brown vines that snake through shattered windows and yawning hoods.

"For months, I ran into dead ends," Sharice says, gazing outside. "I searched through abandoned research papers others had failed to publish until Heath had me listen to auditions for the new announcer since our current one was retiring. Hour after hour, I'd listened to the same intro: 'A thousand years ago, the oceans rose, and a terrible monster emerged, starting a war that left our air poisoned and a government in ruins...' Then it hit me. What is different about today than what they had back then?"

"No clue," I answer dully, too distracted by the despair the sight of miles of desolate landscape inflicts upon me. I'm so very fucked.

"The mystyl," Sharice answers for me. "Something about them being exposed to mystyl had triggered the druadans to hatch. So, I flew home to see Mom a week later, told her my theory, and she said she had a contact with access to archived mystyl samples."

Druadans and mystyl are linked. Druadans were created to be the mystyl's worst enemy, and recently, I learned their riders can see the slimy monsters that regular people couldn't. But this...this was something else.

The eggs remain dormant until they're needed.

The realization slams into me, a puzzle piece snapping into place where I didn't even realize a gap existed. Oriana hatched because there were mystyl nearby.

"You *wanted* Oriana to hatch, so you stored mystyl in the caves and then let them loose?"

Sharice smirks. "Timed locks rigged to look like they broke. Very clever design by our manufacturing team, if I say so."

The flames of anger waft into a raging inferno inside me.

"People were hurt. People died. Ember was shot, and Logan's stallion turned rogue because of *you*."

Sharice must sense my anger because she takes a step back. "There was no other way. We were running out of time."

"Time for what?"

Sharice narrows her eyes but doesn't respond.

"Fine." I snap. "So, you wanted the eggs to hatch. But why let those monsters loose again during the gala?"

My sister turns away, but not fast enough to hide the flicker of doubt in her eyes. It's small, barely there, but it unsettles me. She's always been composed, always certain. That hesitation doesn't belong.

"That wasn't exactly my idea," she says at last.

I step closer, watching her. "Then whose was it?"

She exhales slowly, the moment of uncertainty erased as she turns back to me, expression smooth. The sister I know is the one who plays her cards too closely to see.

"I am only one piece of ITM. There are others who direct other projects."

It's no surprise she isn't working alone but something about the way she says it, the way she lets that last sentence settle between us, sends a chill through me. She's warning me. Or maybe daring me to ask the next question.

And exactly what I want. Sharice spilling secrets.

We move again and she directs me farther into the building. "Three eggs would be too difficult to smuggle out, but one fit easily enough in my suitcase. I left the comm messages to keep Circuit from seeing you as an accomplice. I swear I wanted to protect you."

I think of those messages, watching them by myself and again with Heath. I studied every trace of fear in her eyes, every tremor in her voice. She was so convincing, playing the role of a woman trapped and desperate for help. Even now, remembering them makes my chest tight. As furious as I am with her, I know she's telling the truth about this. At least, she believes she is.

"So," she continues, "Afterward, I connected with other like-minded individuals. Scientists, scholars, engineers, and ITM provided the resources we needed."

All this time, I was worried sick, imagining her in danger while she'd been working with a terrorist group.

She gestures to a plastic bench, and we sit facing a dry fountain with faded teal and pink tiles.

"You said you came here for answers, and I'll tell you what I can. But it's complicated and I'm not sure you're ready for the truth."

The resentment from keeping me in the dark is still present, although her assurances that much of what she did was to protect me, has lessened the fire to smoldering embers. "Try me."

She lets out a laugh, but it's a hollow sound like she doesn't do it often. "Oh, Brigid. You have no idea how lucky you are, living blissfully unaware with the riders at the station while Oriana hatched. Thousands of credits spent, months of research, and people dedicating their months of their lives researched and planning, all for the chance to let her hatch. And you were the one to see it."

Her words hit like a splash of cold water, and I blink. No way my sister is jealous of me?

In all our years together, Sharice has never been jealous of me for anything. Not once. She's always been the confident one, the steady rock while I stumble through life.

But there's something in her eyes now, a tightness around her temples that I've never seen before.

It isn't my fault. I didn't want Oriana to hatch and up until a few weeks ago, I didn't think that was an option. From the moment I saw that egg, I felt this overwhelming need to protect it, and that feeling had only grown when she hatched.

I wish I can tell Sharice all of this. Confide in her all the confusion and fear I carry, but the words stick in my throat. Opening up would only make things worse right now, when she's looking at me like I'm a stranger.

None of it matters anyway. I'm here arguing while Oriana is at Blackhawk dying or possibly dead already.

The thought summons the feeling of a sharp blade twisting between my ribs. I am connected to Oriana, there's no point denying it anymore. I know that truth in my bones, and I'll try everything I can to keep her alive.

But not like her. I won't become someone who endangers innocent people to save one animal, however rare, however special. "If you want a thank you, you're not getting it."

Sharice's smile fades. "I'm not expecting a thank you. I only want you to be aware of how much sacrifices were made for your benefit."

"All the more reason for you to tell me what's wrong with her and help me save her," I say.

"I will," she replies, "but I need something from you in return."

"What?" I ask, my tongue pressing briefly against the roof of my mouth. A phantom itch crawls between my shoulder blades as I imagine the possibilities. It might be nothing major and my fear is unfounded. Maybe drafting a carefully worded note to slip to a politician at the next exhibition. Or perhaps she needs my help understanding more about the druadan stations.

She lets out a soft sigh. "A promise you'll stay here."

Dammit, I should've known. Once again, I've underestimated my sister. It's wickedly clever in its simplicity. She's not asking me to risk my life as a solider with ITM, or plant bombs at the Circuit's warehouses. She's just asking for me to not try and escape. Obviously, I want to tell her no. I'll never stop trying to escape, but the chance to save Oriana is the very reason I came here.

"Why?" I ask after a minute. It's not a promise, but it's not a no.

She arches a brow. When we were kids, she had freckles like me. However, time spent indoors, or age caused them to fade.

"I need you here with me. We're family. I want you to be here, to be a part of this."

At Tritan, the senior marketing team mentored us interns on the true tactics behind marketing and public relations. Emotional manipulation was the key, although no one ever dared speak it out loud. Marketing and PR rely heavily on psychology. When boiled down to it, people are motivated by three things. Love and fear and hope.

Hook them with one, say, you'll save more money if you buy this, or your family will be safe if you quit your job; you're doing well.

Hook them with all three, and you're unstoppable.

Sharice had known this from the start. She's been dedicated to marketing since freshman year, while I had switched tracks late in grad school.

And now, she had me.

Bingo.

If Oriana truly is dying... I swallow hard, weighing my options. The smart move is to wait for backup, but if Zane and Circuit's team haven't shown up by now...they probably never will, or by the time they do, Oriana will be dead.

"Okay." I force the word out. "I promise I'll stay." The weight of my decision sinks in my stomach like a lead ball.

Sharice doesn't react right away. Instead, she studies me,

her sharp gaze peeling away layers, searching for cracks. She's always been good at this, knowing when I'm lying but I'm not the same girl I was two months ago. I meet her stare with a steady, serious gaze, willing myself to look like I mean it.

Her lips press together like she's weighing whether to call me out. Then, after a beat, she tilts her head. "Well, just in case," her voice deceptively light, "I feel like there's one more thing you should know just to be sure."

Without a word, she taps her comm, and a shimmering image materializes between us. My breath catches at the sudden sight of Heath and Jess's room at Blackhawk.

The familiar gray curtains, polished stone walls, and plush furniture. Heath is in the bottom corner, drink in hand. Logan leans against the kitchen counter while Carter paces, gesturing animatedly about something I can't hear. The timestamp in the corner reads Live Feed.

The realization scrapes my throat raw. Zane was right. There is a mole at Blackhawk.

She had the rooms bugged. How much has she seen? The night of Kaeden's memorial, the four of us had been together. Then with Carter, Heath, Jess, and I...

My skin prickles at the invasion of privacy. "How long?" My voice is steady, but each word feels like glass. "How long have you been watching us?"

"Long enough to know you'll do anything for your riders."

My nails dig hard enough into my palms to draw blood. Marshal and I kept our sibling relationship on the down low, and it was the right choice. The only time we spoke of it was in his room. If she knew he was my brother, she absolutely would've said something. Sharice never misses a chance to gloat.

Sharice's lips curve into a smile that shows no warmth. "One call from me, and the police will arrest them all for suspected collaboration with ITM terrorists. Imagine the scandal, three druadan riders caught aiding the very people Circuit is fighting." She lets the threat hang in the air. "So perhaps you'd like to reconsider your position on helping me?"

Three riders. She didn't know about Marshal or about my ability to shift the bonds. I refuse to break eye contact as a cooling sense of relief rushes through me.

"I'll take that as a yes." Sharice sniffs and lifts her chin. "It's because of the riders, Brigid. They're the reason the druanera is dying."

Four

CARTER

We're falling apart.

Heath looks like I feel. Shitty, tired, and the stick that is usually wedged up his ass has sprouted thorns, and not in the fun, kinky kind of way but the *'holy fuck I can't sit down'* kind of way.

"We got your call," I say. "Please tell me you have good news."

Heath's brown eyes darken. "I'm not making any promises."

"Why the hell are we here, then?" Logan snaps. "I've got swing shift patrol to do."

Heath lets out a small sigh. If it were possible, Logan has been an even bigger asshole since Brigid took off. You can barely have a conversation with the guy without him storming off, and that's if you can find him. He's dodging us, still drowning in the guilt that his fucking temper sent her running.

And he might be right.

I should be the better man. Tell him it isn't his fault. That Brigid made her own choices. That none of us are blameless. I should remind him we're brothers, that we stand by each other even when we fuck up.

But I don't.

Truth is, I want him to suffer. To feel every ounce of regret so he understands what he destroyed. Brigid was the best fucking thing that ever came to us, the tether that held us together beyond the bond, and his impulsive anger ruined it. And I'll be dammed if I make it easier for him to move on.

Lately, Heath doesn't say much, but his irritation simmers beneath the surface like mine. He's not ready to forgive, either.

Maybe someday, when we know Brigid is out there, alive and whole, I'll find it in me to let this go.

But not a goddamn second before then.

Heath clears his throat. "The investigator I hired has had limited success tracking her from the station, but there are a couple of updates I thought you'd like to be apprised of."

Logan and I share the briefest of looks, his gray eyes as cold and hard as steel.

He barely holds my gaze before dropping it to look at the bottle of whiskey on Heath's table.

He reaches for it, spins off the lid and takes a swig.

Heath's jaw ticks before he continues. "The PI found flight records from Delford and cross-referenced all the photo IDs used to purchase the tickets, so even if she'd used a fake name, her photo would still match her."

"She could've used a disguise. Dyed her hair," Logan says.

My mind whirls at that. Would she really go that far to hide herself from us? My theories had run the gamut of why she left so quickly.

Everything from Logan's stupid remark about not needing her to harassment from the other riders if they heard about her wanting to bond with Oriana. The latter would lean into her needing to change her identity, which is why it's so hard for us to find her.

"So," Heath continues. "Since it wasn't likely she took a ship out of Delford to Gaergan, he dug deeper into security cameras around the city. Still nothing."

"What about her friends? Laura and Vince?"

Heath sighs. "They haven't heard from her."

"They could be lying," Logan says.

Heath takes the bottle and tops off his own glass. "Hagar was pretty sure they were telling the truth. They let him search their place and their comms and even let him link theirs to his. In case Brigid tried contacting them, he'd get an alert, also."

Heath pauses long enough to sip, his hand trembling as he brings the glass to his lips. "It appears," he says after setting the glass down. "They're just as eager to find out what happened to her as we are."

I really fucking doubt that.

No way is anyone wanting to find her more than me. I've tasted shit most people can't even imagine with her, felt hair like liquid silver running through my fingers, and had the kind of sex that ruins you for anyone else. Every second with her was like being high on the best drug ever invented.

And now I'm supposed to just...what, move on? No. Fucking. Way.

While I might want to punch Logan every time I see him, the flow of steady resolve lingering in the bond whenever we're near each other tells me all I need to know.

We'll never stop looking for her.

And yet, where my connection to Ember hums behind my breastbone, there's an undercurrent of *wrongness*.

I've never experienced it before, but I'm not so stupid to not see it for what it is.

Brimming.

I, Carter James, am brimming.

The sensation coats my tongue like fish oil supplements from childhood, rancid and thick that no amount of whiskey will wash away.

It's beyond what anyone tells you. The constant restlessness, like I'm coiled too tight and about to explode. I'm starving, but food tastes terrible. I'm feverish, but no shower is cold enough.

And at night, it's worse because at night, I dream of fire.

Flames scorching my feet and legs, consuming me until I can hardly breathe, and I awaken, panting and drenched in sweat. The only thing keeping it under control is the OS.

I feel the packet in my pocket, rolling it between my fingers. My supplies are running low.

I'll have to hit up a dealer in the Village. Not ideal, but I can't go without it.

Heath watches me. His judgment practically radiates off him when I take a hit.

Whatever. He can think what he wants.

The empty bottles in the trash tell me all I need to know about how he's coping.

With full-out war looming over us, neither of us has the luxury of slowing down to recover from Brigid.

I never wanted to be a soldier, but the druadans are the one edge we have against ITM's mystyl attacks.

I can't bail now, no matter how much I hate putting on the Specter uniform.

It's only a matter of time before we're sent out, and the other riders on the team need me to bring my A-game.

And if that means keeping my system loaded with OS, then so be it.

"So, what do we fucking do now while we're waiting?" Logan asks.

Heath takes another long drink. "The investigator said the only other option is she left on a Circuit-owned shuttle. They don't have to identify passengers like public, civilian ones do."

"The only way she'd be on a Circuit chartered shuttle is if she were arrested or working with the police," Logan says. I grind my teeth, remembering how she'd been interrogated by Agent Ewensen and Zane when they accused her of being connected to her sister and ITM, but of course, she wasn't, and they released her.

Heath shakes his head. "The first thing Hagar investigated was arrest records. Nothing new."

Nothing new, he said, but not *nothing*. After the attack at Meridian, she confessed she accidentally killed a boy in self-defense when she was a teenager growing up in Uncy'lia.

Holy shit. I push myself back from the chair. "Uncy'lia."

"What about it?" Heath asks.

"You said the investigator has Circuit's flight plans," I say. "Not just names on the roster? Check for any flights to Uncy'lia last week. Specifically, a research facility. It's all scientists and grad students, so there's very little crime, which would make it highly unusual if a Circuit police shuttle went there."

"He's right," Logan says, and I grind my teeth at the fact he's trying to cozy his way into my good graces. "I bet they don't get more than a handful of calls a year there."

Heath frowns but taps on his comm anyway. He opens the window so the holographic image floats a few inches above his wrist, and we can all see the lists of dates and flight routes.

"There." I point at the fluttering blue image of lines and letters. "Uncy'lia R. Station. 6 AM the day after Logan's trial."

"If I had to guess, I'd bet that was the shuttle she was on."

Heath highlights the flight number and closes the hologram. "I'll have Hagar look into it."

Neither Logan nor I move.

Heath's mouth curves into a smirk. He taps his comm with his finger and starts a call on speaker for all of us to hear.

"What is it?" a gruff man's voice says after a couple of seconds.

"It's Lockwood. I sent you something I want you to look over."

"Oh yeah? Well, it'll have to wait. I'm in the middle of downtown Parnia surveilling an attorney with a wandering eye for blonde waitresses."

"Cancel it," he says.

"Listen here, son. Your rider status and fancy last name might be enough to push lesser folks around, but unless you want to skip to the front of the line, you're going to have to wait like the rest of my clients."

"Greedy cocksucker," Logan hisses under his breath.

He shoots Logan a glare, warning him not to piss off the already edgy PI. "I'll pay whatever you want," he says, his voice taking the tone of his father during one of his family's thousand-credit-a-plate dinners he'd drag me to when Jess couldn't be his plus one.

There's a long, drawn-out silence, and I almost think he hung up when Hagar says, "There's no way I can get the names of the people that were supposed to be aboard unless I hack into Circuit's internal version of Network and probably end up in some prison or choking on my own vomit in a TZ. However."

He pauses again, and the vein in Logan's neck looks like it's about to pop.

"If it's more credits, I can send more —"

Hagar laughs. "The money isn't the issue; it's the jail time I'm looking at if I keep digging." He pauses, and there's a click from the other line as if he's closed a door. "Look," he says, his voice quieter, "there is one thing I can give you: the name of the person who requested the shuttle. They may or may not be on it, but at least it's a lead."

"Who?" Heath's eyes flit between me and Logan's. It's killing him to depend on someone else for answers.

"The request was made the night before by a CSU Agent. Zane Giles."

"Agent Zane? He is the one who arrested Brigid. Why the hell would she be with him?"

"No clue," Hagar says. "But that leaves a lot of questions, doesn't it?"

Heath's lips thin. "It certainly does. Keep digging. I'll transfer more credits by the end of the day."

Heath taps his comm, ending the call.

I pace the floor, avoiding looking at Logan. My boots thud against the tile floor, each step echoing my frustration. "What the hell was she doing with Zane?" I ask.

"Good fucking question," Logan says, his voice strained. He's thinking what we all are. Brigid *had* heard from her sister and is trying to work with CSU to get Sharice arrested. But why the need to leave? Can't they just interview her here?

Ignoring us, Heath places a call. It buzzes once, twice, and then Ewensen's familiar voice answers. "Lockwood? This is unexpected. What can I do for you?"

Heath's jaw tightens. "Deputy Ewensen. Sorry to call you like this, but Brigid left the station, and we have records showing she left with Agent Zane. Is there any way we can contact him?"

There's a long pause, the kind that makes my stomach sink, and I stop pacing.

"Yeah, I can get you his number," she finally says, "but it's not going to do you any good. He's out on administrative leave."

Logan straightens in his chair, his eyes finding mine across the room. Despite being pissed at him and shutting him out, I lower my barriers, letting his emotion breakthrough. A chill breeze washes over me, not just cold, but that specific icy sensation that hits your skin when dark clouds suddenly block the sun. It prickles the skin on my arms.

His worry for Brigid mirrors my own.

"Did he say why?" Heath asks.

"Personal reasons." The way she says it makes it clear there's more to the story. "I can't push it, or HR will have my ass. I'll see what I can do until Agent Zane is back and let you know if I hear anything before then."

Heath curses under his breath. "Thanks, Ewensen. We appreciate it."

He hangs up.

"Fuck lot of good that did," Logan says, grabbing the back of the nearby chair so tight his fingers make dents in the padding.

Heath runs a hand through his dark, nearly black hair. It's longer than I've ever seen him wear it, and the thick strands now curl around his ears and brush his collar.

"I know it's frustrating," he says. "But at least it's something. We must be patient and—"

Logan slams his fist against the wall. "Fuck patience. Waiting is just us sitting here with our thumbs up our asses while she's out there in danger or floating face down in the ocean with her neck broken."

"God dammit," I shout. "Don't say that. We don't—."

"That's right," Logan interjects. "We don't know *shit*."

Logan glowers, his gray eyes leveling with mine. I flex my fingers, curling them into hard balls by my side. My self-control is rapidly approaching its limits.

During our latest one-on-one check-in, Marshal suggested the two of us bare-knuckle it out as it'd also help with my early stages of brimming. I wrote it off as his way of humoring me, but damn if it wasn't tempting. Especially now, even more so if I can't get more OS soon.

"Enough!" Heath bellows, drawing our attention from each other. "This is getting us nowhere. This fighting between us won't find Brigid any faster. We need to keep our heads." He pauses and meets my gaze. "We'll find her. I promise."

I exhale and feel the tension in my shoulders ease. Heath's certainty doesn't magically fix anything, doesn't bring Brigid back, or erase the heat in my chest. But right now, his unwavering conviction is the only lifeline I have. I sharply nod.

If I can't believe Heath, then I have nothing left to hold onto at all.

Five

BRIGID

Oriana is dying because of the riders.

"Why?" The single word escapes me. Already, my mind races ahead, trying to fill in the blanks of what Sharice just told me.

"That is a very complicated answer I'm not sure we have time for."

"Tell me."

"ITM is fortunate to have access to resources and literature not known to the public, and as such, it's easy to see the correlation. That's what science is: observation and correlation. Everything is just a theory waiting to be proven."

"So, you *have* a theory then?" I ask, my voice sounding

overly eager, but I don't care. Here it is. The answer that will save Oriana.

"I do." Sharice crosses and re-crosses her legs. "Since the druanera hatched, how many riders experienced brimming? Fevers? Insomnia? Mood swings?"

I blink at the rapid-fire questions. "None," I say after thinking it through.

"And how many had even worse symptoms and died from...what is the condition called?" She taps her chin. "Flaring?"

I'm ashamed by how quickly I want to say one did: Kaeden. The urge to prove her wrong twists with something darker because admitting it means part of me is glad he died.

Shit. Wait, no, Kaeden died *before* Oriana hatched.

Responding to my silence, Sharice sighs and laces her hands together. "Would you like me to continue, or are you seeing the pattern here?"

Holy shit. Oriana is the reason why? How did I not see this? It's so obvious now.

Before I left, there was a significant decline in brimming side effects that left Fiaro and Marshal puzzled. Could that be why I felt my ability to sense her and the others decline? Whatever power they'd been siphoning off Oriana to prevent them from brimming, am I a part of it as well? Somehow, unknowingly tapping into her power while I manipulated the bonds of Logan and Heath?

"But again, this is all a theory," she says after some time. "One that I have no way of testing."

"Get her out of there," I say before I lose my courage. "Save her. You can do it, right? You have connections there? Someone on the inside who can have her shipped to another station or somewhere safe?"

Sharice's throat bobs as she swallows, and sadness flickers

over her dark eyes. "I might know a way." She straightens her back so she can look down at me even though we're the same height. "Come with me. We're going on a little field trip."

Not far from where we were sitting, I follow her through a heavy door that hisses as it opens, revealing a wide, circular chamber. The sight stops me cold. People, dozens of them, move with purpose across the space. Some wear lab coats, and others wear tactical gear and fatigues.

Machines line the walls, their screens flickering with streams of data I can't begin to understand.

"Welcome to the heart of it," Sharice says, her voice softer now, almost reverent. "This is where it happens. This is where we fight back."

I open my mouth to ask what "it" is, but the words catch in my throat. Across the room, a figure steps into view from one door leading out. She's in her mid-sixties and carries a stack of books.

She sets them on the table next to another woman, who promptly flips it open and waves a small device over the pages.

There's a glow of blue light and a beep before she taps something on the keyboard and flips the page.

She's scanning them into the computer.

Sharice notices me staring. "We're building our own information database here." The overhead lights cast harsh shadows across my sister's face, highlighting her sharp cheekbones and the determination in her eyes. "Network hides things from us because Circuit forces them to, and we've discovered so much more than we ever imagined. We didn't have all the information when we took the first egg, and it cost us dearly. But we do now."

I can't help but be impressed. Network is entirely funded by Circuit, as is a massive information system that has everything from scientific articles to images to media projects and entertainment programs. It's everything Circuit has for the past three hundred years and is growing daily.

It's a serious undertaking what they're attempting to do.

"So, why do you want me?" I ask.

A relieved smile crosses Sharice's face. "I'm pleased to see you're coming around, but there's still more I need to show you." She gestures for me to follow.

We move deeper into the facility, and I notice other people. There are so many. We pass clusters in hallways and common areas, at least thirty that I can count, and glimpses of more down branching corridors. Men and women of all ages, some barely more than teenagers, others with gray in their hair. It's what I should've expected. Their assault on Meridian was too well organized, but seeing it up close like this confirms my deepest fears.

This isn't some ragtag group of radical environmentalists.

This is an army in the making.

The realization churns my gut. "The break-ins at the labs," I say as understanding dawns. "You weren't sabotaging the labs. You were *stealing* equipment."

My sister purses her lips. "We were reclaiming what was taken from us. Taking back what they'd built on stolen knowledge and stolen lives."

There she goes again with the *they*.

I start to ask who *they* are but stop myself.

Circuit. She means Circuit.

I already feel inept around her, and secretly, I'm glad I figured that out on my own.

She leads us down a sterile hallway, its walls coated in layers of eggshell-white paint that barely disguises the mall's original plaster surface beneath.

Through a set of double doors, the laboratory that awaits us looks like it's been lifted directly from a high-security research facility because it *has* been. Sleek equipment lines the walls, holographic displays flicker with data streams, and in the center of the room are rows of giant bathtub-sized tanks bubbling with lime-green liquid.

"Mystyl," I breathe, moving closer to one of the tanks. Inside, hundreds of mesh grids stacked like slices of bread, each lined with creatures no larger than my thumbnail. A subtle current pulses through the water, and in perfect synchrony, they ripple, shivering in tandem. A prickling sensation skitters across my scalp.

There must be thousands in this tank alone.

I clutch the metal bar surrounding the base as the ground shudders under my feet. Each one of these tiny, fragile-looking creatures will grow into a literal nightmare of a monster until recently was believed to be extinct.

How long before they'll be the size of dogs, fully matured, with venomous tendrils capable of killing a person in seconds?

I scan the room. The tanks line the walls, disappearing into the distance. This is just one room. Are there more here? More rooms? Or hidden at other bases?

A sickening realization coils in my gut. No one is prepared for this.

My heart stutters as the room tilts.

Sharice grips my arm. "Breathe," she says.

I yank free and whirl on her. "What the hell is wrong with you? How could you think this is a good idea?"

Sharice flinches, just for a moment, before her expression hardens. "We were out of options. We tried reasoning. Negotiating. Even working with Circuit. Nothing worked. So, we're escalating."

"Escalating?" My voice shakes. "Do you have any clue how dangerous these are?"

She lifts the hem of her shirt. Angry, whip-like burns snake across her ribs. "I know exactly how dangerous these are." She lets the fabric fall. "But we've developed safety protocols, containment measures, and failsafes. If a tank fails, we neutralize the threat."

I search her face for doubt, guilt but there's nothing. Just cold determination.

What happened to my sister?

"*You're* breeding them," I say.

"Not quite," Sharice corrects. "We have yet to nail down their reproductive cycle, but using technology similar to the kind used for druadan reproduction, have been able to clone them."

She moves to another door, pressing her palm against a biometric scanner, clearly ready to move on. "Come. This is not all we've been growing."

The heavy door slides open with a pneumatic hiss, revealing a brightly lit chamber. As my eyes adjust, I make out a wooden barrier constructed of pallets and plastic crates. Straw litters the floor, and a massive form shifts in the shadows. A low rumble fills the air, and my heart nearly stops.

"The other egg," Sharice says softly. "It's a female as well. We've named her Initial Rider-Infused Specimen. Iris for short."

And just like that, Sharice unknowingly revealed the answer I wanted since Oriana hatched.

Another druanera exists.

The animal moves forward, blue coat gleaming like oil on water. Though horse-like in size and form, she's delicate with a slender neck and fine-boned legs that seem almost too fragile to support her weight. Her eyes, faintly glowing but strangely dull, scan the surroundings with the wary intelligence characteristic of her kind.

Idly, I wonder which bloodline she's from, as she's clearly

not from Oriana's Solara line. Raven, maybe, with that midnight-blue sheen to her coat? Or perhaps Gemini, given the subtle dual-toned markings along her flanks? But whatever her lineage, she seems nervous and wild-eyed in a way that only an unbonded druadan can be.

"You haven't bonded with her," I say.

"Not yet." Frustration bleeds through her tone. "We're still working on it. But we've made progress, thanks to the journal."

I pull my gaze away from Iris. "Journal?"

"Rosaline's journal." Sharice watches me closely, gauging my reaction.

My breath catches, adrenaline still coursing through me from the sight of the mystyl tanks. After Heath and I read them, Rosaline's journals had disappeared at Blackhawk.

We thought Fiaro confiscated them, or perhaps another curious staff member had caught wind and taken them for themselves. But no, it was her. Anger seethes inside me. She snatched them from under our noses, and just when we'd been so close to understanding how druanera bond and how to care for them.

Mentally, I replay what she just told me, wondering who at Blackhawk they'd hired to steal it. My thoughts screech to a halt.

Steal it.

She said journal. Singular.

She didn't know about the others which meant whoever stole them for her was keeping them for themselves and lying to her.

"It's been most illuminating," she continues. "All those secrets she kept in it. How her Sentinels played a pivotal role in the final days of the war. All that knowledge about the true nature of the bond and how it's so much more than telepathy with your druadan."

I want to ask her what she means, but she's walked away and is holding the door open for me.

We walk the short distance to the metal stairs. I learned they were called escalators in elementary history class and used to move with a motor to aid people in places like this. Since Circuit dictates universal health care, stairs are considered part of the *health-centric lifestyle* except for the disabled, elderly, or very young. Elevators are an option in every two-story or greater building. But if you want to be silently judged by anyone nearby, you best take the stairs whenever possible.

Sharice walks ahead. Lights flicker above us from the high ceiling. Ancient fixtures, their bulbs missing or broken, dangle like the husks of dead snails. My eyes sweep the area, and I openly stare at the dark interiors of what used to be stores. A pile of old clothes rests near a metal bench, and as we draw nearer, a skeletal hand steals my breath.

Sharice doesn't spare a glance at the skeletal remains tucked into a corner, their clothes disintegrating into the tile, their bony hands locked in some final gesture of prayer.

I do. The sight turns my blood to ice, even as I tell myself it shouldn't. Of course, there are corpses here. This place has been abandoned for centuries, and it's not like Circuit made an effort after the war ended to search for survivors.

The bombs were dropped, and the land ruined. The end.

Sharice must hear my gasp because she comments, "When we took this place over, we tried to move them, but they're fragile and turn to dust. Lots of members of our group are extremely superstitious and voted against attempting further, so unfortunately, you'll find some are part of the decor now."

"Dead bodies are part of the decor?" The words are out before I can stop them.

Sharice rounds on me, eyes narrowing, and I can't help but wilt a little. "What exactly do you think we're working with here, Brigid? We don't have access to clean warehouses or whole apartment complexes. This isn't some government-backed group with unlimited resources. Everything we have here, everything we use, comes from what we can scrounge, trade, or drag out of places like this. And half the time, we're packing up just as fast when Circuit inevitably finds us."

My cheeks burn, and I find I can't look at her.

"I know what you're thinking," she says, softer now but still cutting. "That we're cold and heartless. That we don't care, but we do. Every single one of us is here because we care, and we're doing the best we can with what we've got. So maybe think about that before you start judging."

My eyes drift back to the brittle, dust-colored forms in the corner. I didn't think about how much work it must take to hold this place together or what it costs them just to survive.

When she starts walking again, I follow her, my eyes snagging on the store names, letters missing from signs spell nonsense: G P or O Mart. Others, surprisingly intact, like Genevieve's Secrets, Bath Warehouse, Tanning & Nails.

The air smells stale and dusty like it's been trapped for centuries. If they're the first people to be here, it has.

Plastic mannequins stand frozen behind glass, draped in clothing that makes no sense. Skirts that barely cover thighs, shirts with slogans like YOLO and Team Bride. One mannequin has fallen, its blank face cracked, and its plastic arm stretches toward the aisle.

"This place was called a mall," Sharice says over her shoulder, her tone oddly light, like she's giving a history lesson. "People used to come here to buy things they didn't need. Clothes they threw away in weeks, toys that broke after using, and lotions and candles that were mostly chemicals."

Sharice slows, letting me catch up. We stop at a store that was converted into a storage room. Its shelves are piled high with crates of ammunition and various building supplies like rolls of metallic tape for sealing vents, plastic tubing for masks, and coils of electrical cord. Across from it, a space that once sold office furniture now holds cots lined up in neat rows.

People mill about, some sharpening weapons, others sewing what look like uniforms.

She leads me down another corridor, past what was once a jewelry store. The cases are smashed, their contents long gone, but the signs remain: 20% Off All Wedding Bands!

Two more skeletal remains lay on the ground, and I tear my eyes away when I see they're entwined. What had their last moments been like when the bombs fell? I imagine them on an ordinary day, shopping for clothes they'd never wear or food they'd never eat.

Had they heard the shuttle engines first? Had they rushed outside, hands shielding their eyes against the sun to watch? Or had it been instantaneous, one moment alive, the next obliterated in poison so deadly it wiped out every living organism within days?

All the records claim they received no warning. Official reports stated coldly that the region had become too heavily infested with mystyl to save, that containment was the only option. But these weren't just statistics, these were people—mothers, fathers, children.

At least these two found some small comfort in holding each other as their world ended.

We stop in front of a curtain strung across an archway made from mismatched fabrics. A grin spreads across her face. It's the kind of smile that makes my skin crawl like she knows something I don't, and it amuses her.

"Are you ready?" She reaches out to smooth a lock of hair from the side of my face.

I resist the urge to flinch. "For what?"

"You'll see." Her grin widens, and I'm taken aback that she looks genuinely happy.

She pushes the curtain aside, revealing what must have been a food court. I can tell by the arrangement of tables and chairs, though most are broken or missing. The ceiling is high, a patchwork of light fixtures dangling precariously. Vines creep through cracks in the walls, pale yellow and brown, starved for sunlight.

The smell hits me first. Something savory, though I can't place it. A stew, maybe, or roasted meat. I don't see where it's coming from, but the people gathered around the tables clearly do. There are about twenty of them, their faces worn but alert, and they stop eating the moment I step through, all eyes turning to me.

I freeze, my pulse quickening as I recognize the look of expectation etched onto each of their faces.

Sharice steps forward. "As promised, my devoted, I present to you my sister, Brigid Corsair. Our Wayfinder has arrived."

Six

Logan

The security team's dormitory door is ajar, and I hear the soft thumping of the hoofbeats in the arena down the hallway.

Marshal is working with the novices on phasing safety. The rise and fall of his voice calling out instructions is intermixed with the occasional shout of a rider from the direction of the arena.

Taking the stairs two at a time, I retreat to the security team's apartments. Once inside, I check the battery on the laser gun, waiting for the rest of the morning team to get off their shift and come in.

I've laid low since meeting with Heath and Carter the day before yesterday.

Heath promised me an update when he had one, so no sense in pestering him.

He hid it well, but every time I mention her name, he gets

that pinched, pained expression like his stallion has stepped on his foot.

So, since then, I've kept my mouth shut.

For once in my twenty-three years, if I'd *not* said the first thing to come to mind, Blondie would still be here. The two closest things I have to brothers would still be talking to me, and although I wouldn't be a rider, I'd be part of something. Still needed and wanted and not even more of a fuck-up. I had only just started believing we had something special, even beyond that. And now she's gone. I go through the motions, existing. But she got under my skin. More than I want to admit. More than I am ready for.

I lied to myself that she was just another passing thing, but the emptiness is almost as bad as when I lost Galaxyla.

My hand shakes as I load the freshly charged clip into the handle.

Fuck me if I have to aim at anything too far away.

Elena returns with Bush and Stevenson. They just got off the night shift and yawn as they enter the room.

"Pretty quiet tonight," she tells me. "Nothing but some drunk riders that tried pranking a pair of novices by stashing chili powder in their boots. They ended up in the clinic with a rash but nothing severe. Also, a group of teens from the Village was throwing rocks at the gondola from the edge of the bridge. We reported to the police, and they said they'd look into it."

I grunt an acknowledgment. Bush and Stevenson sit on their bunks and unlace their boots.

"You've got an hour until you're up with Sanders for the morning shift," Bush says, tapping the screen on his comm. I grind my teeth. Fucking newbie.

Elena grabs my arm as I get up to leave. "Are you sure you're okay? I mean, with everything, I just want to check that your headspace is right. You don't have to do this. I know

Marshal said you could take some time off after the trial and—"

"I'm fine," I say. "I want to work."

Her eyes narrow on me. The scar above her left eyebrow prevents the skin from creasing. "All right, but just know my door's always open if you ever wanna talk."

"Security shares this room," I reply.

She rolls her eyes. "Tides, Logan. I mean *metaphorical* door."

This time, I don't miss the heat in her voice. It's an invitation to go to her bed tonight when I get off the shift. Fuck if that doesn't sound tempting.

I have my whiskey, and I'm up to five miles a day on the treadmill, but this is only gonna get worse since I can't ride Galaxian. An insatiable appetite that must be fed.

Before, it used to just be about sex. Easing the tension in the bond and preventing flaring. The faces of women blurred as I pounded their mouths with my dick or grabbed them by the ass from behind. But now, the thought of Elena under me makes bile rise in my throat.

And I hate it. I hate Blondie did this to me. That she's hell knows where, and yet still wrapped around me like an invisible chain, pulling even when she's gone.

Carter and Heath are feeling it, too, because the bond burns with their anger for me, but underneath the heat is the icy weight of longing.

"Thanks," I tell her. "But I'm good."

Her arm slowly drops, but her eyes remain locked with mine. "Don't bullshit me, McCelroy. We've worked together for over a year. I may not be a rider, but I know signs of brimming when I see it." She licks her lips, and I hate myself for looking at them. "You *need* to do something. I am willing to help you."

I shift my weight, suddenly aware that Bush and Stevenson

are watching from across the room, so it's not like we're having a private conversation. They've both had a go with Elena before. Bush was even close to proposing at one point but decided they were better off as friends. Relationships get messy when your job is as dangerous as ours. I'm sure they heard about me fighting Garrett to defend Brigid, and now they're probably curious to see if I'll take Elena up on what she's offering. Knowing them, they've got a bet going.

Dickheads.

I shake my head. "I gotta get out there before Sanders shoots himself in the foot," I say, tucking my pistol into the holster. I head for the door.

"Fifty credits," I hear Stevenson say behind me. "Pay up, asshole."

The door shuts behind me, and I stride down the corridor, away from the arena.

I meet up with Sanders near the West entrance and it doesn't take long to do an initial pass around Blackhawk's resident halls.

We do a top perimeter sweep on the roof, followed by a bottom sweep around the courtyard. Stopping for a break at the mess hall, we sit alone and away from the other riders.

If I felt like an outcast before, I was a freaking pariah now.

Five hours later, my shift ends, and we brief the swing shift team before returning to the dormitory.

I quickly change out of my security uniform consisting of black cargo pants, a long sleeve shirt, and vest, and hang it in the closet as I've done countless times before. My eyes linger on my riding jacket on the hanger next to it. The carbon-fiber-infused fabric is black with dark gray embroidery, and polished brass buttons march down the front. Decorative silver bars mark the shoulders that signify my rank as a Master Rider.

I'll never wear it again. The thought pierces my side like a cold blade, and I shove the closet door closed, the sharp bang echoing in the still room.

Nearly everyone is at dinner.

I plug my comm in the charger station my bed, and leave to the barn under Blackhawk.

The subterranean stables are empty as most of the riders are either at dinner or in the evening meeting with Marshal, so I take advantage of the privacy.

Beyond regular security patrols, part of my punishment is not to linger in the barn.

And while there's no one here dumb enough to stop me, I still play it safe by going during off hours.

Truth is, I probably would just get my ass chewed and maybe a week of leave.

The whole sentencing with dickwad Peterson Junior was glossed over on the news, and his father, Mr. Circuit President, hasn't even come to check on him since.

While fifty years ago, a rogue druadan might have been an issue, and it seems like Circuit has more pressing matters to handle.

I'll be damned. I've caught a lucky break.

My stallion is in one of the larger paddocks. Since he's not being ridden, they opened up several stall walls to allow him more room to move around.

The idea he'll bond again once I flare is bullshit.

He's a rogue, so they'll never let a novice work with him long enough to bond.

The pressure in my chest lightens as I approach his stall at the far end.

"*Where been?*" His voice is low and gravelly, and Goddamn, I've missed it.

A smile pulls at the side of my mouth. "*Trying to keep a low profile,*" I reply back in my head.

"*Where your woman?*"

The question is like a bucket of ice water to the face. "She wasn't my woman."

Druadans are honest. It's in their nature not to lie or sugarcoat things. Part of their breeding to be formidable in battle, I'd guess. No time for subtleties. It's why I always liked them, but damn if *he* didn't exactly know when and where to push.

Galaxian snorts at my reply, and it's as close to a scoff as he can manage with a horse shaped mouth. "*I felt you with her. Why?*"

While I'm used to his stilted, fragmented way of talking, it takes me a second to piece this one together. He speaks telepathic words in my head, but most of the meaning is felt through the bond. And with his rogue status throwing everything off balance, it was like trying to listen to a comm call with bad service.

"*She left, buddy, Sorry.*" I tense as a wave of confusion tinged with sadness ripples through me.

"*She hurt?*"

There's so many layers to this question that I stumble on an answer. No, she wasn't physically hurt. Is she hurt now? Or had I hurt her because of what I said?

"*No. She's not hurt.*" I pause, feeling his relief, then add. "*At least, I don't think so.*" It's no use lying to him. "*Listen, I am pretty sure I screwed everything to hell. I said something I shouldn't have, and now she's gone because of that.*"

Galaxian is silent as if mulling this over. Druadans are more intelligent than regular horses because of their heightened senses and years of refined breeding, but what they can and can't understand still surprises me. He chews and licks his lips, and I reach for him through the bars and pet him barehanded. The heat of his hide sucks the breath from my lungs. Uncomfortable but not dangerous. At least not to me.

The tremors evaporate as soon as I make contact, and my stomach growls like I haven't eaten in days.

It's like being plunged into frigid water after working in the blistering sun at Meridian. It's a short-lived relief but I'll fucking take it.

"Tell her come back," he finally says. When I don't reply, his voice deepens, causing my back teeth to chatter. *"You fix this."*

I release a long sigh and rest my forehead against the cool bars of his stall. *"I wish I knew how."*

My eyes stay shut for a short while as I just absorb the presence of my stallion. He eventually grows tired, and I hear him flop down in the stall.

"Where Oriana? Where Female?"

I move back. He's lying in the stall with his massive legs tucked under him. His teal tail swishes, stirring up the sandy bedding.

"They moved her to a different place," I tell him. *"They said she'd get better there."*

A trickle of relief tingles through the connection, and I scratch my chest absently.

"Good. She will heal," he replies, almost as if reassuring me. I find I believe him, which is odd because how the hell would he know?

"I don't like you leave." A trickle of golden warmth permeates through me.

"Don't get all mushy on me," I reply, confused at the sudden sensation. *"I'm only going upstairs. Until they drag my ass out of here, I'm not going to leave."*

Galaxian snorts, flicking his ears back and forth.

I hear footsteps from the hallway, and I know my time is up. *"I'll be back later."*

He watches me for a long while with wild green eyes, which only the Galaxy line possesses. The bond between us pulses, but it's a different feeling than before. It's more superficial, like he's pulling back, letting go, and every time I visit, it's worse.

My ribs cinch tight at the thought that he can somehow sever the bond between us. There's no way it's fucking possible.

But at this point, after Brigid's presence brought me back from the dark place and Oriana hatching, I don't know anymore.

The voices grow louder, and I shove my hands into my pockets and get the hell out of there.

LATER THAT NIGHT, after pounding out five miles on the treadmill, I lie on my bed staring at the ceiling. I need sleep, to rest, but my mind won't fucking shut down. The ceiling has thirty-seven cracks. I've counted them eight times now.

Memphis snores like a damn freight train, and Newton's mumbling about spanking some girl's ass.

Again.

For someone who prays before meals, the dude has one perverted ass mind.

The door creaks open and Elena comes in, hair dripping from the showers, wearing one of those oversized shirts she prefers over pajamas. She knows what she's doing when she bends over her footlocker, giving me a view that would've had me out of this bed a month ago. She catches me looking, a coy smile on her face as she peers at me over her shoulder. Those hazel eyes promise everything I can't have.

Hell, it would be so fucking easy.

But I can't. Won't. It's like the drive is there, but just the thought of touching her makes me nauseous.

Fuck. I turn to the wall, ignoring Elena's disappointed little sigh. My hands shake so badly that I have to stuff them under my pillow to sleep. The tremors are the fucking worst. Won't be able to hide this shit much longer.

Won't be able to do *anything* much longer.

The fever drags me under, and the dream takes hold like it always does.

I'm in that damn field again; grass whips around my legs like razor wire. The sky's gone toxic green, and people run past me like ants from a flooded hill.

The whine of aircraft engines mingles with screams and the horrible wet coughing of those already breathing the toxic fumes from the bombs.

Swarms of mystyl crawl up the sides of broken buildings, their iridescent skins glinting like glass in the sickly light. More bombs fall. More screams.

The ITM rebels emerge from the smoke, and yellow bands wrapped around their left arms. Behind them, a sign looms overhead: Inland Dreamland Amusement Park. The name rings a faint bell, dredged up from some forgotten history class where my teacher had droned on about the history of the tox zones.

The sign disintegrates into dust, and my hands find the familiar weight of a rifle, dream logic making its presence natural even as part of me knows this isn't real. I raise it, muscle memory taking over.

"*Wait,*" Galaxian's voice rumbles in my mind. "*Look.*"

The rebels fade like mist until there's only her, and I lower my finger from the trigger.

Brigid walks through the battle like she owns it. Wearing the same ragged clothes and yellow armband as the ITM. Her silver hair catches the sideways light.

Her hand finds my face; it's cool against my burning heat, and her turquoise gaze meets mine.

I tense, and I fight back the surge of emotions. I try to speak, to apologize for what I'd said, but no sound comes out.

Of course, you can't. *This is a dream, dumbass.*

"Still trying to save yourself?" she says, "Some battles are meant to be lost."

Not-real Blondie lowers her hand, running a thumb over my bottom lip, sending electric currents through the contact. "Smile at fate," she coos. "And who knows, maybe she'll smile back."

Fate and I have never been more than distant fuck buddies. The conniving bitch teases me just enough to keep me in the game, never enough to let me win. From the start, she dealt me a losing hand. Born dirt-poor at a filtration plant before one dumb mistake forced my enrollment at Vanguard.

Galaxyla had been my way out, my chance at something better. Then he died.

I clawed my way back, bonded again, and thought maybe this time would be different. It isn't. Fate ripped that one away, too, toying with me, seeing how much I can take before I break.

So no, I'll never smile at fate. I'll bare my fucking teeth.

She offers me a sad smile. "Logan, there is a war coming. Stop fighting. Give *in*."

"What do you want me to do?" I ask, but it comes out garbled.

She laughs, a trilling sound, and *fuck*, I never want to forget it. It feels real.

"Your instincts have always been your guide. *Trust* them with the answers."

"Answers to what?" This time, my voice is clear, as if I finally got control of my subconscious.

She tilts her head, eyes growing distant. "To everything."

Not-real Blondie's thumb gently caresses my cheek, and I lean into her touch, closing my eyes. She disappears for a second and is replaced with the image of a pistol lying on cracked concrete, rain splashing the ground around it. Then, with a sickening twist deep within my core, I'm propelled backward, back to the moment.

Feeling the dream fading, I curl my hand around her neck and draw her face to mine. She doesn't resist, and our kiss deepens. The heat intensifies to the point of discomfort, and I reluctantly pull back. As I release her, she begins to unravel. Her form flickers and the edges fray like smoke caught in a breeze. Golden mist curls where she stood, dissipating into the void and leaving nothing but silence.

When I awake, the room is still dark.

I reach for my comm on the charger, and the screen lights up with a notification.

A message from Heath.

Ewensen got in touch with Agent Zane. He said he gave Brigid a ride to Uncy'lia. Said she had information for him about her sister, but it turned out to be a bust. Then she asked to spend time with her mother, who is ill. I went ahead and reached out to the research director there, and Brigid's mother requested a sabbatical for the next year. I had a few agents swing by to check the place. The house still has furniture and everything, but no sign of them. We brought in a cadaver dog, and had the place dusted for prints. Nothing. Dead end. Sorry, I don't have better news.

I stare at the message until the screen dims, then goes black, leaving me alone in the darkness once more. And even though six other bodies sleep nearby, I've never felt so very fucking alone.

Seven

BRIGID

Wayfinder.

What the hell does that mean? The tops of my ears burn as the group of people's stares press down. Sharice stands beside me, grin as sharp as a blade, and I realize, too late, that I walked straight into whatever trap she's set.

A man rises from his seat first, his movements slow, cautious, like approaching a wild animal. Then another. Murmurs ripple through the crowd, growing louder.

"She's here," a middle-aged Asian woman says.

"Our Wayfinder is here to guide us to our future," another, older man says.

They close the distance and my body tenses.

Sharice gives no indication that she will intervene, even going so far as folding her arms as she steps backward, all with a smug smile. She lets them come to me, and I freeze, muscles locking up as I brace myself for the mob.

They stop short, and a warm hand slips into mine. It's a woman. She's in her forties, with brown hair pulled into a loose braid and eyes the color of ripe cherries. Tears shimmer there, threatening to spill.

"Wayfinder." She squeezes my hand, and a tear rolls down her cheek. "You have no idea how long we've been waiting."

Others closest begin openly weeping, and they fall to their knees. It spreads like a wave. Soon, they're all kneeling, heads bowed.

"What the hell is going on?" I look to Sharice.

She gazes adoringly down at the group of people bowed before us. "The Wayfinder is a prophesized member of the Inherited Terra Movement. They are the beacon that will light the path. A chosen that will assist the High Navigator's quest, to ensure a future without suffering, but one filled with hope and love."

"Light of the Wayfinder, guide us," the group chants. The words rise and fall, their fervor increasing, pressing in from all sides. My stomach twists, and the edges of my vision blur.

Sharice remains at my shoulder, unmoving. This is her doing. Her handiwork. She manipulated them into believing I was special.

A man, tears streaming down his cheeks, leans forward and presses his lips to the toes of my boots. I retreat backwards. "No!" The shout tears from my throat, my voice cracking through the murmuring voices. The chanting halts and dozens of confused faces stare up at me.

I force myself to stand taller, trying to ignore the trembling in my legs. "Please. I'm not who you think I am. I'm not staying—"

Sharice sets a hand on my shoulder, stopping me. "My sister has had a tiresome day. I only wanted to bring her here before taking her to her room to rest."

The crowd rises to their feet, and parts like water making way for a stone. Sharice slides her arm through mins as if were the closest of sisters. Her grip is firm, but there's a possessiveness that makes my skin itch.

She leans in, her voice low but audible enough for them to hear. "If you could please return to your duties, I promise you will each get your chance to speak with her. Join us tomorrow evening by the south fountain, I will announce the next phase of our journey."

There's no hesitation. They bow their heads, murmur their compliance, and disperse. As Sharice leads me out of the cafeteria, my neck prickles as I feel their gazes follow us.

When we're out of earshot, I yank my arm free and pull her to a stop. "What the hell was that about?"

She blinks at me, feigning innocence. "You're the Wayfinder. I thought that was clear?"

I scoff. "You've got to be kidding me. Wayfinder? Really? That's the best you got. Seriously, how long have you been feeding them those lies?"

Sharice crosses her arms, her expression hardening. "It's not lying. It's ITM's doctrine. The tenet that encouraged them to come here. To use their skills and work together. It's allowed progress to be made rather than stifled. Progress that will benefit everyone. Even the non-believers."

"Bullshit," I snap. "You've brainwashed them into thinking I'm something I'm not. You've turned me into some kind of—"

"Savior?" she offers. "Good. Because that's what they need."

Holy shit. It's so obvious now. My PR-trained sister knows what she's doing. She's weaponizing their faith, turning coincidence into divine confirmation.

Create a prophecy that conveniently comes true, and you'll build an unshakable conviction.

I'm not so naïve to see this for what it is. A cult, and my sister is one of its architects.

"But why me? Why not just make it easy and call yourself the Wayfinder?"

She purses her lips. "Titles only carry the power that's given to them. I helped record the tenets, so how believable would it be if I just spontaneously declared I was a chosen one in something I had a hand in writing? Believe it or not, Brigid, they're not idiots. They'd *know* I was lying. But you're a stranger. An outsider. My sister, yes, but it only strengthens the declaration since the egg hatched at the same time you were with it, signifying the next wave of the prophecy."

"But it didn't hatch because of me," I argue. "I just happened to be near it."

Sharice shrugs. "True. But there are too many other details that match the prophecy to be ignored."

I roll my eyes. "Such as?"

Sharice shakes her head. "The teachings of ITM's doctrine are limited to only the highest-ranking Navigator's interpretations."

I snort. "Let me guess, you're one of them."

"I am one, yes. There are others at other bases, eight Navigators in total. We're fortunate to have a High Navigator here. The highest ranking in our organization, which you'll meet soon."

"Come on," I say. "You can't honestly believe all this crap?"

Sharice's mouth pinches with annoyance. "You minored in history. Well, then you might find it interesting that ITM's roots date back to the mystyl wars and are mentioned by reputable scholars in documents dating to circa 400 PF."

I school my face, even as this information does intrigue me. I've been a history nerd my entire life, but still, my irritation simmers beneath the surface. "Okay. Fine. But I'm still pissed you're using me so more people would believe ITM's bullshit."

Sharice comes to a stop and stiffens. "Isn't everyone using everyone?" Her voice is harder than before. "You came here to get answers? Wouldn't you have done the same to me if it meant saving your riders or Oriana?"

I chew the inside of my cheek until I taste copper. She's wrong.

I would have done so much worse.

"I didn't join ITM because I was bored," she says, "I did it because I saw all the people that have nothing left. The ones busting their asses at the filtration plants or overworked nurses trying to keep the birth rate from falling more. They need someone to believe in. Every day, I carry their best intentions in my heart as we progress onward and tides how we've made progress. Every accomplishment gives them more than Circuit ever did. That's what I'm doing. I'm giving them an honest chance, a future. I'm giving them hope."

"By bringing back those goddamn monsters?" I shake my head, feeling like I'm shouting into a void. Everyone is nodding along to this madness while I'm the only one who can see it for what it is. "You really have lost it. I thought maybe, just maybe, you weren't completely nuts, but this just seals the deal."

Her gaze pierces mine. "Think what you want, but if they believe you *are* their savior, then you are. And you can call me crazy all you want, but you'll see it soon enough they're right."

She checks her comm before I can reply. "All right, we have a few more minutes before I need to get back. There's one more thing I need to show you."

She starts walking but I don't follow. I've seen enough. The whole interaction has left me drained, and I want nothing but to retreat to a private space and decompress or scream into a pillow. Whichever one makes me feel like I'm not losing my mind.

"Please, Brigid," Sharice pleads. "It'll only take a minute, and I believe it'll give you something to think about. I promise I'll take you back to your room as soon as we're done and even have meals sent, so you don't have to be around anyone else if you'd like."

Damn her sisterly connection and knowing just what to say to convince me.

"Fine."

She flashes me a small smile, and we double back the way we came. We take a right, then a left in what used to be the employees' hallways with doors leading into each of the stores.

Finally, we enter one and find racks of shelving reaching the ceiling.

A warehouse. An abandoned forklift sits in the corner, its tires flat, and a torn seat is leaking foam like a gutted animal.

We take a right again and through sheets of plastic draped between the metal shelves.

The room is piercingly bright, with every mismatched set of lights hanging from the ceiling.

"What the hell is this?"

"Our lab," Sharice says proudly. "This is where we're going to change the future, with your help, of course."

Two people are asleep in hospital beds, IVs tethered to their arms, along with a plethora of monitoring equipment. The skin on their faces is mottled red, and they stare blankly at the ceiling.

"There's someone else who'd like to see you," Sharice says,

gesturing to a workstation where a pair of people stand near a microscope and computer screen.

One of the figures straightens, and the blood drains from my face.

Standing in a lab coat and clearly important to whatever is happening here is Elton Nunson.

Dane's older brother. *The boy I killed.*

A cold sweat breaks out across my neck, trickling down my spine as I'm instantly transported back to that night in the boat house seven years ago.

My world tilts, past and present colliding violently. He's the reason I had to leave Uncy'lia. The reason my relationship with my mother became so strained. The reason I fled to a Delford private school away from my friends, Sharice, and everything I knew, rather than face criminal charges that would have permanently ruined my future.

I struggle to keep my face neutral, even as I want to dissolve into dust.

Elton is here, *and* he's working with Sharice.

I spin, pinning my sister with a glare. "What's going on? Why is *he* here?"

Sharice leans closer. "I'm sorry I didn't tell you earlier. Elton is the High Navigator."

Holy shit. The realization jolts like an electrical shot. He's the highest-ranking ITM member, the one Sharice reports to. "You can't be serious? Him?"

Sharice gives me a pitying look. "I knew how you'd react, and I wanted you to be rational about this."

"Rational?" I screech, causing Sharice to wrinkle her nose. "You know damn well he lied about Dane not being at fault. He told the cops *I* lured him out there, like I was some sex-crazed teen, and then got angry when he rebuffed *my* advances. He ruined my life!"

Sharice takes my arm and draws me aside so that our backs are to where Elton converses with another lab tech. "There were no other witnesses. It was your word against his. Of course, he took his brother's side. Wouldn't you have taken mine if the roles were reversed?"

"Like you did for me?" I yank my arm free. "Or did you forget the part where I told the truth? Where I stood there, alone, while you and Mom did nothing?"

Sharice tucks a loose strand of dark hair behind her ear, composing herself like she always does when I get too loud, too emotional, or too inconvenient.

"I wrote a statement," she says, as if it were some favor.

"You wrote words on a piece of paper," I reply. "Then you turned around and let Mom sell me off like a problem to be handled. You stood there while they called me a liar. You let them *banish* me, Sharice." She flinches, but I don't stop. "You *agreed* to it. You let them lock me away at Delford like I was the one who did something wrong, all so they wouldn't have to deal with the scandal. So don't stand here and act like you were on my side. You were on *Mom's* side. You were on *their* side."

Sharice crosses her arms, eyes flicking to the other side of the lab where Elton and an assistant are still talking before settling back on me. "I see how you might think that, but I was on no one's side. Mom was already planning to send you to a boarding school since it was clear you were struggling and needed more assistance than the teachers there could provide. She wanted to wait until the end of the semester, but the incident made her transfer you quicker."

I shake my head, a bitter laugh bubbling up. "You're lying."

"I swear, I am not."

Tides how I want to believe she's telling the truth.

"The Nunson family is powerful," she continues, her voice

lower in case anyone is trying to overhear us. "Right up there with the Petersons, Drakefords, and Lockwoods. If it'd gone to court, every juror there would've been paid off, and you would've been found guilty of murder. Even at sixteen, your future would've been forever tarnished, hindered even."

Reason dowses my seething anger. I don't want to hear sense. I want to cling to my rage, to the betrayal that kept me going after I left when nothing else would.

Sharice steps closer, her voice gentle. "I'll let you in on a little secret. I never wanted you to leave. For a month after, I begged Mom to send me, too."

I blink. "You did?"

She nods, sincerity softening the usual steel in her expression. "I was about to graduate, and my mentors were at Uncy'lia's station. I had to stay to finish my senior project. I was glad when I moved to DU, and we got to spend time together. And now that you're here, we get to make up for lost time."

A golf-ball-sized lump forms in my throat. Why tell me this now? After all this time?

To keep me from losing my shit about Elton and making a scene.

"So," she continues, watching me carefully, "Elton has put the past behind him. I assure you, he's only looking toward the future. If he can, then you can." She hesitates, then adds, "Just...please. You don't have to like him. Just tolerate him. For me."

"Please, Brigid. Remember how I told you this is bigger than me or you or him?"

I grit my teeth and nod.

"Just listen to him," she says, "I promise you'll see. The past is in the past." Sharice's smile widens, the tensions draining from her face as Elton strides toward us.

He wears a khaki button-up shirt, sleeves rolled to his

elbows, black cargo jeans, and a white lab coat. A yellow armband circles his left bicep, one I've seen others around the facility wear. Mostly the ones with guns, but not just them. What do you have to do to earn that badge? Kill someone, probably. Or maybe swear some oath, perform a blood ritual. My mind wanders, diving into half-remembered stories of cults in history, anything to avoid the fact that he's now looking this way, closing the distance with each step.

It's been years, so it's no surprise he looks different. He has a neatly trimmed beard framing a jawline that's lost its boyish softness. Two black tattoos— one of a compass and one of a sword — curl down both sides of his neck, disappearing beneath his collar. His brow is thicker, his features sharper, more defined.

And then his eyes, a shade lighter than his brown hair, are too damn similar to Dane's.

Dane was more handsome, and while I'd had a crush on him once, it had never been *me* who advanced on him. "Ah, Brigid," Elton says, extending a hand. "It's been ages." His voice, deeper than I remember, carries the same lilt of his Gaergen Island accent. It instantly reminds me of Carter, sending a sudden burst of pain in my chest.

I don't shake his hand. I agreed to *tolerate*, which is not the same as being friendly in my book. "It has," I reply coolly.

His thin lips mold into a grin that doesn't reach his eyes. "I'll admit, I was hesitant about Sharice's insistence on bringing you here, given all that occurred between us. However, our progress has hit some roadblocks, and I'm eager to see if you will help alleviate those."

I grind my teeth so hard, I swear I hear them crack. I promised Sharice I'd help her, but that was *before* I knew he was here. My sister's gaze heats the side of my face, and I don't dare look at her. I know what she's doing. The sister telepathy goes both ways. She hopes I choose my next words carefully because they could mean harm to Oriana or my riders.

"I'm still not sure what exactly you need my help with," I say, willing my voice to stay neutral. "Perhaps if you explained it more to me?" The question is testing the line but not crossing it.

He narrows his eyes, but it's a mix of curiosity alongside arrogance. "It's all a bit technical." His tone sounds patient with a touch of patronization. "I'm not sure you'd understand it all if I did." He tilts his head, the corner of his mouth curving into something that isn't quite a smirk but holds the same condescension. His gaze appraises me, and suddenly feeling self-conscious, I cross my arms. "Try me."

My sister shifts nervously beside me.

Whatever game they're playing, whatever truth they think they hold, I need to understand it. For Oriana's sake, for my riders, and for everyone else in the country while the slow spread of toxic air ticks the clock of another apocalypse to midnight.

"Very well," Elton says. "What is it you would like to know?"

"You told me the TZ's air is spreading. People must've noticed the TZ's spreading," I continue, "Scientists, meteorologists, farmers even?"

"Sure, they have, but whenever they try to draw attention to it, Circuit buries it with other trivial news. Create enough smoke; the fire will always go out."

"But *why* are they keeping it from us? What purpose does it serve to keep their people in the dark about this?"

Sharice gets a contemplative look and rubs her chin as if considering her next words. "You are asking all the right questions, but I have no easy answer for you. Governments are only as powerful as the faith the people they rule have in them. If that faith wavers, they must snatch it back by whatever means necessary. In some cases, lying or at least withholding the truth."

It's widely accepted that Circuit skews information on Network's news programs. Of course, they want to cast themselves in a good light. I'm in public relations. I get how public image is the key to any successful business.

But after I saw the doctor's video when Sharice first brought me here, admitting they were forced by Lannett to falsify the air quality reports, it planted a seed of doubt that has only grown with each passing day.

Circuit is doing more than just bending the truth.

They're hiding it.

"All right," I say. "Our government is lying and doing nothing to help save us, so how do we stop the toxic air from spreading?" It's bold but dragging up a buried piece of my childhood stripped away what patience I have left.

Elton's hand goes to his beard, stroking it like he's still deciding how to react around me.

Good. That makes two of us.

"We don't," Sharice finally answers.

I shake my head. "Then what the hell are you guys doing all of this for?"

"The spread of the toxic zones is inevitable," Elton says. "Our only hope is gas masks and oxygen tanks or building biodomes in which we can live. All of which will take time to build, something we don't have much of. But I do believe I have a way for us to adapt to the toxic air." His dark brows bunch together. "While Circuit is busy trying to get their bills passed or increase their board member's stipends so they can buy another yacht, people like us are searching for answers."

I work my tongue in my parched mouth. My sister believes it. They all do.

A slow, creeping dread settles over me.

We really are all going to die soon.

It doesn't matter if Oriana lives. I'll never get the chance to ride her.

A hollow, sick feeling claws at my insides. All of it was pointless. The long hours in the archives with Heath, pushing Marshal to train me as a novice, convincing Fiaro to keep Oriana at the station. Leaving my riders to come here in search of answers.

I have fought so hard for a future that might never come.

"Here," Sharice says, taking my hand. "It's not all hopeless. Look at this."

Elton steps to the end of the table behind us, and Sharice leads me over. "We've already made so much progress. Full metabolic convergence in the absence of spirulina supplementation, *and* under conditions of photonic deprivation and exposure to hypertoxic gaseous substrates."

I squint at the petri dish, utterly confused by everything he just said. He senses my confusion and adds, "These liver cells are thriving in the equivalent of the toxic gas outside."

My brain works to wrap itself around the idea that they might actually have a solution to save the world as the door to the lab opens.

A man steps in, cradling his arm, a fresh bandage wrapped tight around his elbow. His face is pale but composed as a lab tech guides him toward the exit. Their voices are low, reassuring.

Behind him, two others enter. A second set of lab assistants greets them with soft smiles, gesturing to the reclined chairs along the far wall. A man and a woman, both in their mid-thirties, sit and roll up their sleeves.

The lab techs wrap the rubber tubing around their arms

and draw several vials of blood. Once that's done, they start an IV line and hang a bag of pale yellow liquid next to them.

"You're all set." The tech's hands are gentle and careful, and it is easy to speculate she has a medical background. Elton said Sharice recruited the best.

"Do you want a tablet?" she asks. "I saved that romantic comedy you liked last time."

The woman nods. "That would be nice."

The older man doesn't ask for anything, only offers a faint smile as another tech ties a tourniquet around his arm. A needle slides in, blood rising through the tube. A second syringe follows, injecting something clear. His fingers twitch slightly.

Everything about the moment is normal.

No one is screaming. No one is being strapped down on gurneys like in those horror movies or documentaries about cults with robed people chanting around alters.

There is warmth in the medical tech's voices, a reverence and their mannerisms display nothing but a careful kindness.

And yet, something deep down doesn't feel *right*.

That says a lot, considering everything that's happened in the past couple of days, so I'm quick not to dismiss it.

I force myself to speak, my voice low. "You're experimenting on people."

Sharice frowns. "Volunteers. I assure you."

"We recruited many of the country's top scientists, all thanks to your sister's efforts," Elton says, eliciting a tinge of red on my sister's pale cheeks. "She's a brilliant strategist when it comes to identifying talent and cultivating it. She's a symbol for ITM's values, and few are as dedicated to saving the country as her, but I'm sure you're well aware of that."

I force a tight-lipped smile and shrug. Is my sister brilliant?

Absolutely. But the jury's still out on whether I think she's going to help the country or make it worse. My sister has never been what I considered noble or selfless, so the idea that she is investing time into something entirely altruistic is hard to comprehend.

Sharice never did anything without her own benefit. She's seen as a leader here, respected and clearly valued, but knowing her as I do, I still don't think it's enough.

"What would take Lannet's scientists years," Sharice says, "we're accomplishing in weeks. Unrestrained by regulations, unfettered by bureaucratic hoops, budget committees, or..."

"Ethic's boards," I finish for her.

"We adhere to ITM's code of ethics here," Elton says. "And believe in the greater good over singular individuals."

"Even if that means subjecting people to potentially dangerous procedures?" I ask.

"We do everything in our power to limit the risks," Elton says, "and are proud to say the number of incidents is negligible."

Negligible? "S-So, things have gone wrong?"

Elton's gaze meets Sharice's, and something unspoken passes between them. A confirmation. A shared understanding. My stomach tightens. Oh God. People *have* been hurt.

Volunteer is such a vague term. These people could be coerced, manipulated, or even lied to about what's happening to them. Maybe they're paid. Or perhaps they really *do* want to help. But this isn't the way. There *must* be another option. A better one.

The room collapses in around me, suddenly stifling. The sharp scent of antiseptic becomes overpowering, and the low beep of monitors grates against my nerves.

"No, screw this. This is insane. You're *both* insane. I want nothing to do with this."

I can't be here another second. My pulse thunders in my

ears, mimicking the rush of anger and frustration rising in my throat.

I need to get out. Now.

I make a break for the exit.

Two large men appear, broad-shouldered, with scruffy beards. One has thick black hair pulled into a low man bun, and the other is older, with streaks of gray in his beard.

The one with the man bun lifts his shirt, revealing the pistol at his hip.

"Are you serious?" I face Sharice. "Either you shoot me or let me go. What's it going to be?"

"Let her go," Sharice calls out from behind me.

The guards move, and I'm out the door before anyone else can stop me.

Eight

JESS

The sterile scent of antiseptic lingers in the air as I pace the length of the apartment I share with Heath.

I stare at the disposable cup the test came in, and I urinated in a minute ago. The instructions say results will appear on the side in less than ten minutes. Ten agonizing minutes.

I turn sharply, crossing the room again, ticking off the mental list of everything I'll do after I know the results.

The call to my mother will be the first step. She'll be delighted to have a grandchild. Then, a trip to the village clinic for a prescription of prenatal vitamins. Then, I'll book a shuttle to visit our family doctor to confirm everything is healthy before Heath and I release the public announcement I drafted and proofread. Canterbury's for a baby shower registry. Nunez's for nursery furniture, and then Heath and I will need to discuss finding a bigger place in the Village, as the Blackhawk apartments are limited to one or two bedrooms.

Heath will tell his father, and they'll have no choice but to call an emergency meeting to reevaluate the merger. A child changes everything. With an heir in the picture, my family and Heath's will leverage the family image and focus on stability and legacy. The filtration plant will stay open, and jobs will be saved.

My pulse quickens. I stop and place both hands on my stomach, staring down as if the answer is there, hidden beneath my toned stomach from years of Pilates and swimming.

It isn't. There's no sudden revelation, no instinctive sense of what's happening inside me.

I feel...nothing.

It's ridiculous. I've never been one for superstition, for listening to my body. I should know, right? An intuition. A feeling. Marshal is wrong. I don't have what it takes to be a mother.

The clock on the wall ticks louder than it has any right to, each second a drop of water carving its way through my resolve. I move to the window; the city sprawls below me in a patchwork of light and shadow. It's a kingdom I've spent years building. One move at a time, one deal after another, each piece carefully selected and placed on the board.

I glance at the clock again. Still two minutes to go. I force myself to sit, though the urge to rise and pace gnaws at me. I rest my hands on my lap to still the shaking. I know what's at stake. I planned for every possibility. But I can't shake the dread, the gnawing thought of failure.

Would it really change everything? Can I still proceed with the merger if the answer is no? I don't want to think about it. But the question won't leave, hanging in the air like a storm cloud ready to burst. Without the child, I lose my strongest bargaining chip.

A positive result is the only option. I'll use it to cut through the board's hesitation, to push the merger without opposition.

The alarm chimes and my head jerks toward the sound.

It's time.

I rise, legs like jelly beneath me, and cross to the small device sitting on my desk. My hand hovers over the screen, hesitation creeping in where there should be certainty.

I tap the screen.

The lights of the city dim, and the ticking of the clock fades. All that exists are the words glowing on the screen in front of me.

SHORTLY AFTER, I find Heath in the gym setting weights on the bench press. He hasn't been sleeping well, and I hear him sneak into the apartment well past midnight. He sleeps on the couch while I have the bedroom but it's still obvious he's shaken from Brigid leaving. I'm not jealous, though, not like I would've been months ago.

Another rider sees me and eyes Heath before gathering his water bottle and rushing out. The first-floor gym is open to all of Blackhawk's residents. However, since it's closer to the barracks, the equipment is often busy, and many residents prefer using the smaller, less crowded one on the upper floor.

Heath spins the stopper on the bar and looks up when I approach. He wears dark blue jogger pants and a sleeveless shirt that shows off his pumped muscled biceps and forearms.

Even though it's very much over between us, I can't deny he's quite handsome.

He narrows his eyes at me, and it's enough to tell me he

knows why I'm here. We hadn't spoken in days, and he opted to sleep on the couch, only using our apartment for bathing and changing clothes. True, I spend most of my spare time in the Village shopping or at cafes in an effort to avoid him.

I stop beside the bench. There's no need for pleasantries. He knows why I'm here. "I took the test," I say.

Heath raises a dark brow. "And?"

I tilt up my chin. "And I'm not pregnant. The test was negative."

Heath is very good at keeping his emotions in check, but I sense a sense of relief as he drops his gaze to pick up another weight.

"Well, that is unfortunate," he replies flatly.

As if I expected anything else. "Is it? We were bringing a baby into the world for a purpose, not because we loved each other and wanted to share that love. It was a necessity to promote a stalled business transaction. How screwed up are we that we thought it was okay?"

"It's not," he says. "But it was the best option we had." He pauses, looking up to me. "How is it possible? I thought you took a fertility pill?"

"I did. Obviously, it didn't work."

Heath runs a hand over his dark locks, still perfectly styled even during his workout.

I pick an invisible piece of lint off my shoulder. At the time, it seemed a no-brainer, a duty to assure thousands of people kept their jobs for a small price to pay. But now...since I had time to think about it.

Since I came to Blackhawk. Since I met Marshal.

"You're right. So, now, what do you want to do?"

"You tell me."

The cold indifference bothers me more than it should, and I

snap. "Oh no. Don't you dare put this back on me. You know what we need to do next."

His jaw flexes, and he gives the slightest nod.

"I'll call them today."

"Good. And I'll do the same." I suppress the glee in my tone.

The engagement. The wedding. The possibility we'll be tied together forever is gone.

Finished.

I start to turn away when he says, "Are you okay?"

I'm caught off guard by his rare empathy. "I..." I take a breath to compose myself. "Yes. I'll move on, and you should, too. For what it's worth, I'm glad it's over, and we can put this all behind us."

"Me as well," he says softly, offering me a gentle smile. "Perhaps we can look into alternate paths to help our families and Venovia. I will move to the barracks so you can stay have the apartment a little longer."

"Thank you, Heath."

"I wish you the best, Jess. Truly. I'll have my bags packed and move out tomorrow."

I leave before he says anything else, and tears sting the back of my eyes. Heath and I grew up together; our families have known each other since we were born, and while relieved to no longer be obligated to him, a small part of me is scared. Terrified, if I'm being honest with myself, that I am now free. I wipe my eyes as I hurry up the stairs back to our apartment.

My heart stammers and I'm lightheaded. It feels as if I'm staring at a crossroads with a hundred different paths leading in every different direction, and it's disorienting.

For the first time in my life, I have no plan.

Twenty-three years, I walked this earth with every choice,

every decision planned and mapped out for me, first by my parents, then by myself.

I rest a hand against the wall, fighting the tightness in my chest and nearing the verge of hyperventilation.

Days of accumulated stress culminate into the dizzying letdown of relief, and I close my eyes, willing my breathing to slow.

A minute passes before I regain control. I stand on steadier legs, and the urge to panic eases. Heath will move to the barracks.

What's another day or two? There is nothing to rush back to the city for, especially with it locked down and Circuit threatening a curfew. I have more than enough properties listed, and any incoming offers can be handled via Network or postponed until the current disruption in the city is contained.

I straighten my shirt and start down the hallway. I only make two steps before stopping.

An idea strikes me, and my mood lifts. I spin on my heel and head up the stairwell.

Minutes later, I'm facing a familiar door.

I draw in a shaky breath and knock twice.

Nine

BRIGID

Right now, my only desire is to put as much space between me, and my sister, Elton, as I possibly can, and I'm not paying attention to where I'm going.

The hairs stand on the back of my neck, and a glance over my shoulder reveals the two overgrown apes I faced off with are tailing me. They're around thirty feet back. Annoyance tightens the skin around my temples, and I walk faster.

I detour into the bathrooms, and they follow.

Dammit.

I use the facilities and wash my hands. Their grim reflections stare at me in the mirror. Since they're obviously new fixtures in my life, I give them nicknames.

Man Bun and Grandpa.

My feet move of their own accord, taking me in and out of corridors, past other storefronts that were converted to apartments, until I eventually end up back in the main walkway, passing by the old shells of stores, when a pile of garbage forces me to veer right down another arm of the old building. I hear laughter and see little shadows bouncing on the walls.

Children.

I move closer and find what appears to be a daycare. At least twenty kids of varying ages scramble around on mattresses, play with blocks, or sit at plastic desks with veneer wood tops.

A classroom at the far end of the hall is covered in faded posters of letters and numbers. A group of children sit cross-legged on the floor, listening to a woman teach them about oxygen and hydrogen molecules and how they bond to form water.

It shouldn't surprise me that children are here, yet it does. Sharice told me they welcomed anyone who wanted to join, including families. Yet, the sight of so many children still catches me off guard. I assumed ITM was made up of hardened adults with radical beliefs and violent tendencies, but that assumption dissolves in an instant.

Light filters through the grimy windows, turning the air dusty and golden.

Then I see her.

Mom.

On the far side of the room, sleeves rolled up, mixing powdered goat's milk like it's something she's always done. Children gather around her, their voices excited, as she hands out packets of oatmeal and dried fruit.

My stomach twists into a hard knot. Sharice told me she was here, but I thought she'd be in a lab, shut away with microscopes and tissue samples. Not here like this. Not handing out bowls of food to eager children like some kindly grandmother.

She glances up, and her face brightens with a smile. "Bridgie. I was hoping you'd stop by. Come here. Give me a hand."

I have no choice but to walk over. She passes me a jug of thin milk. I pour it into glasses, pretending my hands aren't shaking from anger.

"Did Sharice show you her lab?" Mom asks.

I nod stiffly, not wanting to talk about what I saw in there.

"She's doing good things here. Groundbreaking work that the government refuses to invest money or time into. These kids would've died if their parents hadn't brought them here. The treatments, your sister's treatments, are helping. Hyper oxygenated detox aerosols with pulmonary hyperplasia. These kids are getting better."

My grip tightens around the jug, knuckles white. "She's experimenting on *people*."

"They're all volunteers."

I scoff. "Nice. She's got you brainwashed, too."

"I've seen it myself." Mom doesn't even look at me when she says it, like the statement's too obvious to question. She pours oatmeal into a bowl for a small boy who starts coughing halfway through. The sound rattles like broken glass.

A woman approaches. She's mid-thirties, her skin tan, her bright red hair tied back in a braid. "Laurel, this is my younger daughter, Brigid."

The woman does a weird half-bow thing with her head. "Pleased to meet you."

"Laurel helps run the daycare," Mom says. "And over there is her son, Ronan."

A boy with equally red hair is at a table with teenagers,

hunched over a tangled mess of wires and tools. Sparks jump as he solders pieces together, quiet concentration on his face.

"They're fixing heating units," Laurel says, following my stare. "Ronan just turned thirteen last week. He's a smart kid, good with machines. More than once, he's helped our mechanical crew when the gennies cut out."

I can't look at her or at any of them without feeling like the outsider I am.

Instead, I glance at the walls. The cracked plaster is covered in drawings. Childish lines and bright colors. Trees and mountains and suns.

Broken buildings I recognize as the ones outside the windows we passed during Sharice's tour of the building.

Druadans gallop across a yellow backdrop. Concentration etches the riders' faces as they lean forward in their saddles, arms stretch over muscular necks as they grip the reins. The scene feels startlingly real and I can almost hear the rhythmic pounding of hooves against the earth, feel the vibration traveling through the ground beneath my feet.

Above them, rocky hills cover the wall, with flowing navy rivers and then more druadans grazing or laying down. I squint at the details. These are different. All of them are red with patches of black and red glowing eyes.

Odd.

I shift my gaze to another mural, and one image stops me cold.

It's me.

A woman is drawn standing atop a mountain with a golden sun shining above her. Her face is calm, and silver-blonde hair drapes her straight shoulders. She wears a suit of all white, and a violet-colored cape flutters behind her as if she's facing a gust of wind.

In one hand is a gleaming silver sword, and in the other a compass.

Unlike the more childish ones, it's extremely detailed and well done, bordering on professional.

Wayfinder is scrawled underneath with flourishes of rays of light silhouetting her.

Laurel asks, "Do you like it?"

I withdraw my hand, feeling like I've done something I shouldn't. "It's very good." My voice is distant, with a reverent quality, and I drop my hand to my side.

Laurel beams. "Ronan drew it when he heard you were here. I hope it doesn't offend you?"

"Offend?" I scoff. "No," I quickly say. "It's..." I pause, licking my lips, and return my gaze to the mural. "He's very talented."

Laurel bobs her head. "Thank you. He inherited it from his father; rest his soul."

"Oh, I'm sorry."

"Don't be. He knew what he signed up for. We chose it together, and he died with honor in his heart, knowing it would give me and Ronan a better future."

My mouth goes dry. Was he a fighter at Meridian? Is Heath, Carter, or Logan responsible for his death?

Mom comes to my opposite shoulder. "Have you eaten, dear?"

I shake my head, surprised at the question.

"I didn't think so. You always got impulsive when you were hungry." She gestures to Man Bun and Grandpa. "See to it my daughter eats?"

I swallow down the protest, suddenly feeling like a defensive teenager again.

"Will do, ma'am," Grandpa says.

They both look at me, and I know my mom will have no qualms about dragging me to the cafeteria. I guess Sharice's promise of getting to eat alone in my room went out the window when I stormed out of the lab.

"I'll come see you later," Mom says. She squeezes my arm. "I'm so glad you're here. Be sure and save me some leftovers?"

A wave of nostalgia pummels me. From out of nowhere, I'm thrust back into my childhood when she told me the same thing: she'd have to work late, and I wouldn't see her at dinner.

I mumble a reply, but Man Bun's hand on my back steers me away.

Out in the main hallway again, I'm at once drawn by the smell of food.

The food court is crowded. People laugh and tease, slurp soup, and shout for the salt or hot sauce to be passed down. I tuck my arms in, my body pressing against the throng of people waiting to go to the counter.

I'm not particularly hungry, my appetite suppressed by the days of swinging cycles of crippling anxiety and hair-pulling rage. Tides, I wish I could wake from this nightmare of a day and find myself in my room at Blackhawk, with a silly Network reality show on, wearing my pajamas, and with a full glass of sweet rose in my hand.

However, despite the noise, the room is surprisingly cozy, reminding me of the family restaurant parents bring their kids to for birthdays, and the servers clap and sing to them over a slice of cake. I breathe in deep, settling my nerves. The food does smell good. Judging by the amount of people eating, something special must be on the menu today.

At the counter, a young woman, barely in her teens, with dark hair and thick eyeliner, greets me. Her eyes lift just a smidge upon recognizing me. "Oh, Wayfinder, it's good to see you," her voice wavers. "It's chili bean soup, cornbread, and goat cheese today, but I can see if there's anything else if you want?"

"No," I say quickly. "Chili is great." The last thing I want is to make a fuss. This is my first time in the base without Sharice as an escort, and I don't want to draw any more attention than necessary.

She gestures to her helper, another teen boy who ladles the soup and sets the cornbread atop a smear of goat cheese.

I take it, thank them, and find an empty table in the corner by a fake palm tree. The oversized pot it sits in has a long crack down the center, and the paint on the trunk has faded to this weird yellow-brown color.

I never noticed before how much of a time capsule this place is. Everything is old and dusty, but surprisingly, a lot of it is intact. Since mining and forestry are limited, nearly everything we use is recycled from plastic. And ITM finding a place like this was incredibly lucky.

The overwhelming scent of roasted tomatoes and chili spices draws my attention to the present. Steam rolls off the thick chili, and I blow on it before trying a bite. It's not bad if a bit underseasoned. I shove two more bites, then move to the cornbread. Suspicious dark flecks coat the sides of the slice, and I convince myself they're un-ground bits of cornmeal and not the added protein of weevils.

I wolf it all down, anyway. I'm hungrier than I realized, and by the time I scrape the last of the bowl, my eyes droop.

I lick the last bits of goat cheese from my fingers and stand to put away my bowl in the wash bin when a hush falls over the room.

Elton enters. Everyone's chatter lowers in volume.

Gone is the lab coat, replaced by a fitted blue Henley that stretches across broad shoulders, cargo pants tucked neatly into scuffed boots.

A worn baseball cap sits low over his sharp gaze, the emblem of Parnia's soccer team stitched across the front.

As Elton goes to the food line, a young boy approaches hesitantly, a delicate paper snowflake clutched in his small hands. He holds it up without a word. Elton pauses, then grins and tugs off his cap. He settles it onto the boy's head.

"Fair trade," he says, voice warm. "Now, make sure you get something good for that."

The kid beams and does a little half-jump. "I'm never giving this one away."

"Everything seems valuable until you realize it serves no purpose," Elton says, tapping the boy's head. His gaze shifts, locking onto mine as he says it. "But if you find something *truly* worth holding onto, don't let it go."

A trickle of ice slides through my veins.

His eyes quickly return to the boy. The crowd parts and he strides to the counter, stopping occasionally to pat someone on the back or greet them.

The teen girl's eyes brighten upon seeing him, and a faint blush appears on her cheeks.

"High Navigator Nunson, I didn't know you'd be eating with us today. Otherwise, I would've set aside an extra portion."

He rests an elbow on the counter. There's something calculated about the way he leans, just casual enough to seem approachable but still maintaining that air of authority. His posture radiates an easy confidence, like someone who's never had to question whether he belongs in a room. "It's no problem at all," he tells her, "I found myself with some time on my hands and figured I'd drop in and see how lunch is going."

"It's going well. Thirty-one plates served so far."

He flashes her that grin of his that makes my toes curl in my boots.

He pauses and takes a fork from the cup on the table. "Well, make it thirty-two," he says, his voice low as if they're sharing a secret. Her smile widens until she's positively glowing.

Gross.

"Now, don't overdo it," he says as she ladles the chili into a plastic bowl. "You know I take the same portion as everyone else."

"Here you go." She hands him the tray. The chili serving and cornbread are normal, but the hunk of goat cheese is twice the size of mine.

Either he doesn't care or doesn't notice because he thanks her and takes the tray to the other end of the room. He sets it on a table, then fills a mason jar at a barrel of water with a pump.

On his way back to the table, he's stopped by a couple of older guys in bulletproof vests and cargo pants. The skin on their faces is patchy skin and scars and faded tattoos decorate their arms.

Only when he sits, do the conversations resume at their normal volume and intensity. No one joins him, and I try as a might. I find my eyes drawn to him as he eats.

He sets the extra plate beside him and meticulously plucks each individual piece of food out of the chili. Kidney beans on one plate, chunks of tomato on another, bits of onion on a third, until finally only the ground, whatever meat is left. I guessed goat at first, but the taste was off, so it most likely was a soy-based product.

Once satisfied everything is separated, he begins eating the tomatoes with a knife and fork. It's painfully slow, but he appears in no rush. Once finished, he takes the next plate to his left of the beans and places it atop the now empty one.

This guy is something else.

Obsessive does not begin to cover it.

I finally force myself to lose interest in his strange eating habits and walk to the exit. He looks up as I hurry past.

"Did you find what you were looking for?"

I miss a step.

"Sharice and I talked after you left the lab in such a hurry. We're troubled that you found our mission so overwhelming. We both really want you to be happy here. I'm proud of the tight-knit community we've formed here, and you're a very welcome addition."

Dozens of eyes watch me. I take another step, praying he loses interest and lets me go.

"Jessica Drakeford ordered a pregnancy test from her doctor." My body stiffens as if struck by a bolt of lightning. The news lodges in my brain like a bullet. Does Heath know? Did she already take it? The sour taste of jealousy coats my tongue as I imagine her telling Heath and the joy on his face. I'd hurt Oriana to help their family's business empires keep the filtration plants open and prevent mass layoffs. And what did I get out of it?

This. I am here, and they are out there.

That dull ache, ever since arriving, pulses in my chest.

"Why don't you join me and I can tell you all about what you're missing on the outside."

"I'm good, thanks," I say, even as I'm dying inside.

The room is silent now. Everyone waits, watching to see if I will defy their leader's orders.

"Don't make me ask twice," he says, with that eerie calmness.

More guards are stationed just out of sight, but Elton won't dare show force. Not here.

I'm the Wayfinder. Their chosen one, and that knowledge is the only thing keeping me upright.

The chili churns in my stomach.

The walls feel too close as the weight of everyone's stares presses in.

No, I refuse to play his games. I refuse to submit.

I break into a run, not caring who sees. Not caring what it looks like.

Slowing to a jog in the hallway, I hear footsteps fall in behind me. Man Bun and Grandpa are right on my heels.

The corridors blur until I find an empty storage room.

Once inside, I slam the door shut. Chest heaving, I grab the nearest thing, a blanket pieced together with scraps of different colored print shirts. I press it against my face and scream until my throat is raw and sore.

I hate this. The frustration.

Dread clings to my skin until I break out in a cold sweat.

Outside of here, the world is moving on without me. My friends, my riders, people I know and love are —

The door clinks behind me, interrupting my spiraling thoughts.

Quickly, I wipe away the tears on my cheeks.

I've only begun to compose myself when I hear the squeak of hinges.

I pray it's Sharice, but my hopes are dashed when Elton enters.

Suddenly, I feel like a cornered animal. How stupid I was to think he'd let it go.

"Get out," I say, willing my words to sound hard.

He tsks and closes the door behind him, but not before I spot my two guards waiting in the hall.

"We're long overdue for a chat, just you and I, and since you clearly didn't want to do it publicly, then private will have to do." The way he says the word private makes my skin crawl, but I do my best to hide it.

"A chat? Is that what this is? 'Cause from my perspective, it looks like an ambush."

He scoffs. "An ambush? No. A discussion."

He looks at the single chair by the table. Dirty towels, scraps of napkins, and other trash towering on it. His lips curl in mild disgust. "Your sister thinks you're the key to our salvation. She believes people will learn of the prophesized Wayfinder and flock to us in droves, giving us the numbers we can use to force Circuit to expose themselves as the liars they are."

I don't reply.

He waggles a finger in my direction. "It does sound rather fantastical, doesn't it? Believe me, when I first read the Inherited Terra doctrine, I struggled to believe it also. Great armies said to reclaim the land. Navigators to lead the mission. A foretold Wayfinder the key to it all."

My jaw shifts. He went to law school, and it shows. The few lawyers I've interacted with all loved to hear themselves talk. But he's so hard to read. Does he really believe this crap, or does it just align with his desire to gain power?

I feign a yawn. "Do you have a point?" I'm treading on thin ice here, but I want him to finish whatever he's doing and get the hell out.

Elton chuckles. "Just as vivacious as I remember. It's no wonder Dane was smitten with you."

At the mention of his dead brother's name, my a tightness squeezes my chest. Elton is more like his father than his brother. Dane didn't like to hear himself talk like this. He was more of a thinker, and we spent hours in quiet company reading books or sketching. Elton is the opposite.

"Very well, I'll get straight to it." He leans his head to the side, cracking his neck.

For a sliver of a second, his confident poise disappears, and

I glimpse the tiredness in his posture. The sag to his shoulders, the shadows around his eyes.

Looks like someone else isn't sleeping well, either.

"Your sister is an excellent scientist." His tone is conversational, but there's a hard edge beneath it. "I know how it can be between siblings. My brother and I had our ups and downs, and I fear her relationship with you is clouding her ability to get the work done."

I bristle. "Sharice is dedicated. She'll find what you're looking for."

His soft chuckle sends a shiver down my spine. "I know how hard it can be to motivate someone, but I take pride in my gifts to do that."

He holds up my comm and the screen glows blue, notifications blinking in a steady rhythm. Missed calls. Messages from my friends Laura, Vince, and Carla, among others, but then I spot Carter and Heath's names in the list.

He taps the screen closed before I can check if Logan's name appears, too. I catch myself hoping—stupidly, pathetically hoping—that maybe Logan sent an apology. But who am I kidding? That's not him. I know him at least that much. His pride is too massive for a simple text message apology. If he did want to make amends (a cosmic-level "if"), he'd do it in person.

Which the chance of me seeing him again seems to be growing slimmer by the second. I shudder at the thought of them keeping me here forever, trapped as a prisoner with no way out. I'll die before then. The thought sobers me, the cold reality of my situation crystallizing like ice in my veins. This isn't just some temporary inconvenience. This could be my life now.

Or what's left of it.

A mix of longing and frustration fuels the flames of anger

inside me, and I glare at him. "Give it back." I try to inject confidence into my words, but to my ears, I sound like a whiny brat. Elton doesn't miss it, either.

"Ah, but this is such a distraction," he muses, "and you are far too busy to be distracted right now."

He spins the comm between his fingers. "It seems you made quite an impression on this trio of riders. Should I put them out of their misery and tell them to stop contacting you?" His eyes flick toward me with a challenge.

I don't respond. How do I? Yes? No? Does it even matter? Will they even believe me, or will it make it worse if they know I'm alive? No, that's wrong. They'll hope I'm alive, but they're not stupid. Logan especially will question if it's even me who has the comm.

He swipes the screen, and my face falls. "Where are you?" he reads in a mocking tone. "I'm sorry, please come back. Are you safe? Blondie, please tell me, are you alive?"

The last one stings the most since I know who it's from.

"Blondie?" he says, eying me up and down. "A pet name? How adorable."

My molars tear into the side of my cheek.

He forces a frown. "Ah, pity. It looks like they've given up on you. It's been a week since the last one came through."

A rawness pulls at my throat, trying to hold back the tears that threaten to escape. A week? It feels like an eternity since I was taken captive. A week of mind games and threats, a week cut off from the outside world.

They had given up on me.

"I could reply back if you like?" he continues. "Give them one last goodbye, put an end to their misery?"

He's enjoying this, getting off on seeing my pain and vulnerability. A tear escapes the corner of my eye, and I quickly wipe it away before Elton sees it, but I'm too slow.

"There, there. There's no reason for that. This is a good thing. They've moved on, and so should you. No more distractions."

With a deep breath, I try to compose myself. I can't let him see me weak. It's what he wants. Instead, I put on a brave face and look at him with defiance. "Sharice promised me—"

Elton scoffs, cutting me off. "She can promise all she wants. She knows her place. I permit her to do her little experiments, so long as they align with the bigger picture." He leans closer. "One that you are the center of. Which means you need to fully cooperate with her every order, or you'll be dealing with me."

His words linger in the air between us. He's waiting for me to break, to challenge him, but I won't give him the satisfaction.

I think of Dane, his brother, and the way his life ended in that boathouse.

The way I ended it.

I remember his jealousy, the way he tried to claim me after overhearing his parents' plans. Always lurking, always sneaking into the lab, eavesdropping. I wonder if Elton knows. Would he even care? Or is this just another piece of the puzzle he's manipulating to fit his vision?

"This is all because of Dane, isn't it? Your way of punishing me?" My voice is steady despite the turmoil roiling inside me.

Elton's gaze turns razor-sharp. "I'm finishing the dream we both shared. A future where everything makes sense. Where the last of humanity isn't struggling day by day. One where science rules above all else, and the human race can reclaim what the sea and dirty bombs stole from us. And while I will never forgive you for taking my brother from me, I am not so narrow-minded as to place my personal vendettas ahead of the future. And you are the key to that future, Brigid."

He shifts his weight closer and rests a hand on my thigh. I physically recoil, but he doesn't seem to notice.

"You and your sister are incredible women," he says. "But Sharice is also a dreamer, and while her ideas are flashy and make for great propaganda to recruit more to our cause, they've proved in several cases to be just that. Just dreams." He moves closer, and I smell the chili powder on his breath. "So, tell me." He dangles the comm next to his face. "What are you willing to do for *this*?" He dangles the comm next to his face.

The edges of the room darken, shrinking down to a single focal point of his sand-colored eyes. I grit my teeth and, with a fluid motion, knee him in the balls. *Hard.*

He doubles over, clutching his crotch. "Fucking bitch."

I stare at him, but the victory is short-lived as he recovers and slaps me across the cheek. My ears ring, and I stumble backward into the side of the cot. Eyes stinging with unshed tears, I press my palm against my cheek, feeling the heat radiating from my flushed skin.

"I thought you'd be reasonable," he says, his polished facade finally cracking to reveal the cruelty underneath. For just a moment, his features twist into something ugly, revealing the hideous monster visible beneath his carefully constructed charm. "Clearly, I was wrong," he says, smoothing the single hair that fell on his forehead when I smashed his goods. "You want to behave like a selfish brat, then you'll be treated like one. Starting right now until you prove you can behave. You will remain in your room until summoned and will be escorted at all times. If you step out of line, if you try to flee or interfere with any of our work here, my guards have permission to restrain you by any means necessary. Your time here is tenuous, and your immunity is solely centered on your usefulness to the cause. Once said usefulness is gone, that immunity will go with it." His nostrils flare, but he's regained his composure.

"You're an asshole."

"I've been called worse." He taps his comm, and the door opens, revealing the two brutish guards. "Please take Brigid to her assigned room."

The two move in, flanking me and gruffly taking each of my arms.

"Playtime is over, *Wayfinder*," Elton sneers. "Work starts tomorrow."

Ten

Marshal

An insistent knock at the door arouses me from a deep sleep. I sit up in bed, running a hand through my hair, shaking the exhaustion from my thoughts.

Who the hell is up at this hour?

Finn lets out a half-hearted woof but doesn't raise his head from where he's sprawled at the foot of the bed.

I rest my hands on my knees. "Some guard dog you are." I shake my head and push back the covers.

"Coming!" I yell and stand. I tug on a pair of sweatpants but am too tired to care about finding a shirt. Another knock echoes through the quiet, and I mutter under my breath as I cross the room. Every muscle in my body protests. I pull the door open, fully prepared to give someone a piece of my mind.

But it's Jess. She looks tired, with shadows under her eyes.

Her presence is like a splash of ice water to the face, and I'm instantly awake. "Jess? What is it? Is everything okay?"

"I'm sorry it's so late, but I can't sleep," she says, the words rushing out of her. "And I was hoping we could talk?"

I step aside, holding the door open wider. "Come in."

She enters, and I close the door behind her. The spacious room feels small with her in it, and the air between us instantly charged.

I rub the back of my neck, still half-asleep, unsure of what to do with my hands. "You want tea or something?" Though I can't even remember if I have any. I wander into the kitchen anyway, reaching for a glass. "I've got water."

"Water's fine," her voice low.

I fill a glass and hand it to her. Her fingers brush mine for the briefest moment. I can't help but notice the slight tremble in her hands. She's been crying, or close to it.

She takes a sip, then lowers the glass. "I took the test."

Even in my groggy state, I know what she's talking about.

There's only one test that she could be referring to, and I'd be lying if it hadn't been weighing heavy on my conscience as well. "And?"

"I'm not pregnant."

The words hang in the air, heavy. I blink, trying to process. "Oh," I whisper, not sure what else to say. "What does that mean?"

"It means..." She blows an exhale through her mouth, fluttering the black strands on her forehead. "It means I'm relieved. And I hate that I am. I feel like a complete idiot for believing the fertility meds would work." Bitterness coats her words. "Maybe it's not meant to be? Maybe I can't get pregnant or... maybe Brigid screwed something up."

I frown. "Brigid? Is that why you did this?" The words tumble out before I can stop them. "Because of her?"

She tenses, her expression hardens, clearly irritated for letting it slip. She looks away, lips pressed tight. "Guess it doesn't matter now," she says flatly. "It didn't work, anyway."

I drag a hand through my hair, my mind racing. A rider having a child. It changes everything. It should be studied and understood. If it's possible...

I catch myself.

Jess is right. Brigid is gone, and unless she miraculously decides to come back, I'll have to content myself with not knowing.

I exhale sharply, glancing at Jess. The resignation in her face stops me from pressing further. She already made peace with this, or at least she's trying to. Digging into it won't change anything.

Instead, I lean back, staring at the ceiling. "Yeah," I say finally. "Guess it doesn't matter."

Jess sniffs and paces to the window to gaze out.

I watch her carefully. "What will you do now?"

She shrugs. "Return to Delford, I suppose. Not much left for me here."

Panic spikes through me at the thought of her leaving. Delford? She can't go back. No, that's wrong. She can. I just don't want her to.

"I could hire you," I blurt out before I can stop myself.

She spins on her heel, confusion tightening her brows. "What are you talking about?"

I scramble for an explanation, my heart pounding in my chest. "The greenhouse. You could take care of it. The chefs could use fresh herbs, fruits, vegetables...whatever they need. You'd have a place here. It's not much, not like your salary now, but you'd be able to stay."

She stares at me, incredulous, like I've lost my mind. "You're kidding."

I shake my head. "Nope."

She laughs, but it's a dry, humorless sound. "Marshal, I don't know the first thing about running a greenhouse."

I cross my arms, standing firm. "You're smart. You'll figure it out."

She tilts her head and studies me, her lips twitching into a smirk. "What exactly would the terms be?"

I relax, sensing the shift in her tone. She's considering it. "Full autonomy over the greenhouse," I say, thinking quickly. "You decide what's grown, what's needed. Set your own hours."

She watches me for a moment longer, weighing my words before she shakes her head, a smile tugging at her lips. "You're really serious?"

"You have no idea."

She takes another sip of water and peers at me over the glass. I hold my breath as time stands still.

She shakes her head, and my stomach sinks. "I'm sorry, but I just can't.

"Why not?"

"I have a small team," she says. "People depend on me to keep Drakeford Properties thriving. My offices are in Delford and Parnia, and with shuttle rides becoming difficult to book, I need to be close to where my work is."

"Work from here? Lots of people do it."

She offers me a sad smile. "I can't. Buying and selling property is more than just calls and contracts. I need to set foot in the spaces, connect with the people listing them."

Fuck. I want her to stay, desperately, achingly, but what I'm asking is too much. For her to give up her whole life and her career for me is selfish as hell. It goes against everything I told her in the cable car. She's spent her whole life being told what to do and finally has a chance at freedom, and here I am, trying to take it away.

"I understand," my voice low. "Just know the offer still stands if you decide to change your mind."

She steps toward the door, and for a moment, I think she's about to stay as she turns to me, a strange look in her eyes. Before I say anything, she leans in and presses a soft kiss on my cheek. The warmth of her lips sends a surge of heat through me.

"Thank you," she murmurs as she moves back. "You're a rare man, Marshal Clemmons."

I stand there, stunned, as she steps out the door and disappears into the night, leaving me wide awake, my heart pounding in my chest.

I should call her name and plead with her to stay, but I don't. She's made up her mind, and I've never known anyone who stands firmer in their convictions than she does, although Logan is a close second.

There's nothing I can do. Whatever she saw in me, it wasn't enough to keep her.

Eleven

BRIGID

Grandpa doesn't say much as we walk, not that I'm in the mood for chatting. Elton's visit has left me shaken, and I want to escape to a private space where he can't reach me.

The storage rooms fall away behind us, replaced by a stretch of narrow hallway lined with cracked tile and flickering lights overhead.

He leads me into what was once a storefront for clothing, big windows with faded sale signs and dust clinging to what's left of a display counter. Sheet metal and salvaged plywood break up the space into four makeshift rooms.

He gestures toward the back left. "That one's yours."

I step inside and close the door. It's dense plastic, and the old hinges groans shut behind me. On the other side is a locking mechanism comprised of a metal bar and a ring. I slide it into place, breathing a sigh of relief. It's crazy how the simple luxury of a private room instantly calms my frayed nerves.

The room's barely wide enough for the cot. Peeling plaster maps the walls like old burn scars, and a rusted lamp leans in the corner. It's industrial-grade, probably swiped from a hospital or prison. The cot's mattress is thin and is topped with faded wool blankets and a very sad, very flat-looking pillow.

A desk and chair sit pressed against the far wall, and beside it, a trunk waits with the lid propped open.

Two more jumpsuits like the one I'm wearing are folded, and I find a white t-shirt, sports bras, and underwear. A toothbrush, a small tin of powdered paste, a bar of soap, and a comb.

I examine the space, trying to accept that this will be my new home from now on.

Ten minutes later there's a knock at the door as I'm washing my face in the small basin. Worried it's Elton again, I shout. "Who is it?"

"It's me," Sharice says.

I lift the lock and open it. Sharice stands in the doorway. No longer in the cargo pants and lab coat, she now wears more causal gray sweatpants and a long-sleeve shirt. "You missed dessert, so I brought you some." She holds out a plastic bowl.

I take it from her, and the smell of cinnamon and caramelized sugar fills my nostrils.

I peer at the twisted pastry coated in brown sugar and plop onto the cot.

"Elton told me about his talk with you," she says.

Talk? Is that what he called leveraging my comm if I slept with him? I should tell Sharice. But what if she already knows?

What if she knew what he did? He probably makes her tell him everything anyway. Nothing *had* happened, and until it did, telling her would only make things worse. For both of us.

My jaw clamps shut. I hate him so fucking much.

"And while I know," she continues. "I've lost the privilege of giving you sisterly advice, I feel there is something you *should* know."

I stab the soft dough with a fork, not looking up.

Sharice joins me, and the cot's spring coils squeak. "For the better part of this past year, I read every text, document, or scrap of data pertaining to druadans and their bonds. And then, when Iris hatched, I could finally put my theories to the test. I did everything I could to force a bond with a druanera so I could use my own blood and tissue samples, but it wasn't enough."

She hesitates, and a sad smile crosses her face. The first real emotion I'd seen on her in days. "But my research wasn't in vain because I learned that riders are truly transformed when they bond at the cellular level. Put simply, their bond re-shuffles bits of their DNA. Their temperament is amplified. They don't feel things like normal people do."

She's right. Logan's temper, Carter's appetites, and Heath's control-freak nature. All were what I considered very *heightened*.

"When I was at Meridian I saw it often. You spent time with them so I'm sure you've seen I also?"

I shift uncomfortably away from her. She knew damn well how much time I'd spent with them. When did this conversation drift from her wanting to comfort me to offering me advice about something she had no right to?

"I hope you understand what I'm getting at," she says, staring ahead. "I know you were close to them, but it's all in your head. Their DNA is altered; that's why they feel things about you. It's not real. It's just chemical reactions warping their minds, changing their chemistry. The urge to mate is strong in druadans, and they release pheromones to make them want you."

She's lying. She has to be.

She pivots to face me. "I know you don't want to hear this, but just think about it. If the bonds with their stallions were gone, what would you have? Would you even matter to them?"

"Yes, I know they would," I speak with conviction, but to my ears, it sounds weak and hollow.

Sharice wraps her arm around me. Despite every screaming instinct, every red flag waving in my mind, I let her. My body betrays my better judgment, melting into the embrace like it's starved for touch, which, if I'm being honest, it is.

"I know you think that, but the sooner you accept that what they feel for you isn't real, the better off you'll be."

I want to fight. To tell her she's wrong and what we shared was *real* but what proof do I have? The memories flash vividly: Carter's crooked smirk under the filtered shadows of apple trees, the cedarwood smell of Heath permeating the air as we sat side-by-side in the library, and how his fingers brushed my cheek when he confessed his feelings for me. And then Logan, when I kissed him, the storm clouds cleared from his eyes as I summoned him away from the darkness.

The memory of him is swept away and replaced with his cruel words. *"We were better before you."*

And just like that, my certainty shatters.

I wasn't so naïve to know men, riders especially, were reputed to have healthy sexual appetites.

Maybe I was deluding myself all along that what I was to them was different. Maybe I was so desperate for connection that I manufactured meaning from insignificance.

Sharice continues rubbing circles on my back, each motion

melting another layer of my defense. I don't trust her—I shouldn't—but my body betrays me, leaning into the first genuine touch I've felt in weeks. I'm powerless against it. For just this moment, I allow myself to be comforted by someone who might be my enemy because the alternative is facing this painful truth entirely alone.

"Elton is the High Navigator," she says after a minute. "Our commander and we have to follow him. It'd be best if you stayed out of his way for now. If you can cooperate a little longer, play the Wayfinder role while you're here, just until we finish our project, then I promise to do whatever I can to let you go."

The words are perfect, too perfect, like a beautifully wrapped package with a spring-loaded snake inside.

"Try to get some rest," Sharice says, rising to her feet. "I'll see you in the morning."

I find myself smiling back at her, a hollow thing I wear like armor.

Once she's gone, I lie back on my cot to stare at the ceiling.

I hate everything she told me and wish it was all a lie, but she didn't tell me out of spitefulness or cruelty. She did it as a mercy. To help me come to terms with the reality I refused to see.

Maybe something can be said for surrender, for letting the current take you where it will. But the truth is, it's easier to break someone who's still fighting than someone who's already broken.

Twelve

BRIGID

THREE MONTHS LATER

Bodies don't rot here.
 The bombs that ended the war killed off everything within hundreds of miles, leaving behind very little flora and fauna to assist with the decay process.

My breath catches in my mask. The mummified person is tucked between a plank of wood and a plastic tarp. Only the sun and heat have affected it, leaving it perfectly preserved.

Without the slowed natural process of decay and the beige jumpsuit with Circuit Justice System stamped on their chest, it'd be impossible to tell if this was one of the first inmates dumped out here hundreds of years ago or if they died last week.

Their shoulder and neck are smeared with blood, and their right arm is missing. They're face down, and I use the toe of my boot to kick them over. They're still surprisingly heavy, which I assume means they died recently. Their mouth twists into a permanent snarl, teeth intact and gleaming like polished white marbles in the sunlight.

I crouch, squinting at the surrounding ground. No signs of a struggle, no discarded weapon, or anything useful like a knife or comm.

The oxygen mask is still on their face, but I don't see a tank anywhere. Too bad, that would've been a good find.

"Tides," I mutter, pulling my mask tighter around my mouth.

"Keep moving, team," Sharice's voice crackles in my headset. "We're almost to the crash site."

I shove the wood back over the body as if covering them might grant a shred of dignity.

When in a constant battle with the very air around you, one misstep, one leak in your suit, and you'll unknowingly take your last breaths.

Sharice taps my shoulder and points to the ground next to her, then points ahead.

Stay close.

My breathing is loud in my ears; every inhale reverberates in my oxygen mask, drowning out the howling wind. The suit is hot, bulky, and smells like the last guy who wore it, but I won't complain. Being out here on Reco — resource recovery duty — means I'm not stuck in the base, being mobbed every time I leave the room. Anywhere I go, I can't so much as cough without someone dropping to their knees or whispering blessings under their breath.

Elton's demand to have guards escort me everywhere ended when the ITM's assault frequency escalated, and he couldn't spare the two extra men.

Also, it didn't hurt I never tried to escape. Not even once.

It's not like I hadn't considered it. I contemplated ideas on how to steal a comm or gun from a guard, but two weeks into being here, a person was dragged through the airlock, gasping as their eyes nearly bugged out of their skull, I knew I was wholly and royally fucked.

To be honest, being the Wayfinder isn't *the* worst. Mostly, I stand next to Sharice and Elton during announcements and smile like some politician's kid while they preach about progress and unity.

Sharice is nothing if not devoted to finding a cure or at least an antidote to neutralize the TZ's effects. ITM's scientists have made progress on inserting new genes via viruses and had limited success with exposure to a thirty-percent TZ air atmosphere before side effects occurred. The viruses are hard to replicate, and the materials we need are buried deeper in the cities. Each raid grows riskier.

They're confident they'll get it to a hundred percent before long, but I have my doubts.

At weekly meetings, they hand me the ledger and take the names of volunteers willing to sign up for their "medical advancement" program. I don't choose them. I just write what they tell me, then speak it clearly and loudly while the crowd murmurs their praises.

I've learned to quiet the part of me that is saddened with each eagerly raised hand. Some survive the procedures for weeks. Others don't.

Sharice and Elton didn't hide their deaths. They tell the families they're heroes, and they give themselves for their family's future.

But I leave all of that behind when I'm off the base in the haze of swirling red dust. Here, where the dull rays of sunlight manage to pierce the yellow fog, I glimpse freedom.

Out here, I'm free to remember who I was before the experiments to hold off mass extinction, before living in a cramped room where mystyl creatures are unsettlingly close and only a centuries-old wall keeps the poisoned air at bay.

Out here, I'm not the Wayfinder. I'm the same as the others, in rust-colored jumpsuits and black helmets, looking like the fire ants that scurry about their mounds at Meridian.

There are six of us in total, including Sharice and Elton, and the only identifiers are the yellow armbands on our arms.

"The crash site should be a half mile east from here," Elton says in my headset. He's moved ahead with the others.

I heave the wheelbarrow forward, the hard plastic tires bouncing on the rough terrain.

Ever since that night, I've tortured myself for not getting my comm back. I could've slept with him, given my body to him while my mind was elsewhere, just for the chance to message the riders, to let them know I'm alive and put them out of their misery.

But every time I consider it, I ease the guilt by convincing myself he'd been lying.

He has all the power and even if I had let him do what he wanted, he never would've followed through on his end of the deal.

I've made a habit of staying up well past lights out just to make sure he doesn't try to visit me again. Sacrificing hours of sleep for peace of mind, but he never comes to my room.

However, just to be safe, I've gotten into the habit of barricading my door with the extra chair.

I never told Sharice what he did.

Why should I? She'll just sweep it under the rug, and it's

not like she'll turn against him. He is the High Navigator. Untouchable.

And my Wayfinder status only exists because Sharice made it so.

If I forced her to choose between me and him, I would lose.

There is only one way I can escape.

Which is why I'm out here in the heart of a tox zone, scouring an old town, miles from the base. I can sit and wallow in my fate in my room or volunteer for dangerous missions like this for at least a fraction of a chance I can find a way out.

Just cause I hadn't tried to escape didn't mean I'd given up.

Sharice had asked Elton to bring more, but he dismissed her, saying we'd be less likely detected by any passing shuttles in a smaller group.

It's all a lie, though. Elton said it so the base wouldn't squabble over who gets first dibs on shoes, candy bars, or insulated bottles of wine.

But those luxuries weren't what had Sharice drooling. She was focused on the manifest they'd uncovered by hacking into the shipping company's port on the Network.

No, what they were after was something else much more valuable.

A decommissioned scientific research team was moving to Leviler, and they'd been researching atmospheric decay. This shuttle had crashed out here six months ago and had all their equipment, including a digital chip, quietly packed during the transfer. A storage drive with all of their research data on it, including the air quality samples for the past five years.

It was priceless.

It was proof.

Proof that our government was keeping the truth hidden from us and we could use it to recruit more people to our cause.

I adjust the side strap of my oxygen tank and trudge forward, eyes scanning the area. They didn't give me a weapon, claiming there weren't weapons to spare, but I know the truth. They want me to feel vulnerable and afraid.

Fear means I'm compliant.

Fear means I won't try anything stupid.

Even after three months, they still don't trust me.

And they shouldn't.

The longer I've been here, the more I've learned escape isn't just unlikely; it is impossible. I have accepted that.

This is my life now, like it or not.

This place is my home.

For the most part, they've welcomed me.

Making me feel as though I'm a part of something bigger. While Sharice isn't the warm and fuzzy type, she's seen to it that I'm comfortable.

But that doesn't mean I gave up completely. During the day, I play the part and behave, but the night is mine.

They can't touch my dreams.

When it's light out, I lie awake long after, staring at the swirls on the ceiling and imagining I'm back at Blackhawk, where three overly warm men lie with me.

During the day, I keep busy and occupied with ITM tasks, but at night, resentment festers.

I'm spending what could be my final weeks on this earth without the three men I love most. Without my friends or the people at Blackhawk, I've grown to care about.

When asleep, I lose control. They find me in my dreams, their faces clear despite the time apart. They whisper my name as their hands seek mine, their mouths warm against my skin. And when I wake, the phantom touches are so real they linger long after.

Elton and three others move ahead, and we form a sort of arrow as we walk through an old shopping district.

Metal shopping carts were piled in the street as if someone had tried to build a wall, and we'd been forced to double back to find a way around them since the structure was too unstable to climb.

The shopping district is riddled with ghosts of the past. Every storefront boasts decrepit clues of what it used to be. A bakery's sign hangs by a single rusted chain. A toy store's colorful display faded to dull hues behind cracked glass.

It might as well be another planet for all that I recognize.

Keeping my head low, scanning the ground for anything useful. The others press ahead, their shapes distorted by the haze; red jumpsuits blend into the swirling dust.

A hunk of something metallic is half-buried under a slab of concrete. Squatting, I pry it free, a jagged piece of aluminum siding. Turning it over, faint paint clings to the surface: Inland Dreamland Amusement Park and Zoo, Exit 40. The design is faded but clear enough, with a cheerful ferris wheel, cartoonish trains, and an elk mascot grinning with oversized teeth.

Delford had an amusement park once. I never got to go. The levee broke the summer I turned nine, and it all sank into the floodplain. I toss the scrap into the wheelbarrow, and it rattles against scavenged wires, cracked plastic containers, and a handful of rusted metal brackets.

I keep moving.

Centuries of dust and heat have buckled the asphalt, forming cracks big enough to snag a foot and twist an ankle. We walked most of the morning and the idea of hobbling back to the base on a hurt leg isn't the most appealing.

The wind howls through the broken windows, fluttering

loose roof tiles, and somewhere nearby, a door bangs open and closed.

Thousands of people who lived here called this place home when the bombs had dropped. Kids, women, and families were out shopping at these stores, eating at these restaurants, or driving these cars when, in an instant, they were dead.

The gas from the original bombs was a thousand times more potent than what lingers now. Their deaths would've been relatively quick, a few coughs, then unconsciousness.

I try to take solace in that knowledge, but it doesn't work.

Jack's voice crackles in my ear. "Herd of banshees. North. Quarter mile."

Banshees.

After seeing the drawings in the school room, I learned that the wild black and red druadans, whom people believe extinct, are, in fact, very much real.

On Network, they're myths, whispered legends of creatures that can't exist. No one ventures into the TZ and lives long enough to confirm, and even if they did, the odds of seeing one before it killed you are slim.

Like druadans, they're carnivorous, but somehow, I doubt they'd be satisfied with a bucket of protein pellets.

Sharice estimated the descendants of the survivors from the final battles numbered fewer than a hundred in the entire ten-thousand square miles of Delta wasteland.

I had yet to see one until today.

And here they were. An entire herd.

Scrambling up a collapsed wall, I clawed my way to the top, dust and broken glass shifting beneath my hands.

I finally see them. To the north, moving through the ruins.

The herd turns, galloping in our direction. I count six total, including a foal. Their coats shift in the dim light, shades of black and gray, and their hooves strike hard against the cracked earth as they fight to drive the predators away.

The foal stumbles as a pack of mutated dogs with malformed heads and foaming muzzles, called jackals, close in.

They left us alone for the most part and, with a shout or toss of a rock, ran off for easier prey.

The adults close ranks, forming a protective wall.

Then the jackals dart ahead to cut them off, and the lead stallion moves from a defensive stance to an offensive, chasing after them.

The stallion snags one jackal by the scruff, lifts him in the air, then tosses him aside. Another, possibly a mare, catches a bigger one by the tail and flips it over backward, then stomps it to death.

Cringing in disgust, I can't look away.

Only two jackals remain, and they're fully sprinting in our direction, with the herd hot on their heels.

"Move, move," Elton shouts in my head, overlapping others, yelling to find cover. "They're drawn to movement. Find somewhere to hide and stay put."

I hesitate. Up here, I have the high ground. Maybe I'll be safer staying put. But before I decide, my foot slips.

A jagged gap between two slabs of concrete swallows my boot, and my ankle wrenches sideways. A sharp, searing pain shoots up my leg. I bite a scream and yank, but the heel is wedged tight.

Shit.

My breath fogs the inside of my mask. I claw at the broken concrete, nails catching on dust and grit. My breaths come fast and shallow, and my frantic pulse thunders in my eardrums. Fingers straining, wrists trembling, I tug, but it won't budge.

"FUCK!" I shout, but the mask muffles my voice.

My gaze darts over the rubble, searching for something to

pry the rock. I spot a length of half-buried rebar under debris and reach for it.

I grip the rebar and wrench it free, ignoring the way my scraped palms protest. Wedging it into the crack beside my boot, I press down; every muscle in my arms burns as I force the stone upward. It shifts. Just an inch and I yank my foot free. But the momentum throws me backward, and I lose my balance.

The sky trades places with the ground as I tumble down the pile of rubble. Sharp edges tear at my clothes and scrape my skin, and I tuck into a ball, protecting my face and head.

Finally, I stop tumbling, and my back slams against a jagged slab of concrete. Pain jolts through my ribs. The rebar clatters beside me, ringing out against the stone.

For a moment, I can't move. Dust fills my mouth, dry and bitter.

I lift a shaking hand, wiping away the dirt from my eyes. My fingers press against bare skin.

My mask.

I bolt upright just as my stomach plummets and scramble back up the rubble, eyes darting frantically. It has to be close.

I don't see it.

No, no, no.

I clamp my lips shut even as my lungs are already burning. How long do I have? In some places, it's thinner, but others are saturated with toxins. If I'm lucky, I have minutes. If I'm not—

No. I can't think like that.

My gaze catches on something tangled in the wreckage. A tube. My oxygen line.

Hope surges, and I seize it, pulling hard only to find the other end severed.

No tank.

A desperate sound slips from my throat. My vision swims

as my chest convulses, every instinct in my body screaming for air. My fingers tighten around the useless tube, and I groan.

Black spots collect at the edges of my vision. I'll pass out soon, which means my body will betray me and breathe anyway.

I'm all out of options. I squeeze my eyes shut, feeling tears stream down my cheeks, and inhale.

The air was thick and heavy with a sharp chemical residue. But beneath that, something else. Sweetness, almost pleasant. Like the dried cherries on top of birthday cakes at the base.

It's killing me, but I *can* breathe.

Mind clearing, the panic recedes just enough for rational thought to return.

I hold my breath, testing. If I ration my inhales and limit my exposure, then maybe...

A shadow moves behind me, looming and immense.

Slowly, I turn.

The lead stallion looms above me. Watching. Twin streams of steam unfurl from his flared nostrils, curling in the poisoned air like the breath of some slumbering dragon.

A Banshee.

His long mane falls past his shoulder and is knotted and missing clumps. Muscles ripple beneath his black hide, riddled with scars. His eyes burn red, unnatural, and luminous in the wasteland's haze, and my starved-for-oxygen brain. He bares his too-oversized canines, protruding past his lips, a mutation made for survival.

I freeze, and he lifts his head as if scenting the air. Rushing sensations make me jolt.

Fear. Curiosity. Anger. *Hunger.*

Not my emotions. *His.* A stallion. But how is this possible?

The bond.

After all this time, after centuries of evolution, it's still there.

It's unrefined and nebulous, not tempered by control or centuries of selective breeding. A feral energy sparks over and through me like a raw current, coursing along my spine, crackling in my veins.

Almost like Oriana's.

My chest aches. Sharice assured me they'd moved her to Lannett and she was alive and safe, but when I pressed her for more details, she changed the subject or claimed she knew nothing else.

I focus on the bond surrounding me, a pulsing, invisible current as if the air itself hums in recognition. Slowly, cautiously, I press against it. A small, deliberate push as if testing the springs of a mattress.

The stallion snorts, his ears flick back and forth, muscles coiled tight beneath his thick black coat. The energy shifts and curls around me like a wary predator circling its prey, like a cat winding its tail around an unfamiliar leg. Testing.

My lungs demand oxygen as I clamp my mouth shut. I'm running out of time.

Grabbing the bond with both hands, I force it toward me. I glare at the wild creature, refusing to break eye contact like you do a feral dog. It's just me and you.

"Submit," I will the word to connect.

The stallion lowers his head, nostrils flaring, watching.

"You can breathe here. You will save me," I growl mentally, willing the words to strike true.

The stallion's raw bond flares in response and surges through me, wrapping around my chest my limbs. Heat floods my veins, thick and liquid, like slipping into a bath after freezing rain.

The burn in my lungs vanishes.

I gasp, inhaling deeply, expecting the saccharine poison of the air, the chemical sting of the TZ, but it's just...air. No sour taste, no acrid smell. Just clean, natural.

Spots fade from my vision. My head clears, the pounding ache subsiding. My grip on the bond tightens instinctively, unwilling to let go, unwilling to risk losing this lifeline.

The stallion steps back as I push onto my feet, his red eyes flickering as they glow brighter.

A tremor of uncertainty pulses through the bond. My head throbs from the intensity, my stomach twisting as I stumble under the weight of a mind not my own.

The stallion flattens his ears and snarls, elongated canine points glinting like ivory daggers beneath his curled lips.

I pull back to release the hold, but I don't know how. The bond is still wide open, still pulling, still feeding.

His fury crashes into me. I shield my face, preparing for the attack, when I hear a sharp pop.

There's a bloom of red in the back of my eyelids, followed by an intense pain, and then...

Nothing.

I open my eyes just as the stallion crumples.

The severed bond snaps, yanking me back so violently that I cry out.

Whipping my head to the side, Elton stands with his pistol raised, smoke curling from the barrel.

The stallion's thick black coat rises with fading breaths as dark blood pools from his mouth, soaking the dust, his red eyes dimming with a final, sluggish blink before he goes still.

The silence that follows is suffocating. A void where something vast and wild had existed.

My fingers and toes tingle, and my knees buckle. I can't speak. I can barely breathe. The air tastes wrong again, tinged with that artificial sweetness.

"Are you alright?"

Sharice.

"Where the hell is your mask?" she shouts, resting a hand on my back.

Jack drops beside me, hands fumbling to put the spare helmet on me, but I barely register him. My breath is shallow, my pulse roaring in my ears, and the aftershock of the bond still crackles beneath my skin.

"What the hell happened?" My sister asks. "Are you okay?"

"Get her up," Elton barks. "The others will smell blood. We need to move."

He holsters his gun, and our group starts the walk back to the base. I glance over my shoulder, and despair coils around my ribs like iron wire, tightening with every breath I take in the stallion's lifeless body on the ground. I had felt it. Its strength and fear and soul, we'd connected and for the briefest of moments before...

Sharice hovers uncharacteristically close. "I still can't believe it didn't kill you."

I look to see if anyone is within earshot. "It wanted to, but something happened. I felt it. I felt *his* bond."

Her face doesn't change, even though she's paying very close attention.

"Are you sure?"

I nod. "It saved me and I think I know what we need to do to save everyone."

"So let me get this straight. You think that if a person bonds with a banshee, it will alter a person's DNA and they can breathe the TZ air?"

"Yes," I say confidently.

Sharice peers at me skeptically. "Fine, I'll bite." She takes a tablet from the bin on the table and sits, legs crossed in the chair opposite me, giving me flashbacks of every job interview ever. "Start from the beginning. Tell me every detail."

I explain how I lost my mask, ignoring her disapproving look and comment that I should always have a safety line attached to my shoulder harness. She's right, but there are twenty safety lines and some require someone else to untie them for you to use the bathroom, so most people leave the hip ones undone. I will swallow down the awkwardness and never forget it again.

She makes notes as I tell her how I slipped down the hill and the stallion appeared.

"You're lucky he didn't rip your throat out," she says.

I rub the sides of my temples, trying to stave off the threatening headache. "I don't think he wanted to. I felt him. He was hungry but also curious."

"Odd, all the banshees we've interacted with have shown only primal savagery."

I bite my lip, knowing I'm straying into territory I've kept by some miracle a secret from Sharice.

"I can feel druadan bonds."

Sharice's hand holding the digital pen stills on the tablet. I sit up a little taller, preparing for whatever comes next. *Cat's out of the fucking bag now.*

Her left eyebrow hitches. "Explain."

I inhale sharply. "At Blackhawk station, I noticed that I could detect other riders' bonds. Sense them."

"All riders?"

I shake my head, and a knowing look appears on her face.

"No, just three."

Her lips form a thin line, and she resumes writing on the screen. "I see. Please go on."

"At first, I didn't know what it was, but then I felt Oriana before she hatched, and afterward, I sensed them even more clearly." I pause, licking my lips. This is it. I'm laying it all on the line because I must. There's no other way to save the world. "And then there were times when I could actually *touch* them."

Sharice finishes writing her sentence, and when our eyes meet, her gaze is distant, full of a million thoughts I can only guess at.

"Damn," she finally says. "While I'm upset you decided to keep this from me, I understand your hesitancy." She sighs and rubs her forehead. "But I'm more upset my theory was wrong. I hate when I'm wrong."

I shake my head, feeling like I'm three sentences behind. "Wrong about what?"

She furiously scribbles on the tablet's screen. "My theory pertaining to the riders being responsible for the druanera's failing health. I still believe they are tied to it, but it seems you're more at fault."

"Me?"

She nods like it's not the mind-blowing notion I feel it is. "Think about it. You used a dormant fifth sense to touch and manipulate their bonds and not once wonder where the power was coming from. Everything has a price."

I had no idea.

The truth roots it folds me inward. I thought it was me—my strength, my instincts, my connection with Oriana. We weren't bonded, but there was so little we knew about druanera that I never questioned where my power came from or what it might be costing her.

Sharice is right. I'm an idiot.

I swallow hard, my hands curling into fists against my knees. "I didn't know." But the words feel empty. Excuses.

Nothing changes the fact that I took from her without realizing it, without care. And now...now it might be too late to fix it.

Sharice watches me, eyes sharp. No sympathy. Just the same calculated analysis she always has. She shifts, crossing her legs again. "Back to the matter at hand," she says like my entire world hasn't just cracked apart. "You felt the banshee's bond. So, say you somehow can bond a human to a banshee, you still can't tap into Oriana from here."

I force myself to focus. The guilt will be there later, waiting, but right now, I must push through. I might not have my riders, but having Oriana here would be a significant improvement. I know what I'm asking is big, but I won't miss the chance to at least try. "Then we need to get to her."

Sharice tilts her head, and not for the first time, I wonder if she's secretly jealous of my connection with the riders and Oriana. "Not possible."

"It's too great a risk to transport her here. We're nowhere near that resource level yet. Besides, Elton would never authorize it." She pauses, her lips pursing in the way she does when she's told no by someone. I've pieced together that she's on a leash here, a very long one, but a leash nonetheless. "Your proximity to Oriana is like when our comms are within network receivers. A sort of wireless way to charge and power the abilities you already have. You were born with this gift, Brigid. Whether it be by genetics or exposure to environmental factors, I am unsure." I swallow down the lump in my throat, and my scalp prickles. Marshal. If she suspects it's my genetics, there's a large chance she'll test me and learn we're only half-sisters.

I shove my hands under my thighs, dismissing the worrying thought. So what if she does? That's just a problem for future me to deal with.

"Be that as it may," she continues, "this *gift* is no more than being born with an extra hand. Without neural pathways to control it, it's useless. Like a lightbulb without power is a glass ball. The only way to charge your system, for lack of a better term, is for you to be physically near Oriana. She is the key. Her hatching triggered something in you, flipped a switch on a gene that laid dormant your entire life."

Sharice taps her chin. "However, there is something else one of our lab techs has been working on." She pauses, her eyes dancing between mine as if debating how much to share.

I arch a curious brow. "Tell me."

"From day one, we've struggled with controlling the mystyl, using pheromones, toxins, even bait to coerce them to move where they're needed, and there is one formula we could use with some tweaking for human usage. I think it will enhance or possibly supplement whatever this ability is."

"Okay, so then I can bond it to myself, and you can test my blood."

Sharice is shaking her head before I can finish. "No. It's far too risky. If something happens to you…" Her voice breaks.

Wait. Is she actually *worried* about me?

"We'll get volunteers," she says, composing herself. "People less valuable."

Instantly, I feel icky inside.

She must notice my discomfort because she quickly adds, "This is how it's done, Brigid. Scientists need samples and data; they can't test themselves."

"But I'm not a scientist."

She frowns. "No, but you're the Wayfinder. People will eagerly want to assist you. This bodes well for what they already believe."

"What *you* made them believe," I say.

She reaches out and caresses my hair with the back of her

hand. "I always knew you were something special. You weren't like mom or me."

Don't I know it.

"You had no plans," she says. "No goals you strove for, you just *did*. And because you were the youngest, mom didn't pressure you like she did me."

For a moment, she's not the cold strategist, not the woman who orchestrates plans with calculated precision. She's just my sister. Just Sharice.

"I envied your freedom," she admits, her voice softer than I've ever heard it.

Why can't she be like this all the time?

Her expression tightens, walls creeping back into place, giving me my answer.

She can't afford to be. Not around the others. Not around Elton.

Still, it stings.

I traded one life for another, gave up my friends, the three riders I still cared about, despite learning it was all chemically induced, to be here with Sharice and the rebels.

Neither is perfect. But in reality, there is no way I can have both.

She's my sister. My blood. No matter how different we are, our past binds us. The childhood we shared, the understanding that lingers beneath the distance.

She's the only one who remembers the same moments I do.

"So, as I was saying," her voice brightened, "while the banshees are not near matches to the druadans, they are close enough, which means, given the proper energy source and metabolic state, you should be able to force a bond onto a human."

"And then what happens?"

"I don't know. It's all speculation at this point, but I gather they will have a similar bond as any rider would. We'll know more once we study them. Take blood samples. With any luck, you'll only have to test it a couple of times before I can synthesize the genetic disruption. While I don't want to get ahead of myself, I believe we can transfer the benefits of immunity to the toxic air with a series of injections."

Incredible. My heart shudders in my chest. A miracle drug for everyone who wants to stay. We won't have to leave Venovia. People won't have to die. "So, what now?" I ask, voice eager.

"Now, we need to catch a banshee."

Thirteen

Heath

I steady my pistol, breath held behind my teeth, and line up the sight on the faceless mannequin. Someone painted eyes recently on it, probably a novice on a dare, but they're uneven, giving it a slightly unhinged look.

My feet are precisely shoulder-width apart with my back straight as I stand in one of the firing lanes in a covered shelter on the west hill just outside of Blackhawk.

The weight of the new pistol feels substantial in my hand, not heavy, just present.

This one is sleek and, as Carter rightfully calls it, sexy. A Xalerian X-90, freshly issued for Specter and needing calibration.

We returned from our six-week stint at Clearwater Military

Base yesterday, where the entirety of the Specter team had trained side-by-side with Circuit soldiers, immersed in drills and tech simulations that stripped us down and rebuilt us.

It was Vanguard all over again. Every day started before the sun rose and ended long after it set. The kind of training that leaves your bones aching but your instincts honed razor-thin. They filled in the gaps, performing years of choreographed battles that had been left. Specter wasn't just meant to be good. We were the front line mystyl detection.

We had to be untouchable.

Now we're back at Blackhawk, and the pace hasn't let up. Two instructors from Clearwater rotate in weekly, monitoring our progress.

The range is quiet this morning. Just the way I prefer it. No distractions. No unnecessary chatter. Just me, the weapon, and the target.

I raise the pistol, extending my arm fully. Inhale. Hold. Squeeze.

The first shot breaks the silence with a sharp crack. Dead center in the chest.

I adjust my stance minutely. Second shot.

Another is in the center, although slightly to the left.

By the ninth shot, I've established an almost meditative rhythm. Nine perfect holes clustered tightly in the middle of the target. For the tenth, I adjust my aim, testing the weapon's responsiveness at the edge of the bullseye. The shot lands exactly where I want.

I pluck out one of the earplugs

Someone lets out an appreciative whistle.

I ejected the spent cartridge.

It's Marshal. "Nice, Lockwood," he says, moving into the lane next to me, separated by a low wall.

I reload, feeling the subtle vibration of the charged ammunition as it engages. The balance shifts. The cartridges that came with the gun weigh more than the standard issue.

A negligible difference, but I notice.

I hold the pistol up again and recalibrate based on the new weight. Ten laser blasts in rapid succession, each one finds its mark with absolute precision. All ten land directly in the center of the outline of a human target.

Marshal folds his arms. "You heard from Jess lately?"

I lower the pistol, turning to look at him with a measured gaze. "No. I don't talk to her anymore. Why?"

"Just curious," he says, his attempt at casualness transparent.

I set the pistol carefully on the counter and face him. "If you want to ask me for her number, you need only ask."

Marshal smiles, running a hand over the stubble on his chin. "Nah, I got it." He pauses, then quickly adds, "I mean, I got it from before when she was helping with Finn."

I give him a reassuring look. "Marshal, it's okay. Jess is in my past."

He laughs, tension visibly leaving his shoulders. "All right, well in that case I wanted to make sure it was okay if I..."

"Pursue her?" I offer.

I'll be damned if I've ever seen him look more like an awkward teenager. He's ten years older than me, but you wouldn't guess it, not with the way he's blushing and fumbling for words like his tongue forgot how to work.

He's been stretched thin for weeks, trying to keep the novices sharp, drilling them hard through daily formations like the exhibitions are still coming. Like the crowds will show. Like the world hasn't started flinching at shadows and locking their doors by noon.

However, the truth is that no one feels safe. Not really. And if ITM keeps pushing, those exhibitions will be one more thing we pretend to believe in.

"Yeah, I guess." He shrugs, feigning indifference poorly. "We talked before, and she said she needed space, so that's what I'm doing, but it's been months, and I thought, what the hell if I call her? What do you think?"

I raise the pistol, examining the craftsmanship. "Jess isn't an easy person to understand, so if you're looking for insight, I'm afraid I don't have any."

"Figured as much." He nods toward my gun, changing the subject. "Best two out of three? Loser pays for drinks at Blink?"

Grinning, I point the gun at the target. "Hope you brought your wallet 'cause I never drink anything other than top shelf."

Fourteen

BRIGID

"Don't blink," Edna, one of the base's lab techs, tells me over the headset. "You need to stay perfectly still so the computer can monitor your pupil dilation. It's the only way we know the implant is connecting to your neural pathways."

My hot breath in my helmet fogs the glass as I force my eyes to stay open. A flurry of goosebumps shivers up my arms.

A banshee. I still can't believe it. A real, living wild druadan is here, right next to me.

A week ago, I didn't think they even existed, and now I'm within feet of one. Working with it. Trying to bond it like the stallion did to me.

They're hard as hell to catch, but with the use of the rovers to round them up and bait to lure them in, this is the third one we've managed to capture and sedate.

Since it isn't safe to bring a banshee inside, nor do we know if they can survive in purified air, we'd found a space a short drive from the base for the testing arena. It's partially hidden from passing shuttles under the shadow of a tall rock formation, part of the large circular space was walled off by a collapsed hardware store and reinforced with corrugated metal sheets twelve feet high.

It wasn't until after we'd built it that I considered whether banshees were capable of phasing like druadans. But when the first one ran wildly around the perimeter before the ingested sedative started working, it was obvious they couldn't.

Druadans could only phase with a rider, but then Galaxian didn't have any problem doing it on his own, proving once again that we knew so little about druadans.

I *was* right, however, about putting out rotten meat instead of fresh goat, like Sharice suggested.

Delta is hundreds of miles across, and food must be scarce, which means it has a smell strong enough to draw their attention.

I don't dare move, letting the animal assess me as it will. If it wants to eat me instead, then so be it. I'll be dead in seconds.

This is the third time we've done this, and so far, I'm still alive and breathing.

With a heavy enough dose of sedative to be sure, they all react the same, curious and with limited aggression, unless a pompous ass from maintenance decides the spotlight needs fixed while waiting for the sedative to kick in.

Tough break, Ted.

The heat dissipates as she lowers her head, returning to gnaw on the carcass we'd left in the center.

My heart thumps in my ears, a shockingly steady rhythm.

It's now or never.

I play with the capsule implanted in the back of my neck. Around the size of a grain of rice, it sits at the hairline, making it nearly invisible to the naked eye.

One tap and the chemical will flood my veins.

I tap the receiver strapped to my wrist, where my comm would typically be, and then wait for the beep before tapping the one on my neck. A redundancy, so I didn't accidentally trigger it with an itch or pull my hair into a ponytail.

Crack.

A cool rush of liquid ice pours into my veins. Adrenaline-Laden Therapeutic Augmentation of Increased Reflex, ALTA for short, is a concoction of hormones mixed with herbal infusions.

She upped the dose, and where my muscles usually warmed like I had done light stretching, this time they ached like I ran five miles.

The hazy gloom brightens as if it's midday. Every sense heightens, and I'm overwhelmed by the sensations of smell, sight, sound, and touch.

Despite being outside, the sudden rush of claustrophobia overtakes me.

An aura shimmers around the Banshee, the faintest flicker of crimson red. Normally, it's a flicker at the edge of my vision or a flash when the world tilts sideways and the panic claws up my throat, like the day I lost my mask.

But with Alta, it's clear as daylight. It pulses like a living thing, trailing behind the mare like a loose strand of rope, weightless and untethered, curling through the air as if searching for something to latch onto.

A side door slides open, and a person wearing a full suit and helmet steps into the walled-off area.

The banshee lifts its head, chewing, unfazed by me or the other person, and it reaffirms my theory that their vision is sensitive to movement and poor during the day.

My feet carry me closer, and I snatch it from the air. The banshee lets out a startled squeal as its tether squirms in my grip. The connection pulls taut like a wire, and my knees buckle.

"Stay calm," Edna barks in my helmet. "Your blood pressure is spiking. You're going to metabolize it too fast."

The surge of energy rushes from me, and it's like I'm standing with one foot on a balance beam, ready to fall at any moment.

Once the person is close enough, I spin and launch it toward the person like a fisherman casting a line. A guttural noise escapes me, and the person grunts with the impact.

They're tossed back onto the pile of cardboard scraps they lined the space with.

The banshee rears up, letting out a low growl, and I gasp as it yanks the bond free from my grasp. I rest my hands on my knees, steadying myself, and watch.

"*Please,*" I breathe. A shiver races up my spine, followed by a severe wave of nausea. After effects of the ALTA, but shrug them aside, not daring to look away.

The banshee drops to all fours and shakes its head, and blows its nose.

Tentatively, the person moves to the banshee. The creature arches its neck, and its dark eyes focus on the approaching person. It gnashes its teeth once, then stills.

Holy shit. *It worked!*

As I step closer, the banshee and the person shift their gazes to me.

The person reaches up to the clasp around their neck that secures their helmet to their suit.

"No!" I shout. "Wait! Not yet."

It's too late. Their helmet is off.

It's an older man. Middle-aged, with a receding hairline and pockmarked cheeks.

Shit. Charles. He works in shipping and loading.

He grins at me, showing me his uneven and stained teeth, and squints at the sun.

I hold my breath.

The banshee leans forward, sniffs his face, and his grin widens.

Is she speaking to him?

I count the seconds in my head as I watch. His smile fades, and the left side of his mouth droops slightly.

At first, I think it must just be the way the zone distorts the sunlight, a trick of the mind. Then I see it. The pink of his skin leaches away, transforming into a mottled, sickly green like mold spreading over bread. It permeates from his jaw to his cheekbones, seeping into the delicate skin beneath his eyes. Veins darken beneath the surface. A bluish-green web branches from his temples down to his throat.

"I'm sorry," I yell, backing up. "I thought it would work. I'm so sorry."

Charles looks at the banshee with nothing but adoration in his eyes.

Oh no...no, *please.*

I press the ALTA implant again, feeling a second surge of the chemicals as I reach out for the waning tether between them, but grasp only air. *I can salvage this.*

Frantically, I search for the aura, but the midday sun is too bright, and the automatic dimming shade makes it harder to see.

"It's too dark," I shout. "I can't see through my fucking helmet!"

"Stay calm," Edna says. "I'm overriding your tinting."

The visor clears just in time to see Charles cough blood on the banshee's face.

Crimson on crimson.

He wheezes and his thin lips—already turning blue—curl back in a grimace.

The banshee remains stark still, chest vibrating, and attention focused only on Charles. The bond wavers between them, like the base lights during a storm, flickering and dimming.

Charles falls to the ground, eyes bulging as he grasps his throat.

I draw in a deep breath. My chest tightens as I watch him choke on the poisoned air, instinctively needing to breathe deeper as if it might pull him back.

Even if I wanted to save the bond, it was too late. He's gone.

I step back, and my foot catches on a stray piece of rubble.

The banshee's head snakes toward the sound. Its scarlet eyes glow against the backdrop of its merlot-colored hide, streaked with black as though scorched by fire.

Banshees are predators, and I bonded a person to one, a person who is dying an excruciating death right now, which means it is reacting to the fear and confusion it wasn't familiar with.

And it is pinning it all on me.

We'd never made it this far.

I have no idea what to do.

The side door creaks open, and one of the security team members enters. Before I can react, they draw their pistol and shoot Charles in the back of the head.

Face frozen in a snarl, he falls to his knees and then forward, landing face down on the dusty ground.

The bolts in the ground clank as the banshee struggles to be free, alarmed by the whiplash of another consciousness suddenly appearing, then disappearing.

Fuck.

Panic freezes me in place.

"What did you do?" The word falls off at the end as I'm reeling in shock.

The man doesn't reply as he holsters the gun. He steps over the dead man and gestures for me to follow.

I don't move.

"I ordered him to terminate your failure." Elton's voice echoes over my headset in my mask. I'm too numb to be startled by his presence.

"Failure?" I snap. "But he was bonded. I *felt* it."

"He *was*, and now he's dead."

"So, we try *again*?" Urgency bleeds into my voice as the guard leads me out of the enclosure.

"His mind wasn't strong enough. His consciousness fragmented under the strain of the bonding. The data proves the cognitive deterioration would only worsen with time."

I open my mouth to protest, but then close it. He's right.

That's why I hoped this would be the one. The others were close but not quite.

"This project of yours is taking longer than I'd like. We have the team on a rover bringing in another, so until then, you're dismissed for lunch. The team will analyze the data."

I did it this time. I felt the connection solidify. So then, why did he die when he took off his helmet? Why didn't the bond protect him?

Icy, cold fingers claw at the base of my skull.

The few must suffer so the many can live. Sharice reminded me of that daily. What we were doing was a necessary sacrifice for progress. We stood on the front line, fighting to save humanity while the rest of the country panicked or buried their heads in the sand.

I stuff my hands under my thighs and choke back tears as I ride in the bouncy rover back to the base. I clung to her words, even as the truth pounded my brain.

I had failed. *Again.*

Once inside, I wait the thirty seconds in the airlock for the toxic air to be sucked out, then strip off my suit. Sharice waits for me on the other side. "I'm sorry I couldn't be there this morning. Elton had me recording the weekly broadcast." She holds out a plastic tray covered in foil. "I heard it didn't go well, so I brought you lunch."

The smell of spiced meats and tomatoes fills my nostrils. My nerves are frazzled from the failure, but my stomach seems unbothered. Manipulating the bond draws tremendous energy from me that the epinephrine and other metabolic enhancers only amplify, leaving me tired and starving. Sharice speculates it has something to do with tapping into my subconscious in a way someone going without a REM cycle for a long time will feel.

It's taken days of trial and error to get the balance just right, so I didn't pass out from exhaustion, or the dose was too weak to do anything.

She moves to the side and sets the tray down on the small table. I remove the foil and instantly salivate at the cured pork and beans slathered in a red barbecue sauce.

I sink into a chair, grab the fork, and dig in.

Sharice holds her tablet up. "While you were coming back, I looked everything over, and I know what went wrong this time."

I slow my eating, but only slightly, and look up at her.

"The ALTA dose is correct, but Ch—" The scientists helping

with this insisted we keep the volunteers' identities hidden from me for the results to be honest and non-biased.

They can't have me reacting differently depending on who they send in, or it removes the validity of the tests. And although it's a small base, with the use of shaded masks and plain jumpsuits, they could be nearly anyone when they enter.

"Volunteer C-7 had a severe allergy to peanuts," Sharice continues. "And was taking a daily histamine. I believe the banshee sensed this in their system and rejected it." She hesitates and clears her throat. "Medications in a person's bloodstream are factors we didn't anticipate but will now screen for moving forward."

I mop up the beans with the slice of bread, my thoughts spiraling.

"Maybe the banshees are unbondable with anyone but me," I tell her. "Every time I've tried to force the connection, it's like pouring gasoline onto a fire. Their minds lash out, devouring everything."

"Don't be overdramatic," Sharice says.

I scoff. "The first guy tried eating their own arm, and the second tried attacking me."

"And this most recent one became placid and breathed the air for sixty-seven seconds. Sixty-seven!" she says. "I see that as progress. With every test, we improve the dosage and modify the procedure. It's all we can do. Test, modify, test."

I glare up at her.

The problem isn't just that I don't think I can do this; it's that I don't *want* to do this.

I don't want to be here. The resentment seethes within me. But it's not toward anyone but me. I wanted this. The one who believed it would work. If I backed out now, the banshees' deaths and the injuries to the volunteers would be for nothing.

"We'll figure this out," she says, sensing my dark mood. "I

promise I don't like seeing the failures any more than you do. So, if you're up to it, let's try it again."

She taps on her tablet, then checks the banshee's vital signs on the monitor.

"We have resecured the one from this morning. They sedated it, and it looks stable enough. Why don't you grab some rest, and we can try again later this afternoon?"

I catch an hour-long nap after lunch and expect it to be plagued with red-eyed wild druadans and people gasping for air, but it's not. In truth, I practically black out the second my head hits the pillow and awake only when one of the lab assistants knocks on my door and tells me the rover is waiting to take me out to the testing arena again.

Thirty minutes later, I'm standing in the center of the enclosure again in a mask and suit, preparing to force one unwilling creature to tether itself to another.

Sharice came along with me this time, and her voice speaks in my ear. "Sample B-25 and Volunteer L-31 bonding attempt number four. Vitals and stats look good from my side. You're green to proceed."

I reach up, rub my finger against the implant, and release the first dose. Sharice recharged the three doses but warned me to only use one if I wanted to keep my lunch down.

The banshee mare from this morning's aura swirls a handful of paces from me, fluttering like a red ribbon in the wind. She's sedated, and her side rises and falls in a steady rhythm, her nostrils sending up little puffs of dirt with each breath.

"Proceed," Sharice says in my headset.

In our trials, I've learned I don't need to physically grab it, but it makes it easier. I step quickly to the wavering tether and grasp it between my gloved fingers. It resists, but I hold it long enough to force it toward the volunteer. My body hums with the connection, and a warmth seeps up from both my arms where they touch the banshee.

"Ready," I speak into the headset of the helmet.

I've only ever done it from a distance, but on the rover ride out here, Sharice, and I agreed I should try physically touching both banshee and volunteer as if to reinforce the connection.

"Volunteer L-31 entering the arena," Edna says.

A slight itch irritates the base of my skull, like the first twinge of a headache.

"Wait, something's wrong," I mutter. The banshee's consciousness coalesces with my own. She's grown suspicious since this morning, like a fish in a pond that's been caught too many times by the same lure. However, with ALTA boosting me, I'm able to keep it under control.

"Everything looks good from here," Sharice says in my headset. "What is it?"

"I don't know, I just..." but before I can finish, the volunteer enters, and my heart plummets to my feet.

Their visor is a clear glass one. I see their face.

It's Laurel. *I don't remember her signing up.*

"Uh, cancel the test," I shout. "I can see the volunteer."

"Negative," it's Elton's voice.

Where did Sharice go? I wonder.

"You may continue," he says.

My chest constricts like a shuttle has parked on it. No. I can't. Her son Ronan had already lost his dad. If I fail, he'll be an orphan. Why the hell had she volunteered?

I clench my gloved fists. Because the High Navigator made

her. This is his idea. His twisted attempt at motivating me to try harder.

And screw him, it worked.

I hate this. It's wrong. But I can't fail. Not this time.

I slam a second dose, amplifying my already enhanced senses. Bile rises in my throat, thick and burning, but I choke it down. If I puke in my suit, it's over.

Wait, maybe that's how I get out of this. They'll call the test off until I get them to clean it, and maybe I can talk some sense into Laurel.

I stop myself.

No, Elton will just find someone else I care about in here. Fucking bastard might even use a kid.

Laurel watches me. Her face is pale behind the glass, hands folded in front of her like she's bracing for something.

"You don't have to do this," I say, not caring if Elton is listening. "Please. You can leave right now, and we'll find someone else."

She meets my gaze and offers a timid smile. "It's okay, Wayfinder. I trust you."

My knees turn to jelly.

Trust me?

We aren't exactly close, but she's sat with me at meals, shared her sacred bottle of conditioner, and gifted freeze-dried strawberries when I covered for her in the classroom when she wanted a day off to spend with Ronan or was sick.

She's soft-spoken but firm and endlessly patient with the kids, making her an excellent teacher.

And she never stopped calling me Wayfinder, even when the others had.

"Sedation is wearing off," Elton says. "Proceed, please."

I march to the banshee. It's smaller than the others, possibly younger. Perhaps the herds have gotten wise to our rovers, and they're only able to capture the smaller, weaker ones. I press my gloved hand against its hide and reach for Laurel.

No grasping for threads in the air. If I have to, I'll use myself as the conduit.

It's riskier. The banshee could rip open my suit with one well-placed bite, but I take the chance.

She steps forward without hesitation and clasps my hand, and a pulse of crimson energy envelops us.

The banshee's red aura swirls like smoke, pulsing in rhythm with its heartbeat. I close my eyes, feeling the weight of Laurel's hand in mine. The ALTA surges through me, a vacuum pulling in smoke. Every microscopic burst of energy, every flicker of emotion in this creature—I feel it all.

A sound hums in the distance. A deep, rasping voice. The banshee's, but then it's gone.

My ears pop as the tether snaps around Laurel. White-hot pain sears through my skull, knocking me back. I release them, sagging forward, panting.

When I look up, Laurel stands near the banshee.

She smiles. A pleasant, quiet smile. Almost identical to Charles.

The waning ALTA in my system allows me to see the red ribbons of aura fluttering and pulsing between them.

Please work.

"Volunteer L8, please remove your helmet."

I can't move. Can't speak.

The bond is strong. I did everything I could. There's no turning back now.

She hesitates, then unclasps her helmet.

Over the radio, I almost hear the collective breath being held in the viewing room.

Laurel lowers her eyes. Inhales.

Like before, I count the seconds.

Twenty. Thirty. Forty.

Her skin remains its usual copper tan. No veins bulging. No gasping. No convulsions.

"Congratulations, everyone," Elton says, voice dripping with condescension.

The snap of his smug tone jolts me from my daze.

A bright, trilling laugh escapes her, and the banshee resumes gnawing on the goat's haunch.

She lifts her face to the sky, then twirls and tosses her helmet. It lands with a dull thud beside me.

Laurel levels her gaze on the banshee again, transfixed, looking at the creature as though it's the most beautiful thing she's ever seen. I've seen this look before when Danner bonded to Wraithwind.

She takes a shaky step forward, and her head unnaturally jerks to the right. Her movements are stilted and irritated, and she waves at the air around her face as if fending off biting flies.

The side door hisses open, and I turn. It's Sharice behind the helmet's faceplate.

She spares me no more than a glance before heading straight for Laurel. I snatch the helmet from the ground and stride to her just after Sharice has.

Laurel lowers herself to the ground on all fours and growls. "Stay away," she says, her voice low and unnatural. "Humans bad. Kill family. Make loud noises."

A sinking feeling in my stomach tightens into a fist.

Sharice's eyes widen in abject horror, mimicking mine. I dry heave.

"Rover," Sharice shouts on the radio. "Get me a rover now. We have an emergency and need to get a patient to Dr. Zulkey immediately."

A devastating realization drags me down, submerging me in despair and regret.

I've made a terrible mistake.

Fifteen

CARTER

S pecter isn't a secret anymore.
While we're not exactly a household name yet, we have a following. Specter Sirens, they call themselves, people trading theories, posting blurry videos on Network, and matching our hidden identities to our stallions like it's some kind of game.

It's no surprise we have a fan club. People are looking for anything to get excited about these days, and we look damn impressive in our black tactical gear and helmets. Our stallions, too, are armored in carbon-fiber, ballistic-grade plates, not like the showy sets we wore for demonstrations.

I adjust my grip on Ember's reins. Letting me know he's alert, he swivels an ear back toward me, his breath clouding the air. There are five on the mission here tonight, including me, Ve'loth, Heath, Liam, and Luke.

Life these days consists of mission simulations, combat training, and meetings with Corporal Dickweed or Lieutenant Asskisser. All of whom work under my mom. President Peterson assigned General James the Specter task force and she assures me we're proving effective. Every mission we go on saves lives and keeps fewer weapons in ITM's hands. I can't help but believe her. Believe what we're doing is making a difference, but on nights like this, I miss the spotlights of the arena. I miss the music. I miss the crowds, the energy.

But above it all, I miss not waking up every day and wondering if today's the day someone else is loading Ember on the shuttle back to Blackhawk.

Or I'm seated alone, carrying his bridle on my lap.

We have yet to lose a rider or druadan, and while I pray like hell it stays that way, I know it's not a matter of if but when that changes.

ITM is out of control, and it's common to hear reports of soldiers taken hostage or mystyl being released into police stations or churches.

All of this has made my mom even more overly cautious and one of the reasons she insisted on sending a ground team with us.

It took some convincing from Marshal and Heath to keep Logan on the team after his charges, especially with Garrett already on it. But with the escalating war against ITM, his combat skills are an asset.

Although I'll never forgive him for driving Brigid away, I feel better knowing he is watching the team's six. And despite my grudge, Specter was *safer* with him here.

With General James' blessing, he can tag along without

Galaxian, and he even brought Elena and Seth from his security team for additional training.

A dozen mystyl we can handle. Our stallions take care of the close ones while we shoot the others farther away or relay their locations to the soldiers nearby. The first three missions were meant to be for training purposes, allowing us to get used to traveling with our druadans and working with foot soldiers around us. But a few weeks ago, we were tasked to guard a building while several Circuit board members met. There had been chatter from undercover agents that ITM was planning an assault, and so we were called in.

It was a lot like tonight. Quiet at first, with hours of standing around waiting, but then, as the meeting adjourned, rebels knocked out the security cameras before emerging from a drainage pipe.

They didn't bring any mystyl with them. And at debrief, they'd speculated it was for an information-gathering mission only.

They were sizing us up. And while we took out three of their guys, one escaped on a motorcycle.

Now that ITM knows Circuit has a druadan task force, it's only a matter of time before they amplify their attacks.

We regrouped, pushing ourselves more in training, and the next two missions proved completely uneventful. There is talk that perhaps ITM found Specter too great a risk to challenge and decided to go for easier targets. I don't buy it for a second.

I should be grateful tonight is quiet, but I'd be lying if I didn't say I'm bored.

Restless. And judging by the whispers from the others, I'm not the only one wondering if this is a waste of our time.

Liam's stallion, Ravenwing, paws on the gravel beside me. "Fucking hell," he curses. "I think my balls are freezing to my saddle."

"That'd be a feat since you don't have any," Ve'loth says, voice low.

"Oh really? Your mom sure didn't have any complaints last night."

"Leave my—"

"Silence," Heath snaps. I look at him with a flicker of annoyance that he heard something before me.

He holds up a hand, and all of us tilt our heads to listen.

The alley we guard stretches into darkness, broken only by the faint yellow flicker of a busted streetlamp.

Sensing my unease, Ember shifts beneath me, his tail swishing against my leg. I press a hand to his neck, and the solid warmth of his body steadies me. He's carried me these past months. The one constant in my life was when, for days, I felt like I was drifting.

He's the reason I haul my ass out of bed in the morning. The reason I try and stretch out the OS usage until I can't take it anymore. The reason I make sure I'm eating and sleeping. He doesn't judge like Heath and doesn't demand explanations like my mom or Marshal. I owe my life to him, and he demands nothing but my company in return.

"What is it?" Liam asks.

Heath shakes his head, his eyes scanning the spaces between the buildings. "I thought I heard something, but I'm not sure."

My hand flexes, trying to ease the cramping in my knuckles. I dosed an hour ago, and it's starting to wear off.

"Ship two is loaded and preparing to depart," My mother's voice crackles through the comm in my helmet. "Sweep areas five and six, then head to exfil. Bravo team will meet you there, and I'll be monitoring from shuttle seven."

"Got it," I respond, signaling the others. "Liam and Lockwood go with McCelroy and Seth to five. Elena and Ve'loth with me at six."

Logan scoffs loud enough that I can hear it under his helmet.

"Something you'd like to share with the class?"

"Yeah, that's a stupid idea."

"It's an order."

"And a bad one."

Ember sidesteps, allowing me to stare down at Logan on foot next to me. "You're here as an escort, and as leader of a CSS special ops team, I'm in charge."

"James is right," Heath adds.

I bristle. I don't need him coming to my defense.

Logan peers up at me, his gray eyes visible through the plastic visor of his helmet. "Yes, sir," he shouts, his gaze unwavering. "Let's go, Seth."

He turns and follows Heath and Liam.

Ember steps forward, his shod hooves crunching in the gravel, and Elena and Ve'loth follow me.

As we move deeper into the alley, the shadows stretch and curl like they're alive. Ember and Ravenvein's ears flick in every direction for any sign of movement.

Ahead, the alley opens into a maze of shipping containers stacked three high, and rust streaks the metal walls. The faint stench of oil and stale water clings to the air, mixing with the metallic tang of the cold. I signal for the group to stop, scanning the rows of containers. My eyes sweep the shadows. The bond warms my chest as I search for the telltale glow of tentacles.

Nothing.

I wave my hand and tap my helmet. *Let's go. Listen.*

Ember tosses his head. His tension mirrors the itch in my skin. He wants to move. To fight.

We make it to the others and regroup with Logan, Liam, and Seth.

"Anything?" I ask.

Liam shakes his head as Logan checks the clip on his gun. To our right, flashlights bounce in the misty air above the tops of a container from the Bravo team, helping the distributors load the crates of hand tools, hardware, and lumber.

"Sector five and six, clear," I say on the radio.

"Good," replies Mom instantly. "Hang tight. Cargo is almost loaded."

"Let's fan out here," I say. "But stay within sight."

Logan meets my gaze, and I almost tempt him to challenge me again. The night's pent-up tension has me feeling like a coiled spring ready to snap. Despite the cool air, sweat beads on my forehead. The OS and riding have kept brimming at bay, but I swear I'm developing calluses on my right hand from months of jerking off.

It's not that I haven't had offers from others; my sock drawer stuffed with thong panty offerings is proof enough, but between the exhaustion of working all hours and the bone-deep fatigue that hits me the moment I'm off duty, I usually collapse onto my bunk before I can even consider taking anyone up on their interest. Most nights, I barely have the energy to do more than pass out the second my head hits the pillow.

With my hand, it's easier to let my mind wander to Brigid.

Silently, Logan motions to Elena and Seth, and we form a wall, putting the shuttle and Bravo team at our back.

I guide Ember toward the center, and he snorts his protest but obeys.

The comm crackles again. "All clear so far," Heath reports from a hundred feet to my left, where he and Shadowmane stand near a double-stacked red container.

"Copy that," I reply, my voice steady, though my chest feels tight.

"Nothing here," Liam says next.

A gust of wind whooshes through the containers, and Ember snorts and snaps his head to the left. His ears pin back, a low rumble vibrating through his chest.

"*Mystyl?*"

"*Yes.*" His voice is low, eager.

I lean into the bond, letting my eyes relax so the bond does the weird double vision for me.

Last month, an army squad captured a mystyl alive, so we took the team, stallions included, to Clearwater military base to practice sharpening our senses. It was better than I thought, and I caught up with my baby brother, Derrick, who was recently promoted to corporal in the CNG, Circuit National Guard. He returned from North Gaergen Island with a scar on his cheek and a ring on his finger. He fell for a triage medic named Tyson while working forest fire recovery.

Once I recovered from the shock of my younger brother getting married *before* me, I told him I'd be his best man, only if he let me throw him the bachelor party.

He said he'll think about it.

Heath's voice cuts through the comm, disrupting my thoughts. "You seeing this?"

I whip my head toward his position. It takes only a second before I spot the movement. A ripple in the shadows. Too smooth, too deliberate to be anything other than it is.

"Affirmative," I reply sharply. "Mystyl. Ten o'clock. Wait until you have the shot."

Ve'loth and Liam slowly turn their stallions, and Logan and the others on the ground position to the side. They know better than to get between a druadan and a mystyl.

But before anyone gets a shot off, a screech tears through

the air, followed by a flurry of motion. The tentacled forms scramble up the walls with terrifying speed.

Ve'loth and Ravenvein pounce on one, and the rest of us open fire. The blue-black stallion sinks his fanged teeth into the slimy creature, which lets out an earsplitting screech.

He wasn't fast enough. It's alerted the others. *Fuck.*

I barely have time to register the thought as a swarm of more mystyl, numbering in the teens, scrambles over the side of the container.

I said I wanted a fight. My damn wish is granted.

An orange streak of laser blast races from the muzzle of the gun as I pull the trigger. Blue-black blood splatters against the metal crate beside me, and the acrid stench burns my nostrils. Other mystyl surges, translucent tendrils writhing. I fire, and three collapse in wet heaps, but more take their place.

Ember spins as I blast like a man possessed. All around me, orange streaks flash as the others try to hold their ground.

"*We losing,*" Ember's voice hums in my mind, irritation tinging the edges. "*We kill five. Shadowmane has six.*"

"*Not for long,*" I reply.

Our shared competitive nature flares as I scan the area. I snap another shot off, then quickly shift my gaze to locate Heath's position. He's a blur of movement, his gray stallion tearing through the enemy like a living storm. My grip tightens on the pistol, determination rising to match his kill count.

Forty feet ahead, Ve'loth curses as another skitters up the stallion's legs and wraps its long tentacles around him and his rider, trying to pull them down. The stallion staggers under the weight of the creatures but remains upright.

"Everyone on Ve'Loth," I shout, but my voice is erased by the gun blasts and clatter of hooves. Seth and Elena must hear me because they spin and direct their fire at him and his struggling mount.

But it's no use. There's too great a risk to shoot this close. We need to get them out of here.

My gut clenches as I watch the creatures scramble up the black stallion's legs, suctioned limbs wrapping tight, pulling, dragging. Ve'loth slashes at them, his blade flashing, but they're relentless.

"Liam!" I bark. "Shoot me a path!"

Liam's rifle cracks the night air. The impact sends one creature splattering across the dirt, but more surge in, unrelenting.

This cannot be fucking happening.

Ravenvein rears, hooves striking at the mass of writhing creatures. Ve'loth fights, with his laser sword slashing. Then, in a sickening instant, they vanish beneath the swarm.

"No!" rips from my throat, but it's already too late.

The druadan's agonized scream bellows into the night air. The ground churns where they fell, a mass of twisting bodies, ink-black blood, and the sharp scent of death. My body locks; horror roots me in place.

"*Move,*" Ember growls in my head, his instincts burning hot through our bond. "*More come.*"

I snap back to the fight, fingers tightening around my pistol. "Fall back!" I shout, spurring Ember to pivot as raindrops splash my face.

Pain radiates into the collective bond, searing white-hot and merciless. The agony strikes without warning, a savage knife twisting under my sternum.

Ve'loth and his stallion are gone.

Ember thrums low in my mind, and the hollowness makes my breath stutter.

A sharp ping echoes off the metal container beside me, something hot and stinging grazing my neck and shoulder. I curse, slapping the burning spark away, the scent of singed fabric filling my nose.

My earpiece crackles. "Specter," General James says. "I hear gunfire. Status report?"

I press a hand to my bleeding shoulder and force my voice steady. "Mystyl fucking everywhere. They got Ve'loth."

A long pause. My pulse pounds, my breath ragged in my ears. The onslaught has slowed, but movement flickers at the edges of my vision. A straggler slithers forward, its tendrils flexing, tasting the air.

Logan puts a bullet between its donut-sized eyes before it gets any closer.

Seth, part of Logan's ground team, is leaning too much on his left leg, and the fabric on his left thigh is stained dark with blood.

I tighten my grip on Ember's reins, steel my voice, and shout, "Exfil is compromised. Retreat to secondary."

No one argues.

Trudging through the carnage, leaving Ve'loth's dead body behind us. Mystyl corpses squish and pop like rotten fruit under Ember's hooves. The mystyl's toxins rapidly degrade when they die, and combined with the druadan's resistance to it, it makes this more of a mess than a threat.

We all signed agreements for no extraordinary measures for body retrieval.

May your burning end and your bond be freed. I chant the blessing in my head, promising to honor Ve'loth at Blink when we get home.

My instinct was right. ITM is far from done with us.

Sixteen

BRIGID

The tablet screen casts shadows on the walls of my room as I lie on my stomach, watching a show about a pair of rival co-workers snowed in after the rest of their office switched corporate retreat locations to the beach. They're arguing about who knows how to start a fire. Their playful banter fills the quiet room. It's an old comedy, one I watched in college, but it's better than sitting in silence, stewing. ITM's media library is limited, no Network access, but at least it's something familiar. *A sense of normalcy.*

After what happened with Laurel today, I don't feel like walking around the base. No doubt, word had already spread about how she had a mental breakdown after going to the testing arena.

They might still see me as the Wayfinder, but turning one of their own into...whatever she was now isn't going to win me any points. I have to face them eventually, but that is a problem I don't want to face right now.

The only thing keeping me from completely spiraling was Sharice telling me I was done.

She's convinced she can recreate whatever changed Laurel's blood and allows her to tolerate the poisoned air via a synthetic replication. Which means, at least for now, my part is over. No more tests. No more death.

A soft knock pulls me out of my thoughts. I don't bother pausing the show.

"Yeah?"

To my surprise, it's my mom.

She steps inside, carrying a foil-wrapped bundle and a bottle of water. The smell of sugar and butter hits me before she even speaks. Sweet rolls.

She's eaten meals with me and Sharice, but they do most of the talking. We are long overdue for a real conversation, but I haven't had the energy to drag up everything. The drugging. Her siding with Sharice. The fact that she might have thrown her whole career away for this.

Mom sets the bread on the table beside me. "Did I ever tell you how I chose your name?"

My mouth curves up in thought, suddenly suspicious of the start of this conversation.

"I thought I was named after a relative?"

She sits beside and smooths the wrinkles from her pants. "Your middle name, yes, Elaine, but your name was inspired by something entirely different."

She sighs and rests a hand on my leg. "Your father—" she starts, then pauses. "After Sharice's father passed, I didn't use a sperm donor."

I don't blink. "I know."

Her eyebrows lift slightly. "Oh?" She lets out a dry, humorless laugh. "I'm not surprised. You were always perceptive. Might I ask how you found out?"

"They did blood tests at Blackhawk, and I matched with someone." I lick my lips, stilling my nerves. "They told me their father is Arlin Clemmons."

Her thin eyebrows lift slightly, then she shakes her head and laughs. "Damn him. I always suspected he had other children out there."

"Children? You mean I could have more siblings?"

She tosses her shoulders. "Knowing Arlin, there's a strong possibility. He was devilishly handsome, and anyone who met him fell in love with him. Men and women alike. I never stood a chance."

She smiles wistfully, something I never see her do. Oh my god. She loved him.

"Tell me about him," I ask.

Mom cranes her neck and stares up at the ceiling, then lowers her eyes to mine. "Arlin was a scientist like me. He studied archeology while I focused on biology and genetics. And tides, he had a brilliant, inquisitive mind, while far more bold and daring than I was at that age. He was on a short visit to Uncy'lia at the same time I took on the field experiment along TZ Beta's border, analyzing the beach grasses and sandpiper eggs for mutations. During the day, we hiked the beach dunes marking sandpiper nests, and at night, we made love under the stars."

Yuck, that's not exactly the image I wanted seared into my mind right now. I shift uncomfortably, pushing the mental picture aside. "So, what happened after that?"

She squints at me quizzically. It's not an unreasonable question, and yet I feel like I've overstepped. This is my life. I deserve to know who my father is.

"They didn't allow birth control back then, so while we tried to be careful, inevitably, I became pregnant with you. When he found out, he was overjoyed."

My heart soars more than I thought it would upon learning that my father actually A) knew about me and B) had initially wanted me.

And yet, as Mom sighs, I realize we're getting to the not-happy ending of her story.

"Arlin's tenure ended," she says, her voice tight. "They rescinded his grant and demanded he transfer to West Gaergen for a dig. He had to file a postponement in person, so he left for Delford. A week later, you were born, and he never returned."

She runs a hand over the side of my head, tucking a strand of hair behind my ear. "You were born with this same pale hair and the healthiest set of lungs the midwife had ever heard. She said that since you were born on the spring equinox, where night and day were equal, you had a balance of light and darkness in you. She was a firm believer in ancient religions and told me there was a goddess of both life and death named Brigid." She lowers her hand. "I messaged Arlin, telling him your name, but never heard back."

Mom wipes the side of her face and avoids looking at me.

Is she crying?

Marshal had shown me a photo and said she was in contact with him off and on. Did Mom think he was dead? Should I tell her? Or would it do more harm when it's clear this is still a sensitive subject for her?

I decide to split the difference. "My half-brother is Marshal Clemmons. He's a rider at Blackhawk station."

Mom swivels her gaze to me, her eyes glassy with emotion. "A brother. How old?"

"Thirty-four."

Her face visibly relaxes. He would've been with Marshal's mom before her, proving he was faithful.

"It's been twenty-three years," she continues, "And I've closed that chapter of my life. Whatever reason he had for not returning, I've made peace with never knowing." Her eyes soften, and she reaches for my hands. They're surprisingly warm. "I know my work kept me away from you girls more than I should've, but don't ever think I didn't want you. You and your sister are my greatest gifts. I only ever wanted you to grow up and reach your fullest potential." She pauses, and a smile tugs at the corner of her lips. "And now, with you here, I get the chance to make up for lost time."

A warmth blooms in my chest, and I want to hug her, but I'm not ready.

Not yet.

There's a gentle knock, and Sharice enters.

She wears a gray sweater and leggings.

Her eyes widen in surprise to see Mom sitting with me.

"Is something going on?" she asks.

Mom releases my hands. "Nothing for you to worry about, dear."

My insides twist that Mom is keeping the lie from Sharice. I shouldn't be surprised. Our family was never the most transparent.

I wrestled for weeks about whether I should tell her; she deserved to know, right? But what difference will it make? Will she look at me differently? At our mom, whom she idolizes so much?

"What is it?" Mom asks.

Sharice frowns at me before straightening. "We're having a meeting with the other leaders."

"Regarding?"

"There's an issue with the mystyl." She pauses and looks at me. "Brigid, you should come too."

Ten minutes later, we're all gathered in the meeting room. Headless mannequins with oversized breasts stand like sentinels in the corner, the lingerie they'd been modeling long since disintegrated.

"There's an issue with the mystyl," Edna says. "One that we didn't discover in the texts. While their behavior is unpredictable, we can moderate them with the artificial pheromone trails we lay out. But the substance's durability is low. Any wind or precipitation will disturb and dilute the trails, and they revert to their basal instincts."

I'm not surprised by this as much as I know she expects us to be. I saw them during their attack at Meridian. They scattered and formed groups, much like packs of jackals or wolves. At the time, I assumed it was intentional. Their erratic behavior created more chaos and disruption, allowing the rebels to sneak in and steal the egg. But apparently, it isn't that at all, but a fault of *theirs*.

"While we work on increasing the longevity of the mixture with oils, a certain percentage of every mystyl ambush will not return to the shuttles."

"And you're okay with that?" another lab tech, Rylan, asks.

"We must be. Their drift is an unexpected side effect; however, one I'm confident we will find a solution to."

"Drift?" I ask, feeling Sharice's eyes land on the side of my face. I'm not a scientist, but she wanted me here anyway for some reason, so why not ask the questions I wanted?

"Their drive to migrate is a powerful one," Edna says.

"Going so far as overriding their self-preservation should their desire lead them over a cliff or through water."

Well, that's a silver lining, I suppose.

"Do you know where they're going?" Sharice asks.

Edna shakes her head, her forehead creasing. "The data collected from the trackers in the field is too limited a sample to make an accurate prediction." She pauses, tapping her chin as she looks up at me. "However, I have theories I'll be able to prove soon."

Soon. There's going to be another attack. As much as I hate the idea of being on the front line with the violence, this may be my chance to convince her to take me.

"I'll go," I blurt before losing the nerve.

Sharice scoffs, a sharp sound tinged with disbelief. "While I'm happy to see you showing initiative, you can't."

"With ALTA, I can sense the riders and their druadans." I grasp at straws. There's no way I can know that. Even before the implant, when I felt the rider's bonds, it was three specific ones. Still, it's enough to give Sharice pause and turn her gaze from the door back to me.

"I'll speak to Henderson," she says. "He's the raid leader on this one. If he agrees, go to the equipment supply and have a vest fitted for you."

"Sounds good," I say, not sounding *too* cheery.

She nods and is gone; the door clicks closed behind her.

I release the breath I'm holding. Even as I stare at the closed door, it feels like, for the first time in a long time, it's open.

~

WE BROUGHT A HUNDRED MYSTYL. I overheard the techs loading them up, murmuring about, hoping it would be worth it. This shipment is coming from the Gaergen Region—tools, building supplies, and wool blankets. Things we desperately need. Gaergen has flocks of sheep and lumber mills. We have nothing.

I can't deny I'm a little bit pleased with myself. I convinced Sharice and Elton to let me come to the raid at a Leviler port warehouse, and even if I don't see any druadans, earning their trust enough for them to let me off base is a victory.

Night drapes over the landing zone, and only a few stray clouds cover the stars.

My face is glued to the window. It's been months since I've seen the moon and the constellations.

A tug pulls at my chest, a fleeting memory of sitting in the hot tub with Carter, gazing up at the constellations.

It feels like a lifetime ago. A distant, half-forgotten dream.

I was a different person then. Full of ambition and the belief my sister wasn't the monster I now know her to be. Only weeks into my job, I flirted with him for information, a decision that still left me plagued with guilt. But now, that guilt seems so small, so insignificant, compared to the choices I made since.

Carter wouldn't even recognize me now.

Henderson leads this raid and issues last-minute orders to the six other fighters. He calls me a strap-in, just along for the ride like I'm an intern at some corporate retreat. They don't expect to fight.

Bernie leans over, their braided hair poking out from under their face mask. They must have sensed my hesitation on the flight over because they press a pistol into my hands. "Just in case. No point dying empty-handed."

I tuck it away, hoping I won't need it.

The plan is simple: sneak in while they load the shipment, unleash the mystyl to create chaos, then abandon our shuttle and steal theirs. Stay hidden. Let them do the work for us, then take out whoever remains guarding the ship.

Nathalie, a woman close to Sharice's age with short-cropped hair and a rose tattoo on her neck, checks her rifle. "You think Specter will be here?"

"Possible," Bernie says. "We leaked intel about a raid at Parnia's filtration plant, but it wouldn't be the first time they surprised us."

"Specter?" I ask, forcing my voice to stay even. *Why does the name sound familiar?*

Nathalie scoffs. "The druadan riders Circuit's parading around like soldiers. Performers who think that just because they know how to hold a gun, it makes them some kind of special warrior team now."

My heart stutters.

It makes sense. Circuit would use them. They can see the mystyl.

Carter's family has military ties. Maybe he's here?

Heath is an excellent marksman. Maybe they recruited him, too.

I shove down the excitement before it can show. The others are watching me too closely.

"I can keep an eye out if you want," I offer casually. "Give you some warning if I see them?"

Bernie grins. "Sounds great. Just don't get too close. Those ponies of theirs got fangs."

I manage a nervous smile, playing along.

But my focus has shifted.

I close my eyes, reaching for the bonds, knowing it's futile.

Nothing.

I won't dose with ALTA until I'm on the ground. The duration only gives me about a five-minute window, and I don't want to waste it.

But what if they are here? What does that mean?

Can I wave to them, say hi, and ask for a ride home?

No. There's no way I can slip past the other ITM fighters.

I'm stuck in this. Coming here was a bad idea.

If they see me, any of them, they'll try to save me. They'll be reckless and not care about their safety, and be shot down by the fighters next to me.

Or maybe they won't.

Maybe they'll do nothing and ignore me. What if the pheromones and chemicals have faded with time, and I'm no longer of any significance to them?

Or what if it's worse? What if they see me with ITM fighters and don't hesitate to shoot me?

I clutch my side, feeling like I've been running and have a stitch.

This was a terrible idea.

I shouldn't have come here, but I am here *now*, and I might not get another chance like this.

Whether they ignore me or hate me, I need to see them. Even a glimpse of their faces would be enough.

Just to prove they aren't a delusion or that the reason to escape I've been clinging to is not real, and they don't want me anymore.

But I have to.

How much longer can I keep going? Every night, when I close my eyes, I dream about not waking up. It's like my body is too tired, my soul too heavy. In those dreams, the weight of everything—the guilt, the fear, the loneliness—drags me under. I wonder if it would be easier to stay there, in that dark, quiet place, where I don't have to face what I've become.

And in the paddock, when I stand there, forcing a banshee to bond with me, I feel it. Every time I strip away the humanity from someone, a piece of me slips away, too. A gradual erosion I can't stop.

It's the end of the world, whether by my hand or the toxic air.

What will it hurt to see them one last time?

Seventeen

Logan

"We'll scout ahead," Carter tells me from atop Ember.

Three soft pops are released into the air as they phase, disappearing from my sight.

I hate when they pull that crap.

Jealousy burns like acid in my throat, and I swallow it down. Here I am, hoofing it like a grunt while they get to play their disappearing act.

The bond flutters under my sternum, a steady pulse inside me, but without Galaxian nearby, I don't get the benefit of mystyl-radar vision shit like they do.

I'm just as helpless as the next human. I turn down my radio, listening.

They're everywhere. Slithering across the ground and up the walls.

Without the ability to see their translucent bodies, it's

more of a pray and spray situation these days. I gesture to the entire wall and the others, and I light them up with blasts, shredding their bodies into oblivion, until soon there's nothing but a puddle of goo and ink-stained tentacles splattered with blood on the ground.

I hold up my hand to cease fire and listen. Elena lowers her rifle beside me and exchanges a worried look with me.

I squint for any shimmer in the shadows, then shake my head.

All clear.

Elena nods, and we creep forward.

"Two approaching from the South," Liam shouts in my headset. "Look out for the big one."

We swing our guns toward our left. The occasional spray of translucent blue blood splattered the containers, making it look like someone had fought with water balloons filled with blue paint. I use the mess to my advantage, searching the splatter for any voids that reveal a slimy bastard hiding.

The wounded one appears fifty yards ahead, dragging three of its six useless limbs. It's a big fucker, bigger than Marshal's dog. Its translucent coating flickers and fails, where blue blood smears across its hide. I put it down with a burst of laser fire. The beam cuts through its head and eyes, which are comprised of two large black rings.

Two more swarm over their fallen companions, their tentacles dragging through the bloody remains. Elena drops them both before they can react. Seth sweeps his back and forth as another burst of laser fire echoes in the distance, then there's nothing.

Several minutes pass with no other gunfire, and Liam on Ravenwing materializes from the shadows. "Didn't see any others."

"Great, let's get the hell out of here," Carter says. His words come out rougher than usual, and for the first time in weeks, I lower my guard, letting their bonds wash over me.

Blood pounds in my ears, every nerve electrified. It's been months since I felt this alive.

Fuck me.

I sway at the influx of his high, swinging a glance at Heath and the others. They're all riding this same wave.

This rush is almost better than sex.

Almost.

The urge to hunt, to keep killing, tears at my guts like I'm starving. It hijacks my brain, stomping out any sense of reason.

Heath tries to steady Shadowmane, who jigs sideways and tosses his head. Ember's got his ears pinned back, neck arched tight. They're not even tired. If anything, they're charged up. Buzzing.

I keep my eyes peeled as we march toward secondary exfil. Carter drops the smoke flare, and a yellow cloud billows up.

"Fueling's done. Ten minutes out," the pilot radios in.

Elena strides over, her gaze flicking between me and Carter. "How are you?" she whispers to him. There's a softness underneath, something careful. "I'm sorry about Ve'loth. He was a good man, but I hope you know it isn't your fault. There were just too goddamn many." She rests a hand on Carter's arm, fingers light, but her eyes are anything but. "If you need to talk..."

She's been chasing him ever since I turned her down, and since we're not on speaking terms outside of missions or training, I don't know if he's taken her up on the offer.

Fuck him. Anger hammers inside my skull like a heartbeat.

He found a way to move on. Move past Brigid.

I haven't.

Heath sleeps in the barracks, and I have it on good

authority he's always there alone. At least he and I can be broken bachelors together.

I look at Carter. He glares back. Ten minutes of standing here while he looks like he wants to slit my throat while I sleep.

To hell with this. I turn and walk away.

"Where are you going?" Heath yells. "We can't split up."

I pause mid-step, fingers twitching against my thigh before I can still them. "Just taking a piss. Unless you want to hold it for me?"

"Logan," he protests, but I'm around the corner before he can say anything else.

The headset crackles, and I crank the volume off. My feet carry me silently to the edge of the nearest cargo container, and I peer around it. The air feels strangely still, and somewhere in the distance, chains clank against metal.

I unzip, piss on the gravel, all the while keeping my senses on high alert. I put away my dick and shifted my rifle across my chest. Then I feel it, that prickle at the base of my skull, before my eyes catch the movement. Ever since starting these missions, my senses have sharpened to where it's like déjà vu on steroids.

This isn't the scratchy sound of tentacles on gravel, thought it's *footsteps.*

I press my back against the container, obscuring my body in the shadows. Three rebels rush a hundred yards to my left. They wrapped cloth around their faces and their boots to muffle their steps, and it was damn luck that I heard them.

Their body armor is cobbled together with tape with the pieced-together crap they call guns. *Shit.*

They're too close. If I radio now, they'll hear me. I need to warn the others. The mystyl was the distraction. These bastards aren't here to steal the cargo. They're here to steal the *shuttle.*

As two more hurry past, I hold my breath. One's a girl in a baseball cap, and stray strands of light hair spill from the back of it.

No fucking way.

Still caught off guard by what I saw, I slowly turn the volume back up on my radio. "McCelroy," Carter says in my ear. "The shuttle is here. Where the hell are you?" I grind my teeth, frozen in indecision. But then she's gone, disappearing between another set of stacked containers.

I take a chance. "Hostiles spotted. Get to shuttle two."

There's a brief pause, then Carter says, "Copy."

I start to follow, but then I hear footsteps to my right. I swing around, drawing my gun.

Elena holds her hands up. "Easy trigger fingers. It's just me. Thought you could use some backup." She flashes me a smirk. The whiplash is a hard reset. My mind jerks from Brigid to Elena in an instant. Seth appears behind her, and I know I have to get to the shuttle.

"Let's go, guys," Seth says, voice urgent.

I peer over my shoulder.

"What is it?" Elena squints at me.

I pat my side. "Shit, I left my ammo cartridge back there," I lie. "You go ahead, and I'll catch up."

Elena narrows her eyes. "Don't take long."

I nod, and they start in the direction of the shuttle.

Must be losing my damn mind. No way in hell Blondie is with ITM. But even as I think it, the tiny seed of doubt burrows deep in my skull, refusing to let go.

And I'm not leaving until I know for sure.

Eighteen

BRIGID

The warehouse district sprawls before me. Giant, square buildings of concrete with metal roofs, with metal shipping containers lined between. My breath catches as I watch the group of riders standing in the center below, completely unaware of my presence.

Groups of mystyl skitter across the ground like overgrown jellyfish, their camouflaged bodies catching what little light there is from the security lamps and the stars.

Carter and Heath stand close. They look just like any other Circuit military except for the long black jackets with a ghostly white horse on the shoulder and riding helmets.

Shadowmane and Ember stand nearby. They have carbon-fiber breastplates, and their saddle blankets extend over their hips, looking like the warhorses they're meant to be.

Unable to tear my eyes away, I watch them. Study them. Memorize every curve of their profile. Every outline of their bodies. If this is the last time I ever see them, then I'll commit every second to memory.

One of the other non-riders leans into his space and runs a hand over his neck.

Something shatters deep inside me. Something I didn't think existed anymore.

Elena.

She was on Logan's security team at Meridian. Her boxer braids frame a face that's all sharp angles and confident energy. She rests her hand on Carter's arm.

It's not a casual brush but a deliberate touch.

He smiles at her, and it's a *real* smile. The kind he used to reserve for me.

Logan told me they were better off before me.

I thought I accepted it, that it didn't bother me anymore, but I was wrong because seeing them together now, with her, makes me want to rush over and claw her eyes out.

"You see the eastern quadrant?" she says.

Even at this distance, the area is quiet enough I hear the playfulness in Elena's voice. Carter nods as she positions herself closer until their cheeks are almost touching. It's meant to be innocuous, just one soldier trying to get a better look at another soldier's comm, but then all pretenses are over when she flirtatiously bumps him with her shoulder.

My control slips as primitive rage takes over, leaving me shaking with the effort to keep myself rooted in place rather than giving in to the urge to destroy her perfect face, to make her bleed for touching what I still consider mine.

A feral protective growl tears from my throat.

I've spent too much time with the banshees.

Heath smiles at them with a pleased expression that makes my thigh muscles tense, coiling to spring.

Still, I don't move. Three months of believing they would return. Three months of convincing myself that *I* meant something to them.

I clung to hope like a drowning woman to driftwood, and now, as Elena flashes Carter an ear-to-ear grin, I let go.

My pointer finger hovers over the implant trigger, and I press until I feel the click.

A needle-sharp prick, then cold, seeps into the muscles of my neck, slowly spreading down my shoulders and spine. ALTA, stinging like liquid ice, courses through my system. My arms involuntarily flex, and my vision narrows, sharpening, but it does nothing to dull the sting of betrayal.

They didn't wait for me.

The last shred of hope disappears. Not with a dramatic tear but with a quiet dissolution, like my crackers in a hot broth.

Sharice was right.

I'm a ghost haunting the edges of their thoughts.

The containers blur, transformed by the drug's enhancement and my breaking heart. As the ALTA floods my system, the world condenses into laser-sharp focus. I sense more riders hidden behind the containers.

"There are six druadan riders. To the west by the shipping yard," I speak into the headset.

"Copy," Bernie replies. "It's showtime."

Nineteen

Logan

Once away from Seth and Elena, I fall into a jog, retracting my steps.

I rush around the corner, stepping as light until I hear the murmur of voices.

"...If we take them at the East corner, we can cut them off from the loading bay."

Rebels.

I creep closer and peer around the edge of a container.

There's a group of four in a circle, all wearing masks and armed with a random assortment of guns. Pistols, rifles, and one even has a long machete dangling from their belt.

None is Blondie. Even with masks, I'd never forget the shape of her body.

They split up, and I tail two on the right briefly before I'm forced to find cover.

God dammit. I'm out here chasing fucking ghosts.

When thirty seconds pass, I rise to my feet and see the pair has moved on.

Fuck this. I spin on my heel and start to the exfil point.

I pass three containers when I find her.

She's kneeling at the brick wall of one of the warehouses. Her back to me as she kneels, working to fix a jammed pistol.

She's alone.

This is it.

I tug off my helmet and step out from the shadows. "Hey, Blondie."

Her eyes dart up, feral and wild. Her hat falls off as she jumps to her feet, and her silver hair spills over her shoulders like liquid moonlight.

She aims the gun at me. "Don't come any closer!"

It's the first time I've heard her voice in months. My jaw ticks at the wrongness of it. It's hollow, like coming from the bottom of a well.

I hold up my hands, not risking her getting some stupid idea to run *or* shoot me if she manages to fix the jam. "Look, I'm not here to hurt you."

Ninety feet. If I can get her within arm's reach, I'll grab her, sling her over my shoulder, and haul her ass to the shuttle. I don't care what she calls me or how much she spits or kicks. I'm not leaving without her.

At fifty feet, my footsteps falter. Her eyes narrow at me, the wildness fading into wariness and confusion.

"Hey, it's just me." I keep my voice casual. "You know, the *asshole* who couldn't keep his damn mouth shut?"

She blinks but doesn't reply.

I want to demand what the hell she's doing with ITM, but I feel like I'm one wrong move from spooking her. "Heath and Carter are here."

At their names, her throat moves, and it's the first hint I've seen she's still in there.

"We're here to help you," I shout as a gust of wind drives the rain sideways. "We want to bring you home."

"No." The word is a whisper, yet it slams into me with the force of a truck.

I roll my shoulders back, fighting the tension gripping my neck as my voice drops to a low command. "I am not leaving without you," I say slowly, emphasizing each word.

Her eyes narrow further, the furrow between her brows deepening. The milky film I noticed earlier spreads like cream swirling in coffee. "You need to leave."

I don't move.

"I'm giving you five seconds to turn around and walk away," she says.

"Blondie, I just want to talk—"

"Five." Her voice echoes strangely as if speaking from multiple throats.

I step closer.

"Four."

I risk a dozen steps.

"Three."

I'm sprinting now.

"Two."

My face collides with an invisible wall, and I'm yanked backward. Flat on my back, my chest erupts in pain as if my ribcage is being cracked in half. My spine arches, whipping my head back as an agonizing burn, like liquid lava, pours into my veins.

I roll onto my belly, then force myself to my knees, panting and clutching my chest.

Each breath only intensifies the fire. I look up. Brigid's eyes have turned milky white, and she stares blankly at me.

"What the fuck?" I mutter.

"Go," she commands, her voice distant.

"No," I croak.

The pain amplifies, and I grunt.

What's happening? I don't care. I refuse to back down. It feels like a burning wire is threading through my veins, pulling them taught.

I crawl, on hands and knees, through the puddles of rain, closer to her, and with each movement, searing pain radiates up my limbs. It feels like my body is being pulled in a hundred different directions, hot pokers driving into every joint.

"Please," I groan. "Listen to me."

Right, left, right, left. My hands grasp the ground until I drag myself toward her. The concrete scrapes my palms raw, but it's nothing compared to the blazing inferno in my chest.

Time slows. The thirty feet remaining might as well be a mile. I won't reach her in time.

"Some battles are meant to be lost."

My neck muscles protest as I crane awkwardly to look at her.

Her eyes return to normal, and she blinks. "I warned you to stay away." She turns and leaves. I hear the thud of the pistol on the ground before blacking out.

Twenty

Heath

Something is profoundly, terrifyingly wrong.
Frigid air burns my lungs with every ragged breath, and crystalline plumes escape between clenched teeth.

"*Mystyl gone,*" Shadowmane says in my head. "*I no feel.*"

Logan's body lies crumpled, face down in the gravel. His helmet lies discarded a short distance away, blood seeps from his nose, and fresh scrapes and bruises mar his face.

I open myself to the bond, bracing myself for his pain to give me insight as to what the hell happened. But there's nothing. No pain. No fear. Nothing.

An absolute stillness.

Two soldiers appear beside me. "Get him onboard," I bellow over the drone of the arriving shuttle. One takes his head, the other his feet, while three more keep their guns drawn, scanning the area.

"Has anyone seen Captain James?" I growl as the unease creeps in that he, too, is injured somewhere, and whatever hijacked our bonds is affecting him as well.

"Ember coming," Shadowmane answers. *"I feel him. No feel Galaxian."*

Movement catches my eye, and emerging from the damp fog, the red stallion speeds toward us, shod hooves striking sparks from the wet pavement. Mystyl blood smears Ember's front legs, and his armored breast collar is scuffed, but he appears unharmed.

Carter leaps from his back upon reaching me, and his eyes dance from Logan to mine. The tension etched across his face melts into a flicker of confusion. "What the hell happened?"

"I don't know." The words taste like ash in my mouth.

"Hey!" someone yells. "Specter team!"

From between two nearby shipping containers, a group of Circuit soldiers staggers in our direction, clutching their sides, their uniforms torn and exposed skin cherry red with fresh mystyl burns.

"They took the shuttle!" one of them yells. "The fucking assholes took the whole damn load!"

I open my mouth to ask what, but a cargo shuttle the size of three semi-trucks roars overhead, blades thundering as it skims the tops of the containers, churning up dust and debris. All of us duck, covering our faces as a blast of heat rolls over us as the engines pulse, pushing the craft skyward.

"Motherfuckers," Carter curses, and Ember sidesteps, nervous about the roar of the shuttle.

"What should we do, sir?" Elena asks Carter.

Carter hesitates, his face pained as he tears his gaze from Logan's body. "Call it in. See if they can track it." He turns to the soldiers who are helping load the shuttle. "Everyone, get your asses on board. Now!" He jabs a finger at the lowering ramp. "Elena, Seth, get McCelroy in."

He grips Ember's reins, leading him up the ramp, and I follow with Shadowmane and Liam behind me with his stallion.

He hasn't spoken a word since losing Ve'loth.

Inside, the shuttle smells of smoke and blood. I guide my stallion into the narrow stall and secure him for the flight. My shoulders tense at the space beside him.

One second, he was there. The next. Gone. Specter's first casualty.

The druadans are secured in their stalls, still wearing their saddles and gear. There's an empty stall between them. If Shadowmane mourns Ravenvein, he doesn't share it.

Carter barks orders to the medics while Logan lies with his legs stretched out across four seats. His eyes are closed, and his breathing is shallow.

"We've got three riders injured," Carter says to his comm. "A rider and druadan down, and now McCelroy is unconscious. We're running low on fuel, and we're going to lose our window if we don't move."

Our mission medic, Vito, examines Logan as he fades in and out of consciousness, murmuring words. He checks his pulse, runs a light over his eyes, and triggers his reflexes by running a thumbnail over his hands and legs. "There's definitely some cranial trauma, judging by the goose egg on his head and the slow pupil response, but everything seems to be functioning normally. We'll need to run more tests when we get back."

Vito moves on to address another soldier's mystyl burn on their wrist, and I take a seat across from Logan. The rest of Specter is half-dozing on the shuttle or talking in hushed tones. Liam has his arms crossed, his earphones in, and his eyes focused on the vacant stall on the shuttle. He was a mess at the memorial, and I still don't believe he's gotten over his friend's death.

Once we're well on our way back to Blackhawk, Carter finds me sitting in the corner.

He takes the seat next to me and rests his arms on his legs, hanging his head. "I can't feel him, Heath."

I say nothing, just staring at Logan's still form on the bench. His broad shoulders are too wide, and his left arm has slipped down.

"Did you hear what I said?" Carter snaps. "I said I can't *feel* him."

"I heard you."

"Then why are you so fucking calm?"

Carter peers up at me.

I pin him with a hard look and funnel all my fear and worry into the bond.

His eyes, mouth gapes, and his eyes widen like he's seen a ghost.

"I am far from calm," I say.

He turns away and rubs a hand over his face. "What the hell happened?"

"I don't know."

Anger turns to worry, then fear. "Heath. I can't fucking *feel* him. How is this possible?"

"We won't know until he's awake and can ask him."

"*If* he wakes up."

"Don't," I warn. I know there is still bad blood between them. But I wouldn't let him think that way. "He will wake up, and we'll get him to the doctor, and they will figure out what's going on."

Carter doesn't reply, but his fear saturates the air. He slips a vial from his jacket and drops the OS on his tongue.

The fear eases.

I flex my fists and turn away.

Some time passes, and Vito comes over. "Elena told me you had a burn on your neck that needs looking at?"

Carter waves him off. "Nah, I'm good."

Vito's eyes land on me.

"Let him look."

Carter grumbles but relents and takes off his jacket.

Immediately, the patch of angry red skin is visible, and before Vito can even say it, I know. "That isn't a mystyl burn."

"Nah, a laser ricochet caught me on the side."

Vito's forehead creases, and his glasses slide down his nose. "Hmm. Not a laser burn either."

"Does it matter? Just throw some cream on it and call it good."

The medic's mouth twitches with annoyance, but he sighs and obliges, digging out a metal jar.

Carter tilts his head to the side and lets him apply the mint green paste. Vito is right. It's not a mystyl burn.

The skin is a darker red, blackened along the edges like someone pressed a hot poker into his flesh. ITM was using laser weapons like us, and laser burns are clean. This wound spirals outward like a smoldering brand seared into his skin, and singed the fabric of his jacket where the heat licked through as if the fire came *from* him, not at him.

What the hell kind of weapon could've done that?

Vito finishes, and Carter pulls his jacket back on. "I'll see to that," I say. "You'll have the debrief with General James and the staff officers."

I see hesitation, the impulse to argue. But instead, he leans his head against the shuttle wall, eyes closing. "Looking fucking forward to it."

There it is. That edge, the constant defensiveness he wears like a second skin. I can't even talk to him anymore without him bracing for a fight. The months of stress, missions, and death have worn him down, rubbed away his playful nature, and left him bitter.

He isn't meant for this. He didn't deserve this, and not for the first time. I wish it were me in his place.

I exhale and lighten my tone. "The brewery's grand opening downtown Village is tomorrow. They'll be offering free samples of their ale and those crab puffs hors d'oeuvres you like."

Carter snorts. "Fuck me, those things are good."

"All you can eat."

The bond flares with shared amusement, and it's notable just us.

Both of ours shift to Logan. His eyes are closed, and his face is relaxed.

"Vito gave him something strong for the pain," I say.

Carter nods grimly.

He knows the truth we're both avoiding. The sedative might ease his body, but it's a temporary mercy. When he wakes and reality sinks in, he's going to know the definition of suffering.

I'm not a religious man, but right now, I'm praying to anyone listening that whatever broke in him can be fixed.

Twenty-One

BRIGID

The shuttle engine whines as we return to the base. My back and neck ache from the ALTA as I sipped the bottle of water they handed me once we were safely onboard. It's a two-hour ride back since we had to detour to ditch the shuttle's tracker in Ashburn Lake before swinging back to the southeast.

As we fly over it, I refuse to look at Meridian Station below.

Still, I imagined the boarded-up windows, the landscape dead or overgrown. Dormant and abandoned since the ITM attack forced everyone to evacuate to Blackhawk, which felt like a lifetime ago.

The sight of them with the other woman flooded me with

rage, staining my vision blazing red as I stormed back toward the shuttle until Logan's shout stopped me cold.

I'm not leaving without you.

Logan had been there. Standing inches from me, swearing he wanted to help me.

"Carter and Heath are here, too," he'd said.

I stare at my hands, feeling like I'm disintegrating. Every molecule is splitting and fracturing.

It was a lie to say I wasn't tempted as I stood before the man I'd forgotten was *the* definition of masculine energy. A muscled god with a square jaw, broad shoulders, and a towering six-and-a-half-foot frame. While the memory of his build might have faded, his steel-colored eyes remained true, although a fresh scar marred the side of his neck.

His gaze gripped mine, pulling me in with an unspoken challenge. The sight of him reawakened a pull I'd tried to bury, and tides did I want to give in, but then the radio in my ear told me a team was on their way to my location.

They'd kill him the second they saw him, and even through the haze of betrayal, I didn't want to see him hurt.

He ignored my threats, and if I ran, I knew he'd only chase me, so the only option I had was to scare him.

The ALTA illuminated his bond, revealing a shimmering turquoise tendril, the infused connection of a Galaxian. It was easy to seize it, twisting the ethereal strand until he couldn't move. I didn't want to hurt him, but I had to wind it tight enough to pull him down, buying myself a chance to escape.

And it had worked.

"You doing all right?" Bernie interrupts my thoughts. "You came back to the shuttle paler than Henderson's bald head. You sure you don't want the medic to check you out?"

I muster up a weak smile. "Just tired. It was more overwhelming than I thought it'd be."

"It was a rough one. Lost a whole lot of squirmers. Damn, near a hundred. Those test-tube jockeys are going to be pissed, no doubt." They bump into me with their shoulder. "It was a good haul, though. And Henderson will need the final tally, but it looks like we took out at least five of theirs."

My throat clamps shut as if grabbed by an invisible fist.

Five.

Panic surges, hot and broiling inside me. They can't be one of them. I refuse to believe it. They're too strong, too fast, too...

"I feel you should know," Bernie continues, "these raids aren't always this way. Next time, try not to run off, though?"

"Huh?" I ask only half listening.

"I said, don't run off alone like that." They're being nice, but I don't miss the undercurrent of their gentle scolding.

"Oh, right." I force a half-hearted laugh. "To be honest, I don't think I'll be doing that again."

Bernie's eyes widen. "That bad, huh?"

I rub my face, still not recovered from learning a druadan and their rider were killed. "I think I'm of better use here. You found the riders quick enough."

"True. But next time, there might be more. I'll talk to Henderson. See if we can't get you trained up properly so one of us doesn't have to babysit you."

Logan and I were working on that before I left, and I continued exercising in my room.

"Landing in five," the pilot says over the intercom. I recognize his voice as one of our own and try not to think about what happened to the other pilot. "Helmets, please."

I fasten on my helmet and step down the ramp. The morning sun just peers over the hills on the horizon, and people in suits rush out with dollies and start unloading the stolen crates and boxes.

Once through the airlock, the rest of the raid team disperses to their beds or breakfast.

I round the corner into the main area. Sharice—wearing a navy jumpsuit and white jacket tied around her waist—spots me from across the room.

Her normally neatly braided hair is full of flyaways, and there's a flush to her cheeks that isn't usually present. I wonder if she didn't sleep alone last night. I heard she and the nurse had broken it off, but maybe they got back together.

Not that my sister's love life matters to me.

Tides know at least one of us is having luck in that department.

But I've made up my mind. Love won't find me here. I won't allow it.

Not until this is all over.

Her eyes narrow as she strides over. The ITM commander's insignia on her shoulder catches the fluorescent light as she moves. It's new. She notices my gaze. "High Navigator awarded it to me."

"Congratulations."

Sharice frowns. "Thanks," she says dryly. "We need to talk."

"Now?" I yawn. "I just got back. Can I sleep first, and then we talk?"

"No," she says a little harshly, drawing the eyes of the family beside us, waiting in line for bottles of water. "Come with me."

She grabs my elbow and half-drags me from the main area to a storage room.

Inside, she closes the door and essentially traps me in the ten-by-ten room lined with shelves and boxes. "What the hell happened out there?" She keeps her voice low but sharp. "What do you mean? I went there to sense druadans and riders, remember?"

Sharice's nostrils flare, and her eyes dance between mine. "Correct. But Henderson told me you split off from the group. They had to send fighters to find you."

Heat scalds the side of my face. "The containers block my senses," I lie. She studies my face. Can she see the truth written there? I've gotten better at lying since being here, but Sharice knows me from before. "I needed a clearer place to look," I add quickly.

Her jaw shifts. "You were alone when you triggered the ALTA implant. Do you know how dangerous that is?"

"I know," I snap. "But I had it under control if... Wait, how do you know that?"

Her gaze is unwavering. "A tracker is activated when you dose."

"What?" I blurt. "You're tracking me? You never told me that before."

She lifts her chin and sniffs. "I didn't think it'd ever be needed. Clearly, I was wrong."

I clench my fists. So God damn typical. After all this time, she's *still* keeping secrets from me. My tongue sweeps the backs of my molars as I meet her gaze, forcing myself to stay steady. "Fine. Then clearly, I don't have to tell you what happened on the raid since you're not part of the team."

I side-step around her, open the door, and go.

Twenty-Two

CARTER

The remainder of the shuttle ride to Blackhawk is quiet.

Heath sits back in his seat, fiddling with his pistol again, though he's already checked it a dozen times. My irritation bubbles beneath the chemically induced calm. I lean my head back and close my eyes, but it's useless. These days, it takes an entire bottle to get decent sleep.

The heat at night is unbearable, and I sweat with a fever until I pass out. The dreams are worse than ever. Flames spiraling up my legs, licking at my skin, my lungs seizing, my eyes seared raw. Then...nothing.

I no longer need the heat-resistant pants. Ember's hide no longer burns me, but I wear them anyway, so no one questions it.

I bypassed my latest physical using Specter business as the excuse, but they'll force me into the clinic eventually.

I glare over at Logan. I'm pissed as hell he ran off the way he did, and once he wakes up, he'll get an earful, but until then, I'll have to wait.

Heath murmurs beside me and nudges my arm. "He's awake."

I sit up and see Logan stirring. His eyes flicker open, and they are glassy.

Vito rushes over and shines a flashlight into his eyes. "Can you hear me?"

"I saw her," Logan murmurs, his voice rough.

"It's Vito. Can you tell me your name?"

"Clean your damn glasses. You know my name."

Vito frowns and takes Logan's wrist, checking his pulse.

Logan's eyes swivel to us, and he sits, wincing as he moves.

Heath and I stand and move closer.

"Are you okay?" Heath asks.

"Blondie," he says, her name catching in his throat like it physically hurts him to speak it, "Brigid. She was there. She was fucking there with ITM."

My pulse races, the O-Strike in my system amplifying my already raw emotions. "Don't you dare bullshit us."

"My bond is gone," he says, "I don't know what happened, but I think she did it. She didn't want me getting near her, so she tore it away."

"It's not fucking possible," I say.

"If anyone could, it'd be her," Heath says. "She'd pulled it back before, and we've read that some people bonded to druanera have the ability to completely sever it."

"But how?" I ask, "She's not bonded, and she's hundreds of miles away from Oriana."

"Obviously, she found a way around it," Logan says. "ITM

has been stealing lab shit for months. Lannet's scientists keep going missing, too."

"What if that was why she was there? To take our bonds away?" I say, hating the question.

Logan shakes his head. "No. It didn't feel like that."

"What do you mean? You said you couldn't get near her?"

"She was trying to push me away. I don't think she meant to..." His voice falters. "Break it."

His words hover in the air between us.

"Did she say anything else?" Heath asks.

"Like what?" Logan says.

"Like why the hell she's with ITM?" I say.

Logan scoffs. "We were under attack, and it wasn't like we had time for a whole conversation. I told her to come with me and that we'd help her, but then I was pushed back, and the next thing I know, I'm here."

The muscles in his jaw shift back and forth, and it feels like a vice compressing my chest.

"We'll fix this," Heath tells him. "I'll demand they let you see Galaxian. Maybe that'll be enough for it to reform?"

Logan shrugs and rests a hand on his knee. "I doubt it, but thanks."

Blackhawk's medical team arrives and takes Logan to the clinic.

Heath goes with him.

I can't.

Novices put our stallions away in the barns, and I head up to the main floor debriefing room.

General James enters from one of the side rooms they let Circuit use, her uniform pristine despite the late hour. The medals across her chest catch the overhead lights.

My mother's hair, once a light brown like mine, is streaked

with gray and pulled back in a severe bun that emphasizes the sharp angles of her face.

Three other military officials trail behind her, tablets in hand, faces grim with concentration. I practically see their minds working, struggling to find the best way to spin today's disaster as something other than what it was. A complete fuck up.

Their footsteps echo against the concrete floor as they cross the threshold to what has become Specter's command.

Her eyes find mine immediately. Something in my posture must give me away because she turns to her entourage and says, "Regroup in twenty." Her voice leaves no room for question.

They disperse without a word, leaving us alone.

"What happened?" she asks, not unkindly, but with the military directness that has defined her my entire life.

I straighten my shoulders instinctively. "ITM snuck in under our noses. They must've got off a shuttle miles away, then came by foot or car. Our perimeter sensors didn't pick them up until it was too late."

She nods. "Thankfully, the cargo manifest didn't list any weapons, but we'll use thermal goggles next time. Expand the perimeter to give the transfer team more time." She's already problem-solving, already looking ahead to the next mission, while I haven't even washed the blood off from this one.

Her eyes narrow, watching me. "Casualties?"

"None on Specter." I swallow hard. "Logan's injured but stable."

I don't tell her about his fractured bond. It doesn't matter to her. Not really. Her interest in bonds extends only to their potential as tactical advantages, nothing more.

She studies my face for a long moment. Then, surprising me, she places a hand on my shoulder. "I'm proud of you." Her voice is softer than usual. "I knew you had that James leadership in you."

Something bitter rises in my throat. "Thanks."

"We're making a difference." Her grip tightens. "Sometimes the hardest part of command is standing tall when everything is falling apart around you."

For a moment, I glimpse the weight she carries, the decisions that etched the lines around her eyes and turned her hair gray. And despite everything, I want to believe her, but the moment passes when her comm chimes.

She gives me one more long look, then turns her attention to it.

"Get some rest," she says, tapping on the screen. "Specter is going out again tomorrow."

UNDER THE SCALDING spray of the shower, I stand motionless as sweat, grime, and blood from the battle and mission rinse off my skin, trailing down my body in dark rivulets. I hang my head, watching the dirty water swirl down the drain.

My hand drifts lower, and I grip my shaft. My dick half-hardens in response. I rub my thumb over the head, and a memory, made vivid from frequent use, surfaces: Brigid leaning against the tree, my hands on her hips as I drive into her from behind.

But the image is shattered by the influx of riders' voices in the barracks' bathroom.

My erection flags, and I curse in frustration, letting my hand fall.

I'll come back later, before bed, I lie to myself.

The second I lie down, I'll be dead to the world.

I flip off the shower, snag the towel from the bench, and

dry off. Standing at the rows of sinks and mirrors, I catch a glimpse of myself. I'm shirtless, with a white towel hanging around my hips. I've got about a week's worth of scruff on my chin, giving me the hardened look many of the soldiers have. My green eyes stare back, looking haunted with dark bags under them.

My wheat-brown hair, still wet from the shower, flops over my forehead in a messy tangle, sticking together in uneven clumps, making me look even more worn out and beaten than I feel.

My razor bag sits on the counter, and I reach inside and find the tiny packet.

After a glance assures me no one is nearby, I tear off a strip.

The thin paper feels cool against my fingers, and I place it on my tongue. The OS is sour at first, like a lemon, then drifts sweet as the rush hits.

I tilt my head back as the high ignites, spreading from my chest to my limbs. Confidence surges, burning away the gnawing fear clinging to me since Logan's bond broke. I can face anything, even this fucked up world.

The O-Strike isn't killing me. It's keeping me alive.

Questions swirl, sharp and loud, but the high softens their edges.

I pack up my things and walk past the rows of beds in the barracks before stopping at mine at the end. Heath's bed is on the opposite wall, and I flinch when I notice him sitting there, waiting.

There are no windows down here, and the lights flicker more often.

Heath blends in too well with the shadows. A feat the others haven't missed either, earning him the nickname 'Ghost,' which fits nicely on a team called Specter.

Heath's bed is on the opposite wall, and I catch him sitting there, waiting.

He doesn't say anything, but the way his eyes assess my face says it all.

"Don't fucking start," I mutter, grabbing a shirt from the back of the chair.

"I don't need to start," he says calmly. "You're finishing yourself off just fine."

Ignoring him, I press the shirt to my face and inhale. The high hums under my skin, amplifying my senses until I feel everything. The cotton fabric of the shirt, the soft way it feels against my cheek, and the pungent smell of blood and sweat fill my nostrils.

Dirty. I grimace, and I toss the shirt onto the pile. "You're wasting your time," I say, reaching for another one on the rug by my bed. "Maybe check on Logan instead of babysitting me."

That does it.

In three quick strides, Heath is up and standing face-to-face with me. "You truly consider no one but yourself, do you?" he says, his voice laced with restrained frustration.

Heat radiates across my back. "The hell are you talking about?"

"Do you honestly think these past months have been easy for me?" he says. "Do you think I want to drag Shadowmane into these missions? He's not as young as he used to be; these long rides are hard on him, but what choice do I have? I do this for *you* because you asked me to join you with Specter. I've given you time to figure it out, but this has gone on too long. I won't stand by while OS tears through your mind, shredding your neurons. I refuse to lose you to this."

My mouth twitches as the sting of his words is like a slap to the face, yanking me out of my elevated state. "I've got it under control, all right?"

Heath's eyes darken to deadly slits. "You need to go see him. He needs you."

I scoff and drop my gaze. "I doubt that."

"Remember Morton's."

My eyes drift back up, and I freeze.

"You promised," he says firmly. "We all did."

"We were just kids," I argue. "And long before the world went to shit."

Heath's eyes bore into mine. "Doesn't matter. I still believe it, and I guarantee Logan does too."

The day we put on the Vanguard Academy uniform, we were no longer seen as children to our families but as a badge of honor for them to show off.

Midway through Freshman year, we met at Morton's quarry. We built a bonfire by the pond, passed around a bottle of cooking sherry we stole from the kitchen, and then laughed so hard my cheeks hurt for days afterward. That night, we vowed we'd be there for each other, no matter what.

"He knows he screwed up with Brigid," he says, "and he tried to fix it and look what it cost him. You're better than this. We need you. The real you. You're the one who keeps Logan and me centered."

Dammit. He's right. Without me, they tear each other apart. And without them, I don't even know who I am anymore.

I let out a long, drawn-out sigh. "Fine," I finally say. "I'll go." My fingers flick the towel at my hip, and it lands on the ground with a soft thump. I shake my hips for good measure. "I know how much you *love* staring at my dick, but do you mind tossing me my pants?"

Heath groans, turning away, but not before I catch the hint of a smirk.

He snatches the sweats from the trunk at the foot of my bed and throws them at me.

Choosing to go commando, I pull them on.

Heath sneaks a glance, then, seeing me decent, turns to face me again.

"He's in between shifts in his room. If we hurry, we can catch him there alone. The three of us are long overdue for a chat about what really happened with Brigid."

Twenty-Three

BRIGID

The numbers and patterns blur, melding together until they're meaningless symbols dancing across the monitors. My fingers hover over the keyboard as I try to identify the matching sequences in the banshee data, like Sharice instructed.

"Look for repeating patterns in column D," Her voice is calm but tight with concentration. She leans over my shoulder, her dark hair falling onto the desk as she points to a specific section. "See how this sequence mirrors their heart rates during bonding?"

"I think so." I squint at the numbers, pretending to understand more than I actually do. I'm a fraud here among these scientists, but Sharice gives me manageable tasks and treats me like I belong.

A soft nicker draws my attention away from the screens. In the corner of the lab, separated by a partial glass wall, is Iris. She's lying down, her eyes closed, with an IV on her neck, keeping her suspended between life and death. My heart twists at the sight.

We're losing her.

Sharice follows my gaze and sighs. "Her vitals are dropping again." She moves toward a cabinet of supplies, rifling through various vials. "We need more stabilizing agents, but the last shipment was contaminated. Without the proper feed..." She trails off, but the implication is clear.

We're losing her.

She's always been weak, but between the low-quality feed, her suspected genetic malformations prior to hatching, or the trace amounts of toxic air that inevitably seep into the building, no matter the precautions, she won't last long.

The idea that I was somehow responsible, like I was with Oriana, was quickly dismissed when Sharice showed me no spike in the monitors on Iris while I was working with the banshees.

The lab doors slam open. Elton strides in, two guards flanking him with hands resting on their weapons. Elton wears his lab coat over a white t-shirt and khaki pants. His shirt is wrinkled, and there's a faint sheen of sweat on his forehead.

"Step away from her." His voice is iron. "I thought I made myself clear about unauthorized interactions with the specimens."

"Iris is dying." The words burn in my throat. "We're trying to save her."

"The specimen is ITM property," Elton says. "And while

your concern is noted, please remove your attention from her and focus on your assigned tasks."

Sharice steps between us. "High Navigator, with all due respect, this druanera's biological data is valuable for understanding the bonding process. If we lose her—"

Elton cuts her off with a dismissive wave. "An unfortunate loss, but we'll use one of the wild ones."

Before she can argue, however, two of Elton's thugs enter, struggling with an older man who thrashes in their grip.

"Thy call to us! It sings! Can't you hear it?" he shouts, saliva flying from his lips. "It's in the air we breathe! Don't you feel it?"

His eyes burn with fevered intensity as he continues ranting, spittle flying from his lips. I study his face. Was he one of the test subjects I tried to work with? It's impossible to know for sure, yet the guilt rises like bile in my throat anyway.

Some people went unconscious, and the guards dragged them away without explanation. Could he be another one like Laurel?

He lurches forward suddenly, straining against the guards holding him back. "It's changing all of us! The blood! The precious blood!" His voice cracks with desperation. "You've seen it too, haven't you? The transformation has begun!"

I tense but don't shy away.

"Work in progress," Elton offers to us, turning the raving man away from me as the guards drag him through a side door.

"What are you doing with him?" I ask.

"Don't worry," Elton says. "They're taking him somewhere to rest. There will be someone there to watch him while he recovers."

Before I can respond, he gestures to one of the lab techs. "Prepare our Wayfinder for a blood draw."

I shake my head and cover the crook of my arm. "What? Why?"

His expression hardens. "I'm not asking. Either you cooperate, or we take it from you. Your choice only determines how pleasant the experience will be."

My eyes snap to Sharice. "What the hell is going on?"

"We only need a small sample, Brigid," she says. "Just to test a theory."

"Don't tell me you're getting cold feet?" Elton says, his voice rising. "You can't defy *your* destiny. The reasons the constellations aligned and the doctrine foretold your arrival." He steps closer, copper eyes fever-bright. "None of this was chance. Your sister's love for you brought you here to help us. Salvation is within our grasp, and I refuse to let it slip through our fingers."

The technician approaches with the rubber tube and a glass vial.

He offers me a tight-lipped smile, and I hold out my arm. The rube pinches the skin on my arm, and I glare at Elton as they draw my blood, each pump of my heart feeling like a betrayal.

When the vial is full, the tech hands it to Elton, and he examines my blood with reverence. "Now, let's see if my theory is right." An assistant appears holding a tray with various medicines and vials on it. Elton picks up a bottle and injects my blood into it, turning the milky white liquid pink.

"What are you doing?" I ask.

"Mixing in a little of this, a little of that." He tosses his shoulders. "It doesn't matter. What matters is that this will alter a person's genome just enough to merge with the druadan's that makes their body tolerate the poisoned air." He then takes a new syringe, inserts the needle into the rubber cap, and draws the pink solution into the barrel.

Sharice glances at me briefly, and I catch the flicker of worry in her eyes before she looks at Elton. "Please, High Navigator," she says. "I told you earlier that the compound isn't ready. We need more time to learn about both the short-term and long—"

"We're out of time," Elton says, shaking his head. "Bring in the next volunteer!"

Compound? Sharice didn't tell me anything about a compound.

But before I can ask her, two guards wheel in another volunteer. Jia Huang, a middle-aged Asian woman with dark hair and a yellow jumpsuit, is strapped to the chair. She's in her seventies, and her only son, Zichen, repairs the machinery we find on Reco runs.

She smiles softly at Elton, and he speaks to her in Chinese. Whatever he says causes her smile to widen. An IV line dangles from her wrist, and I don't have to read the labels on the bag hanging on the side of the chair to know there is a cocktail of sedatives in it.

"Wait," I ask, "What are you doing?"

"Finishing what you started." Elton moves to the woman and caresses her cheek with his left hand while holding the syringe with the other. "Just as the sacred doctrine states," he says, staring at her adoringly. "The true children of the land will prevail. Those who see it as a sacred honor to inhabit it. People like Ms. Huang here are pioneers. They will become our future, our hope." He inserts the needle into the IV line and depresses the plunger.

Ms. Huang lets out a soft sigh as her eyes remain half-closed, her mouth agape.

Elton steps away from her and sidles up behind me, too close, his breath warm against my neck. He rests a hand on my shoulder, and I bristle but refuse to flinch. "Now, all that's left to do is for you to activate the serum."

Activate. Force a bond, but on what? There aren't any banshees here...

"Turns out, with this compound, we don't need the banshees anymore. We can use any druadan to do it."

My gaze shifts, landing on Iris lying on the sandy bed of her enclosure, and I grip the nearby counter to keep myself from saying as my mind reels with the implications. With Iris, they aren't inhibited by the catching of dangerous banshees. They'd do the experiments here in the lab. Refine the process over and over, perfecting the procedure in the safety of the base or anywhere until it's successful.

It can't be that easy. Druadans don't bond with more than one person at a time. Unless... unless he wants me to sever the bonds too.

I swivel a look at Iris. Her dark hide is muted under the harsh lights. The curve of her spine juts sharp through the thin skin, and every breath is a gargling gasp. I felt the fear and confusion of the banshees when the bonding failed, and we tried again. Most had to be euthanized after more than two attempts, their minds as fractured as the volunteers.

They'll keep her alive just long enough to finish the tests. Not comfortable. Not conscious. Just... breathing while I force her through a cruel cycle of bond, break, bond again. Each severing would tear away a piece of her, and her final moments on this earth would be torture.

"No," I say firmly. "I won't do it."

Elton's jaw shifts, agitation evident on his face. "Very well." Lightning fast, he lashes out and pulls Sharice to him. He presses the syringe against her neck. "Do it, *Wayfinder,* or your sister will take Ms. Huang's place."

Sharice's jaw drops, shock evident on her face from Elton's

threat. She doesn't cry, doesn't whimper, doesn't fight back. Instead, her eyes meet mine, her face relaxes, and she gives the hint of a nod.

With shaking hands, I approach Iris. Her chest slowly rises and falls, unaware of my presence. This space is all she's known. She's never even been outside. Never seen others of her kind.

I hate everything about this, but I don't have a choice.

Either I bond her with Ms. Huang, or he injects my sister with an untested, potentially dangerous chemical.

There's no contest.

I tap the implant, feeling the familiar buzz as ALTA enters my system. Iris's aura is the deepest of purples, and its energy matches her physical form. It lays draped over her body, barely moving like a kite without wind.

I reach it, and the bond feels different from the others. Thinner, weaker, like trying to grasp smoke.

Elton watches the monitors intently, tracking Ms. Huang's heart rate. The numbers fluctuate as I struggle to establish the connection, and Ms. Huang grimaces.

"Stronger," Elton commands. "Push harder."

I reach deeper, stretching the tether of energy between us, but I feel resistance, not from Iris but from myself. *Something is wrong.*

"Good. Now, connect her to me," he demands, gripping the syringe.

"What?" I ask, thinking I misheard him. "But I thought," I flick a gaze to the woman in the chair.

Elton snarls. "Forget her. She's too weak. Bond her to me."

Horror snatches the oxygen from my lungs, and my hold on her bond wavers. "I...I can't. The banshees are different, but a druanera can't bond with a man."

"After all this time, and still you believe the government's lies," he shouts, the syringe still pressed to Sharice's neck. "As High Navigator, I command you to do it!"

Desperation claws at my throat as I grab the tenuous bond and force it to bend and stretch to encompass Elton. Iris's energy drains, flowing through me toward him, but it's too much. Every second, she's growing weaker.

I will my energy into Iris, trying to balance the flow to keep her breathing, and it creates a strange triangular connection, energy cycling between the three of us in a way that feels fundamentally wrong. Like trying to force together the same poles of two magnets, her aura repels him.

Alarms blare as Iris's vitals plummet. I break the connection to save her, but it's too late. Her aura winks out of existence.

The monitors flatline with a sustained beep.

Elton's eyes roll back in his head, and he crumbles to the floor.

Overcome by confusion and the effects of the ALTA, my gaze lands on the scalpel of a nearby tray.

I could slice his throat with it. The idea is so vivid, so satisfying, and I can almost feel the blade cutting through flesh, the warm rush of blood over my fingers. The intensity of my anger and resentment startles me. All this hatred had built inside me, a molten reservoir just waiting to burst.

I can end it. All of it. Right now. One quick motion while everyone's attention is on Iris and the monitors. No one could stop me in time.

A flicker of doubt tugs at the corners of my mind, keeping me locked in place. What if he's right? What if they could really find a solution to Venovia's survival? My desire for revenge could potentially be killing hundreds of thousands of innocent people. People who might be saved by his research, despite his methods, despite his madness.

My fingers hover near the tray, trembling with indecision as I watch Sharice bend over his unconscious form, checking his pulse.

A small sigh escapes me, and I lower my hand.

The hard truth is ITM is more than just one man. Elton might be their leader, their High Navigator, but the movement has spread throughout the country. His death might falter it, but it won't stop it.

My gaze drifts to Iris's lifeless body. "I didn't mean to kill her," I whisper, tears burning my eyes. "It just happened." My voice breaks as the reality of what I've done crashes over me. "I told him druanera can't—"

"I know," Sharice says softly, looking up from Elton's unconscious form. She stands and rests a hand on her hips. "He's alive, just unconscious, but we need to move quickly." Her eyes dart to the cameras in the corners of the room, reassuring me that not killing Elton was the right decision.

Not yet, anyway.

"Go to your room," she commands. "And don't talk to anyone. I'll clean this up."

I don't move. "What about you?"

"Go!" Sharice yells. "I'll handle this!"

I watch a second longer, then run.

WELL PAST DINNER TIME, in the relative privacy the community bathrooms offer, I peel off my clothes, still reeking of chemicals and antiseptic from the lab.

Sharice found me hours later in my room and said Elton didn't remember anything that happened past him drawing my blood. My failed attempt at bonding him to Iris had left him with a headache and short-term memory loss.

It should've been worse. He should suffer like Iris and Ms. Huang suffered. The memory of his face, that manic look in his eyes, haunts me now. He isn't just egotistical or ambitious; he is truly deranged. The way he ranted about the blood, about transformation, revealed something deeply broken in him.

He isn't the same leader of a revolution to save humanity that he was when I first came here. Months of taking on Circuit have transformed him into a madman chasing a delusion.

At least he won't make me try again.

The relief from that is short-lived, though, when I remember it's because Iris is dead.

I wipe the fog from the mirror. Fatigue from long days and terrible sleep on a hard cot has left its mark.

My silver-blonde hair is darker at the roots, my cheekbones more pronounced, and my collarbones protrude through the thin wool sweater hanging on my thin frame. Even my eyes are dull, no longer the bright blue-green, instead faded to a murky teal, like seawater clouded with silt.

Those from my old life would hardly recognize me anymore.

I barely recognize myself.

The water in the shower runs dark with dirt and sweat, but it can't wash away what I did. I press my forehead against the cool tile, trying to ease the ache in my chest with the knowledge that I didn't have a choice.

The only other druanera in the world is gone.

Because of me.

I sigh and close my eyes, and all I see are the faces of Heath, Logan, and Carter.

I should have run to them when I had the chance. I should have apologized for leaving them and begged them to take me with them.

Then maybe Iris might still be alive.

But if I had, then they'd be in danger.

They were tracking me, and every time I used the implant, it alerted them.

I open my eyes and feel the bump on the back of my neck. I stare at the scissors on the shelf, left by the person before me.

I can cut it out and toss it down the drain, but I quickly dismiss the idea. The odds are good that it'll notify Sharice of any tampering. I curse under my breath, pissed at how trapped I feel.

What range did their tracking system have? Sharice got an alert when I triggered it, but did Elton or any of the others? I can't ask her without her growing suspicious. I towel off and return to my room.

After slipping on sweatpants and a T-shirt, I lie in bed and close my eyes. Iris's violet aura and still body fill my vision. Then I see mystyl releasing from their containers at the storage yard. I remember watching them scatter, knowing they were there to hurt and kill.

I never fired a shot, but the deaths weigh on me all the same.

Standing by makes you just as guilty as pulling the trigger.

This is what war does. It makes us monsters, one small compromise at a time.

There was a time when I hoped I could recover from this. Find my soul amongst the ashes, but I learned hope doesn't make us brave. It makes us cowards, holding tight to ghosts and chasing what's already vanished.

Hope led me to Meridian. Hope led me to Sharice to save Oriana. Hope pushed me out on the mission tonight that had possibly left one of my riders dead. Hope kept me in the lab, helping Sharice find a way to keep people alive. Hope got an innocent and rare creature killed, and dozens more with their minds broken.

Well, I'm done. As far as I'm considered, hope can fuck right off.

Twenty-Four

LOGAN

Darkness pulses, folding in on itself before splitting open. The rusted sign of Blackhawk station swings on broken hinges, creaking in the wind. Shadows move beyond the chain-link fence surrounding the enormous stone fortress.

Another flash as the alarms blared, red lights strobing through the catacombs of underground stables. ITM rebels storm through, cutting locks and throwing open stall doors. Hooves strike concrete. Screams of people and stallions. The scent of sweat and ozone is thick in the air.

Galaxian.

He bursts from his stall, a dun shadow streaking through the mayhem. His teal mane whips as he rears, then vanishes into the night.

A breath. Silence.

Brigid.

She stands in the dark. Galaxian beside her, still and waiting. His luminous gaze pierces through the void, fixing on something unseen. Brigid does not move, does not speak. She only waits.

The vision fractures, and I awake with a start, pulse jackhammering in my ears.

Sweat clings to my back and neck, and my chest heaves as if I'd been running a marathon.

My mind reaches out, seeking Galaxian's reassuring presence, but there's...nothing.

"Fuck!" I slam my fist into the wall to my right hard enough to leave a dent.

Swinging my legs over, I'm immediately nauseous from the mind-splitting migraine I've had since they brought me back last night.

Only part of me was left behind.

Marshal saw me late last night at the clinic. The doctor ran all the tests, but the kicker is there's no way to test whether someone is bonded or not.

You can't see it on a blood test or measure with a scope. It's a *feeling*.

Marshal had done as much, trying to sense mine when Heath and Carter had told him.

"Galaxian is rogue," he said. "You knew he'd never bond again, and it's some luck you're brimming has been as low as it has. This could be a blessing in disguise."

Fuck him and his glass-half-full bullshit.

I clench my fist, feeling the tightness of the skin on the back of my hand where I was marked twice.

The tingling is gone. They're just scars now.

I rise from my bed, dress, and grunt an "I'm fine" to Seth when he asks how I am as I leave.

Word spreads fast, and I ignore the looks from the riders as I stride through the barracks.

Some are of pity, some of fear, as if whatever happened to me is contagious and might spread to them like a bond-eating virus.

Galaxian is in the isolation wing.

I shove down the fear hard, stuffing it somewhere where it'll never come out.

I won't break. Not in front of him.

In his stall, Galaxian looks as he always does. Buckskin colored hide, a stark contrast to his teal mane and tail. His footsteps shuffle in the shavings as he pivots around to face me.

As I do every morning, I open myself to the bond, half-expecting to hear the low grumble of his voice.

Silence.

Some might call me a sadist at this point, but I don't give a shit.

I'll never stop trying.

Galaxian stares at me, ears swiveling back and forth as if listening.

My head feels like it's imploding, and there's a hollowness that makes my breath stutter.

"FUCK!" I grip the bars and rattle the stall door.

It's gone.

It's really fucking gone.

Galaxian doesn't flinch.

"I saw her," I say through clenched teeth. "If she just would've listened, if she just would've let me talk to her." I suck in a breath between my teeth and stare at the ground. "I don't know what to do."

Puffs of hot air brush my knuckles as he sniffs my hands, and I look up. He watches me, teal eyes glowing faintly, and the low thrum of his chest turns my mouth dry.

"I can't hear you anymore, remember?"

The humming stops.

The silence cuts deeper than any knife.

Grief doesn't scream; it sits heavy in the quiet. Thick and stubborn, hiding in the shadowy corners of your mind, waiting for you to slip up. Then, when you're too damn tired to fight, it slams into you until sadness is all you've got.

A brutal darkness wiping out the sun and staining every waking thought.

I turn my back and slouch down the wall until I'm seated on my heels. "If I could just find her. Maybe then there could be a way to fix this."

Galaxian paws the door. "Hey," I scold him, rising to my feet. "Just because we're not bonded doesn't mean you can act like a dickhead."

He presses his nose between the bars, trying to get at something in my pocket.

Druadans are notable snack hounds, and Galaxian complains if I don't bring him one of the vitamin tablets disguised as treats.

"You're out of luck." I feel like a complete ass for not stopping to get him some. I hadn't even considered whether losing the bond would affect him as it had me.

"I'll go get some," I start to leave, but Galaxian snorts.

A clear no.

He twists his head sideways, squeezing his face between the bars. The skin patches on his face rub against the metal, and he nuzzles the holster on my hip.

On autopilot, when I came down here, I'd thrown my belt on with my gun instead of my regular one.

"Yeah, it's my gun. You've seen it before."

I unclip it and take the pistol from the holster. The safety is on, and it's charged for maybe two shots.

Galaxian's lip rubs over the top of it, moving it in my hands, then stops.

It's my service weapon. The one I had since I was in Meridian. I try to figure out what the hell he's showing me when my eyes land on the Circuit Property stamp on the hilt.

The gun. Well, shit.

"You dick." He withdraws his head back into the stall. "You knew? The whole time, you *knew*?"

Galaxian blinks, then drops to scratch his face on his front leg.

The sneaky mother fucker.

I race back to my room and dig out the jacket I wore last night.

Barely conscious when they found me, Circuit's team grabbed the pistol, assuming it was mine.

I pry open my go-bag and find it buried under the chest protector.

Vito must've stashed it in there on the shuttle before I went to the clinic.

It's coated in grit from when she dropped it, and I wipe it clean with my shirt, revealing where a stamp should be from the manufacturer.

I curse loud enough to draw two other guards lounging on their beds' attention.

On the black metal are the two circles encircling a D that appears to be made of chain.

And there's only one place Blondie could've gotten it.

The memory of a dream from all those months ago replays vividly like a Network movie in my head. The rebels running. Seeing Blondie. The sign of Inland Dreamland Amusement Park, which was in TZ Delta before the final war.

This gun came from a prison guard from Tox Zone Delta.

STILL REELING from the revelation about the gun, the door opens, and Carter and Heath move inside.

Everyone else went to lunch, so the shared room was empty.

I knew this would happen. It feels like a damn intervention.

They know better than to give me their pity.

"How are you?" Heath asks, his voice careful.

"Just fucking peachy," I snarl, but it doesn't come out as harsh as I hoped. Ever since I figured out how to find my Blondie, my mood is surprisingly better, like having something solid to chase has put some fire back in my veins.

His jaw shifts, and they move closer and drag the pair of chairs in the corner.

"Carter and I have been talking," he says once they sit near me.

Oh god, it *is* an intervention.

"I shouldn't have let you run off like that," Carter says, leaning forward to rest his arms on his knees. "I should have ordered you to stay."

"Come on, like you could have."

Carter's nostrils flare, and I brace for him to leap out of the chair and attack me. He wants to. He has for weeks, I'd felt it, the restrained rage simmering in the bond whenever he looks at me. I hate it, but I hate this emptiness so much fucking worse.

"I should have tried harder," he says, voice tight. "And for that, I'm sorry."

I don't want their guilt or their sympathy. I want... I don't even know what I want anymore.

"Bond or not," he continues, "you're still our brother."

"And we'll help you fix this," Heath says. "By whatever means necessary."

To my surprise, the sincerity in their voices doesn't make me want to puke. I hate having others see me as a charity case, and if it were anyone else, I'd tell them to get the hell out. Only Heath and Carter get to have my back.

"Okay," I say, voice strained. "Then you believe me, it really was Blondie out there?"

Heath and Carter both nod.

"Good. Now that we've all held hands and got this love-fest out of the way, I think I might know how to find Brigid."

That gets their attention.

"You're serious?" Carter asks.

I show them the pistol I stashed under my pillow. "She wore ITM's armband. She's with them."

Heath rests his hands on his hips. "Dammit. Her sister is connected to this, I'm certain."

"She's been with her this whole time?" Carter says, speaking all our minds.

"We're missing something," Heath says, shaking his head. "For some reason, she went to her."

We're silent for a minute, thinking it over, when Carter says, "Whatever it is, we know she's alive at least."

"True," Heath says. "But it doesn't do any good if we don't know *where* she is."

I hold up the gun. "I do. She's in Tox Zone Delta. That's where this gun came from."

Heath raises a skeptical eyebrow. "How can you be sure?"

"They only issue these to prison guards. They rotate every year where the convicts are dumped, and this year it's TZ Delta." I stand, suddenly energized. "And you two can send me there."

"Absolutely not," Heath says. "Logan, it's suicide."

"My cousin works as a guard," I say. "He says every year they have shit stolen by inmates before they release them in the Zone. Badges, food, knives, guns. There are only two ways this gun ended up in Brigid's possession. Either a guard dropped it while doing an inmate release, or she got it off a convict's body."

Heath is shaking his head before I finish. "So, let's just say she was by some insane chance in TZ Delta long enough to get a gun. How do you know she's still there?"

My jaw shifts. I can't just come out and tell him about my weird ass dreams. They were connected to Galaxian, even if I couldn't feel him anymore.

The truth was, I'd been having them since Blondie left. At first, they seemed like nothing, random coincidences, like when I knew Elena's sister had her baby before the call came in. Or twice when I'd woken up knowing General James would deploy Specter that day, hours before the orders came down.

I'd tried to rationalize it to a heightened awareness, a side-effect from the strained bond with Galaxian due to the lack of time I spent with him.

Until I saw her in that storage facility, I managed to dismiss it. But now? The evidence had stood right in front of me. These weren't just dreams. They were visions, glimpses of truth filtering through whatever wild shit was happening with my brain.

Even with the bond, they'll have a hard time believing what I say, but fuck it.

"You're going to think this is crazy, but sometimes I see things in my dreams. Some are strange as shit and don't make sense, but then others." I turn the gun over in my hands. "I knew I was going to find her, and then her dropping this gun... it has to mean something."

Carter studies me, having been silent the whole time.

"Thank fuck," he says, relief filling his voice. "I've been having strange shit happening to me, too. Not just dreams but...other stuff. Like these fevers that come out of nowhere."

I nod, not sure what to say, but offer him a reassuring smile. Then we turn to Heath. The vein in his left temple pulses, telling me he's stressed.

"I have as well. It's hard to describe, but there are times I feel like people don't see me."

"Are we talking physically or metaphorically speaking?" Carter asks.

Heath buries his face in his hands for a second before dropping them to his lap. "Physically. Like I'm here but not. It's not anything major, just odd."

"Well, shit," I say as a whoosh of relief washes over me. "I hate to say it, but thank the tides. I thought I was going crazy."

Carter sits back and sighs, clearly relieved, too. "So, you were dreaming about Brigid, huh? Probably couldn't help but moan *my* name, even there."

"Something is changing," Heath says, ignoring Carter. "Something we're all picking up on." He looks at me, his expression severe. "Tell us what you've been seeing."

I clear my throat. I've kept this weird crap locked up tight long enough. "Months ago," I start. "Soon after she left, I saw her in a dream with ITM attacking. I saw a sign of the old carnival that was in Delta. It didn't make sense at the time, but now, it's all pointing to what I feel in my gut." *Trust your instincts*, her words replay in my head. "If I were a group of terrorists hellbent on anarchy and needing somewhere to hide out, TZ Delta would be it. It's big, unmonitored, and the weather is shitty, so supply shuttles crash down all the time."

Heath rubs his chin, absorbing it all, and Carter laces his hands behind his head, eyes distant.

"So," Heath finally speaks. "Saying she is there, they're not letting anyone near the zones right now," Heath says, already on board with finding a way to get her back before I asked. "Trawlers are getting searched and licenses revoked. Even if I call in all the favors I can, there's no way we could get you there."

I fold my arms. "That's why I'm going to get arrested."

Heath and Carter exchange a look and I know they're feeling each other's emotions, leaving me in the dark.

Fuck I miss my bond.

"You're serious?" Carter says after a minute.

"I am," I say. "My cousin told me all sorts of shit he wasn't supposed to say at family get-togethers. The convicts are given a mask and sixty minutes of oxygen before they're dumped. Some bullshit about making amends with their life choices before they die an excruciating death."

"If you're trying to convince us this is a good idea," Heath says. "You're failing."

I set the pistol on my lap. "Fine, so we'll pay off a guard to give me an extra tank."

"Delta is thousands of square miles," Carter argues. "You think you can just drop in there and poof, there she is?"

"If Brigid found this gun where I think she did," I say. "Then ITM's hideout must be near where they offload the prisoners. You know I can cover a lot of ground in two hours."

The silence stretches between us.

"I can do this alone," I add, "but it'll be easier with your help."

Heath runs a hand through his hair, his features twisted in calculation. Carter leans back in his chair, eyes narrowed.

"She broke my bond," I say thickly. "How? I don't fucking know, but if she can take it away, then she can fix it."

"There must be another way," Heath adds. "I can make some calls for Carter and me to join you and—"

"No!" I growl. "You can't be near her..." I pause as the realization washes over me like a cold splash of water. "But I can. She can't hurt me. Not anymore."

There's another pause, before Heath lets out a long sigh that seems to deflate his lean frame.

"All right." Carter leans forward, elbows on his knees. "How do you plan on getting arrested?"

Twenty-Five

BRIGID

I make my way out of the showers, carrying my wet towel and basket of toiletries.

In the hallway, the lights flicker and buzz above me before going dark. I curse and squint into the dark, running my hand along the wall until, a minute later, the backup generator kicks on.

It's early, and not many people are out, so there's a chance they'll delay starting them to preserve fuel for the night. With temperatures dropping to below freezing, they need all the gas they can for heat.

I step into the mess hall, hoping to grab whatever is left in the warmer. Two packets of potatoes and hash and one of veggie lasagna. I opt for a nut bar and a vacuum-sealed cup of carrot soup.

Only a handful of people are spread out among the other tables, more empty chairs every day. Those here look drained, probably because they're shouldering the extra workload with the others gone. How many volunteers had gone to the lab? How many more would Elton take until he is satisfied?

Temper flaring as it always did when I thought of Elton, I claim the nearest empty table. I tear off the lid of the carrot soup and sip it with one of the hard plastic spoons.

It tastes like plastic and is barely above room temperature, but I'm hungry, so I eat it anyway. My eyes scan the room, seeing who is here. My stomach dips as I see Ronan and his mother.

Laurel stares ahead at nothing as he gently encourages her to take sips of their carrot soup from the spoon he holds.

Her mouth moves, and she swallows, but there's no life in her eyes.

Sharice told me they were working on a way to reverse the effects, and I needed to be patient, but after the bullshit Elton pulled in the lab — threatening Sharice and forcing me to bond Iris to him, ultimately killing her — I didn't believe it.

I can guarantee if I go to the lab right now, no one's prioritizing a cure for her. She was an unfortunate byproduct of early testing, something they analyzed, learned from, and left behind as they moved on to the next phase.

It should hurt me more to see her this way; I should be wracked with guilt, but I'm not. Not anymore. And the worst part is I know why.

Death literally surrounds us.

It looms around us, pressing in from all sides, searching for a crack to seep through and poison us all. I can no longer deny living in this base has done something to me. Every second of every day, we're one hairline fracture away from a breach, from the toxic air finding its way in.

Initially, that knowledge kept me awake at night. But now? Now, I don't startle at the lockdown alarms.

I no longer much as blink at corpses on Reco runs, and when raid casualty announcements are made, I chew my food like the rest of the people here, my appetite unaffected.

I'm numb.

Despite my best efforts, I am acquiring my sister's ability to shut down emotions.

She made me their Wayfinder. Worshipped and revered by the people here, so I felt like I belonged. Like I'm important. They've called me Wayfinder for so long now that I almost believe it. How can I not? If enough people call you something more than your name and whisper it with reverence whenever you enter a room, doesn't that make it true?

But the part that keeps me up the most at night is wondering how much of my old self remains. Sometimes I catch myself making decisions the old me would have revolted at.

Maybe that's the real horror of this place. Not that it might kill us, but that it might turn us into something we never wanted to become.

And it seems I'm already halfway there.

As I think this, carrot soup dribbles down Laurel's chin. Ronan dabs it with a napkin. He's a head taller than her, with wide shoulders, but still has the gangly limbs of a teenager.

"Please, Mom," he says. "You have to at least try to swallow."

Laurel's tongue works in her mouth and her throat bobs. I sigh a breath of relief and set down my tray. My fork falls from the side and clatters on the ground. I stoop to pick it up and find Ronan rushing toward me.

"You did this to her!" he snarls, darting around the other tables. He jabs a finger in my direction, his face contorted with rage and anger, and hurt like I've never seen in anyone before.

Pure, unfiltered hate for *me*.

"*You* broke her," he says. "You're no Wayfinder. You're sadistic and self-centered. Someone who gets off on using people."

My voice falters as I try to defend myself, but I'm unable to find any words.

"She believed in you. She trusted you, and you betrayed her."

Everyone is watching. Laurel is beloved by all, and no doubt Ronan is not the only one in this room who is angry with me.

"She volunteered," I say coolly, my voice steady though a phantom weight presses against my chest from within. "She knew the risks when she signed up. If there's anything you need, please let me know."

"Bullshit!" he yells. Tears swim in his gray eyes, reminding me so much of Logan's, except lighter, like a storm cloud. "She didn't know what she was doing. They pressured her to do it. And now..." He pauses, chest heaving. "All I want is for you to fix her," he continues, "Make her better. Like she was before."

"I'm sorry but—" I start to say, but he cuts me off.

"Sorry?" he echoes. "*You're* sorry? Look at her. Look at what you've done to my mom!"

Tears prick the backs of my eyes, my defenses crumbling. I can't give him what he wants, and this is only causing a scene.

I can't stay here anymore.

Leaving my tray of unfinished food on the table, I rush out of the cafeteria.

"Where are you going?" he shouts at my back. "You can't run away from this!"

My hands won't stop shaking as I hurry past the group of people filing down the hallway, returning from the day's Reco.

"You did this to her! Ronan's angry words echo in my head.

His face, contorted with rage, is burned into my mind.

It was true. I reduced his mother to nothing but an empty shell and erased the vibrant, kind, amazing woman she was.

I close my eyes, but the image persists. His mother's vacant stare, the drool at the corner of her mouth, the way her hands clutch at nothing.

My fault. My fault. My fault.

I need air. Need to feel the sun on my face and the grass under my feet. Need to escape this suffocating guilt.

At the door to my room, my breath catches. Dozens of small tokens are piled against my door. Miniature clay dolls with crude faces. Strips of fabric are braided into shapes like hearts and miniature druadans. Children's paintings of scenes on salvaged plastic and cardboard.

Offerings for the Wayfinder.

My stomach churns, and I feel like I'm going to be sick.

I drop to my knees, sweeping the items into my arms. The clay figures dig into my flesh. Good. Pain is what I deserve.

Stumbling back, I make it straight for the waste disposal bin. The gifts clatter against the metal sides of the bin as I drop them one at a time.

A sob tears from my throat. Then another. Soon, I'm gasping, tears streaming down my face, struggling to pull oxygen into my lungs.

I can't stay here. My room feels too small, and I need to *leave.*

The thought cuts through the panic.

The atrium. No one goes there anymore. Not since the West Wing collapsed.

I flee my quarters, darting through the corridors until there are fewer and fewer people.

The restoration crews haven't yet reached this section of the building. There aren't any rooms here. It's still very much coated with mold and debris. It's eerie how preserved it is, like walking through a museum of the old world.

The decrepit scaffolding groans under my weight as I climb the ladder. At the top, dust motes dance in shafts of the last of the day's light filtering through the cracked glass dome. The atrium was beautiful once, a garden under the sky. Now, large terracotta pots sit broken or empty, their soil dried and cracked, and the skeletal tendrils of ivy cling to the pillars and walls. It's a monument to death and decay, but still, I come here often when seeking a quiet refuge.

I ease myself onto the ledge and grip the railing before sliding under. The space is four feet wide and encircles the underside of the dome's walls.

It wasn't meant for the public, probably just for maintenance access. My legs dangle over nothing but air and the twenty feet down. From here, I see everything, the entire 360-degree panorama of our failure as a species.

To the east and west, the wasteland stretches to the horizon, its barren soil a rusty crimson, like dried blood. South is the fractured parking lot, and to the north and behind me, the collapsed section of the building.

ITM had installed plastic sheeting with tape to make the area airtight, and it flutters in the incessant wind that blows outside.

I lay my head on the cold bar and close my eyes, trying to console myself, when I hear the clang of scaffolding.

Sharice stands at the top of the ladder, wiping the rust and grime from her hands. "I thought I'd find you here."

With the back of my hand, I swiftly wipe the tears from my face.

She steps onto the narrow platform and takes a moment to gaze out at the wasteland. "The haze is thick today. Can't even see the city ruins."

I huff a dry laugh. "Not like there's much to see."

She lowers herself beside me, and we sit in silence for some time. Sand swirls outside, the grains tinkling on the glass dome.

"I heard about what happened in the cafeteria," she says. "That boy had no right confronting you like that."

"Sure he does," I reply. "I stole his mom from him. God dammit Sharice, he's just a kid. I never should've—"

Sharice grabs my arms and turns me toward her. "Stop it. Right now. Laurel volunteered, thinking only of her son. She did it out of love, to give Ronan a chance at a future."

The flood of guilt consumes me, hot and tangled, but her hands on my arms and brown eyes locked with mine are steady, and something in me eases just enough to breathe.

"Feel bad," She says. "Feel guilt or shame or whatever you need to but wallowing in self-pity for something you can't change won't help all the other people that still need you. I need you here. You—"

"Because I'm the Wayfinder. I know."

She frowns. "Yes, but there's more. There's something I should've told you before, but I haven't found the right time."

Instantly, my mind goes to the riders and Oriana, and I sit up a little straighter.

"After you told me about your ability," her voice has an edge I've never heard before, "I ran some tests on myself to see if perhaps we shared a similar gene from our mother's side."

I swallow. Fear raises its head every time she brings up my

DNA and possibly discovers I have more siblings than just Marshal.

"I ran a full battery. Very thorough, and while I could not discover the element that allows you to tap into the extra sense, I learned one thing."

My mouth goes dry.

The skin around her temples tightens, and tears swim in her eyes. "I'm sick, Brigid."

The words hang between us, as solid as the metal beneath my hands.

"What?"

"It's genetic. Huntington's disease." A tremor in her voice turns me ice cold.

"Do I—?" She shakes her head before I can finish.

"I confirmed it is recessive on my father's side, but I ran a check on your blood to be sure, and you're clear."

"I'm sorry," I say, knowing it's not enough.

She reacts as I knew she would, with a deep sigh and a tight smile. "Typically, it's slow to progress. However, there are factors like exposure to toxins, chemicals, and whatnot that increase the onset of symptoms."

My stomach plummets to my feet when I realize what she means.

I stare at her. "How long have you known?"

"Not long." She looks out at the wasteland. "I'm almost thirty, so there's still time for treatment to slow the effects, but unless we learn how to survive the poisoned air, it won't matter. I'm not making it to forty either way."

The irony slams into me. Here I am, feeling sorry for myself because my actions hurt someone, while Sharice faces something like this. "I don't know what to say."

Her lips curve into a hopeful smile. "Say you'll help me."

Tears prick the backs of my eyes. "I won't do what you're

asking me to do. I'm sorry, but I can't have you end up like..." My voice breaks, preventing me from finishing.

Sharice sets her hand over mine on the rail. "I would never ask you to. The team has enough data. I want your help to analyze."

"But Elton? He tried to kill you. I'm sorry, Sharice, I really am, but he went too far. You might've forgiven him, but I won't. I refuse to be around him—"

She's shaking her head before I can finish. "He's apologized for his behavior and has transferred all research to me. He's granted me full autonomy in the labs. We're no longer using humans for testing and have moved all simulations to digital. Our next phase will involve rats, and the compound will be safe when finally ready for people." She slides her hands down my arms to my hands and squeezes. "I'm really trying to make this right. You were right from the beginning. Progress can be made without horrible sacrifices. You taught me that."

Warmth blooms in my chest, aching and fierce. For the first time in years, she feels close. Like the sister I thought I lost. Her words steady me, and I nod. "Okay. I'll help."

Sharice's smile widens, and she returns her gaze to the domed window above us. The sun skirts the horizon. When it's this low, the divide between the foul air is visible, and for less than a minute, the rays are a natural yellow instead of sickly green.

"Do you remember Mom's edible mold experiment when we were kids?"

I blink, caught off guard by the abrupt shift in conversation. "Yeah, why?"

"She was determined to make the fast-growing mold palatable. She spent weeks on it. Building the right environment, tweaking the moisture levels, everything. But no matter what she did, it always tasted like dirt." She leans back, her hands braced against the platform. "She was ready to give up. Said it was impossible. Then, one day, she left it alone. It sat for a week, forgotten in the incubator. When she came back, she figured what the heck and tried it." Sharice waves her hand. "And voilà. Sweet like a ripe peach."

"I remember," I say, suspecting where she's going with this.

Sharice raises an eyebrow. "I've been thinking about a way to help Laurel. While a cure might never happen, there may be a way to reduce her symptoms and, in the future, with time, mitigate them altogether."

My pulse creeps higher even as I try to keep my expectations in check. "Are you serious?"

"I am," she says, a faint smile tugs at her lips. "If we can isolate the factor that's tethering Laurel to the banshee, with time and resources, our lead scientist told me there might be a way to mimic the immunity to the TZ while keeping their inhibitions."

My hesitation evaporates completely. She really had been working on a cure? "I don't want to make any guarantees, but if we can create an inhibitor for the violent impulses. If it works, it could stabilize the bond, so it's directed to one central tether. No banshees will be needed."

"What?" I snap, cutting her off. "What will they bond with, then?"

Her expression hardens, and I feel the intimate sisterly moment fading. "You don't need to understand. There won't be any bond."

"That's not an answer, Sharice."

Her comm dings, and she stands, brushing dust from her pants. "Look, I have to run, but I'll see you at breakfast with Mom tomorrow, and then meet me at the lab. I'll get you up to speed with everything, okay?"

After she leaves, I stay here until long past dark. The stars are faint specks, their light unable to penetrate the haze of swirling sand.

A real cure. For Laurel and for people to survive the air, but done right. Ethically. I don't know if I believe it, but for the first time in weeks, her promise evokes a feeling in me other than despair. It's as fragile as the cobwebs fluttering the scaffolding, but it's there.

Hope.

Twenty-Six

CARTER

I don't hold back, using full force as my fist swings, catching Logan square in the jaw. Pain bursts across my knuckles. It's like hitting a brick wall, the shockwave traveling up my arm, but he doesn't even budge.

Everyone knows Logan is built like a brick wall, and it'll take more than a few punches to sell this.

I flex my hand, the pain shooting up my wrist. Motherfucker that hurt, and he didn't even blink.

"For years, I've been cleaning up your messes," Heath snarls. "You wouldn't have a job, a place to live. You would have nothing if it weren't for me. Because you're a dick, you push everyone away. I had something good in my life, something decent and real and not forced onto me by my parents, something just for me, and you pushed her away, too."

Heath steps in next, driving two punches into Logan's ribs. The impacts make him double over, and he drops to one knee, glaring up at Heath.

"Is that right?" Logan growls, spitting onto the floor of the barracks.

They sound pissed. Almost enough to make me believe it, which means there's no way the other riders watching will claim he isn't actually angry at Logan.

"You're so fucking self-righteous," Logan continues, rising to his feet. "You forgot she left you too, asshole."

Heath's face hardens as he swings again, but this time Logan's ready. He ducks under Heath's fist and slams his forehead into Heath's face.

Heath stumbles back, wiping the blood from his face. He glances at the blood smeared on his hand from his busted lip. The sight ignites something buried in him, shattering his calm facade, and for a moment, the tame dog retreats, replaced by a feral, snarling wolf.

Heath sneers at him, and it's my turn. I sprint from the side, tackling Logan before Heath can lunge. My weight drives him to the ground, but he twists, throwing me off balance.

I'm strong, but he's stronger, and no one will buy it if it isn't both of us taking him down. Logan's elbow finds my ribs, and I wheeze as he drives into my side, and I'm forced to let go.

Heath recovers quickly, grabbing Logan's arm and twisting it behind his back. Anger flares across Logan's face as he fights against the hold. Heath kicks the back of his knee, and his legs buckle. The two of us pile on, and our combined weight is enough to drag him down and pin him face down on the floor.

"Hold him," I hiss through clenched teeth, digging my knee between his shoulder blades, even as he bucks and curses. I lean down, close to the side of his face. "How are you doing, sweetheart?" I pant in his ear. "You remember the safe word, don't you?"

He doesn't answer, just glares at the ground.

I sit up, feeling the curious gazes of other riders on their bunks. *Holy shit, they're buying it.*

With a free hand, Heath pulls off his belt and works quickly, binding Logan's wrists with my help. "Fucking assholes!" Logan spits as Heath and I release him.

Heath sits back on his heels and wipes blood from his split lip while I keep my knee pinned on Logan.

"What the hell is going on here?" Lugsen's voice booms from the doorway.

Heath and I jump to our feet as Logan struggles with his arms behind his back.

Lugsen's face scowls as he appraises the scene. "You three. My office. *Now.*"

The barrack chief sweeps a hand at the rest of the onlookers. "If you're all standing here, I'm assuming those stalls are spotless. If not, get ready to smell like saddle polish for the rest of your lives 'cause that's all you'll be doing."

The other riders scatter.

Phase one. Complete.

Ten minutes later, we find ourselves in Lugsen's office. It feels like we're kids all over again, getting sent to the headmaster for fighting.

The room reeks of leather oil and stale coffee. Lugsen's office down the hall from the barracks is as depressing as ever. The room is dim with a lamp and a single rectangular slit near the ceiling that lets in a sliver of light. The stone walls amplify every sound, making the ticking of his ancient desk clock sound like a hammer on an anvil. Cracked plastic chairs, with metal legs that screech against the floor whenever you move, are arranged before his cluttered desk.

Along the back wall are three pairs of knee-high leather boots, and a rack of riding coats in vinyl bags hung from a metal rod. They're the new ones for the upcoming season, and the Blackhawk logo shoulder patches are just visible under the fluorescent lights.

Lugsen gestures to the chairs with a heavy sigh. "Sit."

Logan and I lowered into the chairs while Heath remained standing, arms crossed. Lugsen rummages through a mini-fridge behind his desk and tosses ice packs to Heath and Logan.

"For your faces," he mutters, slumping into his creaking office chair. "Though I'm tempted to let you both swell up as a reminder of your idiocy."

Logan presses the ice pack to his jaw, wincing.

Lugsen's gaze sweeps over us, looking like an overworked school principal, and we're the last thing he wants to deal with. "All right. Who wants to start?" Lugsen demands.

None of us says anything.

"Fighting like God damn crows over carrion." His palm slams on the desk, making us flinch. "And in full view of the novices, no less? I expect better from my senior riders."

"He started it," I mumble, pointing at Logan.

"I don't care who started it," Lugsen snaps, then narrows his eyes at Logan. "I'm not even sure why you're down here, McCelroy. The barracks are off-limits unless you're on patrol, and I don't see no uniform."

Logan's jaw works, and the muscles in his neck tighten.

Lugsen swings his gaze from Logan to us. "And you two.

You'll be on unbonded exercise and feeding duty. I'm adding two stallions to your lists."

"Sir, with all due respect—" Heath begins.

"I'm not finished," Lugsen cuts me off. "You're superior officers with Specter will be hearing of this, and I suspect they, too, will want a word."

Fuck. "Come on," I protest, but Lugsen silences me with a hand.

"As for you, McCelroy," he says, looking at Logan. "I had hoped you'd appreciate the courtesy of being allowed to stay at this station. That clearly isn't the case. You will be placed on leave for one week without pay. You will be supervised when not in your room and must check in and check out with me before and after your shifts."

Logan stands so suddenly his chair topples backward, clattering against the stone floor. "No goddamn way. You can't do that."

"I can and I have," Lugsen says firmly. "The transfer order is already—"

"He's mine!" Logan roars, lunging forward and sweeping his arm across Lugsen's desk. Papers fly, and the antique clock falls from its perch on a shelf, shattering as it hits the floor. Before Lugsen can make it out of his chair, Logan punches him square in the jaw. Lugsen's head snaps back from the uppercut.

Phase two.

No going back now.

Heath and I move in unison and grab Logan from behind. He struggles, almost breaking free before we manage to force him to the floor. His eyes are wild and unfocused.

Lugsen rises slowly, rubbing his face, staring at Logan with a look I've never seen before. It's not anger but sadness, a pitying look of disappointment. He'd gone to bat for Logan, and in the end, it'd bit him in the ass. "That's it, McCelroy,"

Lugsen says, holding his jaw. "You're all out of chances." He taps his comm. "Send security to my office."

We don't wait long, and in five minutes, a very confused Seth and Elena enter.

Lugsen motions to Logan. "Detain him until authorities arrive." They do, and Heath and I are sent to the barracks. Soon after, we see a grim-faced Fiaro, Marshal and two Circuit police disappear into Lugsen's office.

When they emerge, Logan is handcuffed.

"Because you assaulted a Circuit government official," one of the officers says. "And violated your probation. By the order of Circuit law, you are under arrest and hereby sentenced to rehabilitation in TZ Delta."

Marshal breaks from the group and strides over to us. "What the hell happened?"

Heath and I shrug.

Marshal scoffs, one brow arched in disbelief. "Seriously? You're not going to tell me?"

"Just a bad day, I guess," I say.

He doesn't buy it. "Well, that bad day cost Logan his last shot. He broke parole. There won't be another trial. No hearing. He's done." He studies us, jaw tight. "I hope whatever it was is worth it."

Then he turns and walks away.

I hope like hell it is.

Twenty-Seven

BRIGID

Three days ago, my sister told me she was dying.

I'm at a loss for how to help her, what to say. She demanded that I keep it a secret from everyone, including Mom, and that I don't treat her any differently.

But that's impossible. Of course, I'll treat her differently. I'll do anything to help her.

I recall the resentment I had for her for keeping me here, but that was before I knew everything. Before, I knew how much our government hid from us.

The flowers will not grow without the light of the sun to draw them upward.

I passed the saying spray-painted on a wall in the west sector daily, and later found out it's part of ITM's doctrine.

Sharice told me it's only supposed to be read with the High Navigator's permission, but she said the Wayfinder, I should at least be somewhat familiar with its principles.

I skimmed through the dog-eared copy one night, most of it read like overripe poetry, long passages about soil depth and seed growth, symbolic of lives and roots and interconnected futures. Dry. Repetitive.

But a few parts stuck with me. Ideas about equal access to medicine, comfort, and a dignified life, no matter where you were born. A whole section on respecting wild animals and learning from them. That part I liked the most.

While we wait for samples to mature in the lab, I help the others sort and label the overflowing storage room. The indirect path to my room gives me time to think, or at least it should, but the faint hum of familiar voices stops me in my tracks.

Pressing myself against the cool metal wall, I edge closer to an open door marked Employees Only. The sign's rusty edges catch the dim light.

"They're growing resistant." Sharice's voice is tinged with frustration. "The pheromones aren't working like they used to. They're developing a tolerance."

I shift farther into the corner, holding my breath.

"We suspected this might happen and prepared for it," a man says. It's Elton. "Up the dosage for the next raid."

"If it doesn't work?" Sharice asks, unease coating her words. "What happens then?"

"It will work," Elton snaps. "The mystyl will do what they're made to do. We'll soon grow beyond the need for the mystyl."

What did Sharice mention before? That the mystyl would naturally drift? That has to be what they're talking about. At the time, I thought it was just another one of her vague, half-shared ideas, the kind she likes to dangle like a carrot to keep me enticed. But now, with Elton here, it feels bigger. Sharice isn't just talking about some strange side effect. The drifting isn't an annoyance anymore; it's posing an actual threat to everyone they send out on the raids.

And I shouldn't be hearing any of it.

My stomach twists. If they catch me listening, I won't get a chance to explain myself. Elton is just itching for an excuse to punish me, and the thought of him cornering me again in my room turns my blood to ice.

I glance back down the hall, my exit farther away than it should be. Every instinct screams to move, to leave before the shadows give me away, but I can't. Not when they're talking about attacking the capital.

"I'll need more of the protein growth serum," Sharice says, her voice fading as if she's pacing. "The last batch had expired."

"Fine. I'll send a team to get more. Whatever you need."

"Doubling might still not be enough," Sharice counters.

"Then triple it," Elton snaps. "I don't care what you have to do; just do it."

There's a long pause, then Sharice says, "I'll need time."

"How long?"

"Thirty-six hours for the amino acids to mature, then twenty-four to homogenize into the oil."

With a grunt of grudging acceptance, he says, "All right. That'll give us time to collect more ammo and transportation to Delford."

A few moments later, Sharice asks, "But what if it doesn't work?"

"It won't matter," his voice cold. "After Delford, you can unplug all the terrariums for all I care."

I press a hand to my mouth, steadying my breath as the

floor beneath me feels like it's about to drop away. Mystyl are dangerous, vile creatures. I shouldn't care if they all die. But it's Elton's cruelty I can't stomach, the way he tosses life aside like it means nothing.

I hate that. I hate him.

If Sharice won't deal with him, then I will. I'll volunteer for the Delford strike, get close enough to him, and...

The light from the open door shifts again. Footsteps. Heavy, deliberate. Someone is moving toward the hall. I lean back farther into the shadows and curl my fingers into fists as I silently pray that they turn the other way.

Elton and Sharice step into the hall, their eyes locking on me.

I casually push off the wall, forcing my expression to stay neutral. "Evening," I say, flashing them a smile. "I was coming to get you for dinner," I lie, looking at Sharice.

Elton's gaze heats the side of my face. "Sneaky sneaky," he says, tone unnervingly even. "We don't need to ask you to refrain from eavesdropping in the future, do we?"

I set my jaw and force my eyes to meet his. "No, High Navigator."

"Good." He offers a smile that's more like a grimace. "I'm sure you have questions, so why don't I escort you back to your room?"

"High Navigator," Sharice interjects, her voice tight. "I don't think that's necessary."

"Nonsense," comes his smooth reply. "It'll be my pleasure. Besides, don't you have somewhere else to be? The lab, perhaps?"

My sister's lips press into a thin line, and she swallows hard. I search her face, hoping for some modicum of support. Nothing. So much for her promises of protection.

Elton gestures ahead of him, and I step out of my hiding

spot, dragging my feet. Walking in silence, the air between us is heavy.

At my door, I pray like hell that he'll leave me, but he follows me inside. In the hallway, two of his helmeted guards stand idly by. He waves them off with a flick of his wrist. Outside the door, the two guards lurk in the hallway. Not the same ones as yesterday. Man Bun has been replaced by another guy in the same black face mask and re-breather setup, and I don't care enough to ask what happened. They're just living proof that Sharice and Elton think I will try something. Although now, if I'm on the base's shit list, maybe it'll be the other way around.

The door clicks shut behind him.

His polished boots tap against the concrete floor. He carries himself like he's always welcome, like he has a right to my space. I don't look at him.

"Brigid," he says, soft but insistent. "I know you don't like me, but I was hoping to sway your opinion."

I turn my head slightly, just enough to see his reflection in the small mirror bolted to the wall. His dark hair is perfectly combed, his uniform immaculate, like every movement he makes is part of some calculated performance.

"I'm not hiding." My voice sounds foreign.

"With every great scientific breakthrough, there's always someone angry about it." He steps closer. "Near-sighted individuals just don't get it like you and me. You shouldn't be ashamed of what you did."

"I'm not ashamed," I lie. I'll say whatever I need to to get him out of here. "I just thought it'd be different," I add quickly.

His head bobs slowly. "Ah, well, we all knew there were going to be some bumps on the road." He lays a hand on my shoulder. "We're not like the others, you and me. We're special. Dane saw it, and now I see it. Can you imagine what we can create together?"

The words slide under my skin, slow and burning, like a splinter of molten glass. "What are you talking about?"

He offers me a tight-lipped smile. "I know your sister told you about the selective breeding programs, but did she tell you they didn't just involve the druadans? They included the riders, too. Selective breeding to enhance traits. Strengthening new abilities. Stronger. Smarter. More durable. They made warriors equal to the animals they rode. Your DNA proves it, Brigid. You are the culmination of centuries of work."

I stare at him, confused about how to respond. *Selective breeding?* What the hell does that mean?

He leans forward, like we're sharing a secret. "I tested my blood also, and carry many of the same markers the original riders had. Our children could be extraordinary. Even more powerful than you. Can you imagine? Together, we could change everything."

His hand reaches for my cheek, and I flinch, but he doesn't stop. His fingers are warm, almost gentle, as they trace the curve of my jaw.

It's been so long since someone touched me like this and spoke to me like this. If I just close my eyes...

"Give yourself to me," he whispers, his lips so close to mine I feel his breath. "I'll make you forget all about your riders."

The word cuts through the fog in my mind. Riders. *My riders.*

The realization slams into me like the electric prods used to force the banshees into the pen, and I shove him away. "No! Get the hell away from me."

He tilts his head, studying me like a puzzle he's determined to solve.

"You need to leave," I forced through clenched teeth.

He doesn't move.

Unease twists into panic, coiling in my chest. My hand reaches back, searching blindly until my fingers find one of my books. I glare at him.

There's a knock at the door. "High Navigator, sir," A man says. "We need to review the cargo manifest that just arrived before distribution."

His expression darkens into something monstrous, and for the briefest of seconds, I think he's going to tell them to go away. My body is rigid as the two of us are caught in a standoff. My teeth dig into the side of my cheek, and the metallic taste of blood fills my mouth.

"This conversation isn't over," he says, his voice low. He rises from the cot, moves to the door, and pulls it open. Without looking back, he leaves me trembling and my heart slamming against my ribs.

No more playing nice. Resolve fortifies in my chest as I remember the vow I just made. I'm going on the mission to attack Delford, and one of us won't be coming back.

Twenty-Eight

LOGAN

My life ending with me in handcuffs was inevitable.

"Move it," a burly guard shouts over the howl of the engines.

The cold bite of the metal digs into my wrists. The wind tastes like rust and death. It scrapes against my face, carrying the grit of what is now thoroughly a hellscape.

A baton prods my back as I and seven other prisoners march down the ramp.

I squint at the ruins of the city stretching out. Skeletons of buildings rise like broken teeth against the gray sky, their jagged edges framed by a green smog I realize is only visible from the ground.

We've been stripped of everything but the tan jumpsuits on our backs. The color of dirt so we blend with the ground and are invisible to any shuttles passing overhead, considering to rescue us.

Which is exactly why they drop us here. No witnesses, no chance.

A crate is tossed out, and without another word from the guards, the ramp closes.

Dumping us in the TZ with the handcuffs is a new level of sadistic bullshit I didn't think Circuit could achieve until I learned my cousin had been wrong.

They don't give us masks.

They make us fight for them.

Dirt swirls around us, and I shield my face as best I can with the cuffs as the other convicts and I are left behind.

My bare feet crunch against broken glass and splintered asphalt as I stumble forward, lungs already burning. The air smells of chemicals caught somewhere between pesticides and the solvent I use to clean my gun. A sharp tang that cuts deeper with every breath.

They warned us it would feel like this. Burning lungs, a knife twisting in your chest, then nothing. George, my cousin's voice echoes in my head. "Don't worry about shoes or water. It's a mask you want. You can live days without the other stuff. Without a tank and mask, you'll be dead in minutes."

Some already have. A guy not far from me takes one look around and pulls out a pistol. Where he got it, I don't know. Doesn't matter. The crack of the shot echoes across the ruins. His body crumples like the rest of the place. A few others start running, desperate for... what? Safety? There isn't any. Not here. The only thing waiting is a drawn-out and ugly death.

I stand still, watching. The wind claws at my skin, whipping through my torn sleeves.

The others are fighting now, scrabbling like rats over scraps. Someone found a mask and clings to it, screaming as two others beat him to the ground. One pries the mask away while the other stomps a boot down on his chest so hard I hear bones crack.

They want this. The ones who sent us here. They want us to kill each other, to tear ourselves apart.

A body stumbles into me, and my instincts engage.

I pin and head-butt the first one. He staggers backward, clutching his face and screaming about a broken nose. I'm on him before he can recover, wrenching the mask from his grip. He's too weak to fight back, or maybe he knows it's not worth it. The mask is a cheap, flimsy thing that'll give maybe thirty minutes of air, but it's enough, and I shove the mask over my face and inhale. The filtered air smells of plastic, but it's clean.

For a moment, I simply breathe so I can clear my mind. I glance back at the guy on the ground. He wheezes, clutching his face as crimson blood pours down his cheeks and onto the sand. I should feel something about leaving him there.

I don't.

The others have scattered or are too busy fighting each other on the ground to notice me. Another guy has a jagged piece of metal sticking out of his throat, and I strip the mask from his face as he gurgles his final breaths.

I can probably take the last one, but it'll cost me what oxygen I had to take this one. I only saw three in the box, and there were seven of us.

Not wanting to waste time, I jog toward the ruins. My bare feet slide on the shifting sand. Behind me, screams echo. The others can tear each other apart if they want.

I have no interest in joining them.

The windows in the high-rise buildings are long gone, the interiors hollowed out by time and decay. This place is a graveyard. Cracked roadways snake through the wasteland, covered in a layer of dirt fine enough to choke on. I catch the faint skittering—tiny claws on concrete—a lizard darts into the shadows of a crumbled wall.

Well, shit. I didn't think anything bigger than a beetle lived out here. I pass what used to be a signpost, its metal warped and illegible, suppressing the fleeting hope it's for the amusement park.

The streets are cracked, and veins of weeds long dead poke through the gaps. A car's rusted shell leans against a lamppost, its tires melted into the ground.

I keep jogging, putting distance between me and where the ship left us.

Beep.

The mask's oxygen is already low. I feel it in the way my breaths get shorter, the faint hiss growing weaker. My legs ache, feet raw and bloody from the jagged ground.

I stuff down the pain and swap it out for the backup one.

The timer on my fresh mask beeps.

Sixty minutes.

The ride to the Village ended with one police officer with a black eye and another with a broken finger, so the judge expedited my sentencing. It'd only taken twenty-four hours to get from fighting with Heath and Carter at Blackhawk to the jail to here.

I jog, ignoring the incessant beep every five minutes, alerting me to my dropping oxygen levels. I scan the sand for signs of footprints or tire tracks.

The wind shifts, carrying a steady clang. I freeze, stilling my ragged breathing to listen, but it's just the sound of the wind banging a loose piece of something against metal.

I'm on the outskirts of the city now, and a building's frame is half-buried in sand in the distance.

I stumble into what used to be a subway entrance. The stairs, cracked and uneven, lead into darkness. The air feels heavier down here, and the smell of mildew confirms my mask is far from fucking sealed.

It's quieter, though. No wind. Just the sound of my ragged breathing.

The mask gives out halfway down. A sharp hiss, then silence. I freeze, gripping it with shaking hands as if I can will it back to full. Staring at the ground, I hold my breath.

Fuck.

I rip it off, sucking in the air. My lungs burn, every breath like a blowtorch is lit in my throat. My vision blurs and spots dance in the dim light filtering through the cracks above. I collapse against the wall, the rough surface scraping my skin.

This was so fucking stupid.

I'm dying, and it's my own damn fault. But part of me knew it would end like this. Maybe that's why I came. To see how far I could push before breaking.

I close my eyes to the spinning world. The sounds of the wasteland fade, replaced by a memory.

Shimmering silver hair glinting under my fingers in the moonlight.

The feel of soft lips against mine. I drop to my knees, head sagging forward.

How long do I have? Minutes? Seconds? The air feels like glass shards tearing through me. Every breath is agony.

My pulse, a relentless thump-thump-thump in my ears.

The sound grows louder and heavier.

I lift my head, blinking through the murkiness. A shadow moves, faint against the crumbled ruins. My hands clench the dirt as I try to focus.

Then I see her. A girl. Long red hair peeks out from the back of her oxygen mask, and through the glass, I see a pair of mismatched eyes.

"Hey," I croak, my voice barely audible. She doesn't respond, just watches with wide eyes.

Before I can say more, hands emerge from the shadows and wrap around her.

Her scream rips through the air as she kicks at the ground and is pulled into the darkness.

Adrenaline slices through the haze of pain and lack of oxygen, and I push to my feet, stumbling toward the sound.

Following her screams leads me up the stairs from the subway platform.

The girl, no older than twelve, is trapped between two of the prisoners dropped off with me. One has her by the arm while the other wrestles a bag from her shoulder. She thrashes and kicks, giving them hell, but it's pointless. They're three times her size.

"Let her go!" I bellow.

The inmates pause, turning toward me. One sneers and stalks toward me, but I'm already moving. My hands are still cuffed in front of me, so I lunge at him with a powerful kick that sends him sprawling. The other lets go of her and grabs a cracked brick from the ground, but I don't give him a chance.

I drive my knee into his gut. Then, an elbow to the face that sends him to the ground.

The first one recovers, scrambling up with a snarl, but I'm already prepared. As he lunges, I sidestep his clumsy attack and slam my foot into his chest. He crashes against the crumbling rock wall hard enough to dent it. He doesn't get up.

I advance on the second guy. "Your turn, fucko," I growl inside the mask.

He tries to punch me, but I pivot, catching his wrist mid-swing with my arms and twisting until he drops to his knees. I tower over him, applying just enough pressure to keep him there. With my elbow, I crack him over the face hard enough to knock him out.

Panting, I flex my fists, and the cuffs dig into the skin. The restraint only fuels my anger.

The girl gets up from the ground and straightens her mask to fit over her mouth and nose. "Please don't hurt me," she whispers through it. Her hair is the exact color of Ember's coat, a fiery red, and her eyes are brown except for the left, which has a slice of blue down the center.

Wild as hell.

I hold my hands up as best I can, but before I can check on her, another man yells from my left. "Get the hell away from her!"

A man approaches wearing a mask that appears to be held together by silver tape and aims an antique rifle at my chest. He's older, his face weathered and bronzed like the sun-baked clay in the cracked basins I passed.

The girl darts in front of me, arms outstretched. "Don't shoot him, Daddy!" she pleads. "He saved me."

The man hesitates, lowering the rifle slightly. He steps closer, his sharp eyes scanning me. Before I can react, he grabs my hand, flipping it palm up. His gaze narrows.

"Shit," he mutters. "You're a rider."

I pull my hand back, scowling. "Not anymore."

He straightens, slinging the rifle over his shoulder. "Since you saved my daughter, I owe you one. I can give you a ride to the clear zone."

"Clear?" I echo, skepticism lacing my tone.

"At the edges, there's an oasis of cleaner air. Gives you a bit of a cough, but it's breathable."

The girl's small frame trembles, but her eyes are curious. I nod. "Fine. Lead the way."

Up out of the subway station, a battered van with tractor tires is parked.

Plastic flutters over the windows, and small air filters are strapped to the roof along with several batteries. He unzips the side and allows his daughter to climb in first, then me.

The van interior is stripped bare except for the front bench seat, and mesh crates are stacked in the back.

He takes the driver's seat and shuts the door. I don't dare take off my mask until they do, and even then, I keep it loose on my neck.

I don't trust them, but at least I'm not walking anymore.

He turns the van away from the subway station, the knobby tires gliding smoothly over the sand. In the interior of the van, the tension in my back and neck eases, melting away.

The windows are blocked by black plastic, so I only see through the cracked front windshield.

"I'm Waylon, by the way," the man says, tapping his chest with one hand while leaving the other on the wheel. "And this is my daughter, Nova."

"Logan," I say, leaning down to pluck shards of glass and jagged rocks from the soles of my feet. The skin around my toes looks like it went through a meat grinder.

"Just Logan?" he asks.

I shrug. What does it matter? My last name means nothing outside the station.

We drive for some time with only the sounds of the hum of the engine and the wheezing of my breath. I'm sure I have lung damage from the exposure out there, but it's not like there's anything I can do about it.

Nova leans her head against the window, an easy smile on her face. Ten minutes ago, she'd been pinned by a con and yet seems unshaken. Girl is tough. Makes sense, given her lifestyle.

A child in the TZ. What the fuck is a kid doing here? She

can't be a prisoner. They don't sentence children to TZ exile, no matter what they've done.

"Who the hell are you guys?" I ask.

Waylon gestures to the crates of random shit piled in the back. "Take a guess."

Bottles, hoses, jars, and other random broken crap overflows from the boxes.

Fuck me. "You're trawlers."

Nova giggles, and Waylon shushes her. "Oxygen deprivation sure did a number on ya, didn't it? We are indeed."

Well, shit. I couldn't have asked for better luck. Trawlers know the zone better than anyone. My chances of finding Blondie have gotten a whole hell of a lot better.

Before I can ask about the amusement park, we stop at what appears to be an war old checkpoint. The gates are rusted but intact, and beyond them, the ruins give way to open space, gently rolling hills covered with tall grasses and pine trees.

More and more trees appear, and soon, we stop in front of an A-frame cabin and a metal airplane hangar.

"Alrighty, we're here," Waylon says, stepping out of the vehicle.

He catches me holding my breath.

"It's safe to breathe here. The higher elevation means less dirty air. We're still technically in the Zone, but it's what you'd call an island. Wind currents change faster than a Chrono seventy winch will fray your cable, and what is safe to breathe one second is filthy as a trawler's bar bathroom the next."

"You have bars out here?"

"'Course, we do." When my eyes widen, he chuckles. "Nah, I'm joking. There's only one that I know of. They'll pop up for a time but disappear when the owner dies or the air fouls. I do have a bottle of Graynier inside, though. I've got a small filter, so let's see if we can't get you acclimated better."

They start toward the house, but I don't move. I'm still wearing my torn shirt and handcuffs, and my feet are coated in blood and sand. "Why are you helping me?" As soon as I ask, though, I regret it.

Waylon studies me and then gestures to Nova, unloading the back of the van and hauling crates to the hangar. "You had a chance to do what those men wanted to, but you didn't. I saw you fighting even with those cuffs. And even with my gun, I doubt I could've stopped you from taking it."

He's right. He's not even six feet, built like a scarecrow. His rifle is old and known to jam. In this climate, there's a slim chance he would've gotten even one round off before I took it from him.

As if seeing me realize all this, he adds. "The way I see it, I owe you one."

"Thanks."

I follow him, still barefoot, but at least here, the dirt has soft patches of grass.

Waylon leads me up the hill past a series of dozens of small, metal pinwheels spinning lazily. Behind them is a line strung with dangling metal chains.

"They're my foul gauges." He says, noticing my gaze. "If they turn that way, their blades hit the metal, and we can hear it even inside."

"What is this place?" I ask.

The man smirks. "Murdock Harbor. Our home."

"I appreciate it and all, but I have somewhere I gotta go." I stop before saying I'm looking for someone.

"Is that so?" He waves in the air. "Cause from where I stand, it looks like the only place you're going is a quick trip to the grave." He opens a drawer packed to the brim with bits of metal screws, pins, and clasps. Then slams it shut before opening another. He rummages around, then withdraws a small key. He proudly shows it to me, his eyes lighting up, and I hold my wrists out to un-cuff me.

I rub my wrists, and he sets the cuffs into another drawer containing at least five other sets and closes it. How many other inmates have come through here?

"It's late. You can stay in the loft. Get you some water, and a meal, and then tomorrow, I'll see if I find you a pair of boots, and you can continue wherever it is you're in a hurry to go."

Nova enters from a side door, carrying a smaller crate to a table, where she begins sorting the various pieces of metal and plastic. The space is small, with the table in the middle, flanked by two long benches, a stove, a fridge, and two bedrooms in the back.

It's around the size of my cabin at Meridian, but it's packed with *stuff*.

Sheets of metal with paint, giant bolts, shuttle propeller blades, wires, fittings, and plastic bottles. Shelves and shelves of items, it's almost dizzying to take it all in, or my short stint in the TZ caused brain damage.

Waylon motions for me to sit at the other side of the long table Nova is at. A second later, I realize it's the wing of a shuttle propped up on cinder blocks. He moves to a shelf and takes down a bottle. "I can't get you too far because the police watch the borders for inmates like you, but I can get you close enough so you might be able to get to Leviler."

"I don't need to go to Leviler. I need to find ITM's base."

His hand stills on the bottle he was uncorking, and Nova stops her working.

"Nah, nah," he says, shaving his head. "Don't tell me you're one of those save the earth, bleed the rich rebels that think the country is better off in ashes than now."

"No. But a friend of mine is, and I need to find her."

"If she's with them, she's gone. You ain't saving her."

I grind my teeth together. "I'll decide that. *When* I get to her."

Waylon brings me a glass of the ivory-colored liquid, and I sling it back without sniffing.

It burns so fucking good.

He sips his, and I feel him and his daughter watching me.

"Most folks I pick up want to get the hell out of here. This must be some friend if you want to go back into the TZ."

"She is."

Waylon makes a crooning sound. "She. We should've known, eh, Novi?"

Nova laughs as he shakes her arm.

"Judging by the glint you got in your eye just now, I ain't thinking this woman is your sister."

I spin the empty glass in my hands.

He waggles a finger at me and tops off my glass.

"Turns out I'm a bit of a romantic. Ever since my Hannah passed, rest her soul. I've done what I can to help others find the ones that make their hearts pitter-patter."

Not sure how to respond since Blondie had done a lot fucking more than that, so I chose to drink instead.

"So, say I *do* know where this base may be. I can't just drop you off there, can I?"

I shake my head, the strong rum seeping into my muscles. "No, but if you can get me close, I can do the rest."

"It's dangerous."

"I can pay."

"Deal," Nova says before her dad can answer.

"All right, then, *just* Logan. You're going to need a plan."

Twenty-Nine

BRIGID

I saw Laurel today.

The doctor says she has violent outbursts, so they keep her sedated.

Ronan wasn't there, but the attendant assured me he came every day to sit with her.

I left shortly after, unable to stay and watch her once-vibrant smile fade into a blank stare.

The rest of the morning I spent in the lab. I'm far from a scientist, but I'm getting better at drawing blood, organizing beakers, and labeling samples.

At least it keeps my hands busy and avoids Ronan and the few others leaving bags of excrement on my doorstep. The trinkets and offerings have decreased from what they'd been.

In the cafeteria, I move fast, grabbing a bowl of whatever passes for stew tonight—some mix of meat and broth. It smells vaguely of iron and spices, but I don't care. I need to get back to my room before anyone notices me or I run into Ronan.

All praise the Wayfinder who hides from thirteen-year-old boys.

I'm nothing but a coward.

I want to apologize. *I should.*

But words are hollow when I'm powerless to change anything.

The belief that I might help her ended yesterday when I overheard a group returning from Reco tell Elton that the banshee she bonded with tore down the pen and, in the struggle to contain it, it broke its neck.

How many banshees did that make dead because of us?

They're feral, dangerous animals that will attack any of us on sight, but that doesn't make it hurt any less. They're living, breathing beings that would still run free if our ancestors hadn't messed up our country to end a war. Now, generations later, we're left struggling with the consequences of those actions.

Eight. The mare's death makes eight banshees dead because of me.

I complained about being sick after that and excused myself for the rest of the day.

I don't know if their bonds work like the druadans, but I pray she isn't hurting like a rider would.

Any chance of fixing her is gone. The bond is severed, and the damage to her mind is permanent.

The thought presses down on me as I head back to my room. I need the quiet, the stillness before I dissolve into another panic attack.

A hard chest collides with mine, stopping me.

I step back and glare at one of Elton's brutes who got in my way. He wears one of the helmets, and his eyes are hidden behind the dark glass.

I sidestep around him. "Excuse me!"

He doesn't move.

I'm so *not* in the mood for this.

My eyes trace the curve of his helmet. It's a sleek, dark thing, but I feel his gaze pierce through the shadowed visor as if he studies me, waiting for something.

The last thing I need is him telling Elton that I was ditching work early or fleeing from the cafeteria. That would only draw more of his attention, and I did not want him to make his evening visits a habit.

"Please." I make my tone lighter.

"Where are you going in such a rush?" he asks.

I flash him a thin smile. "No rush. Uh, I just forgot my toothbrush in the showers and don't want anyone taking it."

He points behind me. "Aren't the showers that way?" His deep voice is deep, muffled by the mask.

"Oh, yeah." I rub my forehead. "What was I thinking? It's been a long day, and I'm tired."

He tilts his head, his expression unreadable through the helmet, but stays silent as I hurry down the corridor toward the bathrooms.

I feel his gaze on my back and shoulders, and refrain from sprinting.

Minutes later, the humid air of the showers clings to my skin as I step inside, and the faint scent of old soap lingers. My shoes echo softly on the wet tiles, and I keep my steps slow and purposeful. I scan the room, though I know no one's here.

I lean against the sink, gripping the edge until my knuckles turn white. Composing myself, I splash cold water onto my face, watching the droplets streak down my reflection in the cracked mirror. It's not like I was doing anything wrong. But it doesn't matter. Guards like him are loyal to Elton. Anything they see or suspect will reach his ears faster than I can spin a believable excuse.

The minutes stretch, and the tension in my shoulders finally eases when I poke my head out of the door. The corridor lies still and empty. No sign of him.

I step out, deciding on the long route to my room.

Inside, I close the door, but a foot stops it.

Thinking it's the guard again, I whirl, ready to lay into him a lesson on privacy, when the smell hits me: sweat and something sour, like rotting fruit.

The lower half of the man's face is covered with an oxygen mask. He's one of the new recruits, but there are so many lately it's hard to keep track.

Maybe he knows Laurel and followed me from the cafeteria?

He steps inside, shutting the door softly behind him. This one isn't part of Elton's usual crew. He's mid-thirties, with thinning hair and a greasy grin that doesn't quite reach his eyes. His clothes hang off him like he borrowed them from someone bigger. Pretty typical for the recruits that they've been bringing in. Most are from filtration plants, and the food rationing has taken a toll on the people still trapped there.

I keep my face blank, but my stomach twists.

"Brigid, is it?" His voice is oily, sliding through the space between us. He moves closer, and I fight the urge to back away.

"Who are you?" I keep my tone flat as I swallow down the heady rush of déjà vu from Elton last night.

He chuckles, low and breathy, like we're sharing a secret. "You don't remember, do you?"

He tugs down the mask.

My breath evaporates from my lungs.

He's changed from the clean-shaven CSU agent in a suit

and tie to this hardened man with a beard. A jagged scar runs from temple to jaw, still pink and angry against his skin. But those cool brown eyes didn't change. He still watches me with an intensity that makes my skin crawl.

Agent Zane.

His grin widens when he sees my recognition.

"No," I breathe.

"You seem surprised?" he says, almost cheerfully.

"What are you doing here?" I already know the answer.

He arches an eyebrow. "Why, devoting myself to the High Navigator, of course."

"You're with them?" I keep my voice steady, even as my pulse hammers.

"I am," he says, grinning wide. All of his teeth are stained black at the edges from years of smoking cigarettes. "Sort of. I suppose you can say I'm hedging my bets. The High Navigator needs me here to tell him about our noble army's next move, and in exchange, I get to share tidbits with my boss to keep my bonus checks coming."

That double-crossing bastard. I glare at him, anger flaring.

This is why no one has come for me. He's been working with ITM all along. He *knew* my mom would take me. Bastard probably earned all kinds of merit badges for bringing me in.

Son of a bitch. I'm so goddamn tired of being played like a fool by people who are meant to be trustworthy.

He laughs, a dry, rasping sound. "You're so wrapped up in yourself that you didn't even notice me. I've been watching you, *Wayfinder*. In the cafeteria, in the lab. In the shower."

My gut clenches.

"What do you want?" I spit through clenched teeth.

"I know you're trapped here. And I know you want desperately to get out. So, let's make a deal, and I'll make sure you get out of here alive. Hell, I'll drive you back to Leviler's headquarters myself."

"And if I say no?" Playing for time now, I scan the room for anything to defend myself. The clock on the wall, the empty water bottle, my books.

Dammit.

Zane's smile widens, and every alarm bell inside me blares. "Then I'll just take what I want, and you get nothing."

He moves into my space, and I catch the gleam of something metallic in his hand. Scissors. The kind in a medical kit, blunt-tipped but sharp enough to cut. Or kill.

Muscles tensing, I open my mouth to scream, but he moves fast, grabs a handful of my hair with the hand holding the scissors, and yanks my head back. Pain blooms across my scalp, and I bite back a cry.

"Relax, sweetheart." He twirls the scissors between his fingers like a magician's trick, then gestures at my hair. "You know, there's a chapter in the doctrine about a woman with silver hair, just like you. It's where your sister got the inspiration for Wayfinder. Course, her hair in the story possesses magical healing powers, and you might've noticed my face isn't as pretty as it used to be, so let's test this theory, shall we?"

My heart kicks against my ribs, panic surging inside me. It's just hair. *It'll grow back.* Still, fear causes my whole body to tremble.

"Hold still," he mutters, raising the scissors.

The door creaks, and I swear I see a shadow shift in the corner.

There's a wet, choking sound, and Zane's eyes go wide.

The grip on my hair goes slack. Hot blood sprays over me, spattering my face.

Zane collapses, clutching at the shears lodged in his throat, his eyes staring blankly with shock.

One of the guards stands over him. His face is unreadable under the helmet. Frozen, my breath shallow and quick, the room spins around me.

The sounds from Zane cease.

He's dead.

Oh my god. I cover my mouth, bile burning the back of my tongue.

The guard takes off his helmet, revealing a square jaw and eyes the color of iron.

My knees turn to jelly. "Logan?" I gasp.

"Hey, Blondie. How you been?"

Thirty

Logan

All color drains from Brigid's face, the pale white of her skin a stark contrast to the crimson spray of blood.

She stumbles backward, one hand flying to her mouth, the other gripping the edge of the table. The blood splatter on her face seems to finally register, along with my unexpected presence.

"Yeah, it's me," I manage, trying to sound casual despite the thundering in my chest.

She scrambles away until her back hits the wall. Her eyes dart frantically around the room, seeking an escape that doesn't exist. Her gaze shifts to the fallen guard, to the blood, then back to me. There's terror in her eyes, whether from me or slicing the guy's throat, I'm not sure. "No," she mutters, half-laughing as she shakes her head. "This can't be real. *You* can't be here."

"Hate to be the bearer of bad news," I say, softer this time, "but this is as fucking real as it gets."

It's been damn hard keeping this secret for days. Infiltrating this place was easier than I thought. Catching a group out looking for scraps, I picked a guy close to my height and build, took him down, tossed him into a ravine, and then dressed in his shit and rejoined the group before anyone noticed.

Playing the role, however, has not been as easy. I've been forced to watch the others leer at her when she walked by or whisper shit behind her back about how she's the High Navigator's toy. The only reason he keeps her here is because she keeps his bed warm.

Every second of every day tested my restraint.

I almost slipped yesterday when that asshole with the earring invited her to a "party" in his room. I know exactly what kind of party he meant.

She said no, but in that moment of brief hesitation, I thought she might agree out of fear or resignation. That split second nearly cost me everything.

"Easy," I try again, setting the helmet down slowly without breaking eye contact. "I'm not here to hurt you."

Recognition begins to dawn in her eyes, replacing blind panic with confusion.

"Logan?" she repeats, this time with a different inflection. "How did you find me?"

I carefully move closer, my hands open at my sides. "Long story."

"But...why?"

My chest feels like it's splitting in two. The weight of what I said to her slams into the front of my mind. *We're better off without you.* Everything was shit then, and I was unraveling, so I took it out on her.

I thought I was doing the right thing, cutting ties, protecting myself from the impending shit storm. But standing here, seeing her like this, I know it was the worst thing I could have said.

"I was wrong," I say, the words rough. The apology feels too small, too late, but it's all I have. "I'm sorry for everything I said. For pushing you away. I—" I stop. Fuck. This isn't working. *Just say it straight.* "We were never better off without you."

She searches my face, studying me like she's reading a map. But there's something different now. A wariness that was never there before. She's looking for the lie, the angle, the hidden agenda behind my words.

Someone's done a number on her while she's been here, turned her natural caution into this brittle distrust. A spark of rage ignites in my chest, hot and sharp, at whoever the hell made her this way. I want to find whoever did this and make them pay. Make them suffer.

A storm of emotions clouds her teal irises.

"You're...you're really here," she whispers.

"I am."

Her calm is short-lived, however, and her eyes widen. "Oh god. You're working for *them*. What did they promise you? Money? Keeping your family safe? Rank?"

She leaps to her feet, swipes a fork from a meal tray on the table, and wields it in my direction. "Elton? Did he send you here?" Her eyes dart to the dead man on the ground, then back to mine.

Guards patrol this area of the building, and if she keeps yelling, it'll draw their attention. She jabs the fork at me. I sidestep and grab her wrist.

"I love you, Blondie."

The words slip out before I can stop them, words I've never

said to anyone but family and Heath and Carter after a night of drinking.

But the way this conversation is going, I might not get another chance to say them.

The fork clatters to the ground, but the fire in her eyes remains. "You're lying," she hisses, struggling against my hold.

I release her but keep her eyes locked with mine. "I've seen what life looks like without you in it, and I'm done pretending I can survive that. You're it. I don't deserve your forgiveness, but I'll spend the rest of my life proving I'm worthy to you." I pause, letting my words settle. "Hate me if you need to," I say, "I don't deserve your forgiveness, but I swear I'm not working for them."

"Words are cheap." She scoffs. "Prove it."

I take my gun from my holster, and her eyes go wide as I place it in her hand and press it so the muzzle digs into my chest. "Go ahead. Look into my eyes and tell me what you see."

Her lips press together as her eyes dance between mine, searching.

"It's your choice," I say, my voice low. "If you don't trust me, then pull the trigger. End this now 'cause I'd rather my blood stain the ground than spend another goddamn second living with you looking at me like this."

Her hand shakes, and emotions flicker in rapid succession on her face before settling as she lowers the gun.

"You really *are* here for me?"

I let out a sharp breath and nod.

Tears swim in her eyes, and her bottom lip trembles. I want to wrap her in my arms, but she still has my pistol.

"How long?" she says, each word slowly but with such force that I nearly take a step back.

"How long what?"

"Fuck you. You know what."

I don't dare lower my gaze. "Five days."

She makes a sound somewhere between a scoff and a laugh. "Five days? You were here that long, and you just stood by, and what, watched me? Why?" She looks up, pinning me with a glare so full of hate, so full of anger. I do take a step back.

"Look, I know you're pissed, but I promise you can yell at me all you want later."

"Pissed?" she hisses. "Pissed doesn't come close to what I'm feeling right now."

Angry tears cascade down her cheeks. "So, what? You just hung out with the other big goons, silent and uncaring, just stood there as people called me names? Left shit on my doorstep? How could you?"

She drops her gaze, and this time, she does laugh, though it borders on hysteria. "How could I have been so stupid? Sharice was right. The bond *makes* you want me. None of this is real."

I stare down at her, shaking my head. "What the hell are you talking about?"

She raises her eyes, leveling me with a look of such pure rage I'm sure would make other men piss their pants. But not me. I like this side, Blondie, this fire, and defiance, not so much when it's directed at me, but fuck, I'll take it.

Shit, I'd missed her.

The blue of her irises is the darkest shade of blue, reminding me of late nights patrolling Ashburn Lake at Meridian.

"A druadan's bond," she says, like she's talking to a child. "Sharice has studied it. It's all chemistry and pheromones. Basic science and biology. Druadans need to reproduce, and at Blackhawk, Oriana triggered something in your bonds that tricked you into *thinking* you loved me, that's all. But it wasn't real. None of it."

I work my tongue against the inside of my cheek. "Bullshit it is."

She purses her lips and shakes her head. "They're going to be back from the raid soon. Please go."

"No."

"God dammit, Logan," she shouts. "You can't be here!"

I don't move.

She pounds her fists on my chest. "Please, you need to go. Run back to the station. Run back to the other riders before they catch you—"

"Brigid." The thumps on my chest miss a beat as I speak her name.

"It's not real. None of it was real." Her voice cracks between sobs, each word breaking apart. "You can't be here. I can't do this again..." her voice trails off.

"Stop." I grab her wrists, not enough to hurt her, but hard enough to get her attention. "Feel me."

She presses her lips together and looks up at me, tears streaking her cheeks.

"Just do it," I command through gritted teeth.

Fear and confusion swirl in her gaze, but finally, she closes them and lowers her head.

Without the bond, I feel nothing change. No flutter or tingling like in Heath's room when I tried to off myself, so I can only hope she's doing whatever she does to sense the bond and find nothing.

The pain of loss I suppressed rises to the surface. It had no place here while I tried to blend with the others until the chance to be alone with Brigid arrived.

And now I finally did, and it's hell.

She opens her eyes and returns them to my face. "Oh, Logan." She says my name like a whisper, and the sadness in her voice dredges up the agonizing memory so it's fresh, as if I just lost it.

"I..." Her voice breaks, "I'm so sorry. I didn't know. I never meant to hurt you, I just wanted to scare you. Keep you from coming closer. If I had known —" her voice does break now, and she collapses against my chest, her arms wrapping around my waist. Hot tears soak through my shirt, and I pull her in closer. Whatever anger I should feel toward her, whatever resentment at her stripping me of my bond, isn't there.

"Why would you come here?" she murmurs into my chest. "After what I did. Why would you ever want to see me again?" Her body shakes violently.

I push her back and stare down at her. Even in the dim light, I see the hollowness of her cheeks, and her silver hair is dull as if tarnished. Even so, she's the most fucking beautiful woman I've ever seen. "You really think you could do anything that would stop me from finding you, Blondie? You could shred my bond a hundred times over, and I'll still come for you. I'll bleed every person dry and wade through their blood to get to you."

I can't wait any longer. My mouth slams into hers. She lets out a surprised whimper, and I kiss her deeper until her body yields. I lower my hand to her back and press close, needing to feel her against me.

She tastes like desperation and longing, and her heart flutters against my chest. Our kisses turn into a frenzied embrace, each of us trying to claim more of the other. My hands roam over her body, reminding myself of every curve and dip.

I break away from her lips and trail hot kisses down her jawline, nipping at her neck as she moans in response. My fingers fumble with the buttons on her pants, needing to feel her skin against mine.

"Fuck," I growl as I finally manage to unbutton them. She

helps me push them down her legs, leaving her in only a pair of black panties.

I tug my shirt over my head and help with hers.

She's not wearing a bra, and I feast on her body with my gaze.

Reaching under her ass, I lift her legs around me and press her against the wall. Her nails dig into my shoulders as she clings to me. She rests her legs behind me, pinning me to her.

My mouth is on hers again, and I kiss her hard.

None of this is tender or soft. This is us taking back what time stole from us.

Our bodies demand from each other what we want, what we fucking need.

And I never needed something more than I needed her right now.

Thirty-One

BRIGID

I can't think, only feel.

The fiery serpent inside awakens from her long-dormant slumber.

This desire. The need overpowers all logic.

Logan's hands slide down my hip and tug my panties aside.

Two fingers tease my folds, gliding effortlessly through the slippery arousal, as he eases them in and out of me.

He moans into my mouth, deepening the kiss, and removes his fingers, leaving me panting. Wanting.

A smirk rests on his face, as he angles my hips, then slowly lowers me onto the massive cock I've only touched with my hand or gazed at from afar when he, Heath, and Carter had pleasured themselves at my command.

The stretch nearly tips me over the edge as every glorious inch fills me. Consumes me.

Once seated inside me, his husky voice asks, "Ready, *Blondie?*"

I bite my lip and nod a little too eagerly. He grunts a reply, then, with a swift movement, lifts and slams me back down.

"Good."

Lift and thrust.

"Don't ever."

Thrust.

"Leave me."

Thrust.

"Again."

Stars clutter my vision as he growls the words into my ear. My thighs tighten, and I feel it coiling inside me.

He's relentless.

His neck muscles, slick with sweat, strain under my hands. He holds me as if I weigh nothing. My hands can't help but explore, absorbing every detail of his corded biceps, broad shoulders, and rock-hard chest.

"I'm sorry," I pant.

"So am I," his voice coated in desire. "And I'll never stop making it up to you."

At his words, I come undone. Shockwaves of ecstasy ripple through me, and I grip him tighter as I ride him. His body becomes the anchor to the exploding tidal waves of pleasure. I feel the frantic beat of his heart in his neck, mirroring mine, against my hands.

He barely lets me recover before he thrusts harder, deeper into me. My muscles clamp down around him, gripping him to me, and heat pools again.

"Come for me again, Blondie. I want you so wrung out from my cock you can't walk straight."

I whimper into his ear and feel his teeth graze my shoulder. His mouth drifts lower until his hot breath washes over my left nipple. The warmth of his tongue laps at the sensitive skin, and my back arches as the next orgasm comes on the heels of the first.

"Oh god," I breathe. "Oh, Logan. Fuck!"

The heat builds, cresting over and I shudder, clenching down on his steel-hard dick.

He shifts his face back to mine, and kisses me hard. He slams into me, burying himself, and the corded muscles in his shoulders tense as his whole body quakes with his release.

A delicious fire blazes from where we're connected as he spills into me.

He holds me for long after, keeping us joined until our breathing eases. His breath is warm in my ear.

"Fuck, I missed you."

A small laugh bubbles from my chest. Reluctantly, he lowers my legs to the floor.

They're so wobbly, I give up trying to pull my pants on, and collapse on my bed.

Logan zips up his fly and turns to the dead Zane on the floor.

Holy shit. I completely forgot he was here.

Logan follows my gaze and frowns.

He picks up a folded blanket from my storage trunk. "You good with blood on this?"

It's so threadbare it's almost see-through, and I was going to cut it into rags anyway. I nod, and he tosses it over the body.

"So, what now?" My voice is still hoarse from getting busy against the wall with a dead CSU agent ten feet away.

I was wrong. I really am broken. This should bother me,

but it didn't. Months of seeing people die either from the TZ's air, banshee attacks during Reco, or coming back with mortal wounds from raids have left me desensitized.

"I'll take care of him," Logan says. "Then we have to be patient."

I scoff. "Well, that should be easy 'cause I seem to recall that's one of your greatest strengths."

His gray eyes darken to the color of storm clouds. "I can when I have to be."

I grab my discarded shirt from the ground and pull it over my head. "Okay, so we're patient for what?"

His forehead furrows. "It's better if I don't tell you. All you need to know is there will be a signal, a distraction, and that's when we make a break for it."

How is this possible? No way Logan figured this all out on his own? Logan is good at many, *many* things, but coordinating with other people is not one of them. Sure, he can manage a small team of security at Meridian, but infiltrating a rebel base *and* getting us both out alive? I can't believe it.

I nod. "All right. Can you at least give me a clue when?"

"A few days, a week at most. But I need you to hold out a little longer. Keep playing nice with your sister and Navigator Dicknozzle, okay?"

I swallow and give him another nod, even as I wilt inside. The euphoric high from our rough, frenzied love-making is waning. It feels like the cloud we'd been floating on has evaporated, and I've landed sharply on hard ground again.

I was swept up in the fantasy of him scooping me up in his arms and whisking me away from here. But that was a fantasy, and this is the reality.

He leans forward and presses a kiss to my forehead. A surprisingly sweet gesture that takes me by surprise.

"Just a little longer? I promise." His steel eyes lock with mine.

He lifts the blanket-wrapped dead body of Zane over his shoulder and then is gone.

My breathing becomes rapid and shallow as I stare at the bloodstain on the concrete, now smeared by our shoes.

I taste vomit at the pool of blood on the floor. Panic cinches my throat shut, and I worry I'm going to hyperventilate. I gag down the disgust and take a towel from the shelf near the sink. I soak it in water, wash my face, then climb on my hands and knees to scrub the floor clean.

The coldness in my gut intensifies until the welcome numbness permeates every cell in my body.

My shield. My protection.

It's how I survived, I can do it a little longer.

Thirty-Two

CARTER

"I sure hope Logan is having a better time than us," The shuttle's wheels touch down at the base in Leviler.

"I doubt that," Heath says.

We don't discuss it, but we're both thinking the same thing. There's a good chance Logan is dead. Either killed by other convicts or the guard we paid off to give him another oxygen tank, went back on his word, or had their shift switched.

Left to the imagination, I think of a thousand ways Logan's hair-brained plan could've gone off the rails.

My hands twitch and jerk, and I curse when I can't lace my left boot. Heath notices my struggle and kneels to tie them.

I choke down the irritation that it came to this. "I feel like a goddamn baby."

Heath laughs. "Yeah, well, maybe you'll think about this next time you think going cold turkey before a mission is a good idea."

There's no point in arguing. He was right. Still didn't mean I regret it.

I needed to drop the O-strike, but I had to convince myself that the time was right.

When ITM quit attacking. When Logan reappeared with Brigid. When the brimming eased.

But it's been a week, and it is clear there will never be a perfect time.

So, I chose today.

My eyes start at the horizon, glowing faintly with the promise of dawn, but the world here remains dim, muffled like it's trying to smother itself in the mist. Ember's unease, a low, mournful vibration, seeps into my chest, mingling with the groans of the wounded men lying out in uneven rows on tarps.

Blood and exhaust fumes from the military vehicles saturate the air.

Across the road, a rider from a station I don't recognize limps toward us. His face is streaked in blood as he sloughs off his saddle.

His stallion is dragging his left leg, and he stumbles, its massive body shuddering as he guides it to its knees. Blood mats its haunches, staining the pale gray hide a sickly brown. The rider moves with mechanical detachment, even as the shine of tears reflects from the security lights. His stallion lies on his side. The rider looms over him, his hands firm but shaking as he takes the pistol from his belt and fires a single shot.

It doesn't fight. Doesn't whimper. It just...stops.

The breath I didn't realize I held escapes.

Nine men lost. Four stallions along with them. I heard the numbers, but seeing the blood of druadans and riders pooling in the cracks of the pavement under my feet drives the truth home. This isn't just another raid gone wrong. It was a slaughter.

My head digs into my pocket, seeking out the packet of papers.

Fuck, I think as I remember I flushed the last of the packets down the drain.

I can't face this raw. Not tonight. Not with the hum of the druadans who lost riders drilling into my skull and the injured three feet away choking on their last breaths.

But I have no choice.

I press my hands into the backs of my eyes. Ember's concern warms my chest, and the pressure eases enough to breathe, enough to stand upright without the world tilting.

"Captain James!" A woman's voice disrupts my thoughts.

My mother strides across the dock, her boots splashing in the shallow puddles of blood and muck. Even here, with the air thick and rancid, she looks composed, her uniform crisp, her hair pulled back in a severe knot. Ember's hum falters as she approaches. The stallion senses the iron resolve she carries like a shield.

Her eyes lock with mine. "Good to see you made it. We've got a tip. A scout spotted a group of mystyl and rebels headed east. It's time to move."

Her words shroud me like a lead blanket.

No time to mourn. No time to process.

We fought mystyl earlier, but then they left. It was strange, like they had somewhere else to be. They don't attack like they used to. Instead, they're either idle, or we chase them down.

When other riders or I bring it up at meetings, we're met

with confused looks and shrugs. No one knows why, and they don't care since it's a good thing. Why question a good thing?

We pack up camp, shoving tents into bags and getting ready to head back. My muscles ache like hell from riding all day, but at least we don't have to fight much. Heath's over with his mount—that big chestnut beast that follows him around like a puppy—fiddling with the straps and talking to it in that low voice he uses when he thinks no one can hear.

That's when Lieutenant Owens shows up looking like he's aged years instead of months. He's a squad leader for one of the escort teams and liaison with the higher up officers. His face is all pinched, stubble darker than usual against his pale skin, and the look in his eyes makes the unease already nestled in my chest curl tighter.

"Where's General James?" I ask. "I spoke to her this morning, and she said she would be here."

"Parnia," he says, clutching the rifle to his chest. "Some emergency meeting about those riots at the filtration plants."

Everyone gets quiet. The riots have worsened, transforming from picket lines to violence and looting. When clean water and food become scarce, people get desperate.

"Got new orders," Owens says, nodding to a soldier next to him. "Get everyone who can still hold a weapon. We're moving out."

The soldier sloughs a bag of ammo and supplies onto the ground.

"Where to?" Heath asks, reaching into the bag to swap his spent cartridges for fresh ones.

"North Cascades neighborhood." Owens pulls out a plastic map and throws it up on the hood of a nearby truck. We've taken to avoiding using Network, as there is evidence that ITM is hacking it. Therefore, we're now using short-range radios and physical maps.

The western part of Delford is all residential houses and apartments, and it doesn't take a genius to know whatever he's going to say is bad fucking news. "They found bombs in the sewers by the levee."

The blood drains from my face. "They're going to flood the city."

Owens nods, a crease forming between his thick brows. "We need to get people out. We have no idea when those things will blow."

Heath's face goes chalk-white. "We need to get everyone out of there."

The words hang in the air between us. Delford's packed with people—workers, families, kids. There's no way we can evacuate in time.

"We've already got analysts trying to predict the fallout," Owens says. For a second, I see actual fear in his eyes. "Best guess, those bombs go off. The streets will flood in four hours."

Heath already has his pack on, his face set in that way that means he's locked in. "How many can we get out in four hours?"

"Not enough," Owens admits. "But we gotta try."

As we scramble to get moving, I call in the other riders who haven't come in yet and can't help wondering if this is why the mystyl are acting weird. What if they somehow knew this was coming and decided to get the hell out? Like how dogs sense earthquakes or seabirds come to shore before hurricanes.

"Move!" Owens shouts, and I swing up on Ember. My mind races with the thought of how impossible this all seems.

They're going to break the levee. They're going to flood Delford.

They're going to finish what the ocean started years ago.

Thousands will die.

Thirty-Three

BRIGID

Logan left shortly after to dispose of Zane's body.

After a night filled with lust-filled dreams of his hands and mouth caressing my body, I did exactly as he asked the next day, continuing my usual routine of eating breakfast in my room to avoid the stares and whispers in the cafeteria.

I then make my way to the less crowded area of the base to assist with organizing the storeroom.

I'm reloading supply bags for the next raid when I overhear someone mention Zane's name.

"When I checked his bunk," an older black man named Ace tells his girlfriend Emma, "it was empty, and I didn't find his comm either."

"Zane didn't seem the type to abandon the ITM," Emma says. "But after we lost our asses at the south port, I wouldn't be surprised if he got cold feet and decided to run."

Ace murmurs in agreement. "The High Navigator won't be happy when he finds out."

"Well, you won't find me telling him," Emma said, setting a spare flashlight into the bag. "I never trusted Zane. He always gave me the creeps."

"You're lucky you didn't share a room with him," Ace says, chuckling. "I'd felt safer with a banshee in the bunk next to me than with him. Some nights, I worried if I'd wake up with missing fingers."

"Well, " Emma says. "Then it's agreed. I won't say anything if you don't."

"I call dibs on that leather jacket of his." Avec hands her a wrapped package of dried granola. "I've always wanted it and saw it hanging on his chair."

Sounds like I'm not the only one who won't miss him. I don't feel guilty about Logan killing him. Not even a little.

Heat gathers between my thighs, just thinking about what happened after.

Tides that had been intense. Wildly dirty, utterly incredible, and probably something I should unpack with a therapist.

If it wasn't the end of the world, that is.

They probably have their hands full.

Zane was a horrible person, and who knows what he would've done if Logan hadn't been there. I shiver at how his hand felt on my cheek and the cold of the scissors as he laid them against my neck.

The moment he set foot in my room, I knew only one of us would walk out.

I pack two charged power cells in the side pocket of the duffel bag.

Good fucking riddance. If it makes me a bad person to be happy that someone was dead, then so be it. I'm long past caring about my soul.

Ace and Emma walk in my direction, and I busy myself with the roll of tape used to cover the reflective metal buckles on the backpacks. Since we lack the budget compared to Circuit's army, we make up for it with the ITM's favorite term: resourcefulness, which is a fancy word for reusing or repairing gear typically tossed in the trash.

Once I hear the door close behind me, I breathe a little easier.

Throughout the rest of the day, I didn't hear his name mentioned again.

Whatever Logan did with his body worked.

Two days passed without a sign or word from Logan, and I'm pacing my room with nothing to do.

We ran out of fuel for the generators, so my room is lit with only a single battery-powered lantern. The brownouts not only affect the lights, but also mean nothing can be done in the lab. While I normally would be grateful for the free time to avoid Elton, the pent-up anxiety from Logan's lack of communication is driving me mad.

Logan is assigned to patrol the South corridors, and so I begrudgingly force myself to avoid that section of the base.

While I trust myself to walk past him without giving him away, it doesn't mean I trust *him* to keep his mouth shut should any of my fan club show up and corner me.

It's not like I get the feeling I am in danger from them. They are intense, sure, but Logan's protective act-first-think-second nature is a real risk.

He was volatile before; I can only imagine what it's like now he doesn't share a bond with Galaxian.

Volatile enough to kill someone and then fuck you next to the dead body.

Okay, so maybe I can.

Once I grow weary of pacing, I move on to organize the few belongings I have in my room. Despite the situation, I tried to make this room cozy, and in the months I've been here, I find that between the gifts worth keeping and items I pick up on scavenge runs, I've carved out a little space in this nightmarish place for my own.

And soon I'll be leaving.

I grab an armload of laundry and head for the linen room.

The laundry room smells faintly of detergent and damp fabric. The hum of the washing machine provides an almost soothing rhythm as I watch the clothes tumble inside.

The rebel base has gone quiet, save for faint laughter from the pub down the old food court and muffled cheers from the gallery where tonight's film plays.

Closing my eyes, I imagine myself back in my shared apartment in Delford, listening to Laura and Vince argue about which restaurant to order takeout from.

I rarely allow myself to think about them. The pain is too much.

The loss of my life before.

But now, with the chance I may soon be free, I let my guard down, indulging in the fragments of memories I have.

All of it is a fantasy, though. Even if Logan manages a rescue plan, I will be a fugitive. I convinced them to take me on the raid, and those soldiers saw my face.

What if that had been her plan all along? Why she was so easily convinced to let me tag along? Sharice is wickedly smart like that. Letting me fight alongside ITM is her insurance policy to keep me here.

ITM has too much blood on its hands now for Circuit to

negotiate. I'll be shot on sight if I try to return to Delford or Blackhawk.

Which means as soon as I get free, I'll need to run again.

If there is anywhere safe to run. I have no idea what the country looks like outside.

Off continent is obviously the best option, but with hundreds of thousands of people and limited boats, most people will die before they can evacuate.

Canna Canna is the nearest country and takes days to cross by boat, and the ocean's currents are some of the deadliest. They're wearing of outsiders, and many captains refuse to take you unless they are compensated enough. The others, like New Columbia, are even farther, taking weeks by boat on rough seas. Shuttles are designed for low altitudes and are incapable of traversing vast ocean distances.

The people of Venovia are thoroughly screwed.

And from the latest I heard, Circuit is struggling. Military forces are spread thin, partly because of our hit-and-run attacks drawing their attention from their own people rioting in the streets over layoffs, food, or fuel rationing.

People are getting sick from the poisoned air spreading, yet don't know why, which makes them scared, and scared people lead to panic and protests.

I feel sorry for their PR people right now.

Footsteps echo down the hall, and someone shouts. I stand, breath held as I strain to listen.

A security officer's clipped voice breaks through the static.

"Attention: A Circuit police shuttle has been spotted one mile to the north. Get somewhere safe. We're going dark."

The hum of the washing machine stops abruptly, and the overhead lights flicker then wink out soon after, leaving me in an eerie silence.

Darkness swallows the room, and my reflection in the

washing machine's glass vanishes. My racing pulse pounds in my ears.

Is this it? The sign from Logan I'm supposed to be waiting for?

Doubt twists in my chest. We've had these lockdowns before, so it's not *that* unusual.

But those are all before I knew Logan was here, secretly working to get me out.

Not willing to risk it, I make a break for my room. No one will question me since it's what we're supposed to do during one of these drills.

If he looks for me, he'll look there first.

In the distance, sounds of boots pound against the tile and shouts echo off the walls. I reach my door and slip inside.

A hand clamps firmly over my mouth. In the darkness, only a sliver of red emergency light creeps under the door, casting just enough glow to reveal the face inches from mine.

Logan.

Outside, I hear murmured conversation, and someone calls out my name. "The High Navigator was looking for her."

"Someone said they saw her in the lab."

The footsteps recede, and Logan lowers his hand.

"You ready?"

I suck in a steadying breath and nod.

Without waiting for him to tell me, I drop to my knees beside the bed, my fingers searching the dark for the canvas bag I packed days ago.

The distant thrum of a shuttle's engines grows louder, vibrating through the walls. Logan pulls me to my feet just as another scream tears through the air, this one closer.

Shouts follow, frantic and overlapping. "They landed outside the airlock! They're on the upper levels now!"

Logan's grip on my wrist tightens as he leads me through the maze of hallways cast in the eerie red glow.

Bodies slam against us as people rush past, their faces contorted with terror under the crimson emergency lights. My stomach lurches as someone's elbow catches me in the ribs. Another shove from behind, and suddenly, Logan's hand is ripped from mine. The loss of contact sends a jolt of panic through my chest, constricting my lungs.

Logan calls out, but his voice barely carries over the stampede. His face appears and disappears between moving bodies. Then he's gone, swallowed by the tide of panicking people.

My heart hammers against my ribcage.

I press myself against the wall, letting the surge of people flow past. My palms are slick with sweat as I tug my bag over my shoulder. I spot a side corridor and slip into it.

I keep my head down, hands tucked close to my sides, trying not to draw attention. I wear a hooded sweatshirt and tug it up over my head and hair. I watch the flow of people, trying to find an opening to dart through and find Logan, but it's pure and utter chaos. People shoving, shouting, yelling, and screaming.

My muscles coil tight, waiting for someone to grab me, to demand where I think I'm going.

"Brigid?"

My head snaps in the direction of the voice. Sharice leans against the wall, and a gash above her right eyebrow weeps blood. Her lab coat is torn at the shoulder, and her brown eyes are steeped with worry.

"The mystyl," she mutters, slurring her words. The wound may be worse than it looks. "They cut the," she pauses, panting. "They cut the secondary power and broke the seals. There's nothing we can do. Elton has a shuttle waiting for us."

My stomach twists. "What about all the people?"

"We have a tunnel." Her eyes plead with me. "Underground in the service floor."

I hesitate, torn. It would be so easy to go with her. In the months, I grew closer to her than I ever had before. I always looked up to her and idolized her charisma and brilliance, and before, she never let me forget who mom's favorite was, but at some point, since being here, that changed.

She stopped looking at me like I was inferior and started seeing me as her equal.

But Logan is waiting. He risked his life coming here.

Even though I destroyed his bond.

Before I can decide, however, a baby's high-pitched wail rises above the din. Screams of panic follow, sending goosebumps down my arms.

I can't leave without helping. It's not even a choice.

I spin on my heel, swallow the bitter tang of guilt of betraying Logan, and race with Sharice to help the others. We direct them to hatches in the ground that lead to the service floor, a level I've known about but never entered. The smell of smoke fills my nostrils, acrid and burning. Flames lick up the sides of the walls.

Someone set fire to the base, either by accident or Circuit's soldiers to flush us out.

"Go Go Go!" I shout as mothers and children step down, then others, and I recognize many faces. Many I consider friends.

Soon, Sharice and I stand above the stairwell. We stare at each other, challenging the other to go in first. Before we can decide, however, there's a crack of a laser gun from the far end of the room.

Sharice's eyes widen in shock before she stumbles forward, falling down the short flight of stairs into the service hallway.

A man catches her, and she stares at me, her hand reaching up.

I avert my gaze and slam the service door shut.

A second later, it locks from the other side, and I stand, bracing myself as dozens of Circuit soldiers surge down the hallway.

This is it. This is what I deserve. I close my eyes as they shout for me to put my hands up, and someone grabs me by the waist, propelling me backward. Lifted off my feet, the air whooshes out of me as I'm slung over a man's shoulder.

"God dammit, Blondie," Logan growls from under the helmet, running with me as the soldiers shout for us to stop. The dark hallways blur, and then I hear the hiss of an airlock. He sets me down and places a mask over my face. I barely have a chance to secure it before I'm outside in the evening air.

The cold wind hits us as we dart through a service exit.

A battered shuttle awaits; its spinning propellers look like they're held together with tape and glue.

The engines glow red, and the windshield is coated in dirt and cracked.

A man waves from inside the cockpit, his silhouette hard to discern.

"Get in!" Logan shouts.

I freeze, glancing back toward the base.

Logan's jaw tightens and his hand reaches out, yanking me up the ramp as the propellers whirl, already taking us airborne. The engines roar louder, and Logan pulls it open, slamming the door shut.

My fists clench around the canvas bag in my lap, and through the small window, I stare at the sea of pitch black speckled with blue and yellow flashing lights from Circuit's shuttles.

I swallow down the emotions of what I've left behind. The violence is unfolding while I'm whisked away to safety.

I'm confused about whom to worry most about. The people at the base are fleeing in tunnels, or the soldiers that are now unknowingly in a building with loose mystyl.

The last count reported that the tanks numbered in the thousands.

Still, I've bled and sweated and eaten alongside those people for months. Many I considered friends.

From the shuttle window, I watch the mall tear itself apart. An orange plume punches through the skylight, rolling up into the clouds, and there's a series of explosions, ripping through the roof of stone and tarps, concrete walls collapsing, glass exploding outward like shrapnel.

I grip the seat in front of me, nails digging in as I watch my home for the past three months implode.

The shuttle climbs, tilts east, and the ruins of the mall disappear from my sight.

Logan's eyes are on my face from where he sits beside me.

I stare at my hands on my lap. "This is..." I hesitate, unable to keep my voice from cracking. "This is because of me. They're all dead, hurt, fleeing because of me."

"Look at me," he says, as I meet his shadowed gaze. "The call to Circuit had to happen. None of this is your fault." His words do little to lift the guilt, but still, I listen. "I would tear down worlds to keep you safe," he continues. "Not because I give a shit about this country or the war, but because a life without you isn't one, I'm willing to live anymore. For months I existed without you, and now you're here, I will never let you go." His hand cups my chin, his thumb painting small circles on my cheek. "They all chose to be there," he says, voice dropping to a whisper. "Just like if I'm ever faced with a choice between you and anyone else, I'll pick you every time."

Thirty-Four

JESS

The greeter waves me through, and I step into the Elmwood dormitory's main foyer. The air smells faintly of old wood polish and musty furniture, triggering a strange unease, like I don't quite belong.

Even though it's been over a decade since I was a student here, the faint hum of male voices and distant laughter from upstairs makes me feel out of place. I shove the feeling aside. I'm no longer a student, and even when I was, I was at the top of my class.

At Thornwick Academy, students are housed in separate dormitories—boys in one, girls in another. My brother is in Elmwood, while I stayed in Hollyhock.

But just because I never stayed there didn't mean I hadn't ever *been* there.

Thornwick prides itself on being home to academically

advantaged students, but the truth is, you don't have to be particularly smart to get in.

Just have a parent or sponsor with deep enough pockets, and the crimson blazer and white shorts are yours.

When I reach Elmwood, I stop at the greeter's desk on the first floor. The man behind it is older, dressed in a corduroy jacket with an Elmwood badge. A few other family members stand nearby, waiting for holiday pickup.

"Hi, I'm Jess Drakeford," I say. "I'm here to pick up my brother, Jace."

The man scans the tablet in front of him.

"I was under the impression Jace's parents would be here to pick him up."

"Yeah, something came up with the business, so they sent me instead. All the guardianship transfer documents should already be on file."

"Just a moment."

As he scans the tablet again, someone steps up behind me. The weight of their gaze settles on me, pressing, expectant. I tilt my head, catching a glimpse of whoever it is that clearly doesn't understand personal space barriers.

We move through the corridors of Thornwick's Elmwood Dormitory. Though all the dorms are well-maintained, Elmwood holds a particular charm, untouched by modernization. Thornwick has always been a school, and the wooden floors, dark with age and creaking underfoot, are polished smooth by generations of students. The walls bear intricate paintings and relics from before the floods.

History clings to every surface. Heavy bookshelves line the hallways, filled with aging tomes that DU history majors frequently borrow, photographing the brittle wallpaper or analyzing the ancient architecture from a time before the ocean covered ninety percent of the planet.

It smells just as I remember, of polished cedar, a blend of wood oil, and the musky aroma of teenage boys.

Three hundred students reside here.

Half as many as when I was here. But birth rates were higher then. Unconsciously, my hand goes to my stomach. I'd be showing by now.

I shove the painful thought down. The last time I walked here, things felt so simple. Everything had felt endless when the future was something to look forward to rather than endure.

The door to Jace's room stands open. Inside, four beds mark the space he shares with his dormmates, though it is neat, each corner and desk arranged with a kind of lived-in order.

He is sprawled on his bed, scrolling through his tablet, headphones in his ears. The soft glow of the screen lights his face. At my presence, he sits up straighter, pulling the headphones out.

"You ready?" I ask.

"Where's Heath?" Jace frowns.

Demanding Heath without so much as a greeting doesn't surprise me. I know he secretly wishes he'd been born first, given the chance to become a rider himself. Instead, he's spent years idolizing Heath.

"He's not here." I lick my lips. "We're not together anymore."

"No shit?"

"Language!"

"What did Mom say?"

"She's fine with it."

"Liar."

I sigh. "Are you ready to go?"

Jace hops off the bed and stuffs his headphones in his

pocket. He pulls his suitcase from under his bed and begins taking shirts from the closet, along with hangers, and sets them inside.

"Well, if it isn't the legend herself," a man says behind me.

I spin and see the reason I knew my way around Elmwood, standing in the hallway. Stephen Mulheim.

Memories I thought were buried rise to the surface like foam on a coffee, as I recall our many times after a tennis match, making out in the recovery room.

Excluding the same preppy polish he always had. A yellow sweater is draped over his shoulders, the sleeves tied neatly in front, and paired with striped chino pants along with genuine leather boat shoes. His pale blond hair, combed carefully to the side, is thinning on top, though he's making an effort to hide it. A neatly trimmed goatee frames his mouth, and his eyes are set just a little too close together.

When I was younger, I thought he'd been the cutest boy at school, and while he's handsome in a generic, sweater-model way, that's the extent of it. Generic. Bland. Pleasing enough at a glance but utterly forgettable beyond that.

And until five seconds ago, I honestly had forgotten about him.

He grins, revealing perfect white teeth. "How have you been, Jessie?"

Jessie. Tides, it's been years since anyone called me that. "Very well, thank you. And you?"

He shrugs. "Been better. Lissa moved out."

Stephen is the third youngest in his family, so he didn't attend Vanguard like many of the boys my age. Instead, he went to Parnia Tech and became an electrical engineer. Since we moved in similar circles, I heard that he remarried after his first marriage ended due to an affair.

"I'm so sorry to hear that," I say.

"Thanks. After Kylie was born, she took all our attention. Between my job and her traveling with Dragonfly City, it kind of just happened."

Lissa had gone into business management but also minored in music theory, so it's no surprise she's the current manager of the rock band Dragonfly City. Heath had asked for my help in acquiring backstage passes for Carter's twenty-first birthday, as he knew Lissa and I had been roommates at DU.

I know she was more than happy to give me the set of tickets, and I also know she was more than happy to sit on the lead singer's lap while we caught up in the dressing room.

"Sorry if this is too forward," Stephen says, "but I heard you and Lockwood called it quits, too. Looks like we've both struck out in the relationship department lately, eh?"

I glance at Jace, who is taking an infuriatingly long amount of time rolling his comm charger into a ball.

"Yeah, just didn't work out either," I say, smiling politely. "You know how it is with riders."

"It can't be easy, that's for sure."

"Becca is finishing her lab project, so she won't be ready for me to take her until this afternoon. I was thinking of grabbing lunch at the commons if you two want to join?"

I start to tell him no when Jace interjects, suddenly appearing by my side with both bags packed. "Lunch would be awesome."

"Excellent," Stephen says. "You ready now?"

Jace nods and moves past me.

The great dining hall stretches before us. Its vaulted ceilings and towering windows let in the last of the afternoon light. The long oak tables are half-filled with staff, parents collecting their children, and students lingering over their meals. The air is thick with the scent of freshly baked rolls, ripe fruit, and smoked meats, mingling with the warmth of the hearths burning in the far corners. In the back, several chefs in crisp white coats move with practiced efficiency, their presence a clear sign that Thornwick is putting on a show with an over-the-top feast for visiting families.

We take seats at one of the long tables, the padded chairs a reminder that, for all its old-world charm, Thornwick spares no expense when appearances are on the line. Two attendants arrive swiftly, ready to take our orders.

Stephen leans forward, affecting an easy charm. "Do you serve wine?"

The young attendant blushes as he reaches for her hand, brushing his fingers over her skin in a way that makes my stomach turn. She glances around before murmuring, "I'll see what I can do."

Stephen looks at me, waiting for a reaction, clearly expecting to impress me. I quickly avert my gaze, unwilling to encourage whatever game he's playing. I cringe inwardly, fully aware of how hard he's trying. I despise men who think making a girl jealous is the way to their heart.

These past months, being single for the first time in my life, gave me time to reflect on what I truly want in a partner. And while I still don't have all the answers, I know one thing for certain: I want a man who loves me unconditionally.

Heath had always been half in, half out. I never want to feel that way again.

The attendant returns with a steaming bowl of squash bisque, freshly steamed scallops, and asparagus grown on-site; the scent of butter and herbs curls into the air.

"So, tell me, how goes? I see Drakeford Property signs all over downtown Delford."

I dip my spoon into the soup. "Good. Surprisingly little impact from the current climate."

"It's a hell of a mess, I'll tell you that." Stephen pauses, running a finger over the rim of the water glass. "Makes me wish I could just escape to my parents' private island off the Amber Coast. You know it's warm enough there to grow pineapples?"

Jace, mid-bite, perks up. "Pineapples? That's Jess's favorite fruit."

Stephen's gaze slides to me, a smirk curling at the corner of his mouth. "Is that so?" He leans in slightly as if this is some grand revelation. "Perhaps you should join me sometime."

"Yeah, Jess," Jace grins, all teeth, eyes glinting with mischief. "Why don't you join him?"

I shoot him a warning look over my spoon, and he grins wider.

But before I formulate some excuse, the hall stirs with commotion. Headmaster Davidson enters, wearing his crimson robe and red cords draped around his neck, in his wheelchair. He's older than I remember, mid-sixties, with a full white beard and bushy matching eyebrows. He's with a group of staff members, but a black riding jacket stands out among the sea of Thornwick's teachers' red uniforms.

I know that jacket.

Marshal's face is passive as his eyes scan the room. For a hairsbreadth of a second, our eyes meet, and the room ceases to exist. The low murmur of voices, the clatter of silverware against fine china, the scent of warm bread and smoked meats, all fade away until there is only him.

The moment stretches, condensing to only us.

Rain-tousled dark blonde hair clings to his head, a single curl slipping down over his forehead as stubble shadows the hard line of his jaw. And his eyes, sky blue and startlingly bright, draw me in with an intensity that steals the breath from my lungs.

Him.

I tear my eyes away, hoping, *praying*, he won't notice me, but it's too late.

He already has.

I toss my napkin on the table. "Will you excuse me? I need to go to the restroom."

Stephen rises from his chair. "Are you all right? Should I go?"

I wave him off. "No. I'm fine." I plaster on a fake smile. "I'll be right back."

I glance at Jace, who's too busy stuffing his face to notice me leaving, then flee to the bathrooms in the opposite direction.

Okay, I'm not exactly *fleeing*; I'm merely avoiding a conversation I am *not* ready to have.

And it isn't like I can sneak into a stall, prop open one of the windows, and climb out. I know, for a fact, the windows are too high.

No, I only need a moment to collect myself, touch up my makeup, and see if the shuttle pilot can come earlier than the planned 2 p.m.

One short call later, I learn he can't. Even with the offer to double his rate. Something about fueling stations being backed up and the Circuit air patrol's technical difficulties with their radios.

Grumbling, I tap the comm closed. I smooth my hair, examining the two braids encircling the top of my head for any flyaways.

Last year, I started growing it out for the wedding, intending to cut it afterward, but decided to enjoy the length even after the engagement ended.

Mother had not taken it well.

I count myself blessed every day I didn't tell her about the possibility of a baby.

I dab on some lip stain and tuck it back into my purse.

As I step out, the door swings open, and a man crowds into me.

"Excuse me," I say, keeping my eyes averted as I pivot to pass by.

The black velvet sleeve of his coat, gold embroidery circling his wrist, stops my hurried passage. I look up at the last face I expected to see today.

"Marshal?" Surprise sends my voice an octave higher. "I—uh—it's good to see you."

Marshal doesn't move; his big form blocks my escape. "You really thought you could avoid me all day, did you?"

"Avoid?" I scoff. "No. You're obviously busy, and I'm not staying long. I'm just here to get my brother for the holiday break."

His eyes drift slowly down my face—my nose, my lips—before returning to my eyes. "You look good, Jess."

A startled croak escapes me at the heat in his words. God. I thought enough time had passed that I'd gotten him out of my system. After Heath and I broke up, I feared he was the knee-jerk rebound. Right guy, wrong time. I needed space. Time to find myself and discover my new life without Heath attached to it. And when weeks turned into months without a call from him, I assumed he had moved on.

"I should've guessed you had family here."

I nod. "My brother, Jace. He goes here."

He angles his head. "And who's the other guy you're with?"

"He's..."

As if summoned, Stephen appears in the alcove. *Seriously, did everyone need to pee all of a sudden?*

Stephen's eyes drift to Marshal, who stands what anyone with half a brain will consider intimately close. "Jessie," he says, turning to me. "Jace needed to grab his soccer gear from the locker room, so I came looking for you. Do you want to stroll the atrium while we wait?"

"Oh, hello," Stephen says, his tone polite but wary. "You're the rider from Blackhawk?"

"I am," Marshal replies. "Marshal Clemmons." Neither hold out a hand to shake.

Stephen waggles a finger between us. "Do you two know each other?"

"Yes."

"No." We answer at the same time.

"It's complicated," I add.

Stephen raises a skeptical eyebrow. "Jace took off to get his soccer gear at the gym, but I thought we could stay here and catch up?"

My eyes dart from Marshal to Stephen. Indecision weighs on me more than I like. If it were my choice, I'd already be on the shuttle with Jace, but my little gremlin of a brother clearly has plans of his own.

"Actually, I——." My voice falters.

"Sounds good to me," Marshal says, clapping his hands together. "I'll join you. I haven't eaten yet, and I am starving."

Stephen's face falls. "Are you sure you don't have to, you know, mingle with the other families?"

Marshal waves a hand. "Nah, I've been answering questions about Vanguard all morning. I could use a change of conversation."

Stephen looks like he's going to argue more, but retreats a step, letting Marshal and me pass.

Jace's suitcase is still next to the table, though his backpack is missing. Grab his soccer gear, my ass. He probably snuck off to hang out with his friends or see a girl.

At the table, Marshal makes a point of sitting on my left while Stephen resumes his place on my right.

I slice off a piece of mini-quiche and take a bite. The tangy goat cheese, smoked chicken breast, sun-dried tomato, and spinach are divine. Thornwick's tuition is steep, but I never remember the food being anything less than excellent.

Marshal orders soup and crusty bread while Stephen snacks on dried potato crisps and sips iced tea.

I contemplate ordering a mimosa, but with two guys deciding to remain in my company, I think better of it. I need a clear head to navigate this minefield.

They avoid looking at each other, choosing to watch me instead.

I lose my appetite halfway through my meal, wipe my face with a napkin, and take a sip of water.

"So, Stephen," Marshal starts, emphasizing his name like it's difficult to say, "why are you here?"

From an outsider's perspective, it's an innocent question, but I don't miss the subtle threat lurking beneath his words.

Stephen clears his throat and glances at me before answering.

"My sister, Becca. She's going to stay with me for the holidays." He pauses, looking at me. "I live a block from the zoo and pulled some strings to get her a volunteer position to help feed the newborn baby tigers."

I read on the Network a month ago that the mother tiger had died shortly after giving birth due to a fungal disease caused by the unusual fall humidity in Parnia.

"Becca adores animals, and it's a surprise I know she'll love. Plus, it'll give her time to get to know her niece, my daughter, Layla." He taps his comm, and before I can protest, he's showing me photos of him and a curly-haired toddler grinning with a gap-toothed grin. "She'll be two in March."

I force a smile as he swipes through more photos. Each one is adorable, and it's clear he's a devoted father. The sour tang of jealousy rises in my throat, and I grab my glass, trying to wash it down.

"You know, Jess is a big animal lover, too," Marshal says casually.

"Really?" Stephen sounds genuinely surprised.

"Sure, that's how we met, actually. She used to walk my dog for me."

Shock replaces Stephen's disbelief. He tilts his head, looking at me. "You...were a dog walker? Funny, you never seemed interested in them at all in school."

Because I wasn't. Aren't. *Dammit.* I stare at the glass in my hand as if it's the most interesting thing, and I'm not secretly dying from the conversation, dredging up memories of Blackhawk. The greenhouse. Trapped in the cable car. His face when I told him I was leaving. "It was a unique arrangement and a long story we certainly don't have time for."

"I'd love to hear it," Stephen presses.

I shoot a don't-you-dare-look at Marshal. If he told Stephen I walked his dog so I could bend the rules and stay at Blackhawk with Heath, it would only lead to more questions—questions I'm not in the mood to answer.

Marshal ignores me. "It was only a few weeks last October, but Finn fell in love with her." He turns to me; a sly smile plays on his lips. "We all did."

I want to stand and run from the room *again,* but I am frozen in place.

My mind stutters over the thought, replaying his words in slow, broken fragments. He can't mean it. Not like *that.*

Before I can piece together a response, the overhead lights

in the dining hall flicker. The chandelier's glow dims, sputtering like a candle in a breeze. A soft murmur rolls through the dining hall, the scrape of forks on plates faltering. I tear my gaze from Marshal to look up at the flickering fixtures, their sharp flashes casting fractured shadows across the room.

"Generators again," someone mutters nearby.

"Typical," another parent grumbles, shaking his head. "This place charges a fortune, and they can't keep the lights on."

The room buzzes with halfhearted complaints and uneasy laughter. A few people glance toward the commons' exits as though expecting a fire drill. It wouldn't be the first time Thornwick's ancient systems failed. I force a breath, steadying myself. Just the generators. That's all.

But even as I think it, I can't shake the tight knot forming in my chest.

Across the hall, staff members whisper to each other, concern sharpening their faces. Headmaster Davidson is nowhere to be seen. Of course, he isn't. He's probably in his office taking one of his post-lunch naps that involves a bottle of scotch and the rerun of last night's soccer tournament.

Marshal seems unbothered, leaning back in his chair as though nothing strange is happening at all. I, on the other hand, can't sit still. My fingers drum against the tabletop, restless energy spilling out of me.

The intercom crackles to life. Everyone's heads snap up, and the murmuring falls to a hush.

"*Students, staff, and visiting family,*" a clipped and strained voice drones, "*we have been notified by the Thornwick Security and Circuit National Guard that mystyl have been spotted a mile north near the Agene River.*"

The words hit me like a physical blow. Mystyl. My heart stutters.

"We take all threats to our students and staff very seriously and are thereby issuing a temporary lockdown until further notice."

Lockdown? My legs move before my brain catches up. I shove my chair back, the metal feet screeching against the floor. All around me, the room erupts. Voices rise in protest, parents demanding answers, students turning to each other in confusion. The flickering lights throw the room into bursts of brightness and shadow, stoking the chaos.

Jace.

I toss my napkin on the table and rise from my chair.

Marshal's voice cuts through the noise. "Jess, where are you going?"

"To the gym. I need to find Jace." My feet carry me forward, weaving through the sea of restless bodies. The voices around me blur—sharp edges of panic, angry questions hurl at an unseen authority. The word *lockdown* repeats like a drumbeat in my ears, steady and unrelenting. A handful of students sit frozen at their tables, wide-eyed and silent as if the air itself grew too heavy to breathe.

"It's probably nothing," someone says near the back.

"It's not *nothing* if they're locking us down," another snaps.

I push past them. Mystyl sightings this close aren't normal. Thornwick's walls are thick, its security tight, but not unbreakable.

As I reach the commons' edge, a group of parents crowd the entrance, arguing with a staff member blocking the doors.

I imagine Jace sitting with his friends at the gym, oblivious to all of this.

A low hum shudders through the building. It's not the generators this time, but something deeper vibrating through the floors.

My gaze snaps to the windows lining the far wall. Beyond the glass, the grounds are empty, but darkness gathers at the tree line. A mile north. That's what they said. Too close. Way too close.

The intercom crackles again, repeating the lockdown message, but I don't wait to hear it. I push forward, cutting through the crowd. My heart races, a single thought pushing everything else aside.

I need to find Jace.

Thirty-Five

HEATH

We sent the druadans home.

A day has passed since we arrived at our makeshift base camp in the defunct Delford office building.

Inside, soldiers and police work together, planning tasks of which neighborhoods are clear and relaying communication on short-wave radios since Network went down.

The ocean mist sprays my face at the edge of the rooftop parking garage. Waves smash against the mile-long levee, sending white water skyward. The structure beneath my boots has stood for five centuries, patched many times to keep the ocean from finishing what it started long ago. Now, it seems ITM wants to help it along.

Since the attack on the TZ Delta station, the army needed all the trained people they could get to help with evacuations. The risk of mystyl moved far down the list of Circuit's biggest worries with the fear of the capital city flooding.

"You should sleep."

Behind me Liam leans against an air conditioning unit, rifle slung across his chest. His eyes are bloodshot, dark circles forming beneath them.

"So should half the people on duty," I turn back to the view. Rain begins to fall, the fat drops spattering my face and coat.

"They're bringing another truck in and want us to look for stragglers or holdouts between fifth and ninth."

Carter paces on my left, eyes sweeping the area for any sign of ITM activity.

Behind us, the city chokes in gridlock. Horns blare. People shout. Shuttles lift off, carrying those with the money to flee.

I crane my neck to the high rises surrounding us, wondering if my parents are still home in the tallest of the buildings, Lockwood Tower.

Odds are high that they took a private shuttle when the evacuation order was announced, but not a hundred percent.

Carter's apprehension drifts around me.

I tighten my grip on my rifle. "They'll be fine at Blackhawk."

He doesn't believe me. *I* don't believe me.

I hate being away from Shadowmane, too, but we're needed here. If the levee breaks, water will flood downtown, destroying the streets and buildings, including Lockwood Tower.

An explosion flares in the distance, followed by a spiral of smoke and a loud boom that shakes the building beneath our feet.

"Fuck," Carter hisses just as the radio crackles with someone's voice. "Breech. Madison and sixteenth. Send all available units to evac."

A soldier rushes out onto the roof. "Captain James, Hernandez is looking for you. We're loading up."

I start toward him, and he blinks as if just realizing I was there. "Oh, Lockwood, good, I was hoping to catch you too."

Carter steps in front of me. "Status report?"

The soldier's face blanches. "The west end is under water."

The three of us rush inside and regroup with Garrett, Liam's brother, Luke, and other riders from North and South Crimela stations.

"Specter team," Captain Hernandez says. "Get on the truck; we've got National Guard teams coming to rescue. They need us up north to help sandbag the streets."

The entire place evacuates, and we climb aboard the three cargo trucks waiting outside.

The truck lurches forward, tires splashing through pooling water as we navigate the abandoned streets. The emptiness is eerie. Buildings loom like silent sentinels on either side, their windows dark, some shattered.

Carter nudges me, pointing to a storefront. "Look."

Spray-painted across the brick in neon green: THE END IS NEAR. Beside it is a crude drawing of a mystyl with its tentacle legs wrapped around a human head. Across the street, another building displays a different take, cartoonish octopuses with oversized eyes, sunlight rays emanating from their bodies. Someone has scrawled: SAVIOR?, beneath it.

"Shit," Liam mutters, taking in more graffiti as we pass.

THEY WERE HERE FIRST, covers an entire wall.

The radio crackles with static before a voice cuts through. "Explosion reported at section fourteen of the levee. Water breaching northeast quadrant." Another burst of static.

"Repeat, water breaching northeast—" The transmission dissolves into unintelligible noise.

The truck's brakes squeal. We jump out, boots hitting the wet pavement. National Guard soldiers direct us to crates of sandbags stacked under a makeshift tent. We form a line and pass the heavy bags from person to person.

Rain pummels us, coming down in sheets now. We splash through puddles, working frantically to build a barrier. My arms burn from the effort, my clothes are soaked, but I keep moving. There's another roar in the distance. More water breaking through, more city being flooded.

My comm unit buzzes against my hip. Network is back online. Out of habit, I look at the news bulletin crawling across the screen: "ITM BASE DISCOVERED IN TZ DELTA. CIRCUIT MILITARY OFFICIALS REPORT SIEGE COMPLETE. NO ITM MEMBERS CAPTURED. NO SURVIVORS."

My stomach plummets to my feet.

"Carter!" I shout over the rain. He must hear the panic in my voice because he abandons his position and hurries over. I show him the message.

His jaw tightens as he reads it, then he slams a sandbag down with unnecessary force. "Fucking Circuit," he growls.

Maybe Logan didn't make it there at all. Maybe they are lying. Maybe they captured Brigid, and she was in custody— No. They made it clear during meetings: Circuit is done taking prisoners. ITM had lost its chance for mercy weeks ago.

I stare at the waist-high wall of sandbags, feeling hollow. This is it. All of the world is ending. I go to switch my comm off when another message comes through from a number I don't recognize.

It might be my parents using a backup communicator, so I check it. It's a series of coordinates I'm unfamiliar with. I tap them in, and the map shows a spot in the middle of nowhere among the hills of TZ Delta.

Logan. It has to be.

I gesture for Carter to follow me to the truck, ostensibly to get more bags. Once out of earshot, I tell him, "Logan's alive. He sent coordinates."

The edges of Carter's eyes tighten; he's conflicted. If we leave, we're going AWOL. We'll be seen as traitors. We might never see our stallions again. But if Logan is in trouble...

Another explosion, followed by the thunderous roar of water. Shouts erupt. "Everyone, back to the trucks! Now! Move it!"

Soldiers and riders scramble toward the vehicles. Carter and I exchange a look.

"We'll catch the next one," he tells Liam, who claps him on the back.

"Don't be a fucking hero," Liam warns.

Carter shoves at him. "Just get on."

The trucks pull away and race from car to car. It doesn't take long to find an old sedan with the keys dangling in the ignition. I wrench open the door, and the two of us climb inside.

After tossing my rifle into the back seat, I slam the accelerator, spinning the car around. We head south, the roar of waves fading behind us with every mile. Each distant explosion feels like the implosion of my own life. I'll be branded a traitor.

So will Carter.

I glance at him in the passenger seat. Despite his rank, despite that he's officially our leader now, there's a question in his eyes as he looks at me. It's the same look I've seen a thousand times before, seeking confirmation that we've made the right call. Even as Specter's commander, he still turns to me when the difficult decisions come.

I've always been our foundation, the rational voice, the level head. The one who thinks five steps ahead, while others react to what's in front of them.

That's what makes this moment so surreal. For once, I'm throwing caution aside, racing toward uncertainty rather than calculating the odds.

"You sure about this?" Carter asks.

His words hit home, and I don't answer immediately. In abandoning our post, I permitted him to do the same.

My moral compass spins wildly, no longer able to find north. I've seen too much blood and death to no what's right anymore, but like always, Carter adjusts his course to match mine.

A year ago, I never would've done this. A year ago, I would've laid out every risk, every consequence, and mapped every contingency. But months of missions transformed me inside.

The country's collapse into anarchy didn't make me more reckless. It clarified what matters.

"Funny," I finally say, swerving around debris in the road. "Usually, I'm the one asking you that."

Carter laughs, looking out at the abandoned streets that slide past us. "Guess things change."

I stare through the windshield as we leave the city and hit the open road.

"All right, Logan," I whisper, knuckles white on the steering wheel. "We're coming."

Thirty-Six

MARSHAL

Thornwick school is in lockdown.

"Damn," Jess mutters, tapping frantically on her wrist comm. "I can't get a hold of Jace."

"I can't reach Becca either," Stephen says, peering at his wrist. "Looks like Network is down."

A knot tightens in my chest. If I wasn't worried before, I am now. I sit up straighter, scanning the room. Staff rushes to lock the doors, murmuring about how it was just a matter of time. A teacher, a middle-aged woman with thick ankles and an armful of gold bangles, steps into the center and claps her hands for attention.

"Everyone, please stay calm!" she shouts. "The chefs are whipping up a fresh batch of scones and cookies, along with hot cocoa and coffee. Don't worry. Circuit has a direct line and will keep us updated."

Her attempt to soothe the crowd falls flat. Around us,

students clutch their comms, frantically messaging friends or family.

"Jace is in the gym," Jess whispers to me. "The locker room. I have to get to him."

No way in hell is she running off alone. "I'll help you find him."

"So will I," Stephen steps closer. His voice has that edge, the one that makes me want to slam my fist into his face. "We'll get you to him, Jess."

Her eyes dart between us, exasperated. "This isn't the time to measure dicks. I need to make sure he's safe."

"Give me a minute," I assure her, ignoring Stephen's smirk. "I'll see what I can do." Overhead, muffled announcements crackle with nothing helpful, just more directives to stay put. Somewhere in the crowd, someone whispers about the shuttles being detoured until the lockdown is lifted.

I stand, my mind racing. Getting to the gym won't be easy. I search the faces of the staff, settling on one of the youngest, a student teacher pacing by the doorway.

As I approach him, my chest tightens. My hostility toward Stephen lingers, even though I shouldn't let it.

Jess made it clear when she left that she needed space. I've respected that, resisting the urge to message her or call her, even during long nights when a drink in hand made the what-ifs impossible to ignore. Seeing her now, though, the scent of her, the way she still moves like she carries the world. It all rushes back.

I consider myself a patient man, but seeing Stephen sitting close to her grates on my every nerve. This isn't just jealousy. It's Nightshade's influence rising within me, responding to Jess's presence. The bond, usually a background hum, flares hot and demanding whenever she's near. For years, I've prided myself on being easy going, patient, even, the calm in the storm while teaching novices to learn how to manage the kaleidoscope of emotions, sharing another consciousness brings. I've mastered the mating drive, caged the territorial impulses, and leashed the carnal urges that come with being bonded to Nightshade.

I convinced myself I was in control. But around Jess, those walls crumble like sand castles against the tide.

Nightshade's influence floods my consciousness, whispering a dark, possessive presence. Mine. Protect. Claim. My stallion doesn't recognize social niceties or human restraint; it only knows she is ours and someone else is too close.

When Stephen's hand grazes hers, a growl rumbles in my throat, sounding more beast than man. This is what terrifies me most, not the jealousy itself, but how right it feels to surrender to it. Around Jess, the battle with my bond tips increasingly in Nightshade's favor. And part of me, a growing part, no longer wants to fight it.

"Hey," I say to the phys ed teacher, my expression schooled even as the tempest of emotions spirals inside my skull. "I overheard you asking about me."

"You're uh, Master Rider Clemmons..." He stammers. "It's an honor to meet you."

I flash him a wide smile. "Why, thank you, and you're Dan Buntin, right?" The headmaster mentioned his name during the meeting earlier. Years of Circuit meetings and functions made me adept at attaching names to faces.

He nods eagerly, and I know I made the right choice picking him. "I've heard you've done great things here, transforming Thornwick's physical education program into a wellness program for the kids."

Dan's cheeks redden.

"You have a son, Danny Jr?" I ask.

Dan blinks in surprise. "That's right. He just turned sixteen."

"I look over all the applications to Vanguard," I say. "And thought I recognized your name." I stoop lower and can practically feel his body vibrating. "I'll be honest. I'm in need of a favor. You see, we need to get to the gym."

He stiffens and frowns. "We're not supposed to let anyone leave during a lockdown."

"I know, but it's just the three of us. We'll be discreet, and I'll claim all liability if anything happens."

He scratches the back of his neck, still not convinced.

"If you let us through, I'll make sure your oldest son gets a commendation for Vanguard. I'll even write it myself."

His eyebrows shoot up. For a moment, he looks ready to argue, then nods quickly. "All right. But you have to be fast."

"You've got it. Thanks." He whispers the code to the door for me, and I thank him again and stride back to Jess and Stephen.

When I return, Jess looks at me expectantly.

"I got the code to the door," I tell her. "He said we can go."

Tension visibly drains from her features as she pats my arm. "Thank you, Marshal," she says.

Nearby, Stephen scowls like he stepped in one of Finn's notoriously smelly and impressively large piles of shit.

"No problem," I say warmly, captivated by her grateful smile.

"What did you promise him?" Stephen quips. "All your salary for a year?"

I offer a dry laugh. "No, actually. The reach of a Master Rider extends way further than most realize." I give him a meaningful look, letting the implication sink in. "Money only opens certain doors. Being a rider, now that's something no amount of credits can buy." I pause, letting my gaze linger just long enough for him to feel the sting. "But hey, we all have our place. Not everyone gets to be chosen for Vanguard."

Sensing the tension, Jess clears her throat. "They're bringing out the food. Now's are chance."

The three of us discreetly make our way to the exit, and when the room is distracted by the appearance of pastries and hot chocolate several minutes later, we type the code and slip through the door.

We hurry down the long, empty hallway, then down a short flight of stairs, until we reach a large pair of double doors and the words THORNWICK HORNETS over the top of them.

Inside, we're greeted by the gleaming expanse of the school gymnasium. The space is impressive, with its polished hardwood floors stretching beneath soaring ceilings that are at least thirty feet high. Championship banners hang proudly from the rafters, gold and black fabric documenting decades of victories. Having attended Green Harbor Junior High myself, a public school in Leveler, I recall Thornwick Junior Academy as our toughest rival. They have the money for private trainers and recruit the best students to fill their team rosters.

Wooden bleachers line the far side of the court, where about thirty young teenagers are clustered together on the nearest set, their excited voices reverberating through the cavernous space.

A young woman stands at the edge of the court, cradling a digital tablet. She looks barely out of high school herself, petite with short ashen hair, dressed in a black tank top and athletic shorts. When she spots us entering, relief floods her face, and she rushes over. "Oh, thank the tides," she says, her voice betraying exhaustion beneath the relief. "Is everything okay?"

"They found mystyl a few miles from here," Stephen replies before I can. "Circuit police are there investigating. But as long as we keep the doors locked, we should be fine."

Relief doesn't begin to describe the look that washes over her face. "The last update I had," she says. "They told me to wait here for updates, but now my comm isn't working." She tucks a strand of hair behind her ear and glances back at the children. "They've been amazing," she says, her voice quiet. "But I can tell they're getting scared. I've been trying to keep them distracted with games, but..." She trails off.

"Mr. Buntin sent us to check on the kids," I say quickly. "We're here to lend you a hand."

Stephen nods emphatically, and my mouth twitches as I suppress an eye roll.

She overlooks my annoyance and lets out a long sigh. "It's appreciated."

"Jess!" a boy shouts from the center of the bleachers.

"That's Jace," she says, striding toward him.

A girl with glasses and two long braids shouts to Stephen, and I assume it's his sister, Becca.

"Jace!" Jess calls out, hurrying past me. Steven and I follow her over. He's sitting with a group of other boys, his face pale but unharmed. She rushes to him, pulling him into a hug.

"We need to get you out of here," Jess says.

He laughs. "Fat chance. No one is going anywhere right now."

"We'll see about that." Jess taps on her comm and then, a second later, curses when she remembers Network is down.

"Relax, "Jace says. "They do drills like this all the time. We just have to wait it out."

Jess looks like she wants to argue more, but then sighs and drops into an empty seat. Jace peers up at me. "So, you're a druadan rider?"

I hold my arms out. "Let me guess, it was the coat that gave it away?"

Jace laughs. "Your scar, actually," he says, pointing to my right hand.

"You know your stuff." I lift my hand, eyes going to where Nightshade bit me a decade ago. "Most kids your age don't know about the mark."

"Jace has always had an interest in druadan riders," Jess adds.

"Is it true you can feel what they're thinking?" he asks.

I shrug. "Sometimes. Depends on whether they're in the sharing mood or not."

"What's yours named?"

"Nightshade."

"That's cool," he says. A warmth spreads across my chest. Getting a real compliment out of a teenager is like getting a two-year-old to hold still for the farrier. Even the most apathetic teen can't fake indifference when they're in front of a real rider.

Stephen's stare practically drills into the side of my head.

There's no denying people of all ages are obsessed with riders. With the body of an athlete, the legacy of a mythical warrior, and the public trust of a firefighter all wrapped into one. No amount of money or a rich family name can top that.

"Thanks," I say, "I'll show you a photo when Network is back up."

He nods and takes a tablet out of his bag, and the music of a car racing game starts up. Jess glares over at him. "Don't you have homework or something? I know you're barely passing geometry."

Jace turns to me. "When's the last time *you* did geometry?"

"Don't answer that," Jess says quickly.

"Actually," I say, resting a boot on the bleacher seat. "We use geometry all the time. Setting up angles and measurements for the riders to follow during performances. If we mess up, it not only looks bad, but druadans can get hurt."

Jace's brow furrows in thought. "So, you have to figure that all while riding? How do you even keep track of it?"

"It becomes instinct after a while," I tell him. "We train until we don't have to think about it. And it becomes a reflex. Our bodies just know where to be. But in the beginning, yeah, there's a lot of counting out loud, marking distances, running drills over and over until it sticks."

Jace leans forward, interest gleaming in his eyes. "And the druadans? Do they understand the angles, too?"

I chuckle. "Not exactly. But they respond to our cues. It's a partnership. Like a dance, in a way. That's why bonding is so important, so we can sense each other, which makes our moves that much smoother, almost invisible to anyone that's watching."

He looks contemplative, absorbing it all, and I can't help but like the kid. He's sharp, just like his sister. He's curious, with the kind of mind that doesn't settle for simple answers and accepts what sounds fantastical to most. Communicating telepathically with an animal is considered, in some parts of the world on other continents, the trickery of demons.

But he's had Heath around as a future brother-in-law, and so the mystery surrounding druadan riders wasn't so obscure to him. I'm a celebrity among riders, and where others would shy away from talking with me or act uncomfortable, he eagerly and boldly asks questions. He's still young but already layering on muscle, and he's nearly as tall as his sister with long lashes girls go crazy for. A natural charisma and light-heartedness remind me a bit of Carter when he was younger.

A shame he was born second. He might've made a decent rider in a different life.

Stephen shifts closer to Jess, draping an arm along the back of the bleacher above her. "Remember that summer at the lake house?" His voice dips. "We went out on the boat with the group, and we dared each other to go skinny-dipping?"

Jess stiffens. She doesn't meet his eyes, staring at her non-functioning comm.

Jealousy flares white hot in my chest, and I snuff it out as soon as it appears.

I let her go, once, and gave her space. If she isn't ready now, I'll make peace with that.

I'll wait however long it takes. She's worth waiting for.

A staff member steps into the gym, clapping his hands for attention. "An update on the lockdown. It's being extended for another four hours."

Groans ripple through the gym. Students slump back on the bleachers, parents sigh, and a few mutter curse words under their breath.

I take the seat on the opposite side of her and don't miss her slight recoil away.

Jess's face pales, her lips pressing into a thin line. She's trapped between me and Stephen.

"I can pull some strings," I say, low enough for only her. "Request private military transport. It'll be allowed to leave no matter the lockdown."

Jess looks up, eyes widening slightly. "Really? You'll do that?"

I shrug as if it's no big deal, even though I'm cashing in a boatload of IOU cards. "I will."

"I'm not leaving without my friends," Jace says, overhearing us. "We have to take them too." Determination is etched into the space between his eyes, and I catch a glimpse of the man he'll grow to be.

"You know we can't take them," Jess replies before I can.

"They're minors, and without their parents' permission, we'd be breaking the law."

Jace stands, so he peers down at us, still seated. He glances over at the other two boys. "Sawyer's aunt and uncle won't be here until tomorrow, and Bodhi's mom won't care."

Jess opens her mouth to argue, but I stop her and stand to face her brother. "Look, this is noble of you, but your sister is right. We could get in trouble for kidnapping, and imagine how your parents would feel if the Drakeford name were in the news connected to something like that?"

Jace's face pales, but his jaw remains set. He knows I've won.

I rest a hand on his shoulder. "I know this is scary, but I have friends working alongside Circuit soldiers. They've got this. I promise your friends will be okay."

The kid's greenish-blue eyes hold my gaze. He's masking the fear, but it's there nonetheless.

I sigh, knowing he's still not convinced, and I don't want this to make more of a scene than it already is. "I'll make a call as soon as I have service, see if they can't get you guys an update on what's happening. Would that make you feel better?"

Jace glances at his friends, then back at me, and nods.

I smile and step back. "Besides, Stephen here will stay with them. Make sure they're safe." I look over at Stephen, and his eyes widen. He's been watching the whole thing and just waiting for his chance to swoop in and impress Jess. "Uh, yeah." He says half-heartedly. He turns to Jess. "I'll get Becca, and we'll stay here until they give the all-clear."

I conceal a laugh when he realizes she's not paying attention, instead focused on gathering her coat and purse.

Jace says goodbye to his friends, hoists his bag over his

shoulder, and Jess and he follow me to the doors leading out of the gym.

Stephen glares daggers at us, clearly left behind with middle-schoolers.

"Let's go." I hold the door open for Jess with one hand and flip him off with the other.

Thirty-Seven

JESS

My parent's primary house sits on a massive lot, a private refuge that feels like it's miles away from the rest of the world. Surrounded by towering trees, the manicured backyard glistens, stretching down to the beach where the waves crash softly against the shore. A private shuttle port is tucked away at the edge of the hillside community, hidden behind manicured hedges, and the gate—massive, iron, and guarded—keeps everyone else out.

When we arrived, their driver drove us through that gate, past armed security, who barely spared us a glance. This is the life I've always known, the kind of world where only the rich and powerful get to be safe, to hide away from everything that happens outside.

It should feel normal to me. It always has. But lately, it doesn't. There's a disconnect growing, one I can't quite shake. My parents, with their constant need to be untouchable, to shut out everything that doesn't fit into their perfect image, feel wrong.

Venovia is struggling to keep the rebels from taking over. People are losing their homes, jobs, and families because of the violence. And yet they choose to be here, carrying on as if nothing is wrong. History shows that it's always the ones with money, those like my parents, who come out on top, no matter the crisis.

At the front door, my mother and father greet us. Both in their fifties, father's rotund belly tells me that mother must've learned of his affair with his personal trainer, Tiffany. He wears a tan polo shirt and slacks. His hairline is receding, leaving him with a noticeable bald spot, but he keeps his head shaved close.

Next to him stands my mother, the epitome of grace and poise. Her hair is dyed a brunette with golden highlights, concealing the gray she refuses to acknowledge. It falls in sleek waves, framing her sharp features and her light blue eyes, nearly like mine.

As usual, her makeup is expertly applied, and the gold rings of earrings catch the fading light. She's dressed in a yellow and white striped halter top maxi dress that hugs her slender frame I know she's proud of.

"Darlings," Mother says, embracing me, then a stiff Jace. She smells of chardonnay and vanilla cigarettes.

She releases my brother, then eyes Marshal to my left. "You brought a friend?" she asks.

I inhale a deep breath, trying to calm my anxious thoughts. "This is Master Rider, Marshal Clemmons. He's the one who secured us a shuttle before lockdown lifted." My parents' heads swivel to Marshal as he extends his hand.

"Pleasure to meet you, Mr. and Mrs. Drakeford," he says and gives them a smile that makes my mother giggle.

I purse my lips, ignoring the flurry of butterflies in my stomach.

He is just a man. No more, no less. So then, why is it that anytime he looks at me, I can't look away?

It's strange, really. From the second I saw him at Thornwick, it felt as if no time had passed between us. As if from the moment in the cable car, when he told me, "I'm simply seeing you for who you truly are," and to the almost kiss was yesterday instead of months ago.

"Please call me Elise," Mother says.

"Preston," Father says, shaking Marshal's hand.

"Well, come in," Mother says, waving to us. "You three must be exhausted."

They move to the side, and we enter, and my teeth tug at my lower lip. Surely they're comparing him to Heath, sizing him up, wondering why in the world a Master Rider would help me and Jace.

But whether they're just relieved we're safe or Mother's infamous cocktail hour has dulled their curiosity, I can't tell. Either way, the calm won't last. Sooner or later, the questions will come and I'll have to answer them.

Mother snaps her fingers at one of the housekeepers, and they scurry out of the room, abandoning the bouquet they'd been arranging for the entry table. The sight of roses and sprigs of baby's breath only intensifies the fresh memories from Marshal showing me the greenhouse at Blackhawk and his offer for me to work there and stay.

The offer I declined.

I told myself it was the right decision. But now, seeing the flowers and smelling their soft scent, the guilt creeps back in, uninvited, and I push it away.

Marshal strides ahead of me. I thought I moved on, and yet here we are, back in each other's lives.

"Headmaster Davidson updated me on the incident," Father says as he leads us inside.

Even though they've only lived here for five years, the renovations have been constant, and each update has only pushed the value higher. The warmth of the house hits me instantly, a sharp contrast to the cool air outside. The walls are lined with polished wood, dark and rich, with beams that stretch across the high ceiling, giving the place a cozy, grounded feel despite its size. Large windows frame the view of the ocean beyond, the glinting water stretching out endlessly.

I sold the one across the street last year with a lesser view for two million credits. They could easily get double for hers if they wanted. That is, if the housing market doesn't crumble like many people are fearing.

The wood flooring gleams with fresh polish, and the house has a modern touch with new fixtures and paintings, but there's a rustic charm to it. Most of the furnishings are imported from Gaergen Island, the kind of luxury you can't buy anywhere else.

Father gestures for us to sit in the living room, consisting of four white couches, and an oversized coffee table crafted from driftwood and scraps of metal molded into uniform shapes, giving it a unique starfish pattern. He sits at the far end, near the giant double-sided fireplace that faces out onto the deck. "Circuit's board and I were under the belief ITM would show restraint in attacking so near a school, but apparently that is not the case. These terrorists must be put in their place. I'll make a call this afternoon and demand our defense efforts turn to retaliation."

Mother laughs, a nervous sound I know she reserves when he's ranting in front of guests. Her face is blotchy red, her eyes watery, and I don't miss the half-drunk glass of white wine on the coffee table. She sits beside him, crossing her legs and smoothing her dress.

I always thought that she was stoic in a way that was supposed to strengthen us. However, as I grew older, it became apparent while watching her interact with her friends or our father that she was incapable of showing genuine emotions. Her rigid upbringing has forced her to filter everything for fear of being judged.

Jace hurries past, heading toward the staircase.

"Wait," Father says, his tone hard.

Jace stops and throws his head back, looking very much like the thirteen-year-old he is.

"Come here."

My brother turns slowly. Father walks to him and gives him a firm shake on the shoulder. He doesn't have to bend to face him anymore. He'll be Marshal's height before long if he keeps this growth spurt up. "You only had two goals last week. I'm severely limiting your comm time over break, and Harry will drive you to the gym every day to practice with Darion." Jace swallows, then nods. He knows it's pointless to argue, as it would only lead to more punishment.

Once a day, practice with the soccer pro is hardly that bad, considering what I had to endure after they caught me cutting roses from the landscape to decorate my room at the end of my sixth year of school.

The whole summer consisted of twice-daily ballet lessons, followed by Latin, and calligraphy.

I was probably the only kid *excited* to return to school in the fall.

"Am I understood?" Father asks.

Jace nods, then quickly adds, "Understood." Father straightens, and Jace disappears up the stairs.

Beside me, Marshal observes it all, but when I steal a

glance, his face is passive. If he thinks my father is too harsh, he doesn't show it. With Jace gone, the awkwardness is even worse. Why is he still here? Should I tell him to leave?

"We'd offer for you to stay for dinner, Mr. Clemmons, but I'm afraid our chef has left for the day."

"I'm quite all right. In fact, I should head back to Blackhawk."

"Are you sure?" Father adds. "I'm certain they could do without you for a little longer, don't you think? Since..." he pauses. "Since my daughter and Heath ended their engagement, I lost my contact with the druadan stations, and I'd like to bounce some ideas off you that the board and I have been discussing." He moves to the double doors that lead into his home office, where he secretly smokes cigars without Mother knowing. "Please, just an hour."

Marshal exchanges a look with me, and the grand space of the living room feels oppressive.

Mother's eyes burn the side of my face. Even buzzed, she's perceptive as ever. "Marshal must be starving, Father. Perhaps we could order some pasta from that Italian place you like so much?"

Father pauses with his hand on the door. "Oh, didn't you hear? They closed down after that fire."

"I can cook," Marshal supplies. "That is, if you don't mind?"

My parents blink in surprise at him. Heath never offered to cook. Not once. Anytime he came here, it was a brief exchange of pleasantries in the living room before he had some excuse to leave.

Before anyone responds, my father's tablet buzzes. He glances at the screen, then at Mom. "It's Headmaster Davidson."

"Finally." She rushes to Father's side to peer at the digital tablet. "Debbie, my assistant, brought groceries yesterday," she adds hurriedly to us before plastering her face with a broad smile.

With my parents preoccupied, Marshal slides a devilish gaze at me, and the breath catches in my throat. He's so damn handsome it makes me dizzy to look at him. "Jess, maybe you can show me where everything is in the kitchen?"

I start to refuse, but he raises an eyebrow just enough to make it a challenge, like he expects me to say no.

"Yes, dear," Mother says, waving to me. "Go with him and open that bottle of Domaine de la Brume in the chiller."

Damn her. She knows that's my favorite.

"Fine." I toss my purse on one of the padded armchairs and stride to the kitchen.

From behind me, Headmaster Davidson's voice fills the room. "Mr. and Mrs. Drakeford, I apologize for not calling sooner. I trust young Mr. Drakeford made it home safe."

"He did. But I'm confused. We pay Thornwick enough to expect better security than this, Headmaster," my father says. "What exactly happened?"

"Reviewing," Mom says, repeating something he said. "That should have been handled before an incident occurred. We send our children there expecting safety, not to have them smuggled off-campus by their friends for their own protection."

In the kitchen, I open and close cupboards, hands moving to keep busy. The shelves are barer than usual. Mother looked thinner, and Father was always out of town and wouldn't be caught dead in the kitchen cooking. Still, I can't help but wonder if the rumors are true. Was it actually harder to get food delivered all the way up here with the shipment disruptions?

Marshal leans against the counter, watching me. It's the first time we've been alone since we were caught in the storm in the cable car. Three months since I told him I intended to have a baby with Heath, and that nothing more could come between us. Three months since he almost kissed me.

I shove it away before the memories overtake me.

I fold my arms and look over at him. "So, what's the plan, *chef?*" I clear my throat, but it's too late.

He's watching me intently, and something flickers in his deep blue eyes, fast and dark, and it's gone as quick as it appeared. *There's no way he's thinking the same thing as me.*

"Got any pasta?" he asks, and just like that, the question fades.

I swallow the lump in my throat, nodding, and grab two boxes from the cupboard. Marshal moves to the fridge, entirely at ease, like it's his kitchen, not mine.

"Growing up," he says, pulling out ingredients, "Mom used to add a clove of garlic for every person she loved. As I got older, and our family got bigger, cousins, marriages, friends, the pasta got more and more garlicky." He shakes his head with a small smile. "No one ever complained."

It's such a silly tradition, but something tightens in my chest.

I don't have stories like that. Our family's traditions include being at the top of one's class, maintaining the Drakeford name, and having an heir or two. You'd think after hundreds of years, humans would've moved beyond these archaic practices of land ownership, but the Bloodline Act is as old as Circuit itself. It isn't going anywhere.

I try to stay out of his way as he chops onions, but the large kitchen feels cramped, and I keep feeling like I'm in the way. He moves like he knows what he's doing. Comfortable, assured, never hesitating. Times like this, the ten years between us are obvious. He's so sure of himself. So confident, and I admire him, even envy him for it.

I can't help but stare at his hands as he works, more than once losing myself in intimate thoughts and having to distract myself with a glass of champagne or wiping down the counter.

Twenty minutes later, I perch on one of the chairs with my half-empty glass and watch him.

He looks up. "Here," he says, holding out a strand of pasta. "See if it's al dente."

I reach out with a hand, but he pulls it back, lifting it toward my lips instead. His fingers brush my mouth, just a whisper of contact, but I feel it everywhere.

I should pull away, but I don't.

Instead, with a surge of liquid confidence from the champagne, I hold his gaze, take the noodle between my lips, and slurp...slowly. His eyes fix on mine, and a spark of heat flares in his ocean-blue eyes.

The sound makes me laugh as I wipe the water from my chin.

He grins. "Good?"

I nod, swallowing. His thumb moves, and I freeze again at his touch as he wipes something from the corner of my mouth. He doesn't pull back right away.

I should say no. Should pull away, but I don't.

Instead, I let his touch linger.

His hands move to my cheek, hot and rough, and I don't dare move. Don't dare *breathe*.

"Is it done yet?" Jace says, entering.

Marshal and I recoil as if struck by an electrical charge, spinning away from each other.

I turn away, my cheeks flaming, and press a hand to my chest, feeling the galloping rhythm of my heart.

"Almost," Marshal says, his voice shockingly smooth despite what we were just doing. "Do you mind setting the table?"

Finally composed, I turn to see Jace watching me, a smug look on his face. *Don't you dare say a word?* I mentally tell him, summoning my strongest threatening look.

"Sure," he smirks. "You want me to tell Mom and Dad?"

"No," I say, at the exact time Marshal says, "Yes."

We exchange a look, and his forehead creases, puzzled. "What I mean is," I say hastily, "let them know dinner is ready *after* you set the table."

Marshal disappears into the pantry to find serving dishes.

As soon as he's gone, my brother looks in the direction he went, then back at me, and makes the vulgar gesture of his pointer finger thrusting into a circled one.

I scowl at him. "Don't be crude," I tell him. "Now, go set the table."

Jace scratches his chin, unmoving.

"Did you not hear me?" I say, my voice rising an octave higher.

Jace frowns. "How can I set the table if I don't know where the plates are?"

I let out an exasperated sigh and pointed to the cabinets behind him. "There."

"I don't know." He rubs his face and fakes a yawn. "Today was pretty stressful, maybe you should—"

"Jace Nathanial Eldwin Drakeford."

He makes a face and holds up his hands. "Fine, fine." He turns and takes a stack of plates from the shelf, then leaves.

Soon after, the five of us are seated at the long rectangular table. It's partially recycled metal and melted pieces of plastic, a marble look without the weight or upkeep.

It was not my mother's first choice, but it was a gift from President Peterson, and my parents never missed a chance to brag about it.

The bowl of pasta, sauce, and steamed corn is passed

around the table. Mother takes a portion fit for a toddler, and Father forgoes the corn altogether. "So, Marshal," Father says once we're all eating. "You mentioned you were at Thornwick representing Blackhawk, did you not?"

Marshal nods, adding salt to his corn. "Vanguard likes to have one or more Master Riders make appearances at the private schools for visibility and transparency. Parents are inclined to resist their eldest son enrolling when they haven't met a rider in person."

"Seems sensible," Father replies. "But I'm curious. How is it you know my daughter so much as to offer a shuttle ride for her and my son?"

Marshal doesn't miss a beat. "As station manager at Blackhawk, Heath and I work together. I consider him a good friend."

A silence settles over the room. Mother takes a slow sip of her wine, and Father clears his throat, nodding stiffly. "Unfortunate how that ended. Though we are grateful the merger was completed before the ITM situation turned into what it has."

"Speaking of, have there been any other issues at the stations since Meridian?"

Marshal shakes his head. "None so far, thankfully. We've upped security just to be cautious, of course."

"Of course," Father replies. "In my opinion, Circuit should've given them up years ago. Waste of money, I say. They should've focused their attention on the infrastructure, the failing dikes, filtration plant expansions that are long overdue." Father pauses. "You've been there what...?"

"Over ten years," Marshal says.

"Ten years? Ah, that's right. You're the one they can't figure out. Well, then, you've been there longer than most. What do you think?"

Marshal chews thoughtfully, then wipes his mouth. He sets

the napkin on his lap, and his foot bumps mine under the table. I suck in a sharp breath, drawing a look from my mother as I pull it back. "I can tell you what I've seen." He briefly meets my gaze before returning to my Father's. "I've seen young boys thrive and grow and find a purpose beyond suits and ties and boardrooms. I've seen friendships and bonds formed and determination unlike any other."

"Shame Jace was born after Jess," Mother says, slurring. "Mothers of riders get first options to season tickets, and that queen bee, Felicia, always likes to flaunt hers at the ladies' luncheons."

Father scowls at Mother's tangent, then says, not looking at Jace. "Vanguard might've done the boy some good, and with Jess, at least the Drakeford line is secure if he'd gone that route. Not that I think he could handle it. Too soft, too self-centered."

I bristle, balling the napkin in my lap. I despise it when he talks about me like I'm not here. Like I'm just another employee at his company, to be shuffled around, used, and then placed back on the shelf until I'm needed again. He might've helped me start Drakeford Properties, but *I* built it into what it is today. In two years, we've tripled our sales.

"Actually," Marshal says, his tone firm. "I don't think Jace is soft at all." He looks to Jace, who's stopped mid-spaghetti slurp to listen, then settles his gaze back on my father. "At Thornwick today, he refused to go with me unless we took his friends. He stood up to me, a Master Rider, when most kids his age wouldn't have dared. That takes real courage and loyalty to his friends." He glances at Jace. "I wish I'd had a friend like him in school."

"Is that so?" Father asks, looking mildly impressed, which, for him, is impressive.

Jace nods slowly. "Yeah, I did."

My brother's body is tense as he's unsure if he's in trouble or not.

Father's mouth curves into a rare, tight smile. "Well then. I suppose your time there has done you some good."

Jace beams, then shoots a look my way, and I give him a small smile.

"So then," Mother says. "Since you're here, Jess. The Stanleys invited us to brunch tomorrow."

I blink. "I don't know if I—"

"I already told them we agreed," she interrupts. "It would be rude not to show."

I sigh and sit back in my chair. I desperately want to return to my apartment in Delford.

"It's getting late," Father says. "And you still owe me that chat?" Father rises from his chair and tosses the napkin on the table.

"I do, don't I?" Marshal says, gathering his plate.

"Leave it," Father barks. "Anita can get it when she comes tonight. Speaking of... they're putting in a curfew tonight, grounding all shuttles until tomorrow. So, unless you want us to send you to a hotel, why not stay for the night, Marshal? We have a guest room, and I'd be lying if I didn't say I'd like to run through my full list with you."

Marshal hesitates for a fraction of a second and blessedly doesn't look at me.

"All right. I'll stay."

The two of them leave, followed by Jace and my mother, and I soon find myself alone at the table, drinking the rest of my glass.

Tides, do I need a long, *hot* bath.

Thirty-Eight

MARSHAL

This bed feels wrong.

The satin sheets are tangled at my feet, and I'm damp with sweat from thick blankets.

It's no use. I swing my legs over the edge of the bed, my feet meeting the cold floor. My fingers trail over the small table by the bed, grazing the edge of the lamp as I press the button.

A dull yellow light illuminates the furniture in the unfamiliar room.

Everything is purple and silver.

Dark wine-colored curtains, a silver-rimmed mirror on the wall, and a silver bed frame.

Drakeford Purple.

The audacity of this family. I doubt if Jess ever had a chance to decorate her own room like I had. Mom had let me paint mine any color I wanted.

I chose black with yellow lightning bolts on the ceiling

because I was a ten-year-old boy. Even after I left, she never repainted it, and last summer, when I visited her, I slept under the same crudely drawn, crooked lightning bolts I always had.

Overcome by restlessness, I stand and move toward the door.

Cooking in the kitchen with her felt like I could breathe for the first time in months. Seeing her, being near her, had sated my soul. It's corny as hell but true.

Her watchful gaze, the way she shifted in her seat when I looked at her too long, the way her long finger kept smoothing her dark hair as if it weren't perfect.

I needed her more than I ever needed anyone.

And it took all self-control earlier not to finish what we started in the cable car when she tried the pasta.

My hand brushes the door handle, then stops.

What am I even doing?

Preston kept me in his study for two hours, and by the time I'd emerged, Jace was lounging on the couch playing his car racing game on the comm with his feet propped on the back. He informed me Jess had gone to bed and then added it was the third door on the right.

He caught us in the kitchen, and his mischievous smirk confirmed he'd seen too much.

I can go to her now.

It's late, and she is probably asleep.

Dammit. I spin away from the door. There is so much I wanted to tell her. So much I regret not saying before. And now, with the country under siege, I don't know how many more chances I'll get.

It's sheer luck she was at Thornwick when I was.

It must have been a sign.

I stride to the door, pulse quickening at the thought of her in bed, dark air sprawled around her like some goddess of night. She made me promise to give her time. The last thing I want is to make her feel trapped, like they do.

My hand slips from the door, but I can't bring myself to step away. I'm stuck, caught between what I want and what she needs.

I start to open it when I hear the barest shuffle of movement.

The light from the hallway dips and then is blocked as someone walks to my door.

For a fleeting second, I panic that Elise, drunk, decided to visit me, but with no lock on the door, what can I do to stop her?

I inhale and open it.

Jess stands there, barefoot, in the corridor. Her arms hug her sides, her black hair loose around her face, and she wears purple satin pajamas. Her nipples are visible through the soft material, and my boxers tighten as her eyes dance over my bare chest.

They drift upward, and I see something raw and fragile lingering there.

"Jess," I breathe, her name almost a question.

She steps closer, and the light catches her face. "I'm sorry." She looks down, then up again, her lips trembling as she speaks. "This is a mistake." She starts to leave, and I catch her by the arm.

"Stay."

She purses her lips, then lets me guide her inside.

In the dim light, she wraps her arms tighter around herself. "After today..." She pauses, her gaze locks on mine. "With everything that happened today, I don't want to be alone tonight."

She stands in the middle of the room, uncertain. Her arms drop to her sides, her fingers twitching like she wants to reach for something but isn't sure she should. I move toward her, slow, careful not to startle her.

"You don't have to ask," I say, my voice quiet.

Her lips part, but she doesn't speak. I want to touch her, to pull her close, tell her it's okay. But I hold back. She's here because she needs something I don't know how to give without overstepping.

I gesture to the bed. "You can take the side you like." My attempt at lightness falls flat, but she doesn't seem to notice. She moves toward the bed, sitting on the edge. Her hands rest in her lap, fingers tangling together.

I sit beside her, the distance between us a canyon I don't know how to cross.

"I thought I wanted this," she says suddenly, her voice low. "I thought I'd be fine without you…" She shakes her head, and a bitter laugh escapes her. "But I can't stop it. The way you make me feel. The way you look at me as if I matter. As if I'm *someone*." She glances at me, her eyes blue as frost. "And then today with Jace. I keep thinking about what would've happened if you hadn't been there." Her voice breaks, and she looks away.

I place a hand on hers, and she doesn't pull away. Slowly, she turns her hand, her fingers brushing mine before curling around them.

The touch sends a warmth through me, and I force myself to focus and keep my breathing steady.

"I've never stopped thinking about you. Not once."

Her grip tightens for a moment before she lets go.

She climbs onto the bed, curling up on her side.

I hesitate, then lie beside her. She doesn't move away, and I drape an arm over her; she leans into me. It takes every ounce of self-control to stay still as she curls into me again, fitting neatly against my chest. My dick hardens, and I curse myself silently.

Even at this distance, I feel her tether to me, a soft, muted glow in my chest. It's been some time since I've been with a woman, and Shade's bond is unfathomably the horniest. That says something, considering they're all stallions.

Whatever prevented me from brimming allowed me to keep it in check. That is, until I am around *her*.

She is my Achilles heel. My perfect poison.

I force myself to think of other neutral thoughts: The new set of practice drills I left the novices to work on. Nightshade, going stir-crazy in his stall.

The vanilla-infused pillowcase.

The silkiness of her hair against my face.

Fuck me.

It's incomprehensible how much I want her. *Crave* her.

Jess shifts, then spins to face me.

My arms remain where they are, not daring to let her slip farther away.

Her breath is warm on my face, and she peers up through her thick eyelashes. "I never stopped thinking about you either."

My body stills with the weight of her confession.

"But after learning I wasn't pregnant, I panicked. Needed space to figure out who and what I am."

"You don't have to justify what—" She presses a finger to my lips.

"There. Just like that. That's why you're different. You're more than you should be for me. More than I deserve."

I laugh, a deep sound in my chest. "You deserve everything."

She leans closer, and we bump foreheads. "I can't, Marshal.

After Heath, I swore off riders. I can't let myself fall for someone like you, knowing any day you could die."

"But isn't that true for everyone?" I take her hand and stroke her knuckles with my thumb, relishing the softness of her skin. "Besides, I'm not like other riders." I look up, fixing my gaze on hers.

She sighs, and a delicious heat appears in her eyes. "Damn you." Then her lips are on mine, and I'm pulling her to me.

They're exquisitely soft and warm and *her*. If I die now, I will die so goddamn happy, and yet...

I need *more*. All of her.

My hands roam her body, stroking, caressing, exploring, and her hands do the same to my shoulders and neck.

Her thumb rubs across the raised skin of the scars on my arms and shoulders, scrapes and bites from a lifetime of handling druadans.

My fingers play with the buttons on her shirt, then drift until they're teasing her nipples through the smooth fabric.

She inhales and arches her back, pressing her breasts up so I can cup them with my free hand while cradling her head with my other.

Blood surges to my cock, and it strains in my boxers. Her lips part slightly, an invitation that allows my tongue to explore the warm, inviting space of her mouth.

I gasp as her hand reaches down and begins stroking my cock through my underwear.

Tides, it feels good. Better than good.

But still, it's not enough. I need more, and from the way her lips are moving on mine, she does, too.

I reach for the buttons of her shirt, deftly undoing them with one hand until the fabric falls open, giving me complete access to her full breasts.

I break our kiss long enough to admire them.

My god, they're perfect.

In the glow of the light, her flawless pale skin transitions to the rosy peaks of her nipples.

Slowly, I lower my face to them, kissing, licking, and nipping, and she moans at the touch. My finger trails down her body, and when I'm near her belly button, she takes my hand and assists it the rest of the way to between her legs.

At some point, she slipped off her pants, and through the thin underwear, I felt the wetness seeping through the fabric.

As I rub the bundle of nerves with my thumb, her eyes roll back in her head, and her teeth dig into her full bottom lip, sending a surge of blood to my already granite-hard dick.

"Fuck yes, Marshal," she breathes.

A smirk plays with my lips at her potty mouth as I continue teasing as she rides my hand through her orgasm.

When her breathing eases, she meets my gaze. Her cheeks are flushed, but her smile doesn't quite reach her eyes. "Before we go any further, I have to tell you something."

"What?" I say hoarsely. Watching her orgasm almost sent me over the edge like some damn teenager, so I'm grateful she's giving me a chance to recover.

"I've never been with anyone besides..." Her blush intensifies, and I swear she's never looked more beautiful than now. Vulnerable. Exposed. "Please don't laugh," she says.

I furrow my brow. "So, you don't want to—?"

"No!" she shouts. "I do. I'm just saying it's been... I don't." She pauses, cursing, and I lay my hand on her cheek and turn her to me.

"I understand. We'll go as fast or as slow as you like. You've got all the control."

She nods nervously, and relief floods her features. Her delicate neck moves as she swallows and rolls onto her back, bringing me with her.

My mouth finds hers again, and the kiss deepens, intensifying into something richer, stronger.

Her movements are bold and more assured as she runs her nails down my back.

I slide a finger beneath the satin band, hugging her hips; the fabric is warm from her skin, and the embroidery catches slightly against my knuckle. The urge to tear it away claws at me, but I savor the slow resistance. With an adorable wiggle of her hips, she helps me pull them down. She spreads her legs for me, and with a tug of my boxers, my cock eagerly springs free. I rub the head against the inner part of her thigh.

Her eyes widen. "Are you...*clean*?"

My eyes dance between hers. "It's standard station practice to check us regularly, and I'll be honest, I haven't been with anyone in an embarrassingly long time."

Since I met you.

She laughs, a soft sound full of relief. "That makes two of us."

I capture her laugh with a kiss, tasting the sweetness of her joy as it mingles with my own desperate need. My lips linger on hers, hungry, as I maneuver my cock near her entrance. The heat from her core brushes against the sensitive skin, a searing reminder of how close we are, and my balls tighten in anticipation. Every nerve in my body is a light, hyper-aware of her beneath me, of this moment I never thought I'd have.

"Are you ready?" I rasp against her cheek, as I stay propped on my elbows above her, careful not to crush her with my weight. My muscular frame towers over her slender body, casting shadows across her delicate form as she lies beneath me, dark hair splayed around her, and I'm acutely aware of how easily I could crush her, hurt her.

She's always so poised and confident. But here, like this,

she is vulnerable, and I wish desperately to capture this moment and form it into a memory.

My heart thunders in my chest, a wild, untamed rhythm as I gaze into her eyes, searching for any hesitation.

She nods, and as if to emphasize her point, she spreads her slender legs wider, welcoming me.

Eagerly, I position myself between them but the damn sheets are so slick and my knee slides out, as I enter her a little harder than I intended.

She gasps, and her fingers dig into my back.

"Fuck, sorry." I breathe, already withdrawing.

"It's fine," she moans, stoking the fire that's been burning for her for far too long. "Don't you dare stop." She arches her hips upward, and I slide into her again a little easier. The muscles of her pussy clamp down around my dick and as I slide lazily in and out of her.

My mind reels as I feel her warmth envelop me, the sensation so overwhelming it nearly steals my breath. I've wanted this, wanted *her* for what feels like an eternity. I thought I lost her for good when she left Blackhawk all those months ago.

The ache of her absence had hollowed me out, a constant, gnawing void I couldn't fill. I'd convinced myself I'd never see her again, let alone hold her like this.

But she's here now, beneath me, her body melding with mine in a way I dared to imagine in the darkest, most private corners of my mind. She's all that occupies my thoughts day and night. She's in my dreams, her laughter echoing softly, her rare, guarded smile a treasure I've yearned to coax from her.

"Tides, I've wanted this for so long," I murmur. I still my hips, allowing her to adjust to let myself absorb the reality of this. "I've wanted *you*. When you left Blackhawk, I thought... I thought that was it. That I'd never see you again, and it nearly broke me. You've been in my head, in my dreams, every single damn day. I missed it so much. Your smile, the way you hold back, but let me see pieces of you. I've been dying to be close to you like this, to feel you, to know you."

Her eyes soften, a shimmer of emotion surfacing in their icy depths as her fingers thread through my hair. "I'm here now," she whispers.

Her words unravel me, and I lower my head to kiss her again, slower this time, pouring everything I feel into it. The longing, the months of quiet torment, the desperate hope that this is real. My body moves against hers as I lose myself in her, knowing I'll never be the same after this, knowing she's etched herself into every part of me.

I kiss her again and again. Savoring and drinking in her blissful moans while the scent of her arousal permeates the air.

The bond hums happily in me, and I wish we were at Blackhawk so Nightshade could feel this.

Her legs wrap around the back of my knees, pulling me deeper into her.

My balls tingle again, and I know I'm close.

I lower my hand; my thumb finds her clit again, and I rub it between thrusts.

"Marshal, oh God." She gasps as the wet sounds of our lovemaking fill the room. "Don't stop. Please."

Her body tenses, the spasms of her orgasm rippling through her are enough to tip me over the edge. This time, I don't fight it.

My balls tingle, and the euphoria consumes me, blinding me, as I release into her with a long groan.

"Jess." Her name is summoned from my lips like a prayer.

For a second, I press my head into the pillow and bask in the lingering effects the most powerful fucking orgasm I ever had.

Slowly, I roll to my side, letting my half-hard dick slip out of her. The bond hums blissfully in my chest, and I know it wouldn't take much for a round two. But for now, I want to savor this. Savor her.

Jess lays there, arms around her head, breasts exposed, with a dreamy gaze staring at the ceiling.

"I never knew what it could be before you." Her voice is soft, reverent. "I never knew it could be like that."

I'm at a loss for how to respond, partly from my mind buzzing from the endorphins and partly because it breaks a part of me to hear it.

I pull her to me, tucking her into my chest, and breathe in her hair. "I love you."

She tenses in my hold but doesn't pull away. "Marshal, I..." She stammers.

"Come with me tomorrow to Blackhawk," I quickly add.

She moves so she can face me. Her face is relaxed, her eyes half-lidded but still alert. "I *am* overdue for a vacation, and the Village has its winter fashion show this time of year." She tilts her head to the side and plays with a curl of hair on my chest. "However, it would mean some cancellations of other plans, and the rearranging of my schedule is a nightmare." Her left eyebrow shoots up defiantly. "So, if you want me to do all that, I'm going to need a lot more convincing."

My dick jerks fully awake at the desire coating her words. "Well, Ms. Drakeford, let me show you just how fucking convincing I can be."

Thirty-Nine

BRIGID

The shuttle's engine vibration is a mind-numbing drone as I rest my head against Logan's shoulder. Exhaustion drags at me, pulling me under in fits and starts, but I'm exceedingly aware of the steady rise and fall of his breathing, the solid presence of him beside me.

My arms and back ache from helping the people down the stairs, and I'm sure there's a bruise on my hip where Logan tossed me over his shoulder.

The shuttle jolts, the landing gear engaging with a heavy thud. I had dozed off at some point, dreaming of iridescent bubbles and vanilla-scented soaps.

Logan shifts; his arm tightens around me for just a second

before he moves to stand. I blink blearily as the hatch hisses open, the night air rushing in heavily with the scent of pine.

A man waits just beyond the threshold, his face lined and weathered, sun-creased, and while he's probably in his forties, he looks older.

His gaze flicks over me, assessing, before settling on Logan.

"Nice to finally meet you," he says, smiling to reveal a row of uneven teeth.

Logan steps forward. "This is Waylon. He's a friend."

My tired mind finally plays catch-up. "You're a trawler?"

He chuckles and motions to Logan beside me. "You caught on faster than your friend here." He takes the hat off the wall and gestures to the hatch. "I kept low so the police can't detect us, but let's get you inside, anyway." Waylon opens the door, and I grab my bag and mask and follow them down the short ramp. Without asking, Logan's arm loops around my waist, taking most of my weight as we step down onto the uneven ground.

The night is black and endless around us, the low-burning lanterns on the cabin's porch casting enough light to guide the way. A light tinkle like a music box in the distance plays. Lines and lines of small pinwheels zigzag along the pathway.

I barely register the creak of the door before warmth surrounds me and the scent of burning wood from a small hearth.

"Welcome to Murdock. This little sprat is my daughter, Nova."

The girl has to be around twelve or thirteen with just the start of breasts and hips. Her square face and sharp features are like her dad's, but it's her eyes that truly catch my attention. Too large for her face, they are golden brown, except for a startling crack of blue splitting through her left iris like lightning in a storm.

Heterochromia—another gift from growing up near a TZ.

Her wine-red hair catches the light from the hanging lanterns and fireplace. The red color is stark at her roots before gradually darkening to black tips, similar to the banshee's red and black coats. The darkening of hair, I'd learned, is a telltale sign of prolonged TZ exposure in children.

My silver blonde has surrendered to dull gray at the ends, but hers holds its vibrancy.

Sharice's theory is right. Some people, especially children, can develop a tolerance to the toxins. Sadness, I worked to keep tamped down, seeps into me, and I forcefully shove it away. I can't mourn her. Not yet.

"I'm Brigid." My voice sounds brighter than expected.

She smiles, then looks at her father. "Nice to meet you."

I shake her hand. It's rough and callused, and her arms are impressively toned for a girl her age. "I spotted two patrols this morning, so I'll tarp the shuttle."

Waylon thanks her, and she leaves.

As if my body knows it's finally safe to rest, I don't make it far into the main room, and Logan lowers me onto the couch. Wearily, I sink into the tattered cushions.

A heavy blanket is draped over me and smells mildly of mildew. A clink of metal, the shuffle of boots, and the murmur of Waylon and Logan speaking all feel distant as I'm slipping between wakefulness and sleep with each breath.

A cup is pressed into my hands, and the warmth bleeds into my chilled fingers. Waylon crouches, his sharp eyes softened just a fraction. "Tea," he says. "Unless you want something stronger."

I shake my head. "This is fine."

I sense Logan, even if I can't see him.

He moves around the couch to sit in an opposite chair, and I watch him through drooping eyelids. He is sharpening a knife with a whetstone. He doesn't look up, but I feel his attention, the quiet watchfulness in the way he moves.

"Thank you," I murmur, the fire, the tea, and the blanket weaving together into something dangerously soothing.

"Get some rest," Logan says. "The others will be here soon."

His words barely register as I slip under.

Forty

JESS

The next morning, I tiptoe out of the guest room like a teenager sneaking home from a party.

The bathroom light is on, but it's probably my dad since Jace never wakes up before sunrise unless he's forced to. I shower, my muscles relax, and I'm in a surprisingly good mood, considering I have to deal with my parents soon.

I take a long time getting ready and wear jeans and a sweater. Mom will disapprove, no doubt, but that doesn't bother me as much as it usually does.

Downstairs, the chef has returned, bringing stacks of French toast, berries, apple juice, and strips of bacon.

Unusually hungry today, I take a full plate. I've started on my second when Marshal appears. He's wearing the same clothes as yesterday and has his rider jacket back on.

His light brown hair is damp, and I kick myself for the missed opportunity.

Since he re-entered my life, two halves of me war with each other, the one like a feral dog released into the wild for the first time, and the other is obedient, trained. Restrained.

Jury is out on who will win.

Our eyes meet, and he pours himself a cup of coffee.

"Good morning," he says. "How'd you sleep?"

"Very well, thank you," I reply cheerily.

He laughs and shakes his head. "I'll be honest, that bed up there might need a handyman to look at it. Several times, it shook, and I was afraid there was an earthquake."

Jace enters, wearing loose shorts, looking like he got in a fight with his hairbrush.

"You're up early," I say absently.

He pins me with a hard look, reminding me of our father when Mom insisted on bringing four suitcases for an overnight trip. "Kinda hard to sleep when you share a wall with the guest room."

Flames radiate up my neck and the sides of my face.

Oh, shit. I was so caught up in what we were doing that I didn't even consider Jace next door.

"So yeah," he says, turning away. "I'm going back to bed." He carries the bacon sandwich out of the kitchen and up the stairs.

Marshal and I share a look before laughing.

His comm dings, and the smile fades from his face.

"What is it?" I sip my apple juice. It's station business and totally not my concern, but whatever is affecting him this way must be serious.

Marshal curses and sets his plate down. "I gotta call the shuttle. Something's happened to a rider."

I hate that I instantly think of Heath, especially after what happened last night, but old habits die so very hard.

"Who?"

"A novice named Callum. An unbonded colt kicked him pretty good last night, and he's being transferred to Delford General."

"Oh, that's awful," I say, covering my mouth. "Is he all right?"

His lips curve into a crooked smile. "Just a dislocated shoulder and some broken ribs. But since Lugsen had to help with the transfer, they need me back." He pauses and taps his comm. "This is Station Manager Marshal Clemmons. I need a shuttle sent to North Delford Hills port."

"Henry can drive you." I pause. Shit. The brunch. I'm going to miss it. Mother is still in bed and will be unbearable if I wake her this early. Consequences be damned. "Drive us," I correct, and the worry eases from Marshal's forehead just an inch.

"Let me get my bag and meet you out front in ten." I slide off the stool and hurry upstairs to pack my suitcase.

An hour later, we sit on a small shuttle as the propellers kick on and lift us into the sky.

I steal a glance at Marshal on my right, staring at his comm, replying to messages he's neglected. Nothing is set in stone, I tell myself.

I promised him one week.

A trial run. On my terms.

It's scary and exciting, all wrapped in one.

Although if my future looks anything like last night, I'm optimistic.

It's a private shuttle, so just the two of us and the one attendant on board. I rise to get my comm charger from the luggage rack. Private shuttles like this often carry additional cargo, such as packages or mail, for extra income. I unzip my bag and hear a grunt from one of the plastic containers.

"What the hell?"

I'm ready to call the attendant when the lid pops off, and my brother scrambles out of the bin.

"Jace?" I shout. "What are you doing? You aren't supposed to be here! You're supposed to be with Mom and Dad."

"Yeah, well," he says. "Spending my holiday break on the yacht with them sounded like no fun."

"You can't go to Blackhawk with us," I say, spinning on my heel to summon the attendant.

Jace grabs my hand. "Wait! I just want to see the station. I've never seen the druadans up close. I promise I'll stay out of the way. Just let me hang out with you until school starts."

"No. Absolutely not. You're far too young and mother and father—"

"Won't even notice I'm gone."

I place a hand on my hip, frowning, even as his words instill a pang in my chest. He raises his eyebrows and gives me his best puppy dog look.

I let out an exasperated breath. "All right. But only if Master Rider Clemmons agrees."

"Deal!" He darts toward the main cabin.

With no choice but to follow, I find him seated in the chair opposite where Marshal and I had been sitting.

Marshal appears mildly surprised and watches me as I sit.

"Stowaway?"

"Yes," I grumble, rubbing my face. "He has something he wants to ask you."

Jace sits sideways, taking up both chairs, looking exceedingly comfortable for a kid who will most likely be grounded until he's eighteen.

He laces his hands behind his head. "So, yeah, after you

talked about the druadans, I thought I could hang out with you guys for a few days. I promise I'll stay out of your way. I just thought it'd be fun to see the station and rub it in Sawyer and Bodhi's faces when I go back to school."

Tense, I wait for Marshal to tell him no and request the shuttle to turn around, but to my surprise, he sits back, studying Jace for a moment. "Yeah, sure, why not?"

"Marshal," I say, astonishment lacing my words. "Surely you have to ask Fiaro before bringing a kid to the station."

Marshal gives me a subtle wink and a smirk that's only meant for me. He knows exactly why I don't want Jace there. This was supposed to be our time. An opportunity for us to determine if there's something truly worth pursuing between us. "What do you say about staying in the barracks with the riders? I might even have you shadow one for the day. You could probably use it as extra credit."

Jace's eyes light up. "No shit? That'd be awesome!"

"Language," I say, but he ignores me, and I'm not sure why I even bother anymore.

"All right." Marshal laughs. "They might put you to work, though, so I don't want to hear any complaints about calluses."

"Deal," he says, grinning. "Thank you!"

An hour passes, and Jace falls asleep after the attendant brings us lunch trays. A tuna melt, with tomato soup and berries on the side. I opt for seltzer water over wine, wanting to keep a clear head back at Blackhawk. The whole station makes me uneasy, like I'm an outsider in a boy's club. I deal with that enough in our family's business meetings.

Marshal's comm chimes, and he reads the screen intently. "What is it?'

"They found Brigid."

"That's great," I smile, even as my voice sounds weak. Truth was, I hadn't thought about her in...well, in months.

"Is she all right?" I add quickly when a slight crease forms between his brows.

"Bruised and dirty, but overall, yeah. Sounds like she has one hell of a story to tell us."

"I bet," I say, laughing.

"Do you mind if we take a detour to see her before Blackhawk? She's staying at a trawler's house, and I'd like to see how she is."

I force a tight smile. Of course, he wants to see her.

Everyone is always so worried about Brigid.

Marshal must sense my mood shift cause he quickly adds. "It's not like that, so you know."

My temper rises, and the first tendrils of doubt claw at my chest. I knew it was too good to be true.

There's a long silence as both of us stare at each other's faces.

Marshal's full lips curve into a half smile. "As much as I like seeing you jealous, I guess I should tell you there's nothing to worry about."

I scowl, crossing my arms. "And why is that?"

"'Cause she's my sister."

"What?" The word comes out an octave higher than I intended. My cheeks burn with embarrassment. All those times I'd spent analyzing their interactions, the way she'd touched his arm so casually, how they'd laughed at inside jokes I couldn't understand. I'd been building elaborate scenarios in my head about their relationship, torturing myself with imagined histories between them, when all along...

Dammit. How had I missed the similarities? The same slight shape to their eyes, the fullness to their upper lips that I found incredibly sexy in Marshal. It seems so obvious now that I feel utterly ridiculous.

"Oh. I didn't know." I try to keep my voice casual, even as I'm cringing at how transparent my jealousy must have been, how Marshal clearly saw right through me.

Marshal laughs. "No one does. We actually just learned it when she started at Blackhawk. We share a dad." He pauses, then adds before I can ask. "You wouldn't know him. He lives off the continent. Before she left, she and I agreed to keep it on the down low."

My shame eases slightly, and I say, "Ah. So, she's a half-sister?"

Marshal nods, and I look at a sleeping Jace; a string of drool hangs from his mouth. I understand what it means to have a sibling. I'll do anything for Jace. "Okay," I say. "I'll tell the attendant to take a detour."

I summon her over for Marshal to give the coordinates to pass along to the pilot.

When she leaves, we sit in silence, answering work-related messages.

Within minutes, I'm restless.

I key in a message to Marshal. "Meet me in the bathroom. Five minutes."

His comm dings, and he takes a second to register what I wrote. His gaze shifts to mine, blue eyes glinting with heat.

"Bathroom. Five minutes," he answers, and I nearly soak my panties at the tone.

Smiling, I unbuckle and step lightly to the pair of lavatories at the back of the shuttle.

The shuttle bathroom is cramped and reeks of the hyper-sweet artificial flowers used for air fresheners. I press my hands to the side of my too-hot face, staring at the scratched mirror. Am I seriously doing this? As if to confirm, my heart staccatos in my eardrums.

Jace has his headphones and is fast asleep. There's no way he'll ever know...

Seconds tick. Then, a minute.

Doubt begins to plague me, fracturing my confidence.

No, Marshal likes to play, but not about this.

Never about this.

More likely, Jace had woken up and wandered into the main cabin, possibly looking for something to eat or just to visit. I stuff down the flicker of irritation that he stowed away without us knowing.

I frown at the mirror. How long am I supposed to wait?

I squeeze my legs together, the pulsing throb not easing.

Tides, it's been ages since I've been this...horny.

Internally, I cringe and search for a less crude word. *Eager? Hungry?*

Another minute passes, and all hope is gone. I reach for the handle, but it opens before I can touch it.

Marshal blocks the opening and steps in.

I move back, allowing him space to turn and lock the door. The small bathroom is suddenly even more cramped.

"So..."

"So," Marshal smirks. "You invited me in here. Now, what?"

I place my hands on his shoulders, and he drops his to my mid-back, snugging me toward him.

"Now, I want you to fuck me. Not all gentle like before, but really fuck me."

Marshal's eyes widen, but the smirk never leaves his face. "I thought you'd never ask." He swoops down to capture my lips in a hot and hungry kiss.

The small bathroom suddenly feels more cramped as we

struggle to position ourselves closer. He spins me around, and his muscular arms easily hoist me onto the counter.

I ignore the sharp bite of the counter's edge against my thighs.

He scoots me farther back, and I feel the shock of cold from the soap dispenser.

I let out a gasp.

"Shit," Marshal murmurs. "Maybe if I move you this way a little."

"Forget it, just fuck me already. Please, I need—" he silences me with his kiss.

His hands are in my hair, and mine are in his, like we can't get enough of each other.

No candles, no silk sheets, no soft music.

This was none of it, and yet it didn't matter because it was him.

The man who liked me for *me*. The man who saved my brother and all those kids when he could've fled to Blackhawk and left us.

The man who coerced me into walking his dog just so he could get to know me better.

I never thought I'd experience this kind of raw passion, but he proved me wrong.

Again.

His hand caresses my neck, and he kisses me. Longing blooms fresh, and I'm panting like a dog in heat. Still, he doesn't stop. His hand glides down my chest, slowly unbuttoning my blouse.

Strong knuckles graze the swells of my breasts, and the growing heat coalesces in the space between my legs. Still kissing me, his hand lowers to the hem of my plaid skirt, teasing it up higher on my thighs.

The narrow confines of the bathroom make everything more awkward than it already is.

His knee bumps into mine, and laughter bubbles from me before I can press a hand over my mouth.

I giggle at the absurdity of the situation. The shuttle's gentle turbulence makes my stomach dip, amplifying the fluttering already inside my belly.

"Are we really doing this?" I manage to say between breathless kisses.

His hands cup the side of my face. "Hell yeah, we are." Then he presses his mouth to mine, and his tongue dips between my lips. I let his mouth roam and explore as mine does the same. I lower my right hand between us, and I find no zipper.

He's wearing the slip-on athletic shorts. Excitement zings inside me, and I reach lower, feeling the outline of his growing erection through the slick fabric.

I hook a finger into his waistband, but he stops me.

"Not so fast," he says, pulling out of my reach. He levels me with a mischievous gaze. I never noticed the dimple on his right cheek before, hidden under the stubble. I want to study his face. Every freckle, every line, every...

Eyes locked with mine, he drops to his knees. Carefully, he drapes my legs over his shoulders, right then left, then looks up at me like a man starved and I resist the urge to squirm "I've wanted to do this for so fucking long," he growls. "You have no idea how much I've craved this, craved you," he continues, his fingers digging into my thighs possessively. "To have you all to myself, to taste every inch of you, to make you come undone on my tongue."

He pauses, his eyes blazing with an intensity that sends a thrill through me. "I want to devour you, to savor your sweetness until you're trembling and begging for more. You're mine, and I'm going to show you just how much I've been aching for this moment."

His words send a rush of heat straight to my core, and as if sensing my arousal, he drops his gaze and tugs my panties to the side. My heart flutters like a wild, feral thing against my ribcage.

At first, he does nothing but keep still as if letting me settle and grow accustomed to his nearness. The sensation of his hot breath and the scratch of his stubble against the sensitive skin of my inner thigh sends a shiver down my spine.

I rarely let Heath do this to me. The intimacy of his mouth on me always felt too exposing, too raw. With him, it was always a struggle to stay present, my mind drifting to safer, less vulnerable places. But with Marshal, it's different. His firm hands on my thighs hold me, steadying me, anchoring me in the moment.

As his fingers press gently into my flesh, a sense of safety envelops me. I take a deep breath, letting the tension in my body ease as I surrender to the sensations he's eliciting within me.

With Marshal, I feel cherished. His attentiveness makes me believe I'm the only thing that matters and damn if that doesn't make me feel sexy. His knuckles trace along the sensitive skin before his tongue flicks over my core.

Relaxing into his touch, I lean my head against the wall and close my eyes.

The shuttle hits turbulence, and I grab onto his shoulders, which seems to encourage him, and his fingers join with his tongue.

Flicking, nipping, tasting.

His fingers thrust in and out, and the movement draws another low moan from me. For a fleeting second, I worry the attendant is standing outside the door listening, but I'm whisked away by the overwhelming pleasure he's inducing.

He increases the speed of his finger's thrusts, his thumb encircling my sensitive clit. Everything fades, except for this. Except for the feeling of *him*. Pleasure overtakes me, and a rising wave of euphoria spills over, flooding my body with tingling warmth. "Oh, God, Marshal," I gasp, sinking my nails into his shoulders as I climax. My legs shudder and tense, and he buries his head deeper between my legs, coaxing the aftershocks with his tongue and fingers.

"This is so..." I can't finish the sentence, and I feel his breath as he grumbles a laugh between my legs. His tongue slows, circling and focusing on the bundle of nerves still raw from his attentions, and he slips another finger in and curves it, hitting a spot that sends a jolt of pleasure through my body, a sensation so intense it's almost overwhelming.

My fingers lace into his hair, clutching the back of his head, while the other presses against the wall of the shuttle. "I can't," I breathe, the words coming out in a desperate gasp as I feel the edge of release hovering just out of reach.

"Oh, I think you can," he murmurs against my skin, his breath hot and tantalizing. "The Jessica Drakeford I know isn't a quitter. Don't overthink this. I'm not going anywhere until you let go and come for me again."

His words send a thrill through me, and I can't help but believe him. Doubts melting away, his words, he'll stay with me, push me over the edge into ecstasy. I see stars, and my entire body contracts as another orgasm explodes.

I moan, not caring who hears, as he grabs my thighs and buries his face between my legs, his tongue making glorious circles right where I need it most.

Finally, the spasms subside, and slowly, he lowers my legs and stands. The piercing sky-blue depths of his eyes, typically so cool and clear, are now clouded with a fierce, almost primal desire. His lips and the rugged shadow of stubble across his jaw glisten with the wetness of my arousal, and his caramel-colored hair is tousled from my fingers, making him look more feral than he already does.

He leans forward and whispers in my ear. "You have no fucking idea how good you taste. Sweeter than anything. It's going to drive me fucking crazy thinking about it from now on. I'm addicted to you."

His words set off a new wave of desire in me, and I wiggle closer, inching my rear to the edge of the sink. The need to feel him inside me is overwhelming. Greedily, I grab his shoulders, pulling his face to mine with a desperation that surprises even me.

Our mouths crash together, and I taste myself on his lips. It's erotic as hell, intoxicating. A heady mix of our shared pleasure, and as his tongue penetrates my mouth, exploring and claiming, he maneuvers out of his shorts.

He takes my hand from his cheek, moving it slowly down his chiseled abs covered with a fine coat of curly hair until, finally, it rests on the silken skin, cloaking the iron underneath. He breaks our kiss. "Do you feel this?" he says. "Feel how hard you make me? Look how much you turn me on."

I bite my lip, glancing at his impressive length, protruding from a small tuft of hair, then back to his eyes.

"I'm going to fuck you now, Jessica Drakeford. Bury my dick inside you until you've soaked my cock with all that delicious wetness you made for me."

I nearly yelp as he grabs my legs again, spreading them. He aligns himself, and before I have a second to react, he thrusts into me. His thrusts are shallow and irritatingly slow, yet each one sends sparks of pleasure through me. The confined space makes every motion more pronounced. My ass rubs on the counter, and I shove away the idea of how unsanitary this whole thing is.

I shift to angle myself better, and my hand bumps the faucet, sending a spray of water over my back.

"Shit," I curse, voice thick with desire.

I wrap my legs around him, pulling him deeper. His mouth finds mine, stifling our moans as our pace quickens. The tightness builds, his dick hardens with every second, and finally, with a long growl of my name, he comes.

I lock my ankles behind him, holding him to me. Marshal's chest rumbles with a chuckle. His eyes are filled with a mix of desire and amusement. Into my neck, he whispers, "Guess it's a weekend of firsts."

I tilt my head, questioning.

"I officially joined the mile-high club."

I press my lips together, lacing my arms over his neck. "I'll ask if they have a badge."

Forty-One

BRIGID

The sound of voices, low and indistinct, the wooden floorboards groaning under the weight of boots. It takes a second to claw my way through the haze of sleep, and my limbs are sluggish.

"She's been sleeping for hours," Logan says.

"Has she said anything?" Heath's voice.

"Not enough," Logan replies.

I rub a hand over my face to clear the lingering fog and push myself upright. The blanket pools in my lap. It's dark out, but the fire in the hearth has burned lower, only embers now, casting a dull red glow in the room.

Logan, Carter, and Heath stand in a semi-circle nearby as if forming a protective wall between me and the door. Their bodies angle toward each other, but their gazes are locked on me.

They're all here. Doubt lingers, whispering that this is just another dream.

The belief shatters, and my heart soars.

My riders.

Carter's expression tightens, jaw flexing. Heath, standing just behind him, exhales slowly.

They wear their military jackets, speckled with mud, their faces pale beneath a layer of stubble, exhaustion etched into every line. Their boots are caked with dirt, even Heath's. Carter has a new scar above his left eye and Heath's cheeks are hollow, his skin paler than usual.

None of them speak.

I grip the edge of the blanket, my pulse thrumming in my ears. "Uh, hi," I say shyly.

"Good to see you, Ms. Corsair," Heath says stiffly, and I wince.

It's been so long that he's defaulted to calling me that again instead of Brigid.

His face is a mask even as I search for emotions behind his chocolate brown eyes.

The ones I used to read so easily are hidden, like the first time we met.

Carter stares at the ground, and my throat cinches closed.

He won't even look at me.

My mouth moves, but nothing comes out. I'm at a loss for words.

What can I say that will replace the months of silence?

"How did you get here?" I realize that I have no idea where here is.

"Logan told us," Heath says. "We drove all night from Delford."

All night?

"I'm glad you're all here," I say softly.

Carter still avoids my gaze.

Before we can say anything else, Waylon enters, asking if we're hungry.

"Breakfast would be appreciated," Heath says brightly, and as if, with a flick of a switch, the tension between us is gone, leaving me with dizzying emotional whiplash. It almost hurts as bad as Carter's cold shoulder. *Almost.*

"So long as we aren't imposing," I add, pasting a tightlipped smile on my face.

"Not at all." Waylon shakes his head. "I traded a plastic sign of a naked lady on a motorcycle, and the guy was so grateful he gave me two of these crates. They're missing their labels. Novi and I like to call it 'Ration Roulette.'"

Logan's comm buzzes, and he looks to Waylon, who's taking cans out of a crate.

"Looks like we got a few more coming," he says to Waylon.

Waylon's sunburned brow furrows. "All right. You trust them?"

"I do," he says, sorting through the cans.

He shrugs and returns to sorting the cans, discarding any with significant dents or bloating.

"Who is it?" Carter asks as we all turn to Logan.

Logan looks over at me. "I told Marshal Brigid was here. Jess and her kid brother Jace apparently stowed aboard, so he's with them, too."

My stomach does a small flip. Marshal's coming here? Would he be mad at me also, for leaving? Tides, it seems like I have a long list of apologies ahead of me.

Waylon looks to Nova, setting out spoons. "There are still the mattresses in the hangar, right?" Nova shrugs, indifferent. "Yeah," he says, returning his gaze to us. "We can make room."

"I swear we'll be out of your hair in a few days as soon as we figure things out," Heath says. "I understand Logan promised to pay you, and I have more money if you—"

Waylon shakes his head. "Don't worry. He settled up. I could use a hand with some things if y'all are eager to earn your keep, though?"

Heath and Carter nod.

"No use waiting for your friends to eat. I've got some unmarked cans to open. Who knows, maybe we'll get lucky and find some peaches?"

All six of us sit on the benches surrounding the table.

Waylon presents a tray of unlabeled metal cans and begins using a can opener to open them.

"I've never met a trawler before," I say.

"That's not surprising." He slides a lid off and plops a blob of creamed corn into a bowl. He sets it in the center, but no one reaches for it. "There's not many of us left, and we avoid the big cities. Meeting up with the brokers at their warehouses, or having drop sites of our own where payment occurs via Network deposits, or useful items like food, clothing, fuel for our shuttles are left for trade."

I notice the others listening. Trawlers were so rare and reclusive that there's a good chance none of them had met one, let alone spent this much time with one. "That sounds lonely. All the way out here from civilization?"

"At times."

"I'll be honest," Heath says, spooning some peas from another bowl. "You're not at all what I expected."

He slaps his leg and laughs. "Expecting a third eye and glowing skin, were ya? I could say the same for you. I see your uniforms. I know riders, and yet here you are, hiding out at my place, hours from the nearest fuel station when the roads are clear, with nothing but dust and folks like us for company. No shops, no restaurants. Hell, not even a decent cup of coffee within a hundred miles."

"There are others like you?" Carter says, ignoring the jab at him and Heath abandoning their posts. I know their choice was hard and what it meant. I also know they didn't need me bringing it up, rubbing salt in the wound. Besides, I was the absolute last person to judge anyone for making desperate and reckless choices.

"You bet," he says, prying open another can. The smell of cinnamon fills my nostrils, and I realize it's apple pie filling. "See, you've got your regular adrenaline junkies, rich kids mostly," I don't miss his pointed stare at Heath, "they're bored and want to get a taste of real danger, so come out here in their custom vehicles or parachute from shuttles, often getting lost or ending up at one of our doorsteps begging to use a comm." He rocks back in his chair. "Then there's the Rust Punks. Shady gangs that think they can control territories. They love to squabble amongst themselves, so I do my best to steer clear of them. Then there are trawlers like me. We respect the TZ, keep our heads low, and if we're lucky, it rewards us enough to keep food in our bellies and a roof over our heads. What we risk our lives to find allows us to live on the fringes, on our own terms and away from Circuit control."

Aside from the rappelling from a hovering shuttle to dig through rubble, it didn't sound that bad. Our disappointing Reco trips are proof enough that trawlers know where the good stuff is, and it isn't just lying around. It's like the old tales of the gold rushes where the first pioneers had tripped over gold nuggets. But then, with more and more people seeking their fortune, they'd resorted to panning, then digging, then mining until it was all gone.

And that happened in less than a decade. Try nearly a millennium.

The fact that Waylon and others like him can find anything of value anymore is astonishing.

There's a murmur of voices outside, and Waylon, faster than I thought a man could move, takes his rifle from the hook on the wall. Logan pulls his knife and strides to the door.

"Who is it?" Waylon yells.

The murmuring stops, and then, "It's me, Marshal Clemmons." Everyone breathes a collective sigh of relief as we recognize Marshal's voice.

Logan and Waylon exchange a glance before Logan lifts the lock and opens the door.

Marshal, a chestnut-haired teenage boy in a designer t-shirt and jeans, and a very disgusted-looking Jessica Drakeford stand on the stoop.

Morning light streams around their bodies, and I notice his hand is in hers. Holy shit, I had missed a lot.

I get out of my seat, and Marshal's eyes scan the room, finding me. He releases her hand and dashes toward me, grinning. The tension of the moment eases as he pulls me in and smashes me in a hug against his broad chest.

"Thank God you're alive."

He squeezes me too hard, and I can barely catch my breath. I urgently tap him on the back, and he releases me. He grips my shoulders, peering down at me. "We were all so worried." His eyes drift from mine to Logan standing behind me.

"Thank you," he says, offering a nod, his eyes softening with gratitude.

Logan runs a hand over the top of his head, fingers running over the ash-brown hair that's recently been clipped short. "I only did half the job. Waylon is the one you should be thanking."

Marshal pivots his gaze and goes to the man in patched

overalls, setting the rifle back on the rack. He claps him on the shoulder. "I can never thank you enough."

"I owed your friend a favor, happy I could repay it."

Jess clears her throat and appears next to him. Beside her is a boy nearly her height with similar colored blue eyes but warmer skin and the same raven black hair. It's trimmed neatly and styled with gel.

"This is Jess," he says, introducing her to Waylon. "And her brother, Jace."

"Ah, nice to meet ya. This is Nova." He gestures to his daughter. "She seems to be around your age. How old are ya?"

"Thirteen, sir."

Waylon chuckles. "My, aren't we the proper one? Well, take a seat. We got some extra."

Logan moves over, letting the other three scoot in.

Marshal grins like he's won the grand prize at a carnival, his gaze lingering on all of us. On his left, Jess doesn't look amused, and I can't help noticing her not looking at me.

Had Marshal told her we were brother and sister, or was she secretly jealous when he hugged me? Whatever reason we kept it secret before seems so pointless now the world is crumbling.

My eyes dip to her flat stomach.

She'd be showing by now if she were pregnant, right?

It hadn't worked. It hadn't been enough.

All those weeks of wondering and waiting. The question hanging over me like a storm cloud since I left Blackhawk all those months ago clears, and relief floods through me, sudden and bright, but in its wake comes a hollow ache of regret.

I drained from Oriana for that chance, pulled the last of her to temper Heath's bond, and let their families merge. All that sacrifice, all that risk... for nothing. The weight of it settles on my shoulders as I stare at the evidence of our failure.

I have no idea if the merger went through with or without the baby or if it failed, and all those people lost their jobs. I was kept in the dark for so long, and now, in some laughable way, it all seems almost trivial. We'd been very small sparks fighting against a tidal wave of disasters. The audacity of it strikes me now, standing here. How naive were we to think we could stop the country's collapse? What did we really think we could accomplish?

Everyone resumes talking, pulling me back to the present, and Marshal fills us in on the terrorist activity causing a lockdown at Thornwick Academy and other news we missed. Food rationing. Network's instability, and wealthy families leaving on yachts or to Gaergen Island.

Jace reaches for one of the half-empty cans of chicken and gravy at the same time as Nova. Their hands brush, and there's a flicker of a moment when they look at each other before each recoil, cheeks flaming.

I smile to myself. No one else noticed.

Jace reaches again, this time sliding it over to her.

Nova smiles sheepishly and digs her spoon into the can.

"You have children?" Waylon asks.

Heath and Marshal look uncomfortable, and Logan is so preoccupied with the collection of antique weaponry displays I don't think he heard.

"Riders can't reproduce," Carter answers. "But damn how we love to try."

Carter shoots me a mischievous grin, and Heath and Jess both take sips from their drinks.

Nova and Jace laugh, earning a scowl from her father.

We are intimately aware of the half-truth this is. Although Jess isn't pregnant, so maybe he is right. I thought pulling back the bonds would allow them to have a child. Maybe I'd missed something.

"It's getting late," Waylon says. "And don't lie to me and tell me you've done all the chores. Why don't you take Jace with you and have him help?" Waylon looks at Jess. "If that's alright with you?"

Jess purses her lips and gives a timid nod. "If it's safe."

Waylon laughs. "It is. We've got two goats that need fed, and more wood brought in."

Seeming to agree, she nods to Jace, and the two kids slide off the bench and go to the door. Nova tugs on her boots and grabs the pail off the hook by the door.

"Don't forget your masks," Waylon calls out.

Nova tilts her head back in annoyance and snags it from the bench. She hands a spare one to Jace, then plops it on her head, not bothering to strap the cord under her chin, and exits through the door.

Waylon massages his temples. "That girl got her mother's red hair and all the willfulness that came with it. The men in her future are in for one hell of a time."

"You really didn't know riders are sterile?" Marshal asks.

Waylon shakes his head and pours another glass of the clear liquor. "You hear things, rumors and such, but since we aren't connected to Network we never can confirm if any of it is true." He takes a sip. "Say, for instance, how some riders die a year or two into their term while others, like yourself, live longer."

To his credit, Marshal doesn't react, at least not enough for me to notice.

"So now we're all here," Heath says, wiping his face with one of the rags that serve as napkins. "I think Ms. Corsair is overdue for a little chat, don't you?"

My cheeks burn. "Oh, I'm ready, alright, if you stop calling me that. I'm Brigid. You know me."

"Do we?" Carter asks, heat lacing his voice. "Cause I sure as hell don't think I do anymore."

Marshal waves a hand. "Easy, James." A subtle warmth blooms in my chest that Marshal re-engaged protective big brother mode so easily.

Under the gazes of everyone around me, my ribs feel like they're cracking in two, and a tear slides down my cheek.

"I'm sorry," I say, speaking the words I've held onto for so long. "I didn't mean to hurt you." My eyes drift between everyone, quickly moving past Jess's. "Any of you."

Heath and Logan shift in their seats, and I stop on Carter.

Emotions cloud the vibrant green color of his eyes that I missed so much.

"Why?" he says, voice low and hard as if it takes everything, he has to speak it. "Why did you leave us?"

The knife piercing my chest twists, and the steel in his voice drives it deeper.

"I didn't want to," I say over a choked sob. "But I didn't know what else to do. Oriana was dying, and there was only one way I could help her. Sharice had the other egg. Agent Zane said they had an ITM rebel in custody, so I promised him I'd help him find my sister if he let me talk to him." I pause, my eyes drifting between them. "The other egg hatched."

None of them move. If this is news to them, they don't show it. Sharice clung to that secret, but perhaps Zane had leaked it to CSU with Carter's connections. Perhaps this wasn't news to them.

"I went to my mom, knowing my sister would still be in contact with her, and then Sharice took me to her base." I pause again, regaining my voice as I remember how they'd drugged me. "Sharice said she could save Oriana but made me promise to stay. She..." my voice breaks again. "She was watching us. The whole time."

Heath squints at me, and Carter's shoulders stiffen under his jacket.

"Doctor Gideon," Marshal says. "He was told to send Oriana to one of the science stations shortly after you left. I knew there was something odd about that."

I nod. "Sharice...ITM," I correct. "They have connections everywhere."

"Did she tell you why she was ill?" Heath asks.

I raise my chin. "It was because of us."

The four riders watch me, their brows creased with confusion.

"When I did what I did at the bonds at Blackhawk," I say, and Jess shifts uncomfortably in her seat. "It weakened her. I didn't know it at the time, but somehow she kept all the riders there from brimming, stabilizing them, but then I tapped into her and it was too much. It drained her, and that's why she was dying."

My eyes flit from face to face, noticing the tight-set jaws and darkened eyes. They're all feeling the guilt, even though it wasn't their fault.

"I knew there was a reason no one was flaring," Heath says, and Marshal murmurs in agreement. "So, moving her away from the station saved her?"

Nodding, I sniff and wipe another tear from my face, months of resentment and, anger and fear crashing down on me. "I wanted to leave," I say, my voice trembling. "but every time I tried, Sharice threatened to use her connections to hurt you or Oriana."

The raw words hang in the air.

"Lovely," Jess says, sarcasm staining her words. "All of us can be found guilty of colluding with a former terrorist now." She sighs. "Isn't this goddamn great?"

Logan cracks a smile at her rare foul language. "I have to

agree with the Ice Queen on this one. You two ditched Specter. Marshal redirected Blackhawk's shuttle, and everyone thinks I'm dead."

Logan's words solidify the direness of our situation.

All of us are branded as traitors and deserters.

As it stands, there is no slipping easily back to our old lives. Every government official and security checkpoint will be looking for us.

Specter would want their operatives back or silenced. Blackhawk would be hunting for Marshal after his betrayal. And Logan—officially labeled a felon and recorded as deceased—was now a ghost, existing in the cracks between systems.

No one is supposed to escape the TZ prison sentence, and I doubt Circuit will take kindly to someone proving their prisons aren't as secure as they claim.

I glance at each of their faces, seeing our shared predicament reflected on me. Freedom and exile, all at once.

"You might have a chance, Marshal," Heath says. "If you leave now, no one can connect you to any of us."

Marshal shakes his head. "I'm not leaving until I know Brigid is safe."

Jess frowns but doesn't protest. There really is something going on with her and Marshal.

"That's a pretty big ask, all things considered," Waylon says. "Parts of the country is either at war with ITM or rioting or choking to death. The damn air currents are some of the worst I've ever seen. I don't know how much longer we can stay here."

A walnut-sized lump forms in the back of my throat. "You can't."

Everyone's gaze shifts to me. "Circuit has been lying to us," I say, my voice timid. "The tox zones are spreading."

Waylon claps his hand on the table. "I knew it! I told Merv

the perimeter was growing, and that asshat didn't believe me. He owes me fifty credits next time I—"

"You're wrong," Jess says, cutting him off. "Circuit isn't perfect, but they'd never cover up something like that."

Marshal moves his hand to hers on the table, drawing everyone's attention. Her mouth twitches, but she doesn't withdraw. "I've worked at the station long enough to know there's lots of shit they keep from the public for all sorts of reasons. Something as big as this would cause panic and add fuel to the fire they're trying to smother."

"You have proof?" Heath asks me.

"Only the data they stole from Lanett's labs." I spoon a helping of peaches from the assortment of cans on the table, trying not to spill any juice.

Logan scoffs. "What's next? Delford flooding?"

Heath frowns, and Carter's eyes widen slightly. "ITM blew the levees last night. Delford *is* flooded."

Logan blinks. "No shit."

"I got an alert before we came here," Jess says. "Everything below thirteenth is under water. They have first responders and rescue teams there, but they expect casualties in the hundreds."

She genuinely sounds sad, remorseful even, definitely not the same woman three months ago who would've callously announced how this would increase her hilltop property values.

The world really has changed while I was gone.

"We did all we could to help," Heath says, "but it was clear ITM had the upper hand. We got our unit on the truck to evacuate before stealing a car."

I don't miss the regret in his voice. They are AWOL. They'll be considered traitors now in Circuit's eyes. My thoughts push ahead. Their stallions. They left them behind, too.

I drop my eyes to my hands furled in my lap. They imploded their lives for *me*. Sacrificed everything to be here.

"How long?" Carter asks.

"It's all dependent on the weather, seasons, concentration levels, but best-case scenario based on..."

"*How* long?" Logan demands.

"February," I blurt. "Best case, we have a month,"

"That can't be right?" Marshal says, eyeing me incredulously.

I frown. "We had scientists there, ones that worked at Lanett and they ran the models in different ways. They said the chemicals are reacting with the soil faster than before and rapidly expanding at an exponential rate." I realize I'm repeating verbatim what Sharice told me in the lab when I asked her the same question. A fresh wave of pain washes over me. She should be here, telling them this, not me. She is the smart one. The brave one. Not the one who impulsively ran from people who cared about her.

A long, tense silence invades the room.

Carter scoffs. "All this time, the world was ending, and nobody thought to tell us?"

I take in their expressions: fear, hopelessness, anger. All of which I experienced when I first learned of it. I carried this burden of knowledge for months, and it feels like a weight is lifted as the truth finally spills into the open.

Jess straightens her shoulders. "There must be something we can do. My father sits on Circuit's board. He has access to the highest levels of clearance and connections. We can tell him what we know. I know he can convince President Peterson to push for emergency research funding to organize mass evacuations. There's still time to fix this."

"Jess," I say carefully, "I understand why you'd think that, but—"

"No, you don't understand." Her eyes blaze. "It's obvious you've given up. *We* haven't. My family can mobilize millions of credits overnight. Someone just needs to pay the right people to find a solution."

Marshal's hand, still on hers, squeezes it gently. Her eyes cool to their ambient frosty expression. It still didn't make sense how the two of them worked. She's like the winter wind seeping in through the cabin's wall and the sun's rays streaming in, pooling on the floor, and filling the room with a warm honey-colored light.

It's growing more and more obvious. When he's near, she softens just enough for the frost to glitter instead of bite. And when she's near, he quiets, his movements more deliberate.

She makes him think before he speaks. He makes her breathe before she strikes.

"Brigid," he says, looking at me. "Jess might be onto something. We could get back to Blackhawk and pool our resources. Maybe they're wrong about the timeline. Maybe it'll spread and then stop. No one knows why it hasn't cleared out and dissipated yet."

I watch him with a sad smile. Tides, I hope he's right.

Logan scoffs. "What the hell is the point of doing anything if we're going to die soon, anyway? None of it fucking matters anymore. It's our final fucking days. We should do whatever we want and not give a shit."

"I've had months to process this," I say quietly. "To rage, to deny, to bargain. To accept. You're all still in shock."

I move to the window, gazing at the deceptively normal sky.

Circuit was so focused on ITM that they missed the even bigger looming threat, or they denied it. The cancerous tumor we ignored for centuries, ignorantly claiming it was benign when, in fact, the malignancy was spreading.

"So that's it?" Carter's voice has lost its edge. "We just wait to die?"

"That's part of what I was working on with Sharice. It's what ITM promises to get people to join the movement. They're trying to find a way to make people immune to the toxic air."

"And did they?" Marshal asks.

I grind my teeth, stalling my response. To tell them about the banshees or my ability to force bonds on them. My hand drifts self-consciously to the implant in my neck. "We started the process, but the side effects were too severe."

"And then the base was attacked," Heath finishes for me.

"But I don't get it," Carter asks. "Why bring back the mystyl? Why attack the cities when they're claiming their purpose is to help people?"

I purse my lips. "To send a message that Circuit can't get away with keeping things from us."

Logan curses under his breath.

Carter barks a dry laugh. "Are you fucking kidding me? All of it was to prove a point? I watched friends die. Watched riders forced to mercy-kill their stallions too wounded to make it back to the shuttle. Saw them afterward, hunched and hollow, clawing at their chests until their fingernails drew blood as if they could somehow reach in and soothe the phantom burn where the bond had once lived, all because ITM needed to send a *message?*"

Before I can reply, Carter shoves himself up from the table hard enough to shake it, knocking over several cans and rattling silverware. "Fuck!" he yells and punches the nearby wall.

The shelf teetering with miscellaneous knick-knacks shifts, a rubber duck and a plastic lid to a bucket slide off and thuds on the floor.

Heath's eyes meet mine, and a glimmer of concern passes over them.

"I'm sorry about your friends, rider," Waylon says. "But do you mind not damaging the cabin?"

Carter lowers his clenched hand and stares at the floor. I see it now, the invisible burden he carries from leading Specter through mission after mission. Each decision, each life lost, has carved lines into his face that weren't there before

No wonder he won't forgive me. He can't forgive himself.

Marshal frowns, then slowly sets the tipped cans upright. "If this High Navigator is as powerful as you say, there's a good chance he escaped before Circuit attacked, which means we have to assume he's still out there and may find a way to continue with his plan."

I tear my gaze away from Carter. "I agree, and there were other bases than the one I was at breeding mystyl. They'll bounce back. If Elton *is* alive, then ITM is still a threat, which means every Lanett lab is in danger." My eyes drift around the room, acknowledging everyone's rapt attention. "He knows Oriana is valuable and will leverage that however he can."

"He's going to kill her," Heath says. "As a way to send a message to Circuit."

"Not if we get her first," I say, with every ounce of conviction in my words.

Forty-Two

LOGAN

It's official. Blondie has fucking lost it.

"Are you serious?" I argue. "Even if we figure out which one of the dozens of Lanett labs she's at, then find a pilot gullible or greedy enough to take us there and get past the layers of security, we still have the big fucking problem of sneaking a whole ass druanera out without anyone noticing."

Brigid huffs a breath, flicking a loose strand of hair from her face. "I didn't say it'd be easy," she says, cocking a hip. "I said it was the only way to keep her safe. Elton wants her, and if we have her here, maybe we could figure out why?"

"Or maybe *you* just want her here," Carter says, his words laced with anger. "Then run back to your ITM buddies like some hero."

Brigid's eyes swim with tears.

Fuck, he's gone too far. She's barely keeping her shit together.

"No," she says, almost too soft for me to hear. "That's not it at all."

Carter steps closer, eyes boring into her. I rest a hand on the hilt of my knife. I've never seen him like this before. To be honest, I didn't know he had it in him.

"Then what is it? Why should we trust anything you say when you've been living with the sadistic terrorists we're fighting? How do we know any of the shit you say is true?"

Brigid scrambles off the bench so hard it scrapes against the floor. "I'm sorry."

She's gone before either of us can move.

The door swings open, then slams shut.

Brigid took my bond. Stripped it from me without hesitation. He should hate her for it. Hell, *I* should hate her for it. But I don't. Because the truth is, she didn't ruin me. She freed me.

If I hadn't gone to her, I never would've found the gun. Without the bond, I walked into that base, knowing no matter how long it took, I could handle it.

Some battles are meant to be lost.

I had weeks to process the loss of my bond and realized Blondie didn't steal something that wasn't already slipping through my fingers. The second Galaxian killed that man at Meridian, my life as a rider ended. She merely nudged the train that was already steaming down the tracks. I wish to hell I knew why.

He caught feelings. And I should know because despite everything in my upbringing telling me not to grow attached to anyone, I had to.

"Carter," Heath says before I can.

"No," he says, shaking his head. "Don't."

"We know—" Heath starts to say, but Carter interrupts him.

"She just left us," he shouts. "And then was with the enemy

we've been fighting for months." He pins me with a stern look. "She cut your goddamn bond, Logan." His voice is pinched, straining now.

I hold his gaze and imagine what I'd feel in the bond right now. Anger. Frustration. Fear. Fear she'd do it to him or Heath. "She didn't mean to," I growl. "She was only trying to push me away before the rebels showed up. It was an accident."

"And so, what, you just forgave her?"

Yeah, and then I fucked her, I think but keep it to myself. Carter has that look in his eyes, and as much as I want to watch him combust, Heath wants me to convince him to make up with Brigid. "Yes, because that's what we do. The four of us. We forgive each other like you forgave me after what I said to her before she left."

The muscles under his stubble shift as he considers my words.

"Don't you get it? There aren't any sides anymore. There's no right or wrong. The world is ending in a month. There's no changing the past." My voice is steady. "But we can change *now*."

"If we're going to die," I continue, "I want to know I did everything I fucking could until the end. No half-assing it. No bullshit regrets. If that mare is somehow the key to stopping ITM, then I'm not wasting time being pissed about the past."

Tension fills the room as Carter's chest heaves, his biceps flexing.

I dare him to throw a punch. I'd welcome the physical pain if it meant relieving his.

"Now," I say slowly. "Go fix this so we can make a goddamn plan."

Forty-Three

CARTER

Outside the cabin, I spot Brigid a short distance away on the path, eyes fixed on the dense forest sloping down toward the TZ.

A well-worn oxygen mask hangs around her neck. I overheard Waylon say the currents were shifted this morning, so the air was breathable, but, like her, I brought a mask anyway.

The morning sun sifts through drifting clouds, casting fleeting shadows over the surrounding hills.

I step up beside her.

How the hell am I supposed to mend a wound when it's already scarred over? I fell for a woman harder than I'd fallen for anything or anyone, and when I needed her most, she was gone. I was forced to become a soldier, to live a life I thought I escaped when I became a rider. It transformed me into something I hate. Hardened me.

"I want to apologize," I say.

"There's nothing to apologize for," she says. "You're right about everything. You can't trust me. I was with ITM. I helped them. Lived with them." She glances at me briefly, then turns back, but not before I see the wetness of tears on her cheeks. "I should've tried harder to escape, I should've fought harder to resist, I should've never taken Logan's bond." She pauses, her voice catching. She turns fully and peers up at me. The blue of her irises reflects the passing clouds overhead. Her face is thinner, her skin paler, but there's still the fullness to her lips, lashes a shade darker than her hair, and the handful of freckles on her perfect nose I know extend elsewhere.

"You have no idea what it was like," I say, voice tight. "Waking up every day, not knowing if you were alive or dead. Wondering if you were suffering or if you chose to leave. It was fucking torture."

"I do know," she says, "because I felt the same way. You, Heath, and Logan are the reason I survived. The reason I kept trying to find a way to save Oriana, a way to stop the air from getting worse, a way to find my way back to you."

Her words do little to ease the tension between my shoulder blades. "I..." I hesitate, then continue. "I tried so damn hard to stay the man you remember. The one who stole champagne for you, the one who made you moan my name in the orchard, the one who loved you from the first moment I saw you. But I watched Heath shut down and Logan unravel, and it changed me. Even though I stayed true, I'm not the man you left, Brigid. He's gone."

Her eyebrows widen at the admission that I didn't sleep with anyone else. I'd be lying if I hadn't been tempted. Three god damn months is the longest I've ever gone without sex. But I could hardly even think about it without instantly feeling sick.

She reaches out and rubs a thumb over my cheek. "No," she whispers. "I still see him. He's bruised and battered, but he's still there."

A vice clamps around my heart, and I want more than anything to believe her.

"I'm not the same either," she continues. "How could I be? The things I did with…" Her voice breaks. "Things I can never take back. Every day, I wonder if I'm even worthy of you."

The tension in my body breaks, and with a swift motion, I pull her to me. The filters of our masks collide as my hands find her waist, overcome by the need to feel that she's real that she's here. "You are worthy," I tell her fiercely before capturing her lips with mine.

The kiss is hard, desperate. Months of longing, fear, and anger all pour into this single moment. I taste the salt of her tears and feel the tremble in her body as she clings to me just as desperately.

When we break apart, I press my forehead to hers, my breath ragged.

This is real. She is real. Everything I felt. Everything we felt wasn't some dream I conjured to keep the darkness away.

I cradle her face in my hands, thumbs brushing away her tears. "Look at me, Brigid." Her eyes are vulnerable and hopeful. "You are the center of my existence," I murmur against her lips. "The axis around which my world turns. Every day without you was like living in shadow, and now—" my voice catches, "—now it's like I can finally fucking breathe."

She presses closer as if trying to eliminate any space between us.

"I still love you." The words spill from me. "I never stopped, not for a single fucking second and I don't care what either of us has done or what we've become. All that matters is you're here with me."

I kiss her again, softer this time, savoring the way her body melts against mine, the way her fingers thread through my hair. Heat flares up my back and neck, white hot.

She yelps and steps back, staring at her hands. "Tides, Carter. You're hot."

I blink. My mind buzzes from the growing bulge in my pants, the kissing has induced. "Damn right I am."

She looks wide-eyed from her hands to my face. "Do you smell that?"

"Smell what?" I lie, I reach out to her, encircling her waist with my hands.

"Something is burning."

The pain intensifies, hovering just below unbearable, and I release her. I draw in a slow breath through my nose, forcing it to steady. This marks the second shirt I've destroyed, something about my sweat reacting with the fabric, an unusual side effect of either the O-strike or my brimming, or both. The doctors can't give me a clear answer.

I strip off my jacket, smelling the burning of the fabric.

I gesture to the cabin, not wanting to alarm Brigid. "Waylon probably tossed something in the fire."

She doesn't look convinced.

"So," I say, wanting to change the subject. "What do you say we go back in there and figure out how to save the fucking world?"

Brigid smiles up at me, and it makes me want to take back everything I said and strip off her clothes right then and there, but then Logan's voice from the cabin snatches that thought.

"You two kiss and make up?"

Brigid laughs and bites her bottom lip. My cock surges fully to attention.

"Oh yeah," I say, my eyes never leaving hers. "We're *all* good."

Forty-Four

BRIGID

Back inside, I sit between Carter and Logan. My lips still tingle from Carter's passionate kiss, and it's hard to keep focused with so much masculine energy surrounding me.

I forgot how much I miss them just being around. Their presence. Their smell, the sounds of their voices, the way they watched me when they didn't think I was looking.

Heath moves to the head of the table and writes on a piece of scrap packing material.

He sketches out four rectangular buildings surrounding one large octagonal one.

Marshal eyes the two of them cautiously, no doubt wondering if he still needs to defend me against him.

I flash him a reassuring smile, and the crease on his forehead disappears.

"Now that you're back," he says, "We talked, and I remember Dr. Gideon saying they sent Oriana to the Lannet lab near Parnia. I distinctly remember because he told the pilot in front of me before he left, and the pilot said it cost extra."

"This is Lannet's station in Parnia," Marshal says. "I've only been there once but have a pretty good memory of the layout."

"Okay, so we know what it looks like. That doesn't help us get in, though. I know for a fact they've increased security since..." I pause. "Since we raided them."

Marshal offers me a reassuring smile and nods. "We could try paying off a guard? Or perhaps I could ask Fiaro for a transfer of—"

"No," Heath says. "No one else can be involved."

Marshal sighs and leans back, lacing his fingers behind his head. "Fine. I'm open to suggestions."

Everyone is silent for a long time, contemplating.

Jess rises from her seat and, with a finger, traces the outline of the octagonal building on the charcoal-drawn map. "I know a way."

"How?" Marshal asks.

"The Drakeford name still holds weight," she says. "For now, anyway. They won't question why I'm there. And if they do, I'll give them a reason they can't refuse."

"What reason?" Marshal presses, frowning from across the table.

Jess lifts her chin, eyeing the room cooly. "I'm going to buy it."

I suppress a laugh, but Carter isn't so discrete. "You're out of your mind. You might have the money, but they'll never sell to you."

Jess gives him a sardonic look. "Don't you think I know

that? Of course they won't. Circuit's got all their research facilities wrapped tight in an iron fist." She slides her hand along the map, her long fingers tracing the outline of the octagonal building. "No, I know they'll never agree to an offer, but unless they want to incur the ire of my father, they'll humor me for some time. Long enough for you to sneak off my shuttle, get the druanera, and then get back on without setting off a single alarm."

My mind races through the implications. "Your shuttle would land inside the gated facility?"

"That's the beauty of it," Jess says, a hint of pride in her voice. "Daddy's daughter wants a tour. They're not going to make me park outside like some common visitor. They'll clear me for landing right in the courtyard."

"We could hide in the cargo holds," Heath mutters, already working through the logistics.

"It'll take time to make arrangements," Jess warns. "And booking a shuttle isn't easy these days. Everyone's either fleeing to Gaergan Island or rushing to their yachts."

Carter and Heath exchange glances. Carter nods slightly.

"I'm in," Carter says.

"Me too," Heath adds.

I'm about to volunteer when Marshal cuts in.

"Logan, you should go with them."

"All three of us?" he asks.

"I'll stay behind with Brigid," Marshal replies.

"You don't trust me to keep her safe?" he says, an undertone of defensiveness in his words.

I suppress a sigh. Here it is, the inevitable showdown that would happen sooner or later. My brother versus guy I fell for, squaring off like two wild dogs establishing territory. Part of me wants to remind them both that I survived plenty on my own before either of them decided to play guardian. Another part understands this isn't really about me at all, it's about them finding their limits with each other, establishing boundaries and respect. I cross my arms, watching them size each other up, and decide to let them work through this particular male ritual on their own.

"It's not about trust," Marshal says evenly. "It's about the division of labor. Carter and Heath know Parnia's layout. You know druaneras better than any of us. I know how to keep Brigid from doing something reckless while you're gone."

"How soon can you arrange the shuttle?" I ask Jess.

Her brows pinch together as she mentally calculates. "Three days. Maybe two if I pull every string I have left."

"Two days," I say, not asking. "We need to move before ITM figures out what we're planning."

The gel lantern flickers again, casting long shadows across our faces. In its wavering light, determination hardens in everyone's eyes. For the first time since this nightmare began, I feel something dangerously close to hope.

Forty-Five

HEATH

We plan to how get Oriana here until well past sundown.

Waylon takes Marshal, Jess, and Jace to the hangar to help them get settled for the night, and I head outside to the wash basin Waylon showed me.

I strip down to my underwear and tug on an extra pair of pants and a T-shirt I had packed for my mission.

Pumping the water, I fill the small cast iron tub and begin scrubbing. The faint scent of damp wood mingles with the tang of soap. The blood stains on my riding pants are stubborn and most likely ruined. I grab the soap, find a bottle of hydrogen peroxide, and lather the fabric, trying to lift the dark, coppery blotches from the fabric.

I scrub the anxiety, the fear, the loneliness that clings.

I gave up everything to be here. My life as a rider. My family. My duty.

All of it, to be here with *her*.

The dull pulse of the bond hums just behind my breastbone.

Shadowmane.

I will see him again, and until then, he's better off at Blackhawk. Safe and cared for until I figure out what the hell, I'm going to do now I'm a deserter. The odds of seeing him again feel dangerously low, but it's a gamble I'd take a thousand times over if it means Brigid is safe. If flaring out is the price to be with her, I'll pay it.

A burst of laughter from the common room pulls me from my thoughts. Carter and Marshal sound like they found a deck of cards.

I rise, leaving the pants soaking, and follow the sound.

Logan, Jace, Waylon, and Marshal sit around the table with a pile of credits in the center, as well as a few buttons and a rusted pocket knife. Nova perches on the armrest of a faded chair, laughing at Jace's attempt to shuffle. The cards slip from his hands, scattering in a flurry of red and black.

"Give 'em here before you hurt yourself," Carter says, snatching them from him.

Jace flips him off, grinning. "I'd like to see you do better, old man."

"Old?" Carter mock gasps, clutching his chest. "I'll show you old." Carter lunges for him, grabbing him by the shirt.

"Are we going to play or not?" Nova quips, tossing a credit on the table.

"Depends if this kid knows what's best for him," Carter says, glaring at Jace.

Wisely so, Jace passes the deck to Carter.

Carter releases him and takes the deck with one hand while ruffling the kid's hair with the other.

Jace curses and shoves him away.

Smirking, Carter leans back, skillfully shuffling the deck before dealing.

"Lockwood, you in?" He looks my way.

I shake my head.

"C'mon. You've got enough credits to cover all our hands. What's a little pocket change for the sake of fun?"

"Stop yapping and place your bet," Logan barks.

It's all so ridiculous and a bit juvenile, and yet, for the first time in days, weeks even, I feel something close to warmth stirring in my chest. The sight of them, laughing and teasing, chips away at the hardness I created to endure the death and blood.

I approach. Carter's fluttering excitement passes through the bond.

"I'll sit this one out tonight," I say, reaching into my pocket. "But I won't stand seeing such a disgraceful pot." With a *tink*, I drop a handful of credits on the pile.

Nova gasps, and her father's eyes widen at the sum. It's over a thousand, and probably more than they've ever seen.

"Hell yeah," Marshal comments. "That's more like it."

Carter sets the stack to the side and eyes his hand. "A generous donation from our Lockwood benefactor."

Everyone laughs and then falls silent to study their hands.

I glance toward the narrow hallway leading to the bedrooms. Brigid must've slipped out without saying anything.

The day she returned, I swore I'd never take my eyes off her again. While she settled in her room, Logan filled me in on what all happened from the time he was arrested to his meeting Waylon to persuading his way into the rebel's base.

Carter and I pressed for details about what they did with Brigid, and immediately, I was consumed with anger. Even as he spoke, he didn't need to finish. I saw the damage the moment I set my sight on her.

Her haunted eyes, her skin pale, her silver hair dull and tarnished like the pocket watch my grandfather had given me.

When Logan told us of Agent Zane being a double agent and having cornered Brigid alone in her room, rage surged through me, hot and consuming, and it flares again now, simmering just beneath my skin. I should have been there. Make them pay for every bruise, every cut, every tear in her voice when she speaks.

The only reason I'm at all rational is because I trusted Logan to do the same.

And from the sounds of it, he had.

Once up the stairs, I find her by the balcony window at the end of the loft, her figure outlined against the setting sun.

The quiet hum of the generator outside drifts in alongside the squawk of two birds squabbling over one of the trees for the night.

Her arms are wrapped around herself as she stares at the valley below. It's like she's still out there while we're in here. Unease creeps down my spine as I realize I'm unsure how to step into it.

She told us so much already about her time at ITM's base, with their leaders, their plan to help people survive the spreading poisoned air, and yet I know more had to have happened. She was there for months. What did she go through that leaves her so haunted? What did they make her do? What did she see? Did people she cares about get left behind or killed during the raid? My footsteps stop.

People she loves?

I grab the folded blanket from the bed. It smells faintly of cedar and old, but surprisingly still soft.

The chill bites as I step outside to join her. Winter has finally reached this far south, its icy fingers creeping into the air. She stands at the widow's walk, gazing out at the horizon, streaked with pinks and oranges beyond the cabin. To our right, the colors shift to deeper blues as the zone air molecules react differently to the sun's rays.

Her hair shifts in the wind, loose strands catch the faint light.

I approach quietly, draping the blanket over her shoulders. She startles but doesn't pull away, and a fresh wave of anger reignites inside me.

"Thanks," she murmurs. Her fingers find the edge of the fabric, gripping it as if anchoring herself.

I lean against the railing beside her, the rough wood cold against my palms. Months have passed since we last spoke or were alone like this, and the distance feels like a chasm I don't know how to cross.

"How are you doing?" I ask finally.

She doesn't look at me. "Oh, you know. Fine, all things considered."

It's a lie, and we both know it.

"Wish things were different," she adds after a moment.

The words I want to say knot in my throat. And tides, there are so many.

I watch her, search for some sign, some opening.

"Ms. Corsair—"

She shakes her head. "Don't do that." The wind tugs at the blanket, and she pulls it tighter around herself.

"Do what?"

"*That.* Acting like we're strangers again. Like we're back in your office on that first day, and you're interviewing me." She turns to me, thrusting out her jaw. "I can feel it, you know. The way you won't let yourself react. Won't let yourself feel." She rests a hand on my chest. "I'm here, Heath. You don't have to hold it in anymore."

"I convinced myself you weren't coming back. I told myself you left for a reason and that I would never see you again."

She watches me, waiting. I don't know what she expects me to say. I don't know what I expect myself to say.

"Carter lost himself on O-Strike. Logan threw himself into his work. I had...nothing. No duty. No purpose. I wasn't a manager anymore, wasn't preparing to be a husband or a father. Just a rider, a soldier, living out my numbered days." I pause, my tongue pressing into the roof of my mouth. "I was a body waiting to be spent in battle because it didn't matter if I was lost. Shut it all down. All of it. That's what I did. That's how I survived." I grip the handrail tighter. "Grieving you, truly grieving you, would have eaten me alive. So, I didn't. I forced myself forward. If I looked back, if I let myself imagine what could have been, I wouldn't have stopped. But you're here. Against all logic, against everything I made myself believe, you're here. And now I don't know what to do with all of it."

She doesn't move her hand from my chest. Her touch is a steady presence, grounding me. I want to pull away before I slip. Before I let her see how close I am to breaking.

"I had to let you go," I whisper. "I had to believe you weren't coming back, Brigid. Or I wouldn't have made it through."

She doesn't recoil. She doesn't look away. "But now I'm back," she says softly with a small smile. "And you don't have to shut yourself off anymore."

The blanket slips from her shoulders, caught in the wind. My hands shoot out to catch it, wrapping it back around her.

She tilts her head, searching my face. "I see you, Heath. I see the way you want to fight this. But you don't have to."

I want to believe her. Damn, how I want to. But control is all I have. Letting go, letting her in, feels like standing on the edge of a current too strong to fight.

She lifts a hand, her fingers tracing the edge of my jaw. "Come back to me."

I exhale sharply, jaw tightening. My hands fist in the fabric of the blanket. If I lean in, if I believe, I'll never come back from this. I'll never be able to let her go.

But it's too late. She's waiting, and I can feel my resolve crumbling, worn thin by months of worry and bloodshed and loss. So much loss. Everything that anchored me to who I once was—my rank, my purpose, my identity. My former life is ashes. My future lies in ruins around my feet.

Except for her. She's all that matters. She's all I have.

I press my lips to hers, and it feels like I'm tumbling off a precipice. I taste the sweetness of her lip and tease her tongue with mine, elated that she needs this as much as I do.

I hesitate at first, my movements tentative and uncertain. This moment I imagined countless times in my room, appears before me. My fingers tremble as they find their way to her hair, those silken locks I have dreamed about for months. I twist a strand gently around my finger, marveling at its softness.

Her scent of soft lilacs fills my senses. Her body presses against mine, and something ignites inside me. My reserved touch grows bolder, hands sliding down to the small of her back, drawing her closer.

Warmth spreads through me like wildfire and burns away my hesitation. For so long, I was bound. Tied to Jess, to my family obligations, to what the Lockwood name demands of me. But now, in this moment, those chains fall away. I cut the cord to that world.

For the first time, I allow myself to truly feel without restraint. My kiss deepens as I surrender to her completely. My body responds with an urgency I can no longer control. This freedom, to want her, to *have* her, overwhelms me, and I get lost in her touch. I'm free from everything but this moment, this woman, this desire I've denied myself for too long.

Breathless, we pull back, our faces inches from each other. I press my forehead against hers and close my eyes, savoring the smell of her presence and knowing she's doing the same.

Below, the faint sound of laughter drifts up from the common room. It's distant, almost ghostly, and it's a world away from where we stand. Brigid's shoulders relax slightly, and she exhales, a long, measured breath that clouds in the cold air.

"I...I don't know how to do this."

A small laugh escapes her. "We don't have to do it all at once. There's no rush. I'm not going anywhere, and you might not believe me, but I mean it. I see it now so clearly. You and the others downstairs are the most important people to me." She pauses, her eyes darkening briefly, affirming the belief she left people behind, including her sister. "You're all I have left."

She steps back, taking the blanket with her. I watch her as her fingers trace the edge of the railing. The ache in my chest deepens. I'll give anything to take her pain, to shoulder it myself.

The wind shifts, carrying the faint scent of pine and snow. I close my eyes and let the cold air ground me. When I open them, Brigid is looking at me.

"Thank you," she says quietly.

The words catch me off guard. "For what?"

"For...being here." Her gaze drops, and she turns away before I can respond.

"There are no thanks needed." I lean closer, lowering my voice. "Never think it is a burden to be with you. "

"Do you regret it?" She returns her gaze to the horizon. "Being a traitor for leaving Circuit's army?"

"No," I reply immediately. "Because I made the right choice. *You* are always the right choice."

Forty-Six

BRIGID

When my teeth begin to chatter, Heath invites me back inside.

Still not used to so freely going in and outside without an airlock, I flinch when I hear the door shut behind me.

Waylon and Nova have bedrooms downstairs but gave me and the others the loft upstairs. It has one large bed and a couch.

Marshal, Jess, and Jace tell us goodnight before leaving for their beds in the hangar. Waylon reminds us the bathroom is outside, but there's a bucket in the closet if it's an emergency, then leaves the four of us alone in the loft. There's only one bed and a deflated-looking couch.

Months of pent-up tension saturates the room, heavy as a blanket of humid air. For a minute, no one moves, as if we're all holding our breaths, waiting for something to break the silence.

Finally, Carter flops down on the couch, and Heath, Logan, and I stare at each other.

I'm conflicted, feeling like I'm being torn in two. I'm not ready. Not yet.

"Bed is all yours," Heaths says, deciding for me. He takes a spare blanket from the foot of the bed and sits on the ground next to Carter. His long legs stretch out as he rests his back against the couch.

I want to yell at him, tell him he's being silly to sleep on the wood floor, but my voice catches in my throat.

Sure, we started on the path to recovering the lost ground, but it's only been a day. Taking those first tentative steps toward healing hasn't been easy for any of us.

I was alone for months, and while it was one thing to have Logan take me against the wall when I was swept up in a whirlwind of feelings, clouded by desire and not thinking straight. Now I'm clearheaded. Logic has returned, with fear and insecurity clinging to it like moss to stone.

Fear that Sharice was right about the bonds.

Fear that we can never return to the way we were.

Fear that I've broken something beyond repair and whatever seed was blooming between the four of us had wilted and died in our time apart.

I climb into the bed, slip under the covers, and close my eyes. Although I'm the safest I've been in months, I've never felt so scared.

Logan pats the dust off the cushions of an armchair and collapses into it. The hum of the generator dissipates, and the light bulb dangling from the ceiling winks off, plunging us into darkness. Seeing only black, my ears strain to listen to their breathing.

They're feet from me, but they might as well be hundreds of miles.

A chasm has formed between us one I'm unsure if I can bridge, and yet I want to try.

"I..." I speak to the darkness, unsure if they're still awake. "I don't want to sleep alone tonight."

Silence.

My heart sinks with each passing second, the quiet amplifying my fears that the dark things I confessed might have been too much for them to accept. Even if I believe there was more between us than just the chemicals of bonds, I'm not the same woman who left Blackhawk all those months ago.

Then I feel it, the subtle shift, the gentle dip of the mattress to my right. The scent reaches me before he does, a familiar blend of cedar and something uniquely Heath. He moves carefully, his weight creating a valley in the mattress as he climbs over me, settling on my left side over the covers.

Another movement follows. To my right, the mattress moves, and the radiating body heat tells me it's Carter. He lays on his back, and I'm instantly relaxed by the steady sound of his breathing. His arm brushes against mine as he adjusts the pillow, and the brief contact elicits an electric current that dances across my skin and settles as butterflies in my stomach.

The mattress shifts a third time, this time at the bottom near my legs. I'm surrounded now, sandwiched between their bodies in a cocoon of warmth. The isolation I felt moments ago dissolves into the darkness.

"Good night," I say, my voice barely above a whisper. I feel warm and snug. Protected in a way I never felt before.

"Good night, Blondie," Logan says from the foot of the bed, his voice a low rumble in the darkness.

I close my eyes, letting their presence envelop me. The steady rhythm of their breathing becomes my lullaby, the weight of their bodies around me an anchor keeping me safe from the storms in my mind. For the first time in what feels like forever, I surrender completely to sleep, drifting off into a dreamless peace.

I sleep the best I ever fucking slept in my life.

I WAKE TO AN EMPTY BED, but their scents and the memory of them staying with me throughout the night lingers. I drag my fingers through my tangled hair, blinking against the morning light spilling through the window. The bed, a thousand times softer than my cot, leaves my body stiff from the unfamiliar comfort.

My jumpsuit is caked with dirt. The fabric is rough against my skin as I pull it back into place. I miss my cotton dresses, my soft sweaters. I miss my hairbrush and, makeup and lotions.

A dusty mirror leans against a pile of junk. Waylon clearly uses this place for storage.

When I catch my reflection, I recoil. My skin is pale beneath the grime, and soot streaks my jaw like war paint. My hair is a disaster, a wild mess that looks like I wrestled a wild boar and lost. I do my best to smooth it down, sighing at the futile effort, before heading downstairs, drawn by the scent of pancakes.

Nova stands at the stove, flipping another onto an already towering stack. Jace devours them as fast as she can cook, barely pausing to chew. Nova huffs, rolling her eyes.

"These are really good. You should've been a cook," he says around a mouthful.

"Nah," she smirks, twirling on her toes, spatula raised like a dancer's fan. "I'm going to be a dancer."

Jace stops chewing, his eyes gliding up and down her body as she moves. I clear my throat as I step into the room, feeling the need to announce my presence. Nova quirks a brow but says nothing as I grab a pancake straight from the stack, eating without a plate. It's warm, buttery, better than I deserve. Then I catch another scent...oh my god.

Coffee.

I pour a mug and moan at the first sip. The warmth radiates through me, the caffeine cutting through the exhaustion still buried in my bones.

"My dad hooked up the antenna if you want to call someone," Nova says.

I reach for my wrist. Old habits die hard, even though I haven't had my comm in months. The girl notices and gestures to a metal box on the table. "We've got a spare if you don't have yours."

I thank her and stare at the comm, contemplating what to do next. Mom is potentially on the run or dead, and Sharice is certainly gone.

Laura and Vince. A dull ache squeezes under my sternum. Last I knew, they were in Delford, and they were safe. They're resourceful. Vince was still dating that cop last I heard, maybe he took them somewhere safe.

I make the call. It buzzes for several seconds before the line clicks, and then—"B? Oh my god, it's you! You're alive! Where have you been?"

"My mom was sick," I add quickly, the lie stitching together instantly. "I had to stay with her while she got treatment, and the center they kept her at didn't allow comms."

Laura's brows knit together. It's odd, sure, but not totally out of the normal. Lots of rich people go to wellness centers to heal both body and mind.

"I'm so sorry! How is she now?"

My tongue sweeps the backs of my molars. "Better."

She offers me a small smile. "Network keeps going out." Laura's voice is breathless, caught between relief and panic. "Since the levees broke, it's a struggle to contact anyone."

"Where are you?"

"They're taking us by neighborhoods to ferries to Gaergen Island. They set up temporary camps there. They're evacuating the whole city."

Her lower lip wavers, a tear trickling down her cheek. "They got me from the apartment, and I didn't have time to pack anything..." She hesitates, and then her voice tightens. "Vince was at work, B, and I can't get a hold of him."

Panic rises in her throat, and I feel it echo in my own.

"He'll be okay. I promise. This is Vince we're talking about. He probably made a new friend on the way home and, for all we know, is on a private shuttle there now."

She sniffs, then lets out a half-laugh. "I hope you're right."

Above her, the lights flicker. A collective gasp ripples through the crowd, and somewhere, a baby starts crying. Her video feed cuts in and out.

"They're unloading us," she says hurriedly. "I'll call as soon as I have service again. Love you, B."

The call drops.

I choke down a sob, consumed by grief and worry for my friends. Suddenly, I feel dizzy, and nearly miss my seat as I sit down.

"Sorry about your friend," Nova says. "You can keep the comm if you want. I'll lie to my dad and say I lost it."

"Thanks," I say, wiping a tear from my cheek.

A rhythmic *thunk* of the axe echoes through the morning

stillness from outside and on the opposite end of the cabin. Jess stands gazing out the window to the west. She doesn't acknowledge me as I move to the other side, keeping a space between us.

Outside, Waylon shouts directions to Logan, Heath, Carter, and Marshal. Heath and Logan load sheet metal into a wheelbarrow while Marshal and Carter chop and stack wood.

None of them wear shirts. I blow the steam on my coffee, watching.

My eyes track their every movement. Sweat-slicked skin, muscles flexing, steam rising from bare shoulders against the crisp morning air.

I glance sideways, catching Jess doing the same.

A silent acknowledgment passes between us. We don't speak, don't smirk, just share a moment of mutual appreciation before turning back to our coffee and watching the display outside.

"Sorry, it didn't work," I say, unsure if she'll catch my meaning.

"It's not your fault. The fertility pill I took was a placebo. My doctor was arrested recently for being an ITM supporter. I believe they discovered what we were trying to do and wanted to prevent it."

I don't remember Sharice telling me anything about her knowing what I could do or mentioning seeing the four of us together. But perhaps she didn't have cameras installed in the bedroom. Or maybe someone else knew, like Elton, and kept it from her. I also know ITM supporters often acted on their own, and there was a chance the doctor did. Either way, it reassures me that it might have worked had the pill been a real one.

"I'm assuming you know Marshal and I are..."

"Siblings? Yes, I'm aware."

I nod, feeling like I'm struggling to make this a conversation.

Behind me, Nova and Jace argue about which bands are better, and Jace is finding ways to brag about all the ones he saw live. Nova apparently has seen none.

Dial it back, kid.

"So, are you and him, like together?"

"It's still undetermined."

"Wait, when did this happen?"

The door opens before she can answer, and the group of sweaty, gorgeous man specimens enter laughing.

"Pay up, Lockwood," Carter says, holding out his hand.

"What happened?" I ask.

Carter smirks as Heath retrieves a plastic card from his wallet.

"There was a large pine round out there, and Carter and I bet who could split it with one hit." Heath sighs as Carter taps the card with his comm, transferring the credits, I'm sure is equal to my monthly salary. If I still had a job, that is.

"I believe it was an unfair trial," Heath accuses, crossing his arms.

Carter scoffs. "Just because you lost—"

"I didn't lose. You rigged it."

"It's not my fault you chose one with a knot in it," Carter says with a smug grin.

Logan and Marshal burst into laughter, Logan shaking his head. "He's got you there, Heath."

Heath groans but doesn't argue.

Their laughter echoes around us, and it feels like something lost, slowly piecing itself back together.

Marshal crosses the room and pulls Jess into a hug, his arms tight around her.

"You're sweaty and disgusting," she mutters, but she doesn't push him away.

His only response is to stare at her, pure adoration in his gaze. I watch them, then glance at the other three, laughing and joking. My heart aches, wondering if we'll ever have that again.

If that kind of lightness can return to us.

Jess sighs, finally pushing at Marshal's chest. "Alright, all of you. Shower. The shuttle will be here in an hour."

The laughter fades as the weight of what's coming settles over us.

It's showtime.

By dinner, Oriana should be here.

Forty-Seven

JESS

"Appreciate you staying late and accommodating me, Dr. Berringer," I tell the lead director of Lanett's Parnia research facility. The sun is just skirting the horizon, and the majority of the staff has gone home for the day.

"Of course, Ms. Drakeford. I have to be honest. We were quite surprised to hear the daughter of Preston Drakeford was going to drop in for a surprise visit."

I narrow my gaze on him, and he shrinks slightly. Good. "I can assure you, Doctor, this is more than a visit. I'm here to appraise the facility and see if it has the viability to be added as an asset to our holdings."

Dr. Berringer clears his throat. "If you don't mind me asking, I was under the impression Drakeford Industries only has an interest in land acquisition and filtration plants. Why the sudden desire to look into research and development?"

I knew he would ask this question because it's the one I would. Interesting.

"We know Circuit is one of your biggest contracts and understand the economic climate is tumultuous," I say, folding my hands neatly on the table. "I have it on good authority that other R&D companies are seeking to diversify their contracts just in case Circuit is unable to fulfill their debts."

His jaw tightens, and I catch the flicker of shock in his eyes before he schools his expression. Bold move, but damn, do I make it sound true.

"Our contracts with the government are certified," he says, leaning forward. "They would never default on a payment."

"Maybe last year," I reply coolly, leaning back, "but if you haven't noticed, the world is changing. Circuit's attention is more divided. If they focus more on security and supplying the military with weapons and resources, they'll have to cut back somewhere."

I let that hang in the air just long enough for him to chew on it. His hesitation is my signal to glance out the corner of my eye at the shuttle on the tarmac. Two security guards pace around it, scanning the hull with their thermal detectors.

My pilot stands at the ramp, stiff-backed, holding his papers as one of the guards reads over them far too slowly for my liking.

"Is that necessary?" I gesture toward the ramp.

The doctor, seated across from me, ducks his head apologetically. "Just protocol, no offense, I assure you. The ITM rebels are everywhere, and we have to be resolute in our procedures."

I arch a brow. "I'm Jessica Drakeford. Do you honestly believe ITM could offer me anything I don't already have?"

"No—no, of course not," he croaks.

"Then I insist you quit harassing my pilot and show me the

facility," I snap, letting my words land like the sharp edge of a blade.

He stammers something unintelligible, then, with a quick gesture to the guards, he signals them away from the shuttle. I don't exhale until they fall back and the large sliding doors begin to close behind us, sealing the shuttle and Heath and the guys inside.

I follow the doctor down the long corridor. He waves his badge over a scanner, and the door ahead hums open with a soft hiss. I glance over my shoulder once to make sure the guards don't double back. The hangar doors lock with a final clang, and I force myself to focus.

The doctor gestures grandly ahead. "This way. I'll show you our most advanced labs."

I nod curtly, falling into step behind him.

Good luck, boys.

I promised them an hour.

The rest is up to them.

Forty-Eight

BRIGID

It's only been an hour since they left, and I'm already struggling to keep it together. My anxiety-riddled brain has decided to run every disaster situation scenario they can be facing on a loop in my head, and I can think of nothing else. Storms. Wind. Police patrols. Elton is already taking Oriana.

Marshal, Nova, and I are seated at the table, and Waylon brings out a dusty bottle of liquor and generously fills our glasses to the brim. I graciously accept, gulping down the alcohol to calm my overactive imagination and frazzled nerves.

"Hang in there," he says, taking the seat at the head of the table. "Shouldn't be much longer now." He offers me a reassuring smile, and I nod.

It's a risk for him to have us here, not to mention the toll we're taking on his limited food and alcohol supply, but he doesn't give me the impression he's the kind of guy who does things he doesn't want to.

If he didn't want us here, we wouldn't be here.

However, the sooner we get Oriana back and find somewhere safe to take her, the better.

All of us being here endangers him and his daughter.

Marshal opens the conversation with specifics on how he survives out here, asking about water, fuel, and medicines, and I drink the whiskey and listen, trying to distract myself.

"We're a mile out from the border," Waylon says, rubbing a thumb on his glass. "But I always have a bag and a mask at the ready should any of the alarms go off. I set the sensors far enough to give us about a 10-minute head start. There's no way to know how dense or thick it is, so you have to be prepared and assume it's a bad one."

Those flimsy, rusty-looking pinwheels will be the only warning. So much for this conversation, trying to calm my nerves. And every second I spend here feels like I'm living next to a ticking time bomb. He said the tech was old, so I can only trust they'll work.

"How often does the wind change here?" I ask.

Waylon and his daughter exchange the briefest of looks, and queasiness settles in my gut. "When Nova was just saying her first words, a late winter storm came through. Me and her mother escaped, but our youngest, not yet a week old, wasn't so fortunate."

"Why do you do this?" Marshal asks. "Why do you stay here, choosing to live next to something so dangerous? You could live by a filtration zone or even up north, where the currents always blow south, and the risk is low?"

Waylon barks a laugh. "Do you think you're the first to ask

me that? Do you think you're the first to think I'm crazy for putting my family in danger? We live here because it's who we are. We're trawlers. Generations of Murdocks have lived in this cabin and made their living from the wreckage of cities long since forgotten by everyone else. While the rest of the world has moved on, we still find treasures of the past.

"A thousand years ago, they had the technology that we can only dream about now. They walked on the moon. Sent satellites to connect us to the entire world. They had astronauts setting up a colony on Mars. They found a way to unite the world into a global, peaceful, and fair economy where the wealth was shared and no one was hungry or homeless. There was no mystyl, no toxic air. You could start walking in any direction and breathe only fresh air.

"So, you ask why I stay. That's why. Like my grandfather and his father before him, my aunts, uncles, and cousins have all made this their life's endeavor. The odds are low that we will find something so incredibly precious and priceless that it will revolutionize our entire existence, but they're not zero. I stay because if I am not out here every day uncovering the remnants of our past, no one will. Now more than ever, my kind is needed; if Circuit's not gonna provide the answers, then we'll have to find our own."

I lean against the side of the chair, steady myself against the dizzying déjà vu.

He and Sharice would find a lot in common.

If she were still alive, that is.

My thoughts darken as I remember her wounded and tumbling down the stairs into the underground hallway before the hatch closed. I cough, clearing the lump in my throat, and let my eyes wander the interior of the cabin.

Every inch of horizontal space is littered with wired contraptions that haven't worked in centuries, preserved plastic cups from non-existent cow's milk yogurt, and bottles that once held soaps and lotions are scattered throughout the room, with a choice piece on higher shelves.

This place rivals DU's Legacy Wing with dozens of pre-flood artifacts locked in display cabinets.

Here, they're strewn about like knick-knacks. A few with certain floral designs or matching sets will fetch pretty prices at most auctions in Delford.

Overall, his home is cozy, and while I'm not thrilled with the geographical location, it's the best option I have right now.

And it's clear I'm not the only one a little on edge. Marshal hasn't sat once since they left, his feet carrying him around the perimeter of the room, eyeing each piece with such intensity that I wonder if he was about ready to give up his own profession.

As if that will happen. Blackhawk would sooner turn their arena into an ice-skating rink for the DU hockey team than let their most prized rider go.

He is the one rider *without* an expiration date. The special one.

I should've told Sharice about him and asked if she had any theories regarding why that could be, but that door is closed, and I never will get the chance.

I suppressed my personal urge and desire to become a rider while at the ITM base. My mind focused on more urgent matters, such as developing a way to save people from the poisoned air and escaping. But now it seems a reality again. Oriana could already be on the shuttle and on her way back here as we speak.

It's really going to happen.

At least, I hope it will.

"Since this bottle isn't finished," Waylon says from the

table, "and we've got some time on our hands, I don't suppose the three of you would mind joining me in a game of Flats?"

A hard lump lodges in the back of my throat, and I swallow it down. I haven't played Flats in years. The last time was with my sister.

"I'd love to," Marshal says, not noticing my discomfort. "But I'll warn you. I'm a bit rusty."

Chuckling, Waylon opens a nearby drawer and takes out the square brown box. "I'll make this first round easy on you till you shake off the dust, and then we'll see if we can't up the stakes a bit."

I missed out on the poker game earlier, and to be honest, it was probably for my own good. I never understood the bluffing part, and my friends always told me I had the worst poker face, not because I looked like I had a good hand, but because it always looked like I *didn't*.

My mom, Sharice, and I played when she wasn't working late or waiting on a printout from the spectrometer. The rounds were short, and the pieces were easy to travel with.

Marshal turns to me. "What about you?"

I open my mouth to refuse, but then Marshal's expectant gaze and warm smile change my mind. "Only if I get to start first," I say.

"Sounds good to me," he replies.

The rules for Flats are simple. You're dealt ten rectangular pieces, about the size of a cracker, each with a different symbol on it. Some stars, others circles, and then others were blank.

You must match them to the ones in your hands or on the table, and the winner has the most flats at the end.

The strategy most people use is watching the pieces on the table, but the real mastery comes from knowing when to steal a piece and when to leave it. When there are only a limited number of pieces to steal, you are forced to take ones you know don't match.

It was the one game I could beat Sharice at.

And I never let her live it down.

The tiles in my hand feel smooth, their corners softened by years of play, and I place down my first one.

Waylon places his next to mine. It's a good match, and the first flutter of nerves disturbs my belly. *I might have a challenge on my hands.*

I glance at Marshal, his brow furrowed as he studies his spread. Across from him, Waylon leans back in his chair, grinning like he already won.

"Your move, master rider," he says, knuckles rubbing the scruff on his cheek.

Marshal doesn't look up. "Don't rush me," he mutters, still staring at the square tiles.

I can't help but smirk. "Strategizing or stalling?" I tease, setting my cards down for a moment to watch them.

Waylon chuckles; the chair creaks under his weight as he leans back even farther. "You call it strategizing. I call it overthinking. We ain't got *all* night, you know."

He's wrong. We do have all night. With the others away on a dangerous mission, I doubt any of us will get much sleep tonight.

Marshal finally places a tile, sliding it into the center of the table. "Top that."

Waylon grunts. Whether he's happy with the play or not is hard to tell. He sets two circle tiles on either side of Marshal's square, essentially blocking him in. It's a risky move since it prevents anyone else from playing a square, but it implies one of two things. Either Waylon doesn't have any squares, or he does and wants to wait until the others are wiped off the board before he swoops in and steals the win.

I stare at the tiles in my pile, pluck a circle, and remove the one on the left. It's a little early to be taking tiles, but early in the game, it is all about learning the other person's hands. If I'm right, Waylon will either take the square or play another, proving once again he wants to reserve his square for the victory.

The door bangs open, the cold wind rushing in as Nova bursts inside. Snow clings to her boots as she stomps them on the rug. "Dad, the goats won't go in," she announces, her tone clipped with frustration. "They're being stubborn again."

Waylon groans, shoving his tiles into the tray face down. "They always know when a storm's coming," he mutters. He pushes back his chair and grabs his jacket from the peg by the door. Marshal rises to his feet. "Want a hand?"

Waylon shakes his head. "Nah, you finish your game. I'll get that Jace kid to help. Those baby-soft hands of his could do with a few more calluses."

"He's in the barn," Nova says.

Her dad shrugs on his coat and hat. "I better top off the gennie, too and lock down the windows while we're at it. Cross your fingers it hits after your friends get back with that mare of yours."

Marshal sinks back into the chair. My eyes follow Waylon to the door. Nova's already outside, her voice carrying faintly as she calls to the goats. Waylon turns back to us, pointing a finger. "Don't go easy on her, just cause she's your sister," he says with a grin, jerking his thumb toward me. Then he's gone, the door slamming shut behind him.

"You got it," Marshal says, grinning impishly, and returns his gaze to me.

He hesitates, his hand brushes against the cards on the table, then finally looks at me.

"The rebel base," he says. "You stayed with your sister.

What tests were they running?" His expression shifts, more serious now.

"Blood work, genetic scans, compatibility trials. They're thorough. There were so many people there. Hundreds, maybe more."

"Hundreds? I had no idea it was that many."

"They're building something big, Marshal. Bigger than we realized."

"I felt so helpless not being able to find you," he admits. "We all did. But those three?" He nods to the loft where we stayed. "They were different, like shells of themselves. Stoic now, sure, but I've never seen anything like it. It reminded me of the druadan riders when their bond mates died. The way they'd wander Blackhawk's halls, half-ghosts."

Marshal reaches across the table, and his hand squeezes mine gently. His palm has that signature rider warmth. When I look up, he's smiling, soft and reassuring. I didn't realize how much I needed that until now.

"I never noticed before," I say quietly.

"Noticed what?"

"The bits of gray in your hair." My gaze lingers on the silver streaks at his temples. "It suits you. Makes you look...*roguish*."

He chuckles, shaking his head. "Roguish, huh? I'll take it."

The silence he leaves behind feels heavier than it should be. I sort my tiles again, trying to focus on the game, but Marshal's too quiet. His eyes flick toward the window, then back to the table. The storm has him worried not just about Oriana but also about someone he cares about out there, just like me.

"She'll be okay," I say, keeping my tone light. "Heath and the others will look out for her."

Dark eyes settle on mine, and his jaw clenches. "That obvious, huh?"

"We might not have grown up together, but you're still my

brother, and I'm definitely picking up on the sibling energy." My mouth hitches into a half smile. "Besides, I've got two eyes."

Marshal slides three tiles out. Two stars and a square. Now things are getting interesting.

"Want to talk about it?" I ask.

"Not much to talk about."

"Come on, you have to give me *something*. I feel like so much happened when I was away. I've seen the way you look at each other. I know it's not exactly my place, but after what she told me about getting Jace and staying at her parents..." I wait to see his reaction.

He clears his throat, looking more uncomfortable than I've ever seen him. "Feeling bold tonight, are we?"

"Just curious," I say, leaning back in my chair.

"Does that mean I get to be curious about you and those three fellow riders of mine?"

"Nuh huh," I say, waggling a finger. "I asked first."

He sighs and rolls his eyes. "It's all early, and I hate to jinx it. To be honest, I'm not exactly sure if there is any sort of a future between us, but one thing I know is that I like it. I like *her*. I guess we'll see where it goes."

I nod, studying him. "I'm happy for you. Jess isn't exactly..."

"Affectionate or the lovey-dovey type?"

"I was going to say friendly, but those work too."

"You wonder what I see in her?"

I smirk and lift a brow. "Your words, not mine."

Marshal runs a hand over his face and lets out a deep sigh. "It's been so long since I dated anyone seriously. I'm woefully out of practice, and tides know I'm a sadist for even trying to pursue her. But she fascinates me and challenges me and tests me, and fuck, when she does this thing with her lips, I almost lose it—" For the first time, I see my brother, Marshal, blush. It's subtle and hidden under the weeks-long scruff, but it's there in all its boyish-crush glory. "Never mind," he adds quickly, "I guess what I'm trying to say is against all better judgment and self-preservation. The heart will do what it wants. You know what I'm saying?"

Tides did I.

Being enamored by not one but *three* men, all destined to leave me a young widow, is certainly not the finest display of good judgment.

We play in silence for a while, the game pulling us back into something lighter, easier. Finally, he breaks it. "So, when are we going to talk about you and those three riders?"

I laugh, shaking my head. "Oh no. We don't have that kind of time. Especially not when I do this."

I play three flats in rapid succession, stealing two of his and winning the round. He groans as I grin triumphantly, the shadows on the walls dancing with my victory.

The first low whoosh of wind threads through the air, rattling the windowpanes. My grin falters as I glance toward the glass. Outside, the trees twist and shudder, their branches slapping against the window like skeletal fingers.

"They're cutting it close," I mutter, my chest tightening.

He follows my gaze, his brow furrowing. "If the wind gets any worse, they won't be able to find us."

"Or worse," I add quietly, my voice edged with worry. "Someone at Lanett realizes Oriana is missing and..."

"They'll send someone after them," he finishes, his tone grim.

They'll have no choice but to change a dangerous landing and risk either crashing into one of the nearby hills or into the TZ.

The game between us forgotten, we stare out the window, watching the storm gather force.

I swallow hard.

Is this how Heath, Carter, and Logan felt when I was gone? I imagine them waiting, months of it, worried, powerless, left without answers. And here I am, feeling this after only one night. Guilt claws at my chest, sharp and unrelenting. I did this to them, left them to wonder if I'd ever come back.

Now, they're out there, risking everything. For me. For Oriana. And all I can do is wait.

Forty-Nine

LOGAN

I slide along the wall of the research facility, keeping to the shadows. Jess has the director occupied, but a few security guards are still patrolling, and scientists are working late. My heart pounds in my chest, but I keep my breathing steady. I've come too far to mess up now.

The facility is bigger than expected, with labs branching off the main corridor. Some studying plants, others viruses. But I know what I'm looking for.

I slip past a guard station, ducking behind a supply cart when a lab tech walks by. The smell of antiseptic burns my nostrils. I make my way deeper into the complex, following the signs to Biological Research Wing C, and find a room with large freezer units along one wall. Each glass door has a digital readout labeling its contents. I scan them quickly: Galaxy, Raven, Ghost, Solara, Inferno, Gemini, Shade, Obsidian. All the bloodlines. All the druadans DNA in test tubes crusted with frost.

I have no clue what I'm looking at, but many rows on the shelves are empty.

The Solara rack is completely empty, and Galaxy has just one left.

"Shit," I mutter under my breath. The rumors are true. They really are running out of good samples.

My nose picks up something else beneath the sterile lab smell, wood shavings, along with a slight thrumming vibration through the floor. I follow both, moving through a secured door into another section.

The room opens to a series of reinforced plastic stalls with spotless floors and bins of protein pellets arranged neatly outside each one.

About fucking time.

Young druadans peer at me curiously through the white mesh windows. I rush down, scanning the interiors. For a moment, I think I see a familiar golden hide and rush forward, but the stall is empty.

Damn it.

A sound makes me turn, and I spin, drawing my gun. Carter and Heath are there, pistols low but ready. Carter is light on his feet, but I swore there was only one set of footsteps. What had Heath said about people not seeing him? Did that include not hearing him either?

"You find her yet?" Heath whispers when they're closer.

I shake my head.

Carter checks his watch. "I'll hit the security room and kill the cameras. You two find the mare."

He disappears, and Heath and I continue down the aisles of

stalls. Two lab techs round the corner ahead, and we have no choice but to take them down. The fight is quick. They're beaker geeks, not guards, and a hard hit to the head knocks them out cold.

We drag them into a storage closet, zip-tying their hands and feet.

We resume our search, and near the end, we find her. Oriana is nearly full-grown now. Her pale gold coat gleams even in the ambient light, and her violet eyes watch us warily.

I can't tell if she recognizes me.

Heath gently slips a halter over her head, speaking softly to keep her calm. I glance at the empty stalls around us, unable to shake the sight of the single Galaxy embryo.

"You okay?" Heath asks, noticing my distraction.

"Fine," I mutter. "Just want to get the hell out of here."

Heath gives me a questioning look but doesn't press the issue.

I check the digital chart outside Oriana's stall for any information that might be useful. My eyes are drawn to the other stalls. There are five foals here. Four newborns and a yearling that looks about ready to be sent to a station.

As I override the security locks, sparks fly from the console, and all the stall doors open.

"Fuck!" I grab Oriana's halter with one hand and draw my gun with the other.

Heath and I run back the way we came, and duck through a side door as running a druadan down the hallway is a terrible idea.

Behind us is the thudding of hooves from the other escaping druadans, and I don't feel bad for letting them free. What does it matter anymore, now that the world is ending? At least let them enjoy their short lives.

Carter waits for us on the shuttle. "What the hell happened?"

"Nothing," I say. "But we got what we came for."

Oriana willingly steps onto the shuttle. I suspect they either sedated her or have trained her to get used to them like any other young horse.

Within seconds of the mare being safely stowed, I hear Jess's voice from across the parking bay. "Thank you again, Doctor. This tour has been most helpful. I'll touch base with you in a few days once I've talked numbers with my team, but you can certainly put my name down for a table at the charity event."

There's a murmuring of goodbye, and then she's climbing up the side ramp.

Her eyes meet ours, and the professional face she wears slips, revealing a slight smile.

She turns and presses the button on the wall, and the door closes.

"Well then," she lifts her chin. "I hope you're all happy. This little trip cost me two hundred thousand credits."

Fifty

BRIGID

I wake before sunrise. Marshal ordered me to go to bed around midnight, and while I stayed up another hour, at some point, I fell asleep.

I sit up and spot Heath in the chair, watching me. "You're back! Why didn't you wake me up?"

"You looked so peaceful. I didn't have the heart."

He was watching me sleep. Okay, it's kinda sweet, I'll admit.

I yawn and offer him a tired smile. "I told you, I'm not going anywhere."

Abruptly, he's out of the chair and sitting next to me. "I know," he murmurs, leaning closer so he can trace his fingertips over my cheek. "But I lost three months I'll never get back, and every second I have with you is already running out. I won't waste another."

His fingers slip to the nape of my neck, and he tugs me closer until his lips brush mine. A soft touch filled with a million unspoken words. I close my eyes, savoring the closeness, the intimacy. Goosebumps prickle my arms even though I'm warm, buried under the blankets.

I reach up and cup my hand around his neck, pulling him deeper into the kiss, and the bed dips as he climbs onto the edge.

My mind scrambles to catch up, and I pull away. "Oriana?"

He smirks. "She's here."

I fling off the covers; the shock of cold instantly makes me cringe, and I frantically get dressed.

Heath's gaze lingers on me, and from the corner of my eye, I catch him smirking.

I pull on my boots and a sweater and race downstairs.

The main room is empty and quiet except for the slight breeze rustling the windows. My heart pounds, listening for the bells.

Nothing.

"Where is everyone?" I ask.

"In the barn," he says, descending the stairs behind me. "The others are with her."

Frantic energy buzzing inside me, I'm out the door, not bothering with a coat despite the cold. The path to the barn is impossibly long as questions race through my mind. What will she look like now? Will she remember me after all this time? Was she hurt? How did they treat her at that facility?

Heath catches up, matching my hurried pace. "Slow down," he says with amusement in his voice. "She's not going anywhere."

The barn door is partially open, and a sliver of warm light

spills onto the frozen ground. I pause just outside, suddenly hesitant, my breath forming clouds in the night air.

Heath places a hand on my shoulder. "Go on," he urges gently.

I push the door open and step inside. The familiar smell of hay and animals wraps around me, but something's different. The goats are gone, having been moved to an outside pen, and in their place are two makeshift stalls constructed from pallets and plastic ties.

A glint of gold in the stall to the left of the goat pen captures my attention. I step forward slowly, acutely aware of the eyes on me.

Marshal, Carter, and Logan huddle together in intense conversation. As I enter, they immediately fall silent, all eyes turning to me, but my eyes are on one thing and one thing alone.

Oriana.

In my time with ITM, I learned that druanera reach maturity faster than druadans. A year is ideal for mental maturation, but by six months, their physical body has grown, and they can safely support an adult's weight. And what a difference months of being fed top-quality feed at Lanett and receiving great care have made.

She's only slightly shorter than the stallions, with her back reaching the top of my head. She is the definition of power combined with feminine elegance. Similar to Iris with her rounded, muscular croup, pronounced withers, but has a proud, arched neck that curves like a breaking wave.

Her coat gleams almost ethereal, not the typical golden hue of palomino but a pale cream that seems to capture and hold the light. Her platinum mane and tail cascade in silken waterfalls, brighter than the silver-gray of my own.

Most striking are her eyes. Deep violet pools that seem to

hold wisdom beyond her years, framed by thick golden lashes. She side-steps to face me, her hooves catching the light, glowing with a soft golden luminescence that leaves faint traces in the air.

The blend of her powerful physique and otherworldly coloring marks her as something extraordinary, even among the magnificence of other druadans.

She strides to the half-door and hangs her head over it. I want to reach out and touch her, but I remember druadans are too hot for bare skin.

Carter clears his throat and steps forward, holding out a deer leather glove. "Here."

I slip it on, trembling fingers, and reach out to pet her nose. Her coat is stunning—the color of sand on the beach and cream, with a metallic sheen under the lights. Her violet eyes glow with intelligence, and she thrums in her chest, the sound light and airy like distant wind chimes.

"Oriana," I whisper, tears streaming freely down my cheeks. "I missed you."

She nuzzles my gloved hand, and all of it floods back.

The connection. The feel of her, like a missing piece of my soul, finally returned. The desire to sit on her back and be her rider.

The intuitive feeling that she and I are supposed to be together. That everything that's happened has led to this moment.

I turn to the others, emotion making it hard to speak. "Thank you," I say, my voice cracking.

They watch me with somber gazes; the weight of what they did, what they risked, lingering in the air between us.

Our presence had hurt her before, and the fear that her being here would cause the cycle all over again weighs heavily on me. I sift through my memories, recalling all the research I either helped my sister with or overheard in passing. There must be something I'm missing. The banshees evolved to breathe toxic air, and when I bonded with them, I gained immunity to the poison. Perhaps that's the key we need now.

If I bond with her, maybe the others wouldn't accidentally drain her energy. Or if they still did, she might be stronger because she can draw from me as well.

"So, what happens now?" I ask.

Marshal clears his throat, exchanging glances with Logan and Carter. "An unbonded druadan is unpredictable, so while we figure out what we'll do next with her, I think you're long overdue to start your training as a rider." His eyes meet mine, serious but with a glimmer of hope. "What do you say, Novice?"

I choke out an unexpected laugh, joy bubbling up through the tears. "I say, hell yes. Let's do it."

Fifty-One

Marshal

I watch my sister fiddle with Oriana's lead rope, grumbling under her breath as she keeps dropping it in the dirt.

I cross my arms as a warmth of pride spreads across my chest.

Or relief.

Or maybe a little of both.

Despite everything, we pulled it off.

And now seeing them together, here, it's like I can breathe a little easier, and judging by the way everyone else is passing a tin of salted fish around and cracking jokes about the terrible smelling gas they're sure to induce, I know I'm not the only one.

After the reunion, we returned inside to eat and talk about the next steps. They stole enough feed for Oriana to last three days, maybe four if we stretched it with wild game, Waylon assured was safe to eat.

Logan, Heath, and Carter watch Brigid like she's the center of the universe. It threw me at first, my sister with not one, but three men caught in her orbit. But I'm slowly growing used to it, and while Logan was a bit of a wild card, their devotion to her was proof enough in my book that they were right for her.

And if anyone could handle a trio like that, it's Brigid. And honestly? One man was never going to be enough to satisfy her.

"Good," I nod, already mentally planning her training regimen. "Now, tie her to the rail over there, and we'll go over physiology."

Carter snorts behind me. "Going full instructor already?"

I shoot him a look. "You got a better idea?"

"The basics first," I continue, ignoring him. "Feeding, grooming, basic commands. Oriana may be bonded to you on some level, but she's been in captivity. She needs to learn to be a proper druadan again."

"Carter can help," Heath says. "Logan and I will take first watch."

It's a good idea. We stole a druanera from a government-owned facility.

They'll be looking.

She struggles with a Tides knows how old horse's saddle, Waylon lent us. Her hands are uncertain as she tries to position it correctly on the blanket on Oriana's back. The mare shifts uncomfortably, and my sister nearly drops the whole thing.

"Easy," I call out, and step in and take it from her. "Even though you're not bonded, she still senses your frustration. Take a breath."

She shoots me an irritated look but does as I say, inhaling deeply before trying again. She's been at this for hours now, and we've barely made progress on the basics. But we don't have the luxury of time. I don't know how long Jess and I can stay here. I called Blackhawk on the way here, telling them I was visiting family for a few days, but the longer I'm away, the harder it'll be to keep the lie.

"Here," I say, and hand it back. "Remember this part goes toward her tail."

"I know that," she snaps, then immediately looks apologetic. "Sorry. I'm just—"

"Frustrated. I get it." I move closer, but not too close. She needs to figure this out herself. "Listen, I promised you before I'd help you become a rider, and I intend to keep that promise." Her eyes drift to mine. "Every novice struggles at first. Even the ones who seem naturally gifted."

"Like you?" she asks, tilting her head.

I snort. "Hardly. I dropped the saddle on my instructor's foot on my first day. Pretty sure he still walks with a limp."

That gets a laugh out of her and smoothes the furrow between her brows.

Once the saddle is secured, I loop a bridle over my arm. "Now, in regards to the marks on her face." I gesture to the distinctive markings on Oriana's nose and brow. "They're unique, like fingerprints."

She pauses and looks more closely at Oriana's face. "Really?"

"Each druadan has their own pattern. And they're incredibly sensitive like the tip of your finger or—" I catch myself, remembering I'm not speaking to a nineteen-year-old boy.

"Or what?" she smirks.

I clear my throat. "Other *sensitive* areas. Which is why we avoid touching them, especially if they're bonded to another rider."

I help her slip the bridle on, careful not to have the leather rub her nose. Oriana is extremely willing and takes the bit without fuss.

Druadans, unlike horses, are practically born trained. They're wild, unrepedicible when unbonded, but when it comes to basics like bridling, saddling, and moving off pressure, it's ingrained into their DNA.

I go over the parts of the bridle, and have her take it on and off a few times. While she practices, I gesture toward the box of feed pellets Logan and Heath stole from Lanett, trying to move on. "We only have enough of those pellets for three, maybe four days if we're careful. Jess is finding another place for us to go. An old warehouse in Leviler, maybe. Or even a boat."

"You'll go back to Blackhawk?"

"I have to," I concede. "With everything going on with the government and the country, they need me." She'd told me ITM had cameras and spies there, and the sooner I get back and cut them off, the better. I'm certain Lugsen is trustworthy, but there are too many doubts regarding Fiaro. He very easily could be in ITM's back pocket now.

She lets out a squeal as she finally gets the bit positioned correctly.

"Good. Now secure it under her chin, but not too tight."

As she works, I tell her more about the bloodlines from which all druadans originate. It's first quarter Vanguard Academy information, but she didn't get the luxury of having this drilled into her for weeks. "Oriana is part of the Solara bloodline, which died out centuries ago. The DNA was too corrupted from the thawing and freezing."

"The egg my sister stole," she says, concentrating on the straps. "That was Raven line, right?"

"Right." I squint. "You saw it, didn't you? The other egg hatched."

Her fingers still.

"What was it?" She's holding back. "Tell me."

"It was another druanera."

My lips part with the breath, and behind me, the other three cease their conversation.

"She was all black, and so I guessed based on the Raven lines always being black."

I wait. A dozen questions pop into my mind.

"Sharice wanted to bond with her. But she didn't have the setup to take care of her, and so..." Her voice breaks off. "She died."

A long silence stretches between us. "I'm sorry. Druadans aren't easy to take care of. ITM was arrogant to think they could keep her."

Brigid sighs and pulls the strap through the ring. I had regular updates from Lugsen. Oriana was started under the saddle, though not ridden. She is exceptionally calm and docile for such a young horse. Or perhaps all druaneras are this way?

I watch Brigid's fingers work, correcting her gently when needed. "Back to the bloodlines. They can influence their temperatures, varying from druadan to druadan. Some are just uncomfortable to touch, while others, like the Inferno line, are at the hotter end of the spectrum."

She nods, absorbing the information while still working on the saddle. "What about phasing? Can you tell me more about that?"

"When you phase, you end up in your own space. Think of the Nowhere as a hotel with a million doors, and each time you go through, it's a new one. That's why we spend so much time training so that when riders phase, they learn to control their trajectory, speed, and angles. They're literally flying blind as they can't see each other, and accidents do happen where a pair of riders collide."

"Great," she says, "One more way I can die a horrible death as a rider."

I hate telling her all of this, but if I don't, no one will. This is a druadan rider crash course, and I need to give her all the information to keep her safe. "Most riders die in accidents. Thrown from their stallions, trampled, or caught in a phase shift gone wrong. If you survive long enough to flare out, you count yourself lucky." I pause, making sure she's following. "The untrained ones can incorrectly phase, leaving behind the rider or the stallion. In worst-case scenarios, half of each." I shudder at the memory of finding such remains. "They call those splices. Thankfully, they're rare, and in my entire career, I've been fortunate enough to witness it once."

Brigid's face is somber, her expression telling me she's heard this before, though perhaps never so bluntly stated.

She finishes with the bridle, stepping back to admire her work. It's not perfect, but it's much better. "Okay," she begins, "So how about one of the *good* things? Tell me more about how bonding works."

I know where this is going. "They have to initiate it," I tell her. "There are no shortcuts. No cheat options. It's a lesson in patience and faith."

"I'm scared." Her voice drops, and a haunted look creeps onto her face. She's been tight-lipped about everything they made her do at ITM, and I'm afraid to press her for details, opting to wait until she is ready.

She looks away, but not before I glimpse the tears brimming in her eyes. "What if I'm not worthy of her?"

"That's not for you to decide," I say gently but firmly. "She'll be the one to choose. I've worked with novices and unbonded for years, and I've never seen a druadan and a person connect as quickly as you two have. Now you need to choose her back."

Two hours later, we put away Oriana. I made her do all the feeding, brushing, and cleaning of her hooves. I try my best not to overwhelm her with training that takes months condensed into a few days.

"We'll continue tomorrow, and might even get you on her back." I squeeze her shoulder. "You've made good progress today, *Novice*."

She wipes at her eyes and nods. "Thank you, Marshal."

"For what?"

"For believing in me, even when I don't."

Without warning, she rushes over and hugs me. I squeeze her back, savoring the feeling. Special doesn't begin to describe what she is to me. The living proof that I'm not alone in this world, that it's not just Mom and me carrying our family's legacy.

I wish Dad could see her now and know the remarkable woman she's become, despite everything. He'd be so proud. I consider telling her more about him. She deserves to know the man behind the stories, the father whose blood runs in her veins. But her slumped shoulders tell me she carries the weight of too many revelations for one day.

Soon, I'll tell him about her, but not today.

Fifty-Two

Heath

I observe from a distance as Marshal teaches Brigid the nuances of druadan care.

They've been at this for three days, and not surprisingly, Brigid is catching on to everything quickly.

Carter and I are more than capable of teaching her, but for whatever reason, this feels right. Besides being more experienced, Marshal is her brother.

And in a way, this is helping fill in for the years they spent apart, not knowing each other.

They'd been robbed of a shared childhood, and these past few days, as they work together, they appear to be reclaiming something precious that was taken from them both.

Brigid furrows her brow in concentration, and Oriana

tolerates her fumbling with a patience rarely seen in young druadans.

When they pause for a water break, I clear my throat. "You mind if I steal her for a moment?"

Marshal glances between us, then steps back. "What for?"

"We need to get measurements. My family's tailor is on standby. You'll need proper riding gear if Oriana calls to you." Brigid's bright eyes shift toward me.

"Riding gear?" she repeats.

"You can't ride in your regular clothes."

She looks at Marshal.

"We've been at this for over an hour. I don't see how a break can hurt. Put Oriana away, and we can meet up again after lunch to go over leg and heel positions."

I wait as Brigid leads Oriana into her stall and then steps beside me as we leave the barn, enter the cabin, and ascend the staircase to the loft.

Carter catches sight of us from the couch, and arousal spiked with a twinge of jealousy drifts from him.

Once in the loft, I rifle through my bag for my spare clothes and uniform. The only possessions I have now after abandoning my position. Everything else I own remains at Blackhawk.

I hand her the pair of riding pants. "Try these. They'll be too long, but we'll get an idea of the fit at least."

She takes them from me but hesitates.

I gesture to the large bookshelf sitting diagonally in the corner. "You can change there if you'd like."

She bobs her head and scurries behind it.

I've seen every inch of her moonlit skin, breathless and bare, knees spread, fingers teasing pleasure between her legs while I watched on my knees and chased my own. And now she hides from me like a stranger.

I find the measuring tape. My fingers hover over it. I measured countless novices for gear, but this feels different.

Because it is. Because this is Brigid.

"Ready," she says, and steps out. The hems of the pants pool around her ankles, and she's gripping the waistband to keep them from falling.

She giggles. "They're more comfortable than I expected."

I step to her and kneel. Her scent has a faint trace of the saddle oil Carter used and the musky note of druadan. "It's the carbon fiber blend with the cotton," I tell her. "Keeps them light but still insulative."

"We could take them in? You think Waylon has a sewing machine I could—?"

"No," I say firmly, standing. "If you're going to be a rider, you'll need a proper fitting uniform."

I gesture for her to lift her arms as I wrap the tape around her waist, my knuckles grazing the bare strip of skin where her t-shirt rides up. She's still, but I catch her biting her lip.

"Turn around," I say. She turns slightly, and I measure the distance from her hip to her heel. The tape slides over the curve of her hip, and a tightness forms in my throat. I'm trapped in a fierce tug-of-war with myself. The desire to maintain a gentlemanly distance warring with the need to strip off her clothes and make her cry out my name.

"How're you feeling?" I need to break the silence.

She exhales. "Overwhelmed. There's so much I don't know, and I worry this is a waste of time with everything else going on."

"All the more reason for you to do this. We can't predict the future, but we can make the most of today. There's a reason Vanguard is two years, but you've always impressed me with your quick learning. If our days really are numbered as you say, why not spend them doing what we want?"

She laughs. "I love your optimism, I just worry all this will be for nothing and Oriana still won't bond with me."

I rise to my feet and peer down at her. "Do you think you're the first novice to be nervous and think you're not worthy? The hardest two months of my life were waiting for Shadowmane to start the bond. Night after night, I wondered if the manager had paired me with the wrong stallion and that it would never happen." I slide a hand over her neck, gently brushing her hair aside. She flinches before gathering her hair and holding it out of the way for me. "But it did. Just like it will for you. I promise."

She grins, and it steals my breath away. "I'll hold you to that."

She disappears behind the bookshelf again, and I put away the tape, marking the measurements on my comm. I see the flurry of messages from my family and friends at Blackhawk, all asking where I am and what happened.

I can't reply without them being able to trace me here. My parents have sent me a picture of them and their friends on the yacht, anchored off the Delford coast near an island. Anger surges, remembering how many people died in the city, lost their homes or loved ones, and my parents pretend like it's a goddamn vacation.

Their obliviousness to others' pain isn't just embarrassing anymore. It's become morally repugnant. And I can't fully escape the knowledge that I benefit from the very system I claim to despise.

"Okay," she says, biting her lip, a playful glint in her eyes. "Since we're playing dress-up."

She steps back into the room wearing nothing but my riding jacket. The black fabric hangs loosely from her shoulders, the hem brushing the tops of her knees. She hugs it closed with crossed arms, the gold embroidery catching the subdued light of the lamp. Her bare legs, long and lean, stretch from beneath the coat, her toes curling slightly against the wood floor.

"Ms. Corsair." My mouth goes as dry as the wasteland outside.

My breath is snatched from me, and not just because she looks sexy as hell in it with her coy smile and pursed lips, it's that she looks perfect in it, as if it's meant for her. As if she's destined to wear it, and the vision of her as a rider fills me with indescribable joy.

"What do you think?" she says, with a seductive tilt of her head.

"It's against the rules to wear another rider's jacket," I reply, but there's no weight to my words, only heat.

She tilts her head further. "It is? Funny, I wasn't aware." She traces her finger along the button holes, inching open the front, her aqua eyes so full of heat I can hardly breathe, never leave mine. "I guess you better take it off me, then."

With three swift steps, I'm next to her. My hands in her hair, my mouth on hers. She gasps, and I capture it with my lips.

The jacket falls to the floor.

Her silver hair cascades over her breasts, and I gently brush it over her shoulders. I feast at the sight of her rosy pink nipples like a man starved.

"My god, you're beautiful," I whisper slowly and move down her neck to the tops of her shoulders.

She moans as I run my knuckles over her stomach until just under a breast. My fingers knead the smooth skin, thumb flicking her nipple. She arches her back, breathing my name. "Heath..."

God, she's here. She's *really* here. Every inch of her is perfection—soft, silken, alive. I want to touch all of her, taste her, feel her under my hands, and reassure myself that she's not slipping away again. I thought I'd lost her. The months without her carved holes into me that I didn't know how to fill.

"I dreamed of this day for weeks," I murmur against her skin, my voice breaking. My hands frame her face, forcing myself to meet her gaze. Her eyes, dark and steady, anchor me in this moment.

"I did, too," she whispers, her fingers brushing my jaw. Her touch steadies me more than words ever could.

I kiss her, pour everything I've held back into the moment. My hands roam her body, relearning every curve, memorizing the warmth of her skin. Her scent, her taste, the sound of her breath hitching...

"I need to remember this," I say, my lips brushing her collarbone, moving lower, trailing across her stomach. "Every part of you. I need to know you're real."

Her hands tangle in my hair, clutching me to her chest. "I'm not going anywhere," she says, and I commit each syllable to memory like a prayer I never knew I needed to hear.

I can't wait any longer.

I release her for a split second. Leaving my boots on, I unbutton my pants and shirt. With shaky hands, I tug my pants down enough, feeling the relief of the erection that had been trapped in my pants.

I need to feel her beneath me, pressed against my chest, and box her in between my arms.

Grasping her hips, I stare into her eyes and guide myself inside of her.

I push into her slowly at first, savoring the welcoming warmth, and she gasps as we're joined for the first time. She's exquisitely tight, and her warmth envelops me as I sheath my full length into her. Her head arches back, her body yielding to my presence, and the sensation surpasses every pleasure I have ever known.

She is my ruin, and I've never wanted to be more thoroughly destroyed by her than I am at this moment.

There's a sound at the door, and she tenses, her muscles clamping tightly around me, ushering a groan of pleasure from my throat.

Her nails dig into my shoulders. "Someone is here," she whispers, her voice coated in heat.

My fingers dig into her hips, keeping her pressed down on me. I don't care if it's God himself, we're not stopping.

Soon, however, Carter's presence, sweet and hot, like liquid caramel, permeates the room. "Helping take measurements?" he says, as a spike of arousal flutters through the bond, coalescing with mine.

Her eyes fix on Carter behind me, but the pain from her nails eases. My desire amplified by his present, I glide her slowly up and down my length, feeling her wetness seep over my balls, no doubt encouraged by her excitement at Carter's appearance.

There's a soft patter of footsteps, and then Carter stands above us. His pupils are blown with desire as he watches.

"Taking measurements for a coat, huh?"

She tilts her head to the side, and he runs a finger along the ridge of her shoulder, gliding slowly down to the swell of her full breasts.

"You didn't honestly think you two could have fun without me?"

She lets out a whimper at his touch, and I continue to rock my hips into her. Her cheeks are flushed, and her erect nipples graze my chest, making my balls ache with every thrust.

Carter slips his hard dick from his pants. It's inches from

her face; she tilts her head, licking her lips with desire as he runs a hand slowly up and down his shaft.

"You want a taste?" he says, voice like gravel.

Brigid's mouth parts expectantly as she stares up at him through long eyelashes. Slowly, her gaze drifts down from his face to his bare chest, to his stomach, and then to his hard length.

She releases her left hand from my shoulder and reaches out, encircling it with her hand.

He releases a shudder of breath as she instantly begins stroking it.

"Take him in your mouth," I command. "I want to watch you suck him while I bury my cock in that tight pussy."

She blinks, her eyes widening as Carter steps closer. He cradles the back of her head and brings her lips to the head of his dick. She resists slightly, her tongue flicking in and out, teasing him, before he coaxes her with a thumb on her bottom lip, and she opens, taking every inch of his length.

"Good girl," I say through gritted teeth as a fresh, hot wave of desire crashes over me from Carter.

The bond ignites, and Carter and I are one. Our arousal feeds into one another's like gasoline in flames; each sensation amplifies our desire in an escalating cycle.

I felt the first whispers of this when we took her and Jess to bed, but I was restrained and guarded. My emotions were tempered by the need for the union to have a purpose.

This has no purpose beyond pleasure.

A carnal, primitive desire. Pure and untethered.

She lifts a hand, wrapping her fingers around the base of his cock, and there's wet sucking noise that fills the room. I slow my thrusts, allowing her to suck and stroke him. My hand drifts up from her hips to her round breasts, and I squeeze their fullness, my thumbs painting circles on her nipples, savoring the delicious sounds the three of us are making.

Carter cradles her head, fingers lacing into her hair as he eases in and out of her mouth.

My body moves with hers, our hips grinding against each other. My balls tighten, and I increase my pace, watching Carter's body react the same.

The pleasure intensifies, and Brigid writhes atop me, her guttural moans growing louder.

Carter's sensations blur with mine, and I catch flickers of the feeling of her soft lips wrapped around my dick, sucking.

It's too much. With three hard thrusts, I bury myself in her and groan with my release.

"Fuck, I'm going to come," Carter warns her, but she doesn't pull back. Instead, she works it faster with her mouth and hands.

Carter's hands lace into her hair, cupping the back of her head, eyes fixed on where they're joined. "Fuck," he curses again and stills as he spills into her.

My dick still hard dick is inside her, and she lets go of Carter's with a wet pop. She shifts back, wiping her mouth with a small giggle.

God, she looks glorious with swollen lips and pupils blown with desire.

She senses my continued arousal and arches a left brow.

My hunger is nowhere satisfied, and neither is Carter's, but the swaying of her head and drooping of her eyelids tells me more will have to wait.

Carter tucks away his dick and grabs her by her waist, easily lifting her naked body and laying her on the bed.

I lie down beside her, and he joins on the other side to create a protective circle around her. She stirs slightly, then nestles between us and closes her eyes.

We doze off and on until Waylon's voice calls up to us from downstairs, announcing dinner is ready. Carter and I exchange reluctant glances, neither of us eager to break this spell.

"We should go down," I whisper without moving.

"You first," Carter challenges.

A smirk tugs at the edges of my mouth. "Not a chance."

He laughs softly. "Then it looks like we're going to starve."

I peer at her sleeping face in the fading light.

For her, it's worth it.

Fifty-Three

BRIGID

Snow falls the next day, melting as it lands on Oriana's golden coat. I stand outside the barn, watching her eat from the bucket of stolen protein pellets, trying to quiet the riot of thoughts in my head. I'm desperate to focus on Marshal's lessons, but my mind keeps drifting to Heath and Carter yesterday.

The memory brings a stupid smile to my face. Tides, nothing was more sexy than the look in his eyes when I came out wearing only his coat. It was totally impulsive, wearing his jacket like that, but I'm glad I did. What started as just trying to crack Heath's serious face actually worked way better than I thought it would.

I don't remember the last time I felt that carefree. The time spent with ITM allowed little room for anything beyond work, sleep, or more work. And wearing his jacket, teasing him, it was like recapturing a small part of myself I thought I lost. And it was clear from the way he played back he thought he lost it, too.

My cheeks burn at the vivid memory, and a pulse starts between my legs, just *thinking* about him letting me tease him.

And then Carter arrived. I panicked, thinking he'd be jealous, but he joined. And tides how I wanted him to. Perhaps he picked up on Heath's arousal upstairs.

But Logan hadn't.

He can't feel them anymore. My stomach twists. It's like we take three steps forward and one step back.

Every time it felt like we were becoming whole again, another wrench was thrown into the gears. All the more reason for doing what we did. *Carpe fucking diem.* I heard Logan say that once at Blackhawk.

I transition back into the present, staring at Oriana, still unable to believe she's actually here. Marshal insists she's ready to ride—maybe she is—but something still holds me back. I'm not a rider. I've ridden a horse twice at a carnival, and even then, it was led. I'm about as far from a rider as can be.

"You're overthinking this," Marshal says over my shoulder.

I grip the lead rope tighter. "I want to do this right." Oriana lifts her head at my voice, ears pricking forward. She moves toward the stall door with a fluid grace that still takes my breath away. Even now, I feel the tentative brush of her consciousness against mine.

Not quite a bond, but something more than nothing. The frustration of almost-but-not-quite makes my chest ache.

I'm tired of this one-way connection. I trust her. That's not the issue. But all riders can speak to their druadan. They share thoughts, feelings. Real communication. And I'm just...guessing.

"And you will," Marshal says.

Oriana lets me put on her halter, and I lead her outside, where Marshal set the saddle and bridle.

Snowflakes catch in Oriana's mane. "I feel like I'm failing her somehow."

Marshal leans against the fence, arms crossed. "She's ready, Brigid. You're the one who keeps hesitating."

I shoot him a look, but he's right. Oriana's grown so much in the past months—her withers now level with my shoulder, her frame filled out into the powerful build characteristic of mature druadans. But every time I think about getting closer, bonding with her, I remember the banshees. How it felt to force that connection, to bend their will to mine. And how it made those people lose their minds.

But everyone is depending on me, and I'm more convinced than ever that bonding with Oriana is the key to saving her if we want her to stay with us.

We spend an hour on groundwork. Doing what Marshal calls lunging, where I take one of the long ropes Waylon found and have her walk, trot, and run circles around me. The slow version of running is actually called cantering, Marshal told me, along with things like changing leads, how to use my body to tell her to change direction, and more.

Once lessons for the afternoon are over, I guide Oriana back toward the barn, the rope loose in my hands. She follows willingly now, her initial wariness replaced with something that feels like trust. Once again, I'm struck with the idea that mares bond differently than stallions. The stallions are aggressive, a tense and dangerous dance that leads to getting bit, but maybe mares are different. Maybe it's easier or more subtle. Maybe it's already happening, and I don't even know.

With renewed hope fluttering in my chest, I lead her into the stall and lock the door.

"You riding her yet?" Carter calls out as he struggles with an armful of wooden planks. He and Heath have been busy while Marshal and I worked with the Oriana, transforming the dilapidated barn into something more functional.

I shake my head, somewhat embarrassed, like I'm taking too long.

Marshal saves me. "Not yet. I'm thinking she'll be ready tomorrow, though."

The sound of approaching footsteps draws our attention to the barn entrance. Logan appears with dirt on the side of his cheek and one hand gripping the arm of a man I never expected to see again. The man staggers forward as Logan shoves him roughly from behind, his hands bound in front of him. I recognized him immediately as one of the guys from maintenance at the ITM base, but I can't recall his name.

"Look what I found," Logan announces as he forces the man to his knees.

Heath drops the hammer he holds, and Carter steps forward, his body tensing.

"Where?" Carter asks, his voice low.

"Southwest, about a half mile from the treeline," Logan replies. "He wasn't alone, but the others ran."

The man's face is bruised, and a trickle of blood runs from his split lip, but his eyes remain defiant. He spits on the ground and says nothing.

I move away from Oriana's stall. The peaceful feeling from

our training session evaporates, replaced by the cold reality of our situation.

If he escaped, then others must have as well.

"Get him inside," Heath says. "We need to know what they know."

Fifty-Four

LOGAN

"Gladly," I tell Heath and hoist up the guy onto his feet.

I shove him to the left side of the barn, making him sit by the goat pen.

"Tell us who you are."

His gaze swings wildly around before landing on Brigid.

"Please," he gasps when he spots her. "Wayfinder! I knew you were alive. Please, you have to leave, they're coming. I can't—I need—"

"Get back!" I draw my pistol and advance. Heath and Marshal flank me, weapons ready.

The rebel pushes himself up and fails, leaving a smear of blood on the wall. His face is gray. "I'm not armed," he wheezes. "Please. I just need help."

"Hate to break it to you, buddy," Carter says, "but I think you're long past help."

I watch Brigid. I see her softening. Consider helping this guy.

I gesture with my pistol. "Do you know him?"

She bites the side of her thumbnail and nods. "Yeah, he worked in maintenance at the base."

"That's right," the man drawls. "You know *me*. You know, we all ran when they attacked us. Please." He winces and clutches the wound on his stomach.

"Who else is coming? I demand. "Who else knows we're here?"

The man wheezes and shakes his head. "I don't know. I don't know."

"I think he's telling the truth," Brigid says.

"I don't." I lift the pistol, directing it at him. He's ten minutes from punching the clock. It would be a mercy killing. "You've got five seconds to tell me how you found us before I end what I already started."

"No," the man murmurs, shielding his face with his hands.

"One."

"Two."

"Three."

"Four."

Brigid places herself between my gun and the whimpering man. She levels me with her gaze, brows furrowed. "He's innocent, Logan. I won't let you kill him."

"Brigid!" Marshal's voice cracks with alarm. "What are you doing?"

"He's hurt." She spreads her arms like some kind of human shield. "Whatever he's done, he needs medical attention, not an execution."

"He's dangerous," I argue, though we know it's not entirely true, not in his current state.

"He's helpless. Look at him. Is this who we are? People who

shoot wounded men in barns? We're no better than them if we do."

Her chest heaves as she locks her gaze with mine. The only sound is the guy's labored breathing and distant thunder.

Brigid doesn't move. I know that look on her face. She's not backing down.

"Fuck," I say, holstering my gun.

I drop my eyes from hers and stare at the guy. "Marshal, see if Waylon has first aid. Carter, keep an eye outside, and Heath, help me secure him."

As we lift him, the two-faced bastard spits in my face.

"Do that again, and I'll break your jaw," I growl.

The man scowls but keeps his mouth shut. Heath wraps a rope around his waist, looping it around one of the barn posts.

"Not so tight," Brigid says. I ignore her and tug the last knot hard enough to make him squirm.

Heath crouches beside the man, keeping his distance. "We can help you," he says quietly. "But we need to know what happened at the base."

The man's eyes dart between Heath and me. His tattered pants are singed at the edges, exposing streaks of raw, reddened burns on his right thigh.

"I already told you, I don't know," he spits, but there's fear under the tough act. His eyes keep coming back to me. Good.

"The base is over fifty miles from here," Brigid says. "No way you made it this far on foot with that leg."

Surprise flashes across the man's face before he can hide it. She hit on something.

I step forward, and he flinches. "Someone brought you here," I snap. "Who?"

"Back off," Heath says sharply, standing up. "You're not helping."

"We don't have time for—"

"I said *back* off." Heath's voice has an edge I rarely hear, and our eyes lock.

He's back. The confident Lockwood who impressed teachers at Vanguard with straight A's and snuck in contraband chocolate for us.

The doubt and hesitation he's had for months is finally fucking gone.

My brothers are finding their way back.

Too bad I'm still out in the cold.

"Let me handle this," he says, voice low.

My jaw flexes, and I step back, giving him space.

Waylon stomps into the barn carrying a pail. His eyes land on the man, then on us, and he sighs, shaking his head. "Just don't leave any mess," he says, scooping a bucket of water from the rain collector.

There's movement from above. Nova and Jace are watching from the hayloft, legs dangling. Nova looks fascinated. Jace is trying to look cool and failing. Waylon catches sight of them. "What in blazes are you two doing? Get down from there!" he barks. "Inside, both of you. Now!"

"Shit," Nova mutters loudly. They scramble out of the top of the loft and down the ladder with muffled giggles.

"Look," Heath says softly, "lately, Circuit's army isn't known for leaving survivors. The fact that you made it out..." He leaves it hanging.

The man's jaw works. Finally, he looks at Heath, then briefly at Brigid. "You really want to know what happened at the base?" His voice is hoarse. "Hell itself opened. That's what happened. And it's coming this way."

Fifty-Five

BRIGID

The man's wet and ragged laugh dissolves into a violent coughing fit. Crimson spatters across his sleeve as he wipes his mouth.

Standing in front of Logan is reckless, but I'm tired of standing idly by as more death happens around me. I can't stand it anymore.

I thought I was past this. The memories of Elton shooting the banshees in front of me and then the volunteers being subjected to an experiment that destroyed their minds and their willpower.

When I was with ITM, I didn't have control, but now I do. So, I stopped Logan from shooting him. And it worked, but I doubt I'll get him to listen again. They are right, and a rebel here is dangerous.

"What do you mean, hell itself?" Heath presses, leaning forward.

Another laugh, more blood. "There were too many. They tried blowing it up, but they're smart. Smarter than you think."

"Who?" Heath asks. "*Who* is smart?"

His eyes go distant, unfocused. "The mystyl. They're not the mindless drones we thought they were. They work together."

The drift Sharice and Elton were struggling to control? Is that what he's talking about?

"Bullshit," Carter says. "They attack recklessly. I've faced down hundreds of them. There is no way they're in control."

"If you say so." He shrugs as his breathing comes in shallow wheezes. He struggles for air; each breath seems harder than the last. His lungs are trashed. The TZ burned them from the inside out. I've seen it before. He won't last long.

Behind me, the others argue in harsh whispers.

"We turn him in," Heath insists. "Make an anonymous tip or send Jess or Marshal. The authorities need to know what happened."

"Are you insane?" Carter's voice rises before he catches himself. "He'll tell them everything he's seen here. Putting Waylon and those kids at risk, too. You know what we left behind, Heath. Circuit won't care they're kids."

Heath's brown eyes darken.

"Carter's right," Logan says flatly. "We end this here. *Now*. He's seen us. Seen Brigid and the mare. We can't let him leave."

Their words fade as my attention drifts to Oriana's stall. Those impossibly violet eyes fix on mine. She lets out a low thrum, so low I can almost mistake it for my heartbeat.

A flicker of movement catches my eye as he hoists himself

upright. Time slows as I see his fingers curl around a rusty pistol buried in the straw and dirt.

He points it at Carter's back.

I don't think.

"No!" I yell and throw myself into him, and the two of us crash against the door of Oriana's stall.

Pain blinds me. White hot and jagged, burning away all thought, all sensation. My body convulses as if being ripped from the inside out, every cell screaming in rebellion. It's as if someone has grabbed each limb and is pulling, stretching me beyond human limits. My bones feel like they're splintering, muscles tearing fiber by fiber. I try to scream, but nothing comes. Mind stretching thin, my consciousness smears, and I'm everywhere and nowhere, disintegrating like sand thrown into a hurricane. Each particle of me spins away, losing cohesion.

A violent pressure builds in my skull until my ears pop with a sickening, hollow sound like I've plunged hundreds of feet underwater in an instant. The pressure doesn't release; instead, it implodes, crushing inward.

Someone curses, and then the world goes dark.

Fifty-Six

CARTER

The laser blast ricochets off the pillar next to me, a sharp, searing crack that snaps me out of my haze. My heart lurches, adrenaline spiking as I leap forward to shove Brigid out of the way, but my hands grasp nothing but air. She's gone. My eyes dart around frantically—Oriana and Brigid are both gone. Vanished. A hollow, echoing pop still lingers in my ears, a sensation I felt deep in the bond, like a string snapping tight then going slack.

"They *phased*?" Logan shouts, his voice raw with disbelief, cutting through the ringing in my head. "Are you shitting me right now?"

I can barely process it myself. Phasing is dangerous

enough, even with a bond. Uncontrolled, unguided, it could tear them apart without a bond.... "It's impossible," I say.

Marshal rests his hands on his hips and shakes his head. "I think we've all been around Brigid long enough to know that word doesn't apply to her."

I rub my face with my hands, the rough calluses scraping against my skin as if I can scrub away the confusion. We're all struggling to wrap our heads around this. Phasing without a bond is like hearing a rule of nature has been broken, like gravity suddenly stopped working. "So," I say. "Let's accept that they *did* phase. What do we do now?"

The thought of Brigid out there, lost or hurt, sends a surge of dread through me.

"You take Waylon's truck and see if you can find her." Marshal's voice pulls me back, steady but grim, as he stares at the guy lying lifeless on the ground. "She couldn't have gone too far." There's a forced confidence in his words, a lifeline we're all clinging to. The farthest phase on record is a mile.

Galaxian escaped his stall the night the mystyl attacked the barn at Meridian. We never figured out how, but either way, it shattered the firm belief that druadans could only phase with a rider. That was supposed to be a constant. A rule.

And that was with druadans. With the druaneras, we know even less.

My brain is on overdrive as the three of us pile into the scrap truck. The three of us grab the masks from under the seat and strap them over our heads.

"Take the south road," Heath tells Logan in the driver's seat. "Waylon says it runs along the lower part of the hill, then we can cut across to the north."

Logan grunts an acknowledgment and starts the engine.

I stare out at the dense forest beyond the scrubland, its shadowed depths swallowing the fading light.

AMELIA COLE

I've faced danger before, but this is different. It's Brigid.

All I can do is hold onto the hope we'll find them in one piece and together and that, somehow, we'll figure out what the hell just happened.

Fifty-Seven

BRIGID

I blink, returning to consciousness, and push my face out of the snow, my head swimming like I just stepped off a carousel spinning at full speed. Pine needles and dirt cling to my face, and I wipe them away, spitting.

The snow falls in soft, fat flakes around me. We're in a forest, the pine and cedar branches heavy with white. A break in the trunks reveals we're somewhere deep in the forested hills surrounding Waylon's cabin.

At least, I think so.

Far to my left, in the distance, a ruined city looks like a mouth of broken teeth against the horizon. I clasp my hand over my mouth, stopping my breathing.

Oh shit. *Where the hell am I?*

"You are safe, and you are with me. What else is there?"

My head swivels toward the sound. "Who's there?"

Oriana stands across the clearing a dozen steps away from me. Her violet eyes watch me, head lowered.

"Hello?" My chest does a weird vibrating, almost itchy, and I press a hand to it. "Wait!" I yell. "I can hear *you?*"

The mare lifts her head, arching her graceful neck. *"And I hear you."*

Her voice is soft and light, like sunlight itself. *"How is this happening?"*

She lowers her nose to the ground, sniffing. *"I do not know. I only know I brought us here."*

I shiver uncontrollably as snot drips out of my nose. *"You did?"*

"You were in danger." She paws at the ground, stumbling closer before collapsing in the snow. Hard. Flakes fly when her massive form collides with the ground with an earth-shaking thump. *"You are safe now, but I'm quite tired."*

I scramble on my hands and knees through the snow to her.

No. This can't be happening. She phased with me. Brought me here to save me from being hurt, but...

My trembling hand moves to my shoulder, pressing against the wound, and warm, sticky blood wells up between my fingers. The crimson stain spreads across my shirt, a dark, expanding bloom against the fabric.

It's bad and hurts like hell, but I don't think it did any major damage. Clutching my arm to my side, I scoot closer. Oriana lies her head down with a grunt and begins wheezing.

My fingers brush the callused ridges on her nose, and she releases a low groan.

"No, no, no. Please. Wait. Tell me what's wrong!"

I lift her heavy head onto my lap; her eyes are half-closed.

Sweat mats her golden hair, and her warmth rapidly melts the snow, exposing the pine needle-littered forest floor.

"You're not supposed to die. God, please."

The bond is dying before her body. I feel it, a strange unraveling, like threads of a tapestry being slowly pulled apart. She used the last of her energy to transport us here and there's nothing left. "Hang on, please. You'll be okay, I promise—"

I glance helplessly around me. "Somebody help me!" I call out their names, hoping, praying they're close enough to hear.

Silence.

"I'm sorry. I'm sorry I didn't think I deserved you. I'm sorry I wasn't good enough. I'm sorry I didn't fight harder. I'm sorry I drained your power. I'm so sorry."

With a final, ragged sigh, Oriana stops breathing.

Fifty-Eight

ORIANA

Before I was born, before I ever saw light, I knew her.

My warrior. My soldier. My chosen.

When I hatched, she was out there, waiting. I was meant to be with her, to fight beside her. My body was supposed to be strong, a weapon, a shield.

Now, I am broken.

I had wished for more time. Time to learn, to run, to explore, to find a mate.

But my time is cut short.

Yet I'm content with it. Strange how that is. Peace eclipsing the pain.

Because I saved her, my chosen, from the bad man, in the

end, I found strength buried inside me. I used it all, every last drop, to pull her through the space between worlds to keep her safe.

That was worth it. That was enough.

Fifty-Nine

BRIGID

О riana is gone.

The loss is like a tidal wave, pressing me into the frozen earth beneath her still body. I don't remember falling to my knees, only that I am here now, fingers tangled in the thick fur of her neck, forehead pressed against her cooling face. My breath shudders, misting in the cold air.

It happened again.

First Iris. Now Oriana. The last of them. Gone.

I shouldn't have been here. I was never a rider. Just a foolish girl with too much ambition and too much arrogance to know better. I thought I could be part of something greater, that I could help, that I could matter. But all I am is death. Everywhere I go, I bring it with me.

A broken sob tears from my throat, raw and desperate. My fingers tighten against Oriana's fur as if I can anchor her here, keep her from slipping into the abyss. But she's already gone. I failed her. I failed all of them.

I should have been stronger, smarter, faster, anything but what I am. Useless.

I have to do something. *Anything.* I can't just sit here, drowning in grief, while Oriana fades into nothing. My hand drifts, almost without thought, to the back of my neck. My fingers brush over the implant buried beneath my skin. My body stiffens.

I can use it.

The thought strikes like lightning dancing in the distance. I gave my energy to Iris once and almost pulled her back from the brink. Maybe I can do the same for Oriana, only not fail.

Maybe I can save her.

Instantly, my thoughts shift from light to dark.

If I do this, it'll reveal my location.

ITM's base is gone, thought. I watched it be destroyed. Whatever monitoring they had, surely, it's gone with it. Circuit wiped them out and burned everything to the ground. If any of their old systems were still running, Circuit would have found them, destroyed them, or ITM's failsafe would have done the job itself.

Sharice was too paranoid to let her research fall into the wrong hands. She had a kill switch. A way to wipe every drive, every file, every trace of her work. The raid was a surprise, but not so much that they wouldn't have had time to press a button.

No one is watching anymore. No one is left to care.

I can do this. I *have* to do this.

It's only been used in cruel ways.

I must trust myself. I *can* endure the side effects.

The darkness. The fear.

Intoxicating. A high like I've never felt before.

If it blows out all my senses, it's worth it to save her. This innocent, beautiful creature.

If the world's air is fucked and we're all going to die in three months, then I'll take advantage of the opportunity to do some good. I'll never clear the red, but I'll be damned if I don't smudge it a little.

My grip tightens against Oriana's mane as I breathe slowly, steadying my trembling fingers. I release my right hand, close my eyes, and activate the implant.

Three times. Three doses.

"I'm not going to lose you, too," I declare in a broken whisper as a dizzying wave of ALTA blasts into my system.

A current of heat sears my veins, igniting a spark in my chest. My consciousness splinters, expanding outward, reaching beyond the boundaries of flesh.

I see it. See *her*.

Threads of energy, delicate and shimmering, were woven through the air like strands of silk. The tethers of our souls. They glow, shifting and pulsing with a rhythm I feel in my bones. Oriana's body is ablaze with it, bathed in a golden light that pours from her in waves. It's not like the Banshee's wild, hungry energy. This is warm, soft, inviting, as if the very essence of life itself is reaching back for me.

As if my subconscious has taken hold, I grasp the glowing threads that bind us. They pulse beneath my touch, a heartbeat of their own. I wrap them around my heart, willing my energy into them, willing her to take what she needs.

Live. Please, live.

This is what I wanted since she first hatched. Yet fear trickles down my spine as I stand on the precipice of bonding with her becoming a reality.

Stark clarity collapses over me like a tidal wave.

I know what I'm doing. This isn't the bond like the riders have. This is enhanced. Amplified. Our fates are sealed.

When she dies, I'll die.

And there's no going back.

The tethers of our bond pull taut. A shockwave explodes outward, fire licking at my skin, searing away the last remnants of cold.

My clothes burn to ash, the air thick with the scent of singed fabric and ozone. The heat should blister, should hurt, but it doesn't. It's inside me now, deeper than flesh, deeper than bone.

Oriana's body erupts in light, golden and blinding as if the sun itself has cracked open within her. It pulses outward, washes over me, consuming everything in its path. The sky flashes white, thunder rolling through the heavens in perfect unison with the surge of energy between us.

My head arches back as exhaustion slams into me, slow and merciless, dragging me under like a rip current. The bond takes hold, siphoning my strength, my very essence.

My limbs twitch. My vision swims. Oriana drinks it in, pulling herself back from the abyss, breath by agonizing breath.

Her eyes open.

Oriana is alive.

And I'm no longer cold.

The pain in my shoulder is reduced to a dull ache. I stare at the exposed skin, watching in awe as the wound slowly stitches itself closed.

"I'm alive?" Oriana's thought slides into my mind, smooth as silk.

She lifts her head and blinks at her surroundings. Violet

eyes glow, a vivid contrast to the green moss and leaves on the ground.

Her white mane catches the moonlight, and her golden coat gleams against the glistening snow.

I flex my shoulder, watching the last of the wound disappear. "I'm healed," I murmur, more to myself than to her. "The bond. It's changing me."

Healing you. She corrects. Her mental voice carries a hint of dry humor. *Changing is a slower process.*

My eyes widen at the new clarity in my vision. Like I was handed a pair of glasses that are a thousand times my prescription.

Pinpricks of glowing light dance in the distance far beyond the trees into the valley below. They're still, unmoving like stars.

Are they vehicles? Shuttles? Nothing or anyone should be down there, and if they are, they're awful stupid to run around at night with flashlights.

"What are they?" I ask a little breathlessly.

"Mystyl," She says flatly. *"They're everywhere. You brought them back. You let them go."*

I should defend myself, but I don't. She's right.

They're miles away but still too unsettlingly close for comfort.

"Are you all right?" I ask and stand on shaky legs. My clothes are ashes at my feet. I wrap my arms around my chest, concealing my breasts out of habit.

Oriana scrambles to her feet, hooves thumping on the ground. *"I am."*

She shakes herself, loosening the pine needles from her mane and tail.

I reach out and pet her.

"Thank you," I tell her. "For saving me."

A throb ripples through me, low and insistent.

Holy fuck.

Heat pools in my core, and instantly, I feel like a cat in heat. I squeeze my legs together, resisting the overwhelming urge to rub against the trunk of the closest tree. *What the actual hell is happening?*

"*And you as well, keeper of my bond,*" Oriana's telepathic voice holds a note of amusement. "*Control yourself. The others are coming.*"

Another intense pulse of want shudders through my body before I can reply.

"Company?" My voice is husky and layered with desire.

I feel them first. Threads of wavering light, two bonds weave around me, testing and teasing, their luminous strands coalescing into mine and Oriana's.

"Hey dickheads," Logan says. "She's over here."

Sixty

Heath

Logan, Carter, and I climb out of the Jeep, our boots thudding against frozen ground. We've been searching the area for thirty minutes, keeping within a mile radius.

I have Waylon's rifle, and Carter and Logan have their pistols at the ready. Although we don't expect any danger, being this close to the TZ increases the possibility of more rebels being nearby.

I still can't wrap my head around Brigid and Oriana phasing out here. It's impossible. They weren't bonded and weren't touching.

It defied all explanations.

So far, there's been no sign of them. Logan turns off the

engine, and the night is still, save for the distant whisper of wind threading through pine branches.

A light rumble flickers in my chest, almost like Shadowmane speaking to me, but he's hundreds of miles away.

I look at Carter as a stronger force shudders through the bond.

I stagger, knees buckling. Carter stumbles, catching himself against the Jeep's door. It's like when Brigid kissed Logan, but a thousand times stronger. It slams into my chest and hollows out my breath.

"Holy shit," Carter breathes. "Please tell me you felt that."

"Brigid," I say, pulse hammering. "It has to be."

Logan stands firm, unaffected, staring down at us as we catch our breath.

"What the fuck is going on?" he asks.

"Something happened." I point ahead of us. "I felt....she's this way." No time for more questions. We move, cutting through brittle underbrush. Charged air, thick with static, prickles against my skin.

I shove away a branch, and the three of us find ourselves in a clearing.

Oriana stands in the center, a naked Brigid beside her.

Silver hair spills loose over her shoulders, veiling the curves of her full breasts. She cradles her hands over her lower half, shoulders drawn tight. Iridescent blue and silver shimmer over her skin like errant electrical sparks, flickering, fading.

Her eyes drift from Oriana to us, they glow bright blue, dimming as we approach, recognition slipping through their light.

The mare's glowing violet eyes are watchful.

The bond flares again, sharp enough to steal my breath.

Brigid's presence appears like a brilliant streak of light. I reach for it, for her, the way I would any other newly bonded, to offer reassurance.

The bond recoils, retreating into Brigid's shadow.

Beside me, Carter inhales. He's doing the same. Testing the edges of this new, unfamiliar connection.

She did it. They're bonded.

Although naked, she appears unharmed, but my gaze snags on the new pink scar above her left breast. Shaped like a sunburst, glinting in the hint of light from the moon.

"It's us." Unsure if she fully recognizes us yet. On bonding nights, there's a reason the rider and druadan disappear from the barn for some time.

Their senses are in shock, running on instinct and adrenaline alone, and the space is needed so they have a chance for the bond to solidify and settle. But that had been at Meridian or in Blackhawk's backfield, where the most significant risk to rider or druadan was a wasp bite or stubbed toe.

Here, I won't give her that option.

I move first, yanking off my coat as I approach her. The cold wind bites at my bare arms, but I ignore it, focusing only on her.

Eyes studying my face, she lets me drape the coat over her shoulders.

Twice now, she's worn my coat naked.

"Hi," she says lazily, and lays her head on my chest. I wrap my arms around her, pulling her close, feeling my heart finally slowing from its panicked race. The cold fear that had gripped me—the suffocating certainty I'd lost her—begins to ebb away as her warmth seeps into me. My fingers trace small circles on her back, reassuring myself she's safe in my arms.

"Mmm," she says against my chest. "You always smell so good. Why is that?"

Logan scowls at where she's tucked against me. "We can't stay here," he says. "We need to get her back."

I release her. "Can you walk?" I ask. She stares at me a little dreamily. "Oh yes. I can walk wherever you want me to go...*Mr. Lockwood.*"

Carter lets out a strangled sound, somewhere between a gasp and a laugh. "Holy shit. She did it, didn't she?"

I nod slowly, my mouth twitching with amusement. "Yes, it appears she did."

Sixty-One

BRIGID

I need them like the air I breathe.

All of them.

Heath is closest, so I grab him by the shirt and pull his face to mine. His lips barely graze mine before he pulls back, a pained expression on his face.

"Son of a bitch," Carter shouts. "I've never been this fucking hard."

Without hesitation, I look to the right of Heath and notice the impressive bulge in Carter's pants.

Carter gestures to his crotch. "I mean, look at it. Wait, scratch that, probably best if you don't, 'cause I guarantee this fucker will poke out your eye."

Logan grumbles something about wasting time.

It's indescribable. This...this *rush*. This power.

"Make love to me," I slur, "All of you. *Now*," I pant.

"Don't have to ask me twice," Carter says, tugging off his shirt.

"No," Heath insists, catching his hand. "Logan is right. It's not safe. We need to get her back."

Carter slides his shirt back on reluctantly, and a small whimper escapes me.

"They're right," Oriana says. *"You're not safe."*

I sigh, then slip out of Heath's grasp and sprint to the edge of the clearing. All three are on me within seconds. They're crazy fast. Have they always been this fast?

The world shudders as Heath and Carter's bonds lead up ahead, then encircle me.

I meet Logan's gaze, and a tendril of sadness creeps into the high. This is wrong. I should feel him, too. *"He does not have it anymore,"* Oriana says. *"I do not feel Galaxian on him."* For the first time since I've heard her, I hear a true sadness in her tone. Regret.

She loved him.

And I broke them.

I wonder how much she can read my thoughts when Carter says, "I've never felt a bonding this powerful before. No way this is normal."

Heath shakes his head. "It's not, but we don't have time to ask questions."

My feet are lifted from the ground as Logan scoops me up, but Carter assists, and I welcome the kiss he plants on my lips.

It's like fire. Scalding yet soothing. "You're like *really* hot," I blurt.

"Thanks," Carter says, voice husky. "I know."

"That's enough," Logan growls, jerking me away from him.

As we walk, I bury my face into Logan's neck, savoring the

smell of him, the wind sky, and the night air. "Since you call me Blondie, I should give you a nickname?"

Logan ignores me, but even in the low light, I see his mouth curl into a smirk.

"I like this idea," Carter says over his shoulder.

"Big L?" I coo. "Logi-bear? Mcgrumpypants?"

Carter laughs. "I like that one."

Logan's steel eyes darken to storm clouds. "You can call me anything you want, *Blondie*."

I shiver at the sound of his words. His voice is the embodiment of lust and heat, and every nerve ending in my core blooms with renewed intensity. I lick my lips, my mouth bone dry.

I'm intimately aware of his arm under my bare legs and his other one cradled around my shoulders. Flashes of memories flicker of him taking me against the wall of my room at the base. Demanding I never leave him again.

"Fuck me," Carter says, voice almost whining. "How much longer?"

"Two hundred yards," Heath says, and he too sounds strained.

Logan's shoulders flex under my arms, and I press into him, wanting every part of my body next to his.

I sense Oriana trailing nearby. She's restless, jigging and galloping between the trees.

At the van, Logan passes me to Carter, and I sit sideways on his lap.

The old vehicle rattles over uneven terrain as we drive slowly enough to allow Oriana to keep up. My fingers skim up Carter's chest, tracing the hard lines beneath his shirt. His heat radiates into me, intensifying the pulsing throb between my legs.

I press my lips against his neck, tasting salt and the

lingering scent of wood smoke and cinnamon. Carter shudders. His grip on my hair tightens as my teeth graze his ear. He curses under his breath, a low, wrecked sound, and tilts his head to give me more access.

"Easy—" Heath's voice is even, but I hear a slight tremor. "Not much longer."

I giggle against Carter's skin, nipping at the pulse hammering just beneath the surface. "I feel amazing."

Carter exhales sharply, his hand slipping to the back of my neck, fingertips pressing into the space just above my implant. I'm too distracted to care. His thumb strokes my jaw as I kiss along his throat, his heartbeat steady against my lips. The bond flares between us, and he groans, letting me know he feels it too.

The front tire hits a rock, and the van violently bounces.

"Shit, Heath," Logan says. "Watch the goddamn road.

I pull back just enough to meet Carter's gaze. His pupils are blown wide, his breathing uneven, but he manages a smirk. "You're so damn beautiful."

The van lurches to a stop, and the cabin looms ahead, lights glowing warmly against the dark.

Marshal is already waiting on the porch, arms crossed.

Carter helps me out of the van and adjusts the coat to keep at least my top half covered. Heath is a head taller than me, so the coat reaches just mid-thigh.

Relief flickers across Marshal's face as he takes me in, but his brows knit together when he notices the way I cling to Carter. His gaze drifts to Oriana as she trots up to us.

His lips part slightly, and I feel him ease around me. His bond differs from the others. Carter and Heath are strong, like golden chains; he is firm, but still delicate, like spider silk.

"You did it," he says, more to the others than to me. His eyes dance between me and Oriana. "You bonded."

I smile sheepishly, the first crack in my hazy euphoria, as clarity creeps back in, along with the sudden realization that I'm standing half-naked in front of my brother.

"Take her to the barn," he says. "I'll get Waylon to bring a bed out there. Brigid needs to stay with Oriana."

"Marshal—" Heath starts to say, but Marshal cuts him off.

"The bond isn't settled. You can feel it, can't you?" His sharp gaze flicks to Heath, to Logan, to Carter. "It's fresh, uncured. You need to watch her."

He's right. The bond, still raw and unstable, tugs at my senses like a butterfly caught in a net. Was it because I used ALTA? Had I forced this to happen prematurely? I sway on my feet, lightheaded, and Carter steadies me with a firm hand.

"Come on," he murmurs, guiding me toward the barn. "Let's get you inside."

I'VE BEEN DRUNK BEFORE, but never like this. This is like I downed a whole bottle of wine and then took some of Laura's pain pills.

However, I then spent the next several hours zoning out with music, mindlessly scrolling Network until exhaustion finally knocked me out.

But tonight, I'm stuck here, defenseless, confused, and bombarded with questions like: How did you bond? Did she bite you? How did she phase you without touching you? What happened to your clothes?

When I don't answer, they finally stop. My mind is working at half-speed, and my tongue feels thick in my mouth. "I didn't *do* anything," I say. "It was like how Galaxian acted on his own, too." I touch the scar on my shoulder, pulling down Heath's jacket. I show them the mark. "She saved me," I say. "Or tried to, but it drained her. She died."

The sadness is there, but muffled, insulated by the high of the new bonding. My mind is high in the clouds while my heart is heavy. It's a very odd sensation.

"Jesus fucking Christ," Logan says.

"Brigid." Marshal kneels in front of me. "Sometimes bonding makes you see things that aren't there. Are you sure?"

"I know what happened!" I snap. "She died, but I saved her! I brought her back."

The four exchange perplexed looks.

"How?" Heath asks timidly.

I flash him a toothy grin and tap the back of my neck. "With this." They all look at each other and then move around behind me. I roll my head forward so they can see. "I told you I was working with my sister on a way to help people. Well, this was part of it."

"What did you do?" Marshal says, voice tight.

"It's complicated, but basically, she figured out a way to amplify my ability to manipulate bonds with a medicine she made. I press this and," I clap my hands together. "Turbocharged me."

"And you used it to save Oriana?"

"Sure did. Gave her some of my energy, hoping it'd be enough to revive her." I smile, pleased with myself. "And it did!"

There are murmurs of surprise from all of them.

"One teeny tiny problem, though," I add, making a pinching motion with my fingers. "Look at my fingers. They're so dirty! I should wash them. My nails are—"

"Brigid," Heath says firmly. "What is the problem?"

I swivel my eyes to him. God, it's so hard to focus right now.

"Whenever I use the implant, my sister can track it. But she's dead now." My voice cracks, and I wipe a tear from my cheek, peering at it curiously. The sadness feels so far away, distant, like a past life.

"What the fuck do you mean tracking?" Logan asks.

"Easy, Logan," Marshal defends. "Her bond is raw and unsettled. She's doing better than most novices right now.

"Circuit seized the base at Delta. There's a chance whatever equipment they used to monitor her implant is either destroyed, in Circuit's possession, or we're too far out of range for it to work."

There's a collective ease of tension.

I lean my head against Heath. "You're so smart," I purr.

"Still," he says, hand resting on my back, "We should take patrols. Maybe Waylon has traps we can set out, and whatever plan you have to get us out of here, Marshal, maybe speed it up."

"Can we take it out?" Carter asks.

Heath shakes his head. "Too risky. It could be deeper or attached to her spinal cord. We don't have anything here, no lidocaine or tools. We need to get her to a medical clinic. Find a doctor we can trust."

The barn door creaks open, and Waylon shuffles in, balancing a plate stacked with misshapen pancakes. "Thought you might be hungry." He sets them in front of me.

I take one, watching Oriana chew her own food across the room. I feel disconnected somehow, like I'm floating slightly above the ground as if gravity were turned to its half setting. The pancake is dense and slightly undercooked, but I keep chewing mechanically.

My legs twitch with restless energy, and I pace the length of the small barn, unable to stay still. The others exchange concerned glances, but I focus on the sensation of movement.

Nova appears at my side, a bundle of clothing from my bag

in her arms. Her mismatched eyes gaze at Oriana with unabashed wonder.

"I've seen the banshees before," she says softly. "When helping hunt and gather, but only from far away. Papa said you got to see one up close?"

I smile, pausing my pacing. "I did. Several, actually."

"Are they as beautiful as her?" Nova asks, her voice hushed with reverence.

I consider this, glancing at Oriana's otherworldly form. "Yes, very much so, but differently. The way a summer lightning storm compares to the glow of northern lights."

Nova seems satisfied with this answer, nodding solemnly before following the others, filing outside to give me privacy to change.

"We'll talk about the coyote traps," Logan says to Waylon as they exit, voices fading as the door closes behind them.

The barn falls quiet except for Oriana's soft breathing and the distant murmur of voices outside. I pull on fresh clothes, grateful for the clean fabric against my skin, though it does little to ease the strange electricity running through my veins.

The door opens again, and Carter steps back in. His eyes soften as they meet mine, concern evident in the furrow of his brow.

"I'll be back soon to check on you," he says, pressing a gentle kiss to my forehead. "Try and rest."

I stamp my foot in frustration. "I don't need rest. I need—" I don't even know how to finish the sentence. The arousal from before has dissipated, and now I'm filled with a restlessness that only moving can fix.

Carter laughs, resting his hands on my shoulders. "I know *exactly* how you feel, trust me, but it'll pass. I'll see if Waylon has something else besides pancakes. Just stay here, okay?"

I nod reluctantly, and satisfied with my acquiescence, he leaves, pulling the door closed behind him.

Alone again, I look toward the stall where Oriana watches me with those impossibly deep purple eyes. Outside, they all discuss plans, strategies, and precautions, all centered around keeping me safe. I appreciate their concern, but they don't understand this feeling buzzing under my skin.

I sip the tea Jess insisted helps her sleep, and to my surprise, my exhausted body gives in, and soon the world quiets.

Sixty-Two

JESS

The slight breeze rustles my hair across my face as I stare at Marshal in front of the hangar. The sun is bright in the sky, casting long shadows across the dried grass and small pine trees. Something inside me shifted like tectonic plates finally giving way after years of pressure.

"We need to leave," Marshal says, taking my hands in his. "They're tracking Brigid here. It's not safe anymore."

"Who is?"

"The rebels. ITM. Something happened, and they know we're here."

Unfucking-believable. Could she not cause turmoil to those around her for a one single goddamn day? I cross my arms, feeling the tension in his words. "And go where exactly? It seems like nowhere is safe anymore." The irritation I've been suppressing bubbles to the surface. Every news alert, every hushed conversation, every strange occurrence points to the same conclusion.

The world is unraveling faster than anyone wants to admit.

"Your parents have a boat," he argues. "You and Jace should go. I can handle this."

I scoff, shaking my head. "Fine. I'll send Jace home to our parents. It's the best way to keep him safe, but I'm staying with you."

Marshal furrows his brow, the thick ridge of it casting a shadow over his eyes, while his mouth quirks up sideways. It's the same expression Brigid makes when concerned, and it's uncanny how their shared genes give them the same mannerisms. "I don't understand," he says. "Why are you doing this? This isn't your fight. You aren't a rider, and you and Heath don't have—"

"Because I have to," I say, cutting him off. "I have the resources to help. You did the same at Thornwick. You put your reputation and *your* career on the line to help Jace and me." I step closer, the heat in my voice replaced by something more tender. "I know the life I've been handed. The privileges gifted to me. The life where I can buy my way out of any discomfort. But in a few weeks, it'll be for nothing. None of it will matter. I buried my head in the sand for too long, and look where it's got me."

The truth of my words hits me as I speak them. How long have I been hiding behind my wealth and status, using them as shields against the real world? How long have I hidden emotions for fear of getting taken advantage of or being seen as weak?

Marshal's steady gaze watches me, waiting for me to continue. "Before, I didn't understand. Didn't know I had any say in my life," I finally say. "But now, with you by my side, it's growing clearer." My voice becomes stronger with each word.

"The world is collapsing around us, and if we're going to die anyway, I want my last days to mean something. I want to be worthy of your love."

The crease on his forehead smooths, and his hands drift up to my wrists, summoning a flurry of goosebumps on my arms. How the hell did his touch *do* that to me?

"You are worthy of my love, Jess," he says.

Tides, I'm not used to this affection. I bite down my knee-jerk reaction to frown at him instead of shaking my head. "No, not yet. But soon I will be."

I look back at the cabin, thinking of Jace inside, blissfully unaware of how quickly everything is changing. For his sake, we need to act now. No more hiding. No more pretending. The time for comfort is over.

"Let me make some calls. I'll get a shuttle here to take us." I glance at the barn, where Logan lurks by the doorway. "*All* of us. Wherever you want us to go."

Sixty-Three

LOGAN

"I think my balls are going to explode," Carter growls, hanging his head between his arms propped on his legs.

With a mattress dragged from the cabin, a pile of warm blankets, and Jess's special tea that helps her sleep, Brigid crashed within minutes of lying down.

Oriana paces in her stall, but so far, is behaving better than most stallions on a bonding night.

Heath and Carter, however, have been squirming like when the all-girls DU volleyball team toured Meridian.

Not being affected by Brigid's bonding night makes me the reasonable one.

Fucking bullshit, if you ask me, but the truth is, if the guy was right about more rebels heading this way, one of us needs to stay clearheaded.

Heath steps back inside, zipping up his pants. That's been three times since she fell asleep. Not that I'm counting.

"There's nothing we can do but wait," he says. "You should go to bed, Logan."

The only thing stopping me from going is them. There's an unspoken challenge to prove they are stronger than this.

Brigid lies sleeping on the cot, sweat glistens off her forehead, and her eyes squeeze shut as if fighting some imaginary demons.

When I bonded with Galaxian, I remember seeing hallucinations in the desert.

Maybe she's seeing the same. Whatever it is, it doesn't look like she's having a good time.

I miss Galaxian with an ache so visceral it hollows out my chest.

His absence feels like a phantom limb, a constant reminder of what I lost.

The thought of leaving—of just walking away from everything—scratches at my mind like a feral animal. *I could just fucking leave right now.*

If Waylon and Brigid are right, there isn't a future for any of us. Barely a month left before the air becomes too poisoned to breathe.

The dream fragments return. Brigid in my dreams, telling me to trust my instincts. Galaxian let her ride him, then told me how to find her even without our bond.

My thoughts drift back to that first night at Meridian's barn during the bonding and how Galaxian had seen something in her then. He protected her.

He knew. Knew she was different. Important.

My dreams...even with our bond shattered, are all I have left.

Heath and Carter sleep nearby, sprawled across extra blankets, reminding me of when, as kids, we crashed at each other's rooms at the academy.

The night creatures chirp and clack in the woods. I rise, drawn by the murmur of voices, and spot Marshal and Jess standing in hushed conversation, their bodies angled toward each other. He reaches out, running a hand across her jaw. She tugs her sweater tighter and disappears into the hangar.

When he sees me, he breaks away and approaches.

"How are you doing?" he asks.

How are you, not *her*. I shrug. "Fine, all things considered."

He lets out a sigh and stares up at the stars. "You know what this means. Brigid bonding with her, don't you?"

The space between my shoulder blades stiffens. "I do."

"It's going to change everything. Fiaro, Lugsen, and all the other managers are going to want to see her. Demand that she go to their station. Demand she..."

"Breed," I answer.

He frowns. "Eventually, yes. Brigid won't get to ride her, not like regular riders. She'll be studied, and when she's old enough, they'll work to maximize her egg production."

"*If* we take her back."

Marshal sighs, resting a hand on his hip. "We're out of food. If anyone is left of ITM, her tracker would've signaled them, putting us all in danger. If she is important to researching ways for us to survive, they will want her. Not only that, but she knows way too much for them to let her into Circuit's hands. We don't have a choice. At least at Blackhawk, I have pull. Jess is looking at a house to rent in the Village for you and the others. Now that she's bonded, and with her confessing everything, there's a chance we can file immunity for her. But we're out of options. We leave tomorrow."

Sixty-Four

BRIGID

Several hours later, I lie on the mattress and fidget with the peeling boards on the wall to distract myself. Sunlight streams through the slats of the barn walls. Sunshine on a rare warm day in winter.

As if reading my thoughts, Oriana's voice whispers in my mind.

"*I feel you are awake. Let's go, Bond Keeper,*" she urges, her mental voice thrumming with the same restlessness that consumes me. "*Let's run!*"

She doesn't have to ask me twice. I grab the pair of deerskin gloves I used before and saddle her.

I'm in thick enough leggings and a sweater, but I touched

her to heal her. If she were going to burn me, she would've done it then.

I'm heat-resistant now. Our bond made that happen.

I won't go far, and it'll be quick before they get back. They won't even know I'm gone.

However, I have enough mental wherewithal left to scribble out a note on a scrap of shipping paper Waylon uses to pack his boxes.

"*Went for a short ride to the big oak to the south. Be back soon.*" I stare at the note, then add, "*Promise.*" Waylon told us the big oak was his deceased wife's burial place and how it'd been her favorite place because of the view. It is no more than a ten-minute walk *and* in the opposite direction from Delta's border.

Oriana prances in place as I struggle to tighten her girth.

"*You are slow.*"

"*I'm trying, okay?*"

The barn has a smaller door in the back, and I led her out of it. I suck in the cold air; the chill nips at my face. I lead her to a barrel and swing my leg up on her back. My entire body trembles as I settle into the seat and the stirrups.

The ground is very far down now. I rode horses before, ponies at country fairs that plodded along with tired-looking handlers, but there's no one holding the reins this time but me.

I swallow down the fear.

"*Any chance we could start slow, please?*" I tell her. Even in the strange vibrating speak, my voice trembles.

Oriana snorts and shakes her head from side to side. "*Slow is not fun! You hold on. We go!*"

I've barely adjusted myself in the saddle before she leaps into a gallop.

The wind is sucked from my lungs, and whooshes in my ears. I grip the front of the saddle with my hand, terrified of being sent backward, and squeeze my legs tight like Marshal instructed me.

I am free. Soaring. It's the best fucking rush *ever*. We are one. Galaxian was just a stallion. Oriana is a *being*. My senses are heightened. The trees blur beside us, transforming into dark green smears. I feel the ground under my feet, feel the air in my lungs, feel the heat in my veins.

Surprisingly, I stay in the saddle. I sense she's holding back.

Holy shit. She can run *faster?*

As if sensing my question, she stretches her neck and kicks it into another gear.

I stand in my stirrups, lean over her neck, trying to keep the wind from stinging my face, and instead get her mane whipping my cheeks. Tears stream from the corners of my eyes, and yet a smile tugs at the edges of my lips.

This is the most incredible rush ever.

We gallop to a trail, and she slows to a trot to ascend.

"We can leap?" she says, and I feel the question more than understand it.

"You mean phase?"

She hums a happy murmur of agreement.

"It's much faster, and I can go farther now we're bonded."

I pull on the rope. The images of her lying dead on the ground are too fresh. Too vivid No. I'm not ready. *"NO!"* I yell out loud and in my head.

Oriana is perplexed. *"Do you not trust me?"*

"No, of course, I trust you. I just...don't trust myself."

Oriana stomps her foot, then snorts, and we begin up the small incline. At the top, we stop under the shade of an unusually large pine tree. It must be old and strong to survive this long in such a windy, harsh environment.

I hop off and adjust my glove. "*Aren't you supposed to mark me, like the stallions?*"

Not that I'm keen on having a druadan bite and scar my hand, but it seems like part of what happens.

Oriana snorts, and I'm rapidly learning it's her way of scoffing. "*No. That's crude. Harsh. Male behavior. Besides, it is pointless since you are already marked.*"

"*I am?*" I ask, my breath making puffs of steam in the air. "Where?"

Oriana nudges my left shoulder, where the star-shaped scar is on my chest.

"*That is the mark of bravery. It is enough.*"

I haven't been brave. Carter was in danger, so I reacted. In fact, some might even call what I did foolish.

"So, you chose me because I stopped Logan from killing a guy who then tried to hurt Carter?"

Oriana flicks an ear to the side, then back to me. "*It is not so simple to explain. I chose you for all you are and sensed you before. It was all of those, however, that ignited the flame that was already burning.*"

Those are just about the best words I've heard in a long time, and my spirit practically sings. She chose *me* to be her rider.

"*We should head back before they start to worry.*"

I mount, and at an easy jog, we make our way back down the trail.

My heart finally beats at a normal rhythm as we approach the barn. The wild run up the trail did what we needed, burning away the frenetic energy that was crawling beneath my skin like ants.

The winter sunshine bathes everything in a sharp, clean light that makes the world feel more real than it has in days.

At the front of the barn, three figures come into focus.

Logan, Carter, and Heath stand like sentinels, arms crossed over their chests. They're dressed in coats and boots as if they've been waiting.

Their expressions are unreadable from this distance, but my stomach knots with preemptive guilt. *Shit.*

Logan's default expression looks like he's pissed anyway, but as we draw closer, I realize it's not anger on their faces at all. It's something closer to disbelief, as if witnessing something they can't comprehend.

"Hi," I say, my voice smaller than intended as I slide down from Oriana's back. Despite my sore leg muscles from clinging on for dear life, my body feels wonderfully solid beneath me now, connected to the earth in a way it hadn't before. A bone-deep satisfaction replaced the restlessness.

"How was your ride?" Carter finally says, his voice uncharacteristically neutral.

My windburned cheeks grow even hotter, and they feel tight when I flash them a timid smile. "Good."

Her presence is stronger in my mind now, and I wonder how much her excitement is blurring with mine. How long has she wanted to run like that, but was stuck in the stalls at the research station?

"Every day," she says, *"Every day, Bond Keeper."*

I lead her into the barn, and they watch me put her away, but no one says anything.

"I stayed close. I left a note. I was safe."

"We know," Heath replies.

"Then what is it? Do I have something on my face?"

"No," Carter says, voice tinged with awe. "It's just that we've never seen a woman rider before."

I tilt my chin up and grin. "Well, now you have."

All three of their eyes dance with fire and something else

that sends a shiver down my spine and heat pooling between my thighs.

I strip Oriana's halter and saddle off and exit her stall.

I dust off my hands. "I think I'm going to take Waylon up on that shower out back. I don't suppose any of you want to join?"

Without waiting for them to reply, I spin on my heel and march out of the barn.

Behind the cabin, Waylon rigged up a rain-catching system and an actual honest-to-good shower head hangs over a polished stone pad with a drain.

The six-by-six space is draped with stitched-together sheets for privacy.

I start to take off my boots when I catch sight of them over my shoulder. Within seconds, their clothes are off, and I'm surrounded by three very naked, very *eager* men. Logan's hard chest bumps against my shoulder while Carter's hand finds mine, and Heath flanks me on the right.

Last night was a blur, and yet I remember how they acted, how they restrained themselves. They could have so easily taken advantage of my vulnerable state, and yet they didn't.

Now, I was more clear-headed than I had been in weeks. *Months.*

And without the effects of the fresh bonding clouding my judgment, I can wholeheartedly say I want them with every fiber of my being.

And they want me.

They watch me with hungry gazes. Even self-controlled Heath fails to maintain composure as his eyes drift down my body, then back up. I should feel self-conscious in the daylight, but I don't. I know my ribs stick out more than before, and the curves of my breasts and hips have barely returned despite my recent feasting on pancakes and canned pie filling, but it doesn't matter.

They gaze at me like I'm the most stunning being they've ever seen, and given that they resemble Greek gods with their sculpted torsos and powerful arms, it definitely gives a girl a confidence boost.

Naked, I step into the shower and pull the lever. The water isn't as hot as I like it, but it's warm enough.

They step inside, their towering frames instantly dominating the space. Each stands well over six feet, with Logan edging out the others in height. They're broad-shouldered and built like the athletes and soldiers they are. Their faces are all chiseled jawlines and piercing gazes.

I still can't believe these men—with their drool-worthy looks—look at me with such raw hunger and devotion. The heat in their eyes when they find mine makes my skin flush and my heart race.

It's a veritable feast of man's flesh, and I am *famished*.

I drink them in, savoring them in their most natural form, pausing on Carter. "What's this?" I say, gently running my fingers over the fresh ink on the firm muscles of his forearm. Strange, I didn't notice it before. They're in coats or long-sleeve shirts most of the time, and when I'd played dress up with Heath's riding jacket, the room had been dark, and I was occupied by other, more interesting parts of their bodies.

"All of us on the Specter team got one," he replies, voice low, clearly affected by my fingers stroking his arm.

"Are they all the same?" I ask.

"Mostly. Mine's the most badass, though."

He's not wrong. The flames licking off the edge of the blades are incredibly realistic. And the word Specter is etched in bold block letters on the hilt.

Heath's has shadows curling around it where the outlines

of the blade disappear and blur. I take Logan's arm and turn over a forearm so massive it's bigger than my bicep. His is a blade with two stars. One for each of the stallions he was bonded to and lost.

Their eyes sear the sides of my face, and when I release Logan's arm, Carter is on me like it'd taken every molecule of his being to be patient.

And that patience was gone.

His lips crush mine with such possessiveness it steals my breath. His tongue invades my mouth, hot and warm, and induces a surge of desire through me.

His hands grip my waist and snug me closer. Heat radiates from his body, and I melt into him. His touch is electric, sending sparks dancing across my skin and making me forget everything else except for him. Except for this.

This. We are all that exist.

I wrap my arms around his neck and pull him closer to me. I don't want this moment to end; I want to drown in the sensation of his lips on mine.

Carter's hands move from my waist to cup my face, deepening the kiss even more. There's an urgency in his movements, as if he's overwhelmed at where to touch next.

My neck. My shoulders. My waist. My thighs.

I press closer as he cups my ass, his eagerness amplified by the bond thrumming between us.

"You feel it," he asks, his voice husky. "How much I want you?"

His arousal, an insistent pulsing, ripples through me, mimicking the same throb between my legs. Heath strokes himself lazily as Carter kisses me. A smoldering undercurrent in the bond, his desire unfurling off him in waves of restrained pleasure.

It's overwhelming, their dual needs feeding into mine,

heightening every touch, every breath. "Holy shit," the words summoned from me before I can stop them.

Logan's broad frame is a shadow in my periphery as he watches us. I can't feel him—like I can with Carter and Heath—but the intensity in his narrowed gaze sends a shiver racing down my spine.

Carter groans, pressing closer, and the hard evidence of his arousal presses against my hip. His hands slide from my face, trailing down my neck and my shoulders, igniting sparks wherever they roam. Heath steps closer, his fingers brushing my waist, tentative at first, then firm as he pulls me back against his chest. The contrast of Carter's urgency and Heath's slow, deliberate touch makes my head spin.

"Brigid," Heath murmurs against my ear, his voice rough with restraint. "Every curve, every inch of you is flawless, and I'm aching to worship it all."

I can't respond, not with words, only a soft gasp as Carter's hands find the soap, lathering it between his palms before sliding them over my skin. Heath joins him, their hands moving in tandem, washing me with care and attention. I let my eyes fall closed.

The stone bench sits cool and solid against the back of my thighs as they guide me to it, their touches lingering as if afraid I'll slip away. Heath's hands pivot my hips. The muscles on the inside of my thighs are sore from riding, and as if sensing this, Heath is especially gentle with his movements.

Once positioned, Carter breaks the kiss and lowers to his knees.

His head between my legs, he doesn't hesitate, instead burying his face like a man starved. His tongue lands directly on the most pleasurable part of my core, licking, lapping, sucking. I roll my head back, and Heath's hand rests on my throat, then lowers to my breast. His thumbs encircle my nipples, gently tugging the erect peaks. My thighs clench with the first stirrings of an orgasm.

Carter slips two fingers inside, and it coaxes me over the precipice. I moan in ecstasy as waves of pleasure radiate through my limbs.

Logan is beside me, his mouth inches from my ear. "You liked it when I took you against the wall, didn't you? I want to watch my brothers do the same. I want to see them drive into you until you scream their names. I want you to make them come so hard it overflows. And when your perfect pussy is swollen and dripping, I'll fuck you so hard you'll forget what it's like to breathe without me inside you."

As I ride the last of the waves of my orgasm, Carter stands and adjusts my hips, then eases into me.

I've barely acclimated to the fullness of Carter buried inside me when Logan dips a finger into my mouth. He smirks as I eagerly peer up at him and suck it.

Heath's hands are on my breasts, in my hair, caressing my neck, and the sensations amplified by the bonds are almost too much to bear. As if reading my mind, Logan's breath brushes against my ear as he speaks softly but urgently.

"Come again for us," he says. "I want to hear you moan with your hand stroking my cock."

Logan and Heath each take one of my hands and guide my fingers up and down their rigid lengths. I moan, arching my back involuntarily as the pleasure builds within once more.

Carter is relentless, and I'm unable to hold back any longer. Leg's clenching, I cry out, shuddering through another more powerful orgasm. I hardly have time to recover as Carter's movements grow harder and faster. His grip tightens on my hips, and with a final hard thrust, he sinks himself into me. His body stills as he spills into me.

There's a moment as he leans forward, letting himself briefly recover, before switching places with Heath.

Heath rests an arm on the bench beside me as Carter tips my chin up and kisses me. I taste my arousal on his tongue and lips and feel the delicious stretch again as Heath slides easily into me. My core slick from Carter's release.

He works slower, easing in and out, and I'm cresting the precipice again.

His rhythm meets mine, and I continue to stroke Logan's thick member with my right hand, feeling the velvet hardness under my grip.

Carter and Logan lean forward, their hands propping me up on their knees as they watch Heath fuck me like I'm theirs to own. My fingers curl into the firm skin of Heath's upper arm, urging him closer, harder, faster.

"Fuck," Heath growls as he lowers his gaze to where our bodies meet. The slick, glistening slide of our connection causes his breath to hitch as he watches the way my body yields to him, clenching and welcoming with every powerful thrust.

He groans, a guttural vibration, and his eyes, dark with unbridled hunger, fix on the hypnotic sight of his thick length sinking into me, stretching and filling me in a way that feels indescribable. With a final, hard thrust, he buries himself to the hilt, and my walls tighten as he finds his release.

His eyes return to my face, and he kisses me gently. Then withdraws to stand behind Carter and Logan, his hands sliding up my sides to cup my breasts through the water.

They lift me higher onto their knees as Logan moves between my legs, grabbing my hips with possessive strength that lets me know precisely who I belong to at this moment.

A wicked grin curves Logan's lips as he pauses, his eyes locking onto the slick, glistening evidence of what came before.

"Look at you, *Blondie*," he growls. "So goddamn wet for me already, aren't you? All from them. From fucking you senseless and leaving you dripping." His thumb traces a slow, teasing path along my slick folds, gathering the warm, sticky evidence and spreading it wider, making me gasp. "See how it makes you even slicker, Blondie? It's pouring out of you. You're a perfect little mess, all primed and eager, just waiting for me to claim what's mine. And I will. Every. Single. Inch."

His words drip with possessive dominance, igniting a fire in my core as he positions himself. The head of his arousal teases my entrance.

"My turn, *Blondie*." He eases himself, inch by glorious inch, inside me. The feel of him filling me is mind-blowingly good as he stretches me. He leans down, bracing on shaking arms.

He pulls sluggishly out, then his hips snap forward, drilling into me. I gasp as my back arches off their knees, and pleasure permeates every cell of my body. His cock feels impossibly thick and hard as it rubs against places inside me that only he seems to know exist.

"You're so fucking tight," he whispers, pumping his hips in a way that has my head spinning.

The heady scent of arousal saturates the air as he nears the edge, my breath coming in ragged gasps.

I peer up at them through half-lidded eyes.

Logan slams into me hard enough that Carter and Heath's holds tighten to keep me from tumbling backward, and he grunts with his release spilling hot and sudden inside me. I gasp as it drips down my legs, mingling with the shower water and the other's sticky release sliding down my leg.

With a rough exhale, Logan slips loose, his dick still hard. My heartbeat thrums in my ears, beating frantically against my chest, and I feel his is doing the same.

He smooths the hair from my face with tender fingers

before brushing his thumb across my cheek. It's a surprisingly gentle gesture from him, considering he'd just fucked me senseless.

All of them did. A giddy giggle escapes.

Steam fogs the cool air as they lower me to the bench.

The three of them watch me intently.

Heath kneels, his hazelnut-colored eyes fierce and unyielding, as if they could strip away every layer of my soul with his look alone. "You're ours, Brigid Corsair," he says, his voice a deep, resonant sound that commands the very air between us. "Even if the seas rise up to swallow the world whole," he continues, his words wrapping around me. "Or the air chokes the very breath from our lungs. Know this. You're ours, completely and eternally. And we'll chase you through every storm, dive into the depths after you, and breathe life back into you if it means never leaving your side again."

He plants a kiss on my forehead and then stands.

I peer up at the three of them surrounding me, and a warm flush spreads across my cheeks and down my neck, my heartbeat quickening. The declaration wraps around me, making my skin tingle. I bite my lower lip, trying to contain the smile of joy threatening to break free.

There's something intoxicating about being claimed so boldly, so completely. I let out a shaky breath, my eyelids fluttering with the comedown of the multiple orgasms as I try to maintain the connection between us.

They take washcloths and soap, washing me first gently from head to toe, then themselves. My body feeling like warm jelly, I rest my head against the wall and watch the suds cascade off their sculpted shoulders.

Carter tilts his head toward the shower head, rinsing his sandy-brown hair and inadvertently giving me a perfect view of his tight, perfectly sculpted ass. To his right, Heath's shoulders and biceps flex as he reaches up to scrub his thick black locks. I shift my gaze to Logan, staring through half-lidded eyes as suds slip further along the sharp V-shape tapering from his massive chest to his narrow waist and the still half-hard cock dangling between his legs.

Network *never* has anything this good to watch.

When the water turns to a trickle, they turn it off, and the chill in the air envelops us once more.

They take towels from a wooden bench just outside, wrapping me first, then tying them low around their hips.

Reality slowly creeps back into my mind. I run my fingers through my hair, realizing I left my hairbrush inside. There's a glorious ache from between my legs, and just as I try to focus on detangling my hair, there's a throb. I'm distracted again by the guy's asses as they pull on pants and shirts.

I sense a rustle in the bond, a shift I'm not sure about, and a second later, Marshal calls out.

It's low, gruff, and tinged with something else. "If you are all...finished." A pause, "We need you in the cabin for a meeting."

Oh shit. The bond. My pulse skitters across my chest. He felt it.

All of it.

I press my hands against my face, reeling from the fiery flame of embarrassment.

"It's no big deal," Carter says, tugging my hands down.

"No big deal?" I say, with a fever pitch. "My brother knows." Dismay clogs my throat, "He *felt* while we were out here..."

"Fucking?" Carter finishes for me and laughs. Then, seeing the mortification on my face, stops himself. "It's okay. He can't feel us like we feel each other. Sure, he knew *something* was happening out here, but he can also tune it out if he wants."

"Oh, thank the tides," I breathe.

Carter laughs, shaking his head, and Heath and Logan step closer. To my dismay, they both wear smirks as well.

"It's not funny!" I shout.

"You're a rider now," Logan says. "Better get used to it."

I worry my lip, and his eyes dart to my mouth briefly. "So," I say. "If he's nearby, every time we do *that*. He'll know?"

Carter rests his hands on his hips and gives me an exaggerated nod. "Sure will, just like *you'll* know when Jess and he." He bites his lip and thrusts his hips forward.

I throw up my head. "Stop it!" I shake my head, backing up. "I don't know if I want to be a rider anymore."

All three of them burst into a fit of laughter.

Sixty-Five

CARTER

Marshal sits at the table, his fingers tapping against the wood.

Jess is beside him, her arms crossed, eyes sharp as glass. If he told her what he felt, she doesn't show it. Across the room, Waylon and Nova sort through a pile of crates, organizing gears and bolts into bins. The air inside the cabin is thick with the unspoken truth we all know.

This place isn't safe anymore.

"We need to move," Marshal says once the four of us are seated. Brigid is to my left, and Heath takes the seat next to her while Logan looms behind her. It was the fucking best treat of my life to see them take her alongside me. Claim her.

I reach under the table and rest a hand on her thigh. I don't miss the subtle shift in her body as she leans just a hair closer to me.

Marshal clears his throat, picking up on the fire I'm gently stoking. "Jess and I talked. There's a vacant house listed in the Village. Heath, Carter, and Logan can stay there while we take Brigid and Oriana to Blackhawk."

We're running, but this isn't just about survival. This is about staying together, about finding a way to make it through…whatever the hell is coming next.

"We could go to Gaergen. I have family there," I offer. Her hand slides under mine, and our fingers lace together.

Logan snorts. "Yeah? Do you think we're the only ones with that idea? The second this news breaks, the whole damn country will be heading there."

The world is ending. The land is turning against us.

"It's still an option," Marshal says. "But I have a whole station full of riders, staff, and druadans to worry about." He pauses, eyes drifting between mine, Logan and Heath's. "When this shitstorm finally makes it all the way north, I want to be next to Nightshade when it does." We fall silent. He doesn't have to say it. We all feel the same.

We would rather die beside our stallions than live without them.

"And Brigid?" Heath asks. I feel her hand tense in mine.

Marshal sighs. "Jess has an excellent attorney on retainer that she's already spoken with, and said that Brigid can withhold her statement when they arrive. Fiaro will have his hands full with Oriana's arrival. I doubt he'll put up much of a fuss."

"If he's not with ITM," Brigid adds.

Marshal's stubbled jaw twitches. "We're rapidly losing people we can trust, but I will be careful."

That's it. After everything we've learned, everything Brigid told us, we're going back to Blackhawk.

As some of the world's famous druadan riders, we're pretty damn recognizable, so unless this house has no windows or a basement, it'll be hard to keep us hidden for long.

It's a temporary solution. I can't be away from Ember much longer. Already, the bond is wound tight, a pressure coiling around my neck, and combined with the O-strike detox, I'm days away from flaring if I'm forced to isolate.

But what choice do I have? If I march into Blackhawk, they'll arrest me on sight. My mother won't hesitate. I was part of a special ops team for Circuit's army, and I abandoned it. Heath too. We'll be tried for treason. And Logan? He's a ghost in the system, a felon walking in plain sight. But none of us has it as bad as Brigid. She lived and worked with ITM for months. In their eyes, she's a terrorist.

I glance at her sitting to my left. Her lips are bruised and swollen, and she still radiates that after-sex glow. I can't lose her. Not again.

I've never felt more alive than when I'm with her. She saved me. Brought me back. Made me whole. I don't care what it takes to keep her safe.

I'll fight the entire damn world if I must.

Outside, we hear the shuttle land, its engines humming through the old wood and corrugated metal walls.

"Ride's here," Marshal says, and we all stand.

Upstairs, we quickly pack, and I shove clothes into my duffle bag, my hands pausing when I see my Specter uniform. The riding jacket. The captain's insignia. It's a reminder of everything I am, everything I lost.

Marshal's doing what he can for us, but I know the truth. I dug this hole. When we get back, I'll call my mom. Tell her I coerced Heath into going AWOL. Maybe he'll still have a future. A chance.

Then again, what does a future even look like now? We're

being hunted, driven from our own land by poison and terrorists who'd just as likely see the world burn as save it.

Waylon and Nova pull us into quick hugs, clinging tighter than they should before stepping back.

We tell them goodbye, wishing them the best, and Logan advises them to stay somewhere else for a while in case rebels show up. Waylon dismisses his concern with a wave of his hand.

"Those nut jobs aren't going to scare me," he scoffs, his jaw set in that stubborn way I've come to know. It's no surprise he and Logan hit it off.

Logan doesn't argue, he just grimly pats him on the back and thanks him.

"I'll try to send for you to visit Blackhawk sometime," Brigid says, pulling back from hugging Nova. "Maybe you can come see a performance?"

Nova smiles weakly. We know it's all lip service. There aren't going to be any performances this spring. There isn't going to be a country.

As we gather our belongings, I catch the glance Jace and Nova share. The boy slips something into her hand. She doesn't say a word, only closes her fingers around it. She gives him a tearful smile and kisses him on the cheek.

Must be something in the water.

Smiling to myself, I sling my bag over my shoulder and step onto the shuttle. We're going back to Blackhawk, and whatever fucked up future awaits us there.

Sixty-Six

BRIGID

E motions crash over me in great torrents as I set eyes upon the place I never thought I'd see again. The giant black stone walls perch regally on the hill. Below, the Village's tile roofs of houses and buildings cluster together, lining the zig-zagging, narrow streets.

The broken bridge spans the rushing river, hundreds of feet in the canyon below. In the distance to the north, the ocean hammers relentlessly against the cliffs, sending up plumes of white spray.

Heath, Carter, and Logan remain behind in a vacant house.

It took every ounce of willpower and Oriana's reassuring presence not to follow them out.

We hugged briefly, and they promised to find a way to see me soon.

Jace stayed on heading north to his parents' house far to the Northwest coast of Delford. Jess made him promise not to go back to Thornwick until it was safe. She told him to keep everything that happened secret, and with the most grown-up look I've seen on a kid his age, he promised he would.

Marshal called ahead, and Station Manager Fiaro and Deputy Lugsen greeted us in the shuttle landing area courtyard.

I study Lugsen's face carefully. His expression remains pinched and suspicious, but I catch the flicker of awe and curiosity when Marshal explains I bonded with Oriana.

"We were informed of Oriana's disappearance from Lanett," Lugsen says, voice clipped. "There will be consequences for the theft."

"However," Fiaro interjects, folding his hands over his substantial belly, "there will be leniency now that she's safe in our custody. If anything, this incident has proven our security measures are woefully insufficient." He sighs heavily. "We have reason to believe ITM has compromised the research station. The other druadan stations are considering pulling all young druadans and halting births until the current political climate stabilizes."

Later, in Fiaro's cluttered office, he leans back in his chair, which protests under his weight. "CSU has been notified. Ms. Corsair can stay here until they arrive tomorrow." He glances at me, his expression softening slightly. "I don't want to separate her and the druanera. The world has gone to shit, but I'm still the manager of this station, and druadans and riders remain my responsibility."

Lugsen nods curtly. "She can stay in the barracks. If there's any hassle from the riders, let me know."

Sometime later, I unpack the box of my belongings that they'd kept in storage for me in the barracks. I plug the old comm into the charger Nova gave me, feeling the emptiness settling in my chest as I realize I miss her. Waylon and Jace, too. I miss the short time we spent together and the family we formed.

This isn't how I planned it. Becoming a rider was this lofty, dreamy goal where everything would make sense when it happened. Everything would be right and perfect.

But instead, it's a hollow victory. The dream was warm and golden, something that belonged to a better version of me, one who had Heath, Logan, and Carter at my side.

Not this. Not an empty barracks, not unfamiliar faces, and judging eyes.

I have Oriana. That has to be enough. I cling to that, gripping it like a lifeline against the creeping doubt.

She's here, steady and real, her presence a tether to something familiar. A piece of the dream that hasn't soured. That means there's still hope.

I have to believe there's still a happy ending waiting somewhere ahead, even if I can't see it now. Maybe the lab techs at Delta were wrong? Maybe the poisoned air will stop short of Blackhawk and Delford? Maybe we have longer than we thought?

Several riders watch me across the room, which is understandable. I am the first woman rider, after all, in a long ass time.

Their expressions range from curious to wary, as though I'm some exotic creature that might bite if they venture too close.

Unlike Heath and Carter's, their bonds are a subtle presence lurking in my periphery.

I'm putting away the last of my clothes when Marshal finds me. "How are you settling in, *novice?*"

I smirk at the nickname. "I'd be lying if I said I didn't like the sound of that."

"Well, I like saying it. About damn time, am I right?"

My grin widens. "Everyone's been fine so far and is giving me space."

"Glad to hear it," he says and sets the shoulder bag he's carrying on my bunk. "I have a gift for you."

"Gift?" I ask.

Marshal rests a bag on the bed. "I figured since you're back now, you might need these."

He opens the bag wider, and I spy a stack of dog-eared journals inside. My heartbeat flits against my breastbone. "Rosaline's journals? *You* had them?"

He nods. "When you told me about them, I had a feeling others might catch word and try and stop you, so I took them for safekeeping. However, when I went down, Yuto said someone had requested one of them, and when I questioned further, he said they showed him an academic transfer card and that DU had requested a loan. He said the guy was rude, though, so he lied and only gave him the one. Thankfully, Yuto's suspicious nature and a tad bit overzealous guard of the archives is the real hero here."

I'm overwhelmed with joy, and after taking a second to let the reality of them being in my possession sink in, I squeal, turn to him, and hug him. He hugs me back, and I feel like my heart is about to explode. "What did I do to deserve an awesome brother like you?"

He shrugs, a tender smile softening his features. "Just doing what family does, protecting each other's secrets and stealing the occasional library book."

I laugh.

"So," he says, "if you're almost done here, what do you say about dinner?"

I grin and nod. "Dinner would be great."

Jess is already seated at the table when we arrive, her sleek hair catching the light. Her face falls when she sees me. She clearly thought it would be just the two of them.

Same, girl.

However, upon seeing Marshal, it vanishes behind a practiced smile. I suppose I'd better get used to her being around more, as it's clear she's rapidly becoming a permanent fixture in Marshal's life.

Just as he accepts how I feel about my riders, I need to accept this.

Over steaming plates of food, we discuss maintaining whatever normalcy is possible at the station. I'll continue riding and developing my skills for as long as circumstances allow.

"A bond doesn't fully cure until you phase together," Marshal studies me over the rim of his glass.

I avert my gaze, finding the pattern on my plate fascinating.

"You haven't, have you?" His voice is gentle, prying, and not at all accusatory.

I shake my head, even as warmth blooms in my cheeks.

"Well," he says, setting down his glass, "we don't want to rush things. We'll keep practicing to help you build your confidence. Phasing is dangerous. I'm not going to lie to you, but it's what druadans were bred for. Whatever genetic piece of DNA altered them to make them faster, stronger, and bond with us also gave them this ability. Think how easy it is for you to blink or breathe. It's the same for them."

"Okay," I say, forcing weight into my voice. "I hope you're right."

I keep my head down, picking at the half-eaten ration on my tray. On the west wall, where a mounted screen cycles through urgent broadcasts. It seems like every city is recovering from one catastrophe after another. Food shipments were disrupted, medicine shortages, people were missing, and the recovery efforts in Delford from the broken levees.

Then the screen glitches with a static crackling, and the room stills. My cup freezes halfway to my lips as the image shifts.

A man's face flickers into view.

I choke on my drink, coughing against the burn in my throat. "Holy shit," the words spill from me.

I blink, but the image doesn't change.

"What is it?" Marshal asks.

I stare at the monitor. "That's Elton Nunson. ITM's leader."

Sixty-Seven

MARSHAL

Brigid looks as if she's seen a ghost.

Chairs creak as people rise from them, and someone curses under their breath.

"How the hell did he hack Network?" I ask.

"I...I don't know," Brigid murmurs.

He's wearing a baseball cap and is clean-shaven.

My mind spirals with the realization. If Elton escaped, had Brigid's sister? If so, why isn't she with him?

"I'm sure you've all seen my face broadcast on Network," Elton says. "Alongside words like *terrorist, radical, anarchist*," he says dismissively. "You might believe ITM is ruining the country. You might believe all the lies and be ready to switch your screen off, but before you do, let me tell you one thing." He holds the camera with his gaze. "We are on the brink of extinction. Venovia's end is numbered in weeks, not months. The TZ's borders have tripled in size. Every minute, the air is becoming more polluted. And what has Circuit done about it? Kept you in the dark."

His eyes pin on the camera.

"And now it's too late. What does our future look like? Masks required every time you set foot outside? What about those outside the cities? What about those who must travel for work? Children never free to play tag outside and climb trees, or swim in the lakes? Never free to explore or roam our country's beautiful landscape?"

He exhales sharply, fingers tightening around the edges of the podium.

The Venovian flag hangs motionless behind him, its three mountain peaks and rising sun stark against the pale wall. His voice hardens.

"Circuit had its chance to act. And it failed."

A pause. A slow, deliberate scan of the camera.

"How much longer are you going to trust them and let them abuse that trust? Until there's nothing left to breathe? Until our fields are barren, our rivers poisoned, our skies choked with toxins? Until we are ghosts walking through our own homeland?"

He leans forward, the overhead lights casting harsh shadows across his face.

"And yet, while we suffocate, while our children live in fear of stepping beyond city walls, Circuit thrives. Their leaders breathe filtered air in their ivory towers, travel in sealed transports, sip clean water from crystal glasses while you ration yours."

He straightens, letting the weight of his words linger.

"I say enough." His voice drops, but the fury in it is unmistakable.

"The time to act is now. We are done waiting. Done watching our people suffer. Venovia belongs to us, not to the same rich families who, generation after generation, fill the seats of the board."

He steps back, hands braced against the podium, eyes burning into the lens.

Behind him, a curtain lifts, and Circuit President Peterson sits bound and gagged, his suit wrinkled, his face red. My stomach drops to my feet.

"The Inherited Terra Movement is here. For you. We have found a way to survive."

"Oh no," Brigid says, voice breaking. "They did it."

Before I can ask what, Elton lifts his hand, a small blue capsule pinched between his fingers. "Just a single pill will make you immune to the toxic air."

The screen shifts. Another video overlays Elton's feed. A group stands in the middle of a ruined zone, houses crumbling in the background. ITM members flank them, masks covering their faces. The music swells, and then, in unison, they remove their masks. Grins split their faces wide and unnatural.

"Thanks to Corsair, I can breathe."

The woman beside him, an older brown-skinned woman, repeats it, her voice too even. One by one, they echo the words, standing tall, sucking in air thick with poison. The camera pans, colors shifting. Flowers bloom at their feet, trees sprouting leaves as if the land itself is healing.

The video ends, cutting back to Elton at the podium again. "We will not abandon you. We will take back our home. We will tear Circuit from its throne. But we can't do it alone. We need your help. You have a choice: stand with us or be buried beneath the ruin they've brought upon us."

The screen goes black, and the transmission ends.

At first, there's a tense hush as everyone absorbs what just happened. President Peterson was bound and gagged. ITM has seized control of a Circuit building and ended with the demand for the people to revolt.

Then, as if the collective consciousness syncs, the hall erupts into chaos. Staff speak in frantic tones, and riders curse and start to argue. Carla clutches her belly, Mac's arm tight around her, no doubt worried about what their future holds for them and their baby.

I tear my eyes away, my breathing coming fast. The hall is a maelstrom of sounds and confusion, with fists slamming against tables, chairs scraping back, and some people hurrying out of the room.

"This can't be happening right now," Brigid says, shock paling her face.

Jess scans her comm's screen. "They have protocols for this. Safe rooms. Just because they have the President doesn't mean they have complete control."

Her eyes dart from me to Brigid. She's trying to stay calm, but she's struggling. She and Heath are part of the families that Elton just rallied an entire nation to rise against. People aren't going to stop and ask whether they deserve it. They'll see the names, and that'll be enough.

Jess taps her comm. I hear her father's voice. "Jessica. Where are you?"

"I'm at Blackhawk." There's a murmur from the other line. "Yes, I saw it on the news. Is Mother there? And did Jace arrive yet?" she asks, stepping away.

Most of Venovia is Circuit-controlled. Public transport, power grids, and food supply. Does he realize what that means? If people revolt, what happens when the roads are blocked and the generators shut down? Will they turn on school teachers? On the police? Where does the line between human and government blur, and when it does, who gets taken out first?

The room is reaching a deafening state as more people scramble to contact family, voices overlapping in frantic tones. Someone at the window, eyes wide with horror.

"There's a fire! The Village is under attack!" a mess hall staff person yells.

Everyone stampedes to the series of windows looking to the west.

But there's no need. Even from where we sit, massive flames lick the night sky and illuminate the silhouettes of shuttles hovering above the town.

Fuck. The entire station is in danger. My mind reels with what to do next.

We could stay and hide, hunker down, and hope the storm passes, but it's too late for that. The storm is at our door.

I look at Jess pacing in the corner as she talks to her family. *I thought we had more time.*

"I'll stay here," I say as Jess returns. "Fiaro and Lugsen will need help to delegate security to remain here, but see if we can spare any to go to the Village. You need to get on a shuttle now."

She tilts her head in defiance. "No. I'm staying here with you," she says. "I can make some calls and see what the state of the rest of the board is."

Brigid slowly rises to her feet, still looking half-dazed. "If they brought shuttles, they brought mystyl."

I curse under my breath. "Dammit. Those three will be sitting ducks there."

Brigid blinks as if processing what's happening. "We need to get their stallions to them. We can help those people."

I shake my head. "There's no *we*. You're not a soldier, Brigid; you're barely a rider."

She balls her fist by her side, and all five feet six of her glare up at me. "I'm not going to hide here while they're in danger. I abandoned them before. Please don't make me do it again."

I exhale sharply, my gaze locking onto hers. That boldness. Damn, the more I get to know her, the more there is no denying she's my sister.

Our father looked the same when faced with impossible odds.

But while she'd been stubborn before, this was different. The softness she once carried, the hesitation that used to shadow her steps, is gone.

In its place is something harder. It's no surprise that her time with the rebels changed her, stripped away the girl who arrived at Blackhawk, and replaced her with a woman who will stand her ground. She doesn't want to fight; she *needs* to.

I scrub a hand over my face, weighing the risks. If I tell her to stay behind, she'll find another way.

"Fine," I mutter. "But you listen to me out there. No heroics. We get them their stallions, and we get out. Understood?"

A spark of triumph flares in her eyes, but she nods. "Understood."

"All right, let's get to the stables."

Sixty-Eight

BRIGID

My boots scuff the cracked pavement as I tug the reins, guiding Ember and Shadowmane toward the idling shuttle. Ember snorts, tossing his head, but he steps up the ramp with Shadowmane and the other five stallions, led by Specter riders trailing behind.

Marshal already contacted Heath, Logan, and Carter and told them about us bringing the stallions to them, and made me promise to message him once I landed and we connected.

The Village's small police force had set up a perimeter around a school playground and called in additional reinforcements from the nearby military base.

Once Shadowmane and Ember are secured in their narrow stalls, I pull Marshal's hooded sweatshirt tighter around me.

The fabric swallows my frame as I lean against the shuttle wall. What we are doing isn't protocol, far from it, and considering I promised to remain at the station until CSU investigators arrived, I figured it was wise to conceal myself.

However, judging by the frantic looks on the faces of the handful of riders and Blackhawk security joining me, no one is paying that close attention.

Although I do recognize Garret, the President's son, slouched in a seat across from me. As we lift off, his eyes flicker my way, and I duck my head, hiding under the hood.

It's hard to tell if he recognized me or not. Or maybe he did, but the memory of Logan's fists rearranging his face after he groped me outside Blink keeps his mouth shut.

My thoughts shift to Galaxian, left behind at Oriana's assurance that he insisted he wanted to stay behind.

He wasn't bonded to Logan anymore. Without their connection, he had no way to alert them about the mystyl's presence, making him more of a liability than an asset.

Heath and Carter can still help people and save lives.

Minutes later, we land, and the doors open.

Outside, it's a warzone.

The smell outside burns my nose and makes my eyes water. A stray dog runs past, its side bleeding from what can only be mystyl burns. Cars speed by, honking and tires squealing as they turn the corner.

The other riders, including several from Specter, mount and gallop off to assist the stressed police officers with evacuation and forming a safe zone.

Thinking only of Oriana, I race down the ramp, leaving Shadowmane and Ember on the shuttle.

I hear their frantic voices thundering behind me. They're scared, but I don't dare take them out by myself.

Thinking it might help, I lean into the bond, seeking them

out like I do their riders, but feel only the slightest connection. Besides being already bonded, they're not mine.

From every direction are screaming and explosions.

They've set up barricades, their vehicle's lights cutting harshly through the evening gloom. Street lights flicker erratically, and I can barely hear anything over the roar of shuttles flying overhead. A scratchy voice crackles through a radio comm nearby: "...*mystyl spotted to the southwest near the hospital...*" Police in heavy tactical gear rush past me, weapons at the ready.

What the hell am I doing?

My throat goes dry as I move, scanning the area until I see a swing set and slides. Would they even be there? What if they got called somewhere else? What if they never got Marshal's message?

Shoving the dark thoughts from my mind, I dart across the road, reaching the playground, my voice breaking as I shout their names. "Logan! Heath! Carter!" I turn around, a creeping sensation overtaking me. They're not here. I am alone.

This was a bad idea. I turn to head back, but before I can reach the sidewalk, a figure steps in front of me.

My heart slams violently against my breastbone, and I freeze.

"Wayfinder," Elton muses, slow and deliberate, as if savoring the moment. "When you triggered that tracker of yours, I thought I was going to have to pay off or kill someone to get to you, but here you are, coming right to me."

Six men flank him, and he signals to them to spread out and form a loose ring around me. My fingers itch to tap my comm, but their guns are trained on me, and I don't dare move.

"Your sister sends her regards and apologizes for not being here," he adds.

She is alive. The ground trembles beneath my feet—

whether from the roar of departing shuttles, distant explosions, or the sheer weight of this revelation, I can't tell. My face remains carefully blank, even as my pulse roars in my ears.

But Elton sees right through it, teeth flashing white in the dim light as he smiles. "Oh, yes. She's a bit worse for wear, as you can imagine, but Sharice is alive. For now."

My hands tighten at my sides. "What do you want?"

He laughs, tilting his head as if I am amusing him. "Do you not watch the news? I don't *need* you anymore. I could kill you right now, and it wouldn't matter. I already got what I wanted from you."

Unease spreads through me, icy tendrils constricting my ribcage.

"However, you have created quite a stir among my members, and I would be remiss if I didn't at least offer you a chance to come with me. Public appearance is everything in our world, as you well understand from your time in Circuit." His smile doesn't reach his eyes. "Sharice would be thrilled to have you with her. She misses you. In fact, the first thing she said when she came out of surgery was, " Did you ask for me?" He pauses, observing my face. "Shame your mother didn't make it."

The words hit me like physical blows. My breath catches, vision blurring as the implications crash over me. "She's... dead?"

"Indeed," he nods, pursing his lips tighter. "Thanks to Circuit. She died fighting for what she believed in, but your sister lives." He steps closer, voice dropping to a confidential tone. "You can join us. Embrace your title as the Wayfinder. We can arrange to care for you and the druanera."

I choke down the lump in my throat. He's lying. He has to be.

"This is just one of many raids tonight. Circuit's fall is

inevitable." His eyes bore into mine, challenging. "Join us. You're smart. Surely you can see you're on the losing side?"

For the briefest of moments, doubt coils in my stomach like a cold, restless serpent. From the first day, he's lied to me and manipulated me. He's the definition of evil, but if Sharice is truly alive... she's all the family I have left. It sickens me to think she's trapped there with him. What if I went with him? I could find a way to convince her to leave later. Rescue her from his influence.

A resounding *no* slams to the front of my mind. Logan, Heath, and Carter. Three men who gave up everything for me. I made them a promise, one I intend to keep.

I snuff out the hesitation. "No," I tell him, my voice steadier than I feel. "I will never go with you."

His eyes flicker with annoyance, then he lifts his chin and points straight at me. "Kill her."

The six men lurch forward. They do not move like men. They're hunched, breath ragged, lips peeled back in something that is not quite a snarl, not quite human. Their eyes are empty, hollow pits of darkness.

Oh my god. He did it. He used the bond to warp them into mindless drones. Soulless soldiers that can endure the poisoned air but will also do his bidding.

I move before my mind can process, muscles coiling to fight, to flee, but then the shadows shift.

A figure appears.

Heath.

He is just *there*, no sound, no warning, as if he emerged from the night itself.

A long laser lance gleams in his grip as he rides Shadowmane. Then he moves, swift and brutal. The blade slices through the first attacker, then the second, cutting them down in a blur of motion.

I scramble back, making room as he turns the snarling stallion on another man.

Beast on the beast.

Shadowmane kicks out, and Elton doesn't move in time. Shadowmane's rear hoof collides with his chest, sending him backward, sprawling on the sidewalk.

He fires his pistol at Heath. There's a *pop* as they phase, reappearing five feet to the left and crushing a man under his hooves.

A truck roars toward us. Clutching his chest and side, Elton curses and climbs into the passenger seat.

The door closes, and they careen down the road and disappear into an alleyway.

I want to chase after him, but my feet lose contact with the ground as I'm hoisted onto his lap. Shadows writhe around him, and his warm mahogany-colored eyes have darkened to something primal and dark.

"What are you?" The words are snatched from my lips as his powerful stallion lunges suddenly, throwing me back into his hard chest.

He ignores me, and we gallop through the streets, returning to the shuttle in a fraction of the time it took me to run.

"There are too many!" A police officer yells nearby. "They're evacuating everyone!"

Blood streaking the side of his face, Logan waits for us. He's barking orders to the police to get on as Heath halts us next to him.

"Where is Carter?" Heath asks from his stallion's back.

"I don't fucking know!" Logan shouts from the top of the ramp over the thumping propellers.

Heath hops off, then pulls me down from the saddle. Riders

and druadans from all directions rush onto the awaiting aircraft.

"We're leaving," the pilot says over the interior speakers.

The three of us exchange a hard look.

"They'll send more shuttles after it cools down," Logan says. "Carter has Ember, they'll be fine."

His words do little to convince me, but Heath's gentle nudge forces my feet to move. Feeling as if I'm submerged in water, I stumble up the ramp as Heath leads Shadowmane aboard.

The doors close, silencing the distance explosions and gunfire, and we're airborne.

Sixty-Nine

CARTER

I tighten my grip on Ember's reins as the cold night air washes over my face, numbing my ears and nose. The quiat, peaceful Village outside Blackhawk has transformed into a living hellscape. Smoke, screams, and the clash of steel. Police officers struggle to hold the line, their faces etched with desperation.

The explosions and gunfire had already drawn us from the house when we got Marshal's message to meet Brigid at the playground. The police chief didn't so much as blink when we ran up to him. Even though he recognized Heath and me as deserters, whatever punishment we face is low on their priority list.

They have bigger problems to deal with at the moment,

and it's clear they are grateful for all the help as they shove guns in our hands and yell at us to help barricade the area.

We'd grabbed our stallions from the shuttle Marshal promised and split up. I hated them out of my sight, but mystyl detection is more effective when we're spread out, rather than clustered together.

Through the fog of ash and smoke, I see what's left of the Specter team advancing. Garret's leading them, and his gaze locks on me.

"Oh, the coward shows up now to claim all the glory?" he sneers when I'm within earshot.

I ignore him, raising my gun and taking aim at an approaching swarm of mystyl.

A rain of gunfire rings out as dozens of creatures collapse, then crawl over each other and keep coming. A crackle from a person's radio catches my attention.

"This is General Allison James. We're holding position at the eighth block, but we need support."

My mom's here. And she's in danger.

"Fuck!" I shout as Ember leaps to the side, narrowly avoiding a mystyl that squirmed its ass between two barricades. He rears and plants his front feet on the creature repeatedly until it stops squirming.

The playground is behind the barricade, and Heath and Logan should be almost to Brigid.

Indecision feels like it's cleaving me in half.

"Fuck it!" I curse, and Ember jigs under me, sensing my frustration. If I hurry, I can help my mom and then meet the others. I spur Ember forward, the stallion's hooves pounding against the pavement.

Liam falls beside me. His face is streaked with soot and sweat.

"Didn't think I'd see you again," he shouts over the clatter of our stallion's hooves.

"Long story," I shout back.

"I bet!" he says, as we weave through the war-torn streets, cutting down any mystyl in our path.

People flee screaming, and flames erupt from vehicles and inside buildings. Clothing stores, restaurants, and pubs alike all have broken windows and dead and injured strewn inside and around them. Despite the cold, sweat drips down my back.

Those fucking bastards did it. They made it all the way up here.

I'm going to kill every one of them.

As we near the coordinates, the wreckage of a transport truck materializes, its metal twisted and scorched. Bodies of her team lie motionless, victims of the mystyl assault. My breath catches when I spot my mother lying beside the open door. Her uniform is burned, blood pooling beneath her.

"Mom!" I leap off Ember, rushing to her side.

She looks up, her eyes weary. "Carter, you're here." A cough racks her body. "I thought I'd never see you again."

"I'm here, Mom." I grasp her hand; it's cold.

Liam kneels beside us, his face grim.

"We need to get her out of here."

"Captain..." he says, voice low.

"Help me!" I shout at him.

He hesitates, then nods, sprinting back to his stallion.

I sense movement, more mystyl closing in.

"*Bad, bad, bad,*" Ember repeats in my head, and his fear and anger hijack my senses, staining my vision red.

My mother squeezes my hand weakly. "Carter, listen to me."

Tears blur my vision. "Don't, God dammit. Stop talking like that. I'm getting you out of here."

She shakes her head. "No, you need to lead them. Promise me you'll find Derrick and tell your father I'm sorry, and I never stopped loving him." She lets out a long, wheezing sigh. "I'm so proud of you. You've grown into such a brave, incredible man. Promise me you'll not lose yourself like I did. Promise me you'll find someone to love and never let them go."

"I promise," I whisper, tears blurring my vision.

Her grip slackens, her eyes closing.

"Mom? Mom!" But she's gone.

I cradle her in my arms, rocking her as I curse and shout for whoever is listening. Grief threatens to consume me, but the approaching slithering snaps me back.

"*She's not here,*" Ember says. "*Sad, must go.*"

As harsh as his words sound, there's genuine empathy behind them. He's mourning just like me, but he's right. It's not safe to stay here. I mount, casting one last look at my mother's lifeless form.

We gallop back to the barricade, and Liam waves to me.

I slow Ember to a trot.

"Do you hear that?" I say.

"No," I reply back but then immediately realize what he means. I'm not shouting. It's quiet. No gunfire, nothing.

"Go go go!" I say, flailing my arms, and Liam's stallion leaps ahead.

They disappear in the smog, and soon the dead appear.

It's a massacre.

Bodies of soldiers, police, and civilians scatter the area like discarded dolls. Red and blue blood smears nearly every surface of the walls and metal barricades.

Smoke hangs in the air from the smoldering buildings, and I reach out, sensing for Heath, but feel nothing.

We pick our way through the carnage, and my throat cinches tighter with every face I see, fearing the next one will be one I recognize. Liam and Ravenwing are nowhere to be seen.

Where the hell is everyone?

Finally, we reach where the shuttle was parked before, and my stomach falls to my feet.

It's gone. The god damn shuttle is gone.

Seventy

BRIGID

Back at Blackhawk, the courtyard is in utter chaos. Station workers scramble to evacuate, their shouts and orders bouncing off the stone walls. Staff and their spouses drag overstuffed suitcases across the cobblestone ground while security guards coax massive crates onto squeaking dollies. Researchers rush around, clutching stacks of files and equipment too valuable to leave behind, ducking between vehicles being hastily loaded with supplies.

Marshal seeks us out, weaving through the frenzy of people.

"Oh, thank the tides," he wraps me in a tight hug, then releases me.

He sees Logan at my shoulder and Heath leading Shadowmane off the shuttle.

"Where's Carter and Ember?" he asks.

"I don't know," I say, voice breaking. "We didn't have time to look for them and..."

He squeezes my forearm. "Don't worry. They're sending more shuttles. I'm sure they'll be on the next one."

I nod, desperately hoping he's right, and it's my panicked imagination thinking he's lying somewhere bleeding out or ITM is taking him and Ember. *If Elton knows what he is to me...*

"The Venovia National Guard sent a barge," Marshal says. "We're evacuating everyone we can. It's big enough for the station, druadans, and many people from the Village that make it over here." He points to the pathway that leads into the orchard and then farther to the steep and windy cliffside path that leads down to the beach.

"It's anchored down there, and we could use all the help we can get to load druadans."

I nod, and the three of us start for the stables, but a sharp snap cracks the air, and everyone turns, gasping as the cable car's lines rupture, sending it lurching. Screams pierce the air as it dangles, swaying over the ravine.

People nearest the edge shout for help. A truck driver leaps from the driver's seat, and others rush forward, securing a winch from a truck.

The man swings it overhead, and the hook catches on the cable car's luggage rack.

There are cheers and sighs of relief as the winch cable holds fast, and then they shout to start the winch.

The winch engine whines as it strains against the weight of the swaying cable car. The people inside clutch at each other, faces pale against the flickering emergency lights. A woman sobs, her hand pressed against the glass.

"Almost there!" one of the workers shouts. The truck shudders as the winch drags the car toward solid ground. The onlookers flinch with every jolt, every sudden tilt, as if sheer willpower might keep the car from plunging into the ravine below.

Then, with one final lurch, it settles against the ledge. Hands grab for the doors, prying them open. The people inside spill out, some collapsing, some weeping, others too stunned to move. A man staggers forward, clutching his bleeding arm, while a teenager clings to the firefighter who pulled her free.

I should help. I should do something. But I can't move.

Everywhere I turn, someone is crying, someone is hurt, someone is screaming. A woman kneels beside a man who is too still. A boy clutches a broken wrist, tears streaming down his dirt-streaked face. Someone is calling a name over and over, their voice raw with desperation.

The world tilts. My breath won't come.

Shock. That's what this is. I know it, but it doesn't matter. My limbs won't listen. My ears ring with the overwhelming noise, and my vision blurs at the edges.

Then—

"Blondie!" Logan's hand grips my arm. "Stay with me. Get your mare."

The panic doesn't vanish, but it cracks, breaking just enough for air to rush back into my lungs. I nod, my movements stiff and unsteady.

With Logan leading, we hurry down to Blackhawk's underground stables. Riders hurry their stallions toward the exits, and I reach for Oriana, not with my hands but with my mind.

I round the corner, and her dark eyes lock onto me, ears flicking forward. I take her halter from the hook beside her stall, slip into the door, and place it on her head. My fingers tremble as I grip the lead rope. She exhales sharply, nostrils flaring as she senses the fear radiating from me.

"*We're going*," I tell her, my voice barely more than a breath.

I turn back to Oriana, trying to coax her into the trailer. A shout cuts through the din.

There's a group of people gathered on the opposite side of the bridge, pleading desperately for help.

I squint at the crowd, and a silhouette of a man on a chestnut druadan appears, emerging from the crowd.

My heart leaps into my throat. "Hey, look, it's Carter!" I shout, pointing. Heath shoulders Shadowmane to the side, trying to get a better view, while Galaxian stands calm, neck arched, ears perked.

"Holy shit," Logan murmurs. "They made it."

It's hundreds of feet across, so it's hard to read his face, and yet a horrifying realization steals the air from my lungs as he backs up Ember. "Wait, what is he doing?" The question tumbles from me.

Logan curses. "The idiot is going to phase across."

"No, Carter, don't!" Heath barks the words, as if it were a command, but they're too far away for him to hear.

Carter spurs Ember into a gallop, and time stands still as the stallion leaps, and they disappear.

Seconds tick by, feeling like hours, and worry gnaws at the base of my skull. Carter and Ember are known for their long-distance phasing, but this is far beyond the length of an arena.

Like really, *fucking* far.

A heartbeat later, Ember materializes, his hooves landing with a thud safely on the intact part of the bridge. Sweat darkens his neck and chest, and pink foam drips from his mouth around his bit.

His saddle is empty.

"NO!" The word tears painfully from me.

Ember slows to a walk before stopping in front of Heath. He takes the stallion's reins, soothing him.

Grief claws at my throat as I sink to my knees. "NO, NO NO!"

Beside me, Heath and Logan curse.

One moment, he was there, solid and real, and the next—gone. Vanished into the Nowhere. Is he still conscious? Trapped in that endless void, alone and terrified, slowly suffocating as the air runs out? The image burns into my mind, unbearable.

Tonight, I learned I lost my mother, and I willingly chose to give up my sister to that monster, Elton.

I *won't* lose Carter, too. Not the man who trusted me at Meridian when no one else would. The man who welcomed me with open arms and stood in awe as I rode Oriana for the first time. The man who always cared for me treated me as an equal when others doubted me. The man who filled every room with joy and confessed his love openly in a world where so many others kept it buried.

I rise to my feet, and Oriana jigs, the lead rope tugging in my hands as she senses my thoughts.

She knows what I'm going to do.

I lead her to a supply crate, grab a handful of mane, and swing my leg onto her bareback. Instantly, her warmth seeps into the fabric of my riding pants, and her steady presence fills my mind. The strong connection between us hums, and her unwavering calm anchors me, reminding me I'm not alone.

We face everything together.

"You ready?" I speak in my head.

"I am, bond keeper." She replies.

My thoughts sharpen a renewed feeling of clarity and purpose, and I click my tongue, urging her forward.

"Brigid!" Heath yells over the sound of the shuttles roaring overhead and people shouting. "He's gone. We have to go!"

Ignoring him, I dig my heels into her sides. "Go," I command Oriana, both out loud and in my head. She shifts her weight to her haunches to catapult herself forward.

We streak past Logan and Heath, and Logan grabs Heath as he tries to chase after me.

Her hooves thunder on the stone bridge, echoing with every stride. She snorts, and my skin tingles like a thousand tiny needles are pricking it.

Oriana was bred for this, *made* for this. Marshal's words stand clear in my mind. *As easy as breathing.* We leap, my ears pop. The white-capped river below, the gray sky above, and the smell of smoke and death all fade as the world vanishes.

Black specks form in my vision, and I'm weightless, although I sense her beneath me. The air shifts, becoming dense and cold, pressing against my skin as if the darkness itself clings to me. My heartbeat slows, muffled, as though swallowed by the void. Every sense dulls. No sound, no sight, just the eerie weightlessness of drifting through nothing.

Like falling without end as we vanish into the nowhere.

Afterword

Stay tuned for the finale of the DRUADAN LEGACY SERIES, Book 4!

Keep up to date with the latest announcements from me by subscribing to my newsletter
Join my Amelia Cole reader Facebook group! https://www.facebook.com/share/g/gVyHbvQXM1cKB1Ei/
Visit my website at:
https://www.ameliacolebooks.com/
Questions/comments?
Email me: contact@ameliacolebooks.com

Acknowledgments

It seems that every book I write pushes me and challenges my writing limits. This one, however, I can wholeheartedly say was the hardest one yet.

Not only is it the longest book I've ever written, but it also explores the complex themes of loss, betrayal, and clinging to hope when you have nothing left. Brigid and the others struggled with the difficult decision of choosing the lesser of two evils when faced with a challenging situation, and I hope this resonates with readers who face similar dilemmas in life.

We're all just doing our best with the situations we're given.

Thank you to Sleep Token for being on repeat during the drafting stage of this book and for releasing a new album the day I sent out ARCs, so I could escape the first reader's fears by immersing myself in the music.

I want to shout out to all the creators who craft the dystopian stories such as Silo, Last of Us, Eternaut, and Fallout. These were all incredible sources of inspiration to ensure my post-apocalyptic world matched the tone and themes. I know that, given the current state of the world, dystopian stories are needed more than ever to shed light on what is often a dark reality.

Thank you to the Forest and Fawn community for being so sweet and welcoming as we discussed battling burnout and revision woes.

To my fantastic editor, Sharon at Devil in the Details! Thanks for slogging through my very rough first drafts ;-P

To my rockstar team of Beta and ARC readers!!! Morgan, Sarabelle, and many others. Your first reads helped shape this story and encouraged me and the characters, pushing me to finish the book.

To my excellent Personal Assistant, Alyssa. Thank you for doing the behind-the-scenes work to ensure my newsletters are sent out and for creating all the beautiful images of my books.

To Michael, Kian, and Megan, you are my whole world. I love you so much!

ABOUT THE AUTHOR

Amelia Cole is a fantasy and sci-fi romance author. She enjoys guessing twist endings of movies, rolling D20s with her friends, and pretending to be an elf archer at Renaissance fairs. She's a short story contest winner and has been published in magazines and anthologies.

She lives with her family in Washington state.

www.ingramcontent.com/pod-product-compliance
Lightning Source LLC
LaVergne TN
LVHW091651070526
838199LV00050B/2146